"No one who opens *The Cloud Sketcher* will find it easy to stop reading before the last vertiginous page.... Passionate and well-researched... remarkable [for] its visceral feeling for architecture.... Rayner's eye is excellent." —*Chicago Tribune*

"Exuberant.... A fast-paced, lyrical novel." —*Milwaukee Journal Sentinel*

"Engrossing.... Rayner is ... an assured and confident storyteller."
—*Los Angeles Times Book Review*

"A whirlwind of passion, obsession, war, art, and undying love that captures both the dark turbulence of the Russian Revolution and the heady sparkle of Jazz Age New York. A powerful, absorbing story about a dangerous and romantic time." —Kevin Baker, author of *Dreamland*

"An old-fashioned novel in the best sense: full of incident and passion, presenting a slice of history and relating a gripping story.... A transatlantic *Great Expectations* of the Jazz Age 1920s."
—*Publishers Weekly* (starred review)

"From the dark backwoods of Finland to the dizzying skyscraper wars of New York City, *The Cloud Sketcher* is as epic in scope and spirit as the new century it chronicles. A marvelously compelling novel."
—Sheri Holman, author of *The Dress Lodger*

"A romantic epic about a Finnish architect intent on building the world's most beautiful skyscraper." —*LA Weekly*

"[*The Cloud Sketcher*] has all the ingredients of good historical fiction, including a strongly told story, an expansive, fascinating setting, and richly drawn period details.... Sure to delight." —*Booklist*

About the Author

RICHARD RAYNER's previous books include the memoir *The Blue Suit* and the novels *Murder Book, Los Angeles Without a Map,* and *The Elephant.* His work appears regularly in *The New Yorker,* the *New York Times, Talk,* and many other publications. He lives in Los Angeles with his wife and two sons.

Also by Richard Rayner

MURDER BOOK

THE BLUE SUIT

THE ELEPHANT

LOS ANGELES WITHOUT A MAP

The Cloud Sketcher

A NOVEL

RICHARD RAYNER

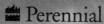 Perennial

An Imprint of HarperCollinsPublishers

A hardcover edition of this book was published in 2001 by HarperCollins Publishers.

HarperCollins books may be purchased for educational, business, or sales promotional use. For information please write: Special Markets Department, HarperCollins Publishers Inc., 10 East 53rd Street, New York, NY 10022.

First Perennial edition published 2002.

Designed by Jeannette Jacobs

Library of Congress Cataloging-in-Publication Data is available.

ISBN 0-06-095613-5(pbk.)

02 03 04 05 06 WB/RRD 10 9 8 7 6 5 4 3 2 1

for Paivi and Harry and Charlie

There is no easy way from the earth to the stars.

—Vladimir Mayakovsky

The Cloud Sketcher

Prologue : 1928

The man in bold pinstripe burst around the corner with a lively step and a handsome face bronzed by the sun. His black hair was swept back from a high forehead, his black eyebrows almost met above the nose, and he was smiling, teeth flashing sharkish against the darker tone of his skin. A pale scar cut deep into his drooping left eyelid and, as he came toward Esko, the energy of his body filled the corridor with threat. He swept by, not turning his head, walking fast and with the swirling suspicion of a limp. An entourage followed in his wake, men with boxy suits and toothpicks dangling from their lips who kept their hands in their pockets, goons whose more obvious allusion to violence was drowned out by the sheer force and drama of their leader's presence. Standing quite still, Esko didn't realize until they'd all gone by that he'd been holding his breath.

At dinner he heard that the man was the ship's most famous passenger, the most notorious personage on board this gilded, throbbing, overheated palace of deco, a bootlegger, a gangster named Paul Mantilini whose syndicate ran eight distilleries in New York alone, each netting more than $10 million a year; yet it was said that Mantilini knew more men on Wall Street than hardened criminals (although the categories often overlapped in these, the nervous, boundless, brilliant, top-speed days of the late 1920s), that he was on first-name terms with the mayor of New York and nineteen U.S. senators, that Gershwin, Caruso, and Darrow were each of them his drinking crony, that he had been with Houdini only hours before he died, that he had personally helped Lucky Lindy gas up his tank. Other rumors were less outlandish but remarkable nonetheless: he was so vain he wore lifts in his shoes; he had given $10,000 cash to a reporter who had described him as the Beau Brummel of Broadway; two of the ship's four masseuses were on permanent standby to rub his smooth, tanned skin with walnut oil; he couldn't bear to lie alone in the dark and went to bed with the lights on, attended by five of his people, a different five every night, lest there should be a conspiracy to murder him while his eyes were blotted out with the mask of fine black silk he habitually wore when sleeping.

The limp, apparently, was the result of a recent attempt on his life. Afterward he had rounded up as many of his rivals as he and his men could capture. When one aging Italian and his son seemed to have proved their lack of involvement, and pleaded for their lives, on condition that they leave New York and never come back, Mantilini told them to decide which of the two should be spared; the father sacrificed his life for his son, and was shot in the head, and the son then hanged himself. Mantilini watched them both die. Still in a rage, he pushed a man down an elevator shaft, and sentenced one of his own associates to have his legs broken for opening a telegram in error. He was predictable only in that he was implacable.

Esko was a Finnish architect, a boy from the backwoods of a country that most people couldn't locate on a map even if they'd heard of it, and usually they hadn't; now, aged thirty-eight, he'd made himself quite a reputation in Manhattan, the new capital of the world, and he'd done so, not only with skill and craft, but with patience and guts, with that quality the Finns proudly called *sisu*, the ability to go on beyond the capacity to endure. Finnish men were stoic. They didn't like saying what they felt, which is what they did, if they drank a little; but they didn't drink a little, they drank a lot, and then they were likely to lurch into your arms, demanding a hug, or stick you in the gut with a knife, a *puukko*, a blade.

Esko had some distance from that now. He'd been in America so long he'd lost his *puukko*. He knew that Americans loved bigness and snap and flair and style — in their language, in their legends, in their buildings, in their gangsters too. They couldn't help but love Paul Mantilini, who never looked down or back, who rode with such nonchalance on the high beam of uncertainty, whose life was crammed with dangers he seemed to find necessary, energizing, as if they were the fuel that made him a phoenix, ever reborn, calmly emerging from the flames.

Mantilini had been on vacation, but even so had acquired a hundred trunks of liquor, made in Scotland, eight cases to the trunk, twelve bottles to the case. When the *Ile de France* docked, it was said, one of his men would simply hand over the keys to the trunks to the customs man along with a three-dollar-a-case "handling charge." The customs man would of course be very accommodating and would make no protest when one of Mantilini's trucks came by the next day to pick up a load that would bring somewhere in the region of $75,000 clear profit. Not bad for a vacation.

In the dining room Mantilini sat in a far corner with his people, a tennis instructor, an Italian poet, a jazz pianist, his mistress (a sinuous black singer who favored shimmering gowns), and the sundry bodyguards and lieutenants. Strolling the deck, he wore smoked glasses and broad-brimmed hats to protect himself from the sun. He sported a selection of swaggering suits and vivid shirts and seemed to have access to doors and passageways that no one else knew about. When the liner inexplicably slowed, halting in mid-ocean, and a Canadian freighter came bobbing alongside, winking a message in Morse, it was assumed that this was his doing. On the last night of the voyage, at the traditional costume ball, he wore the outfit of an Italian peasant, singing arias from *Tosca* and *Cavalleria Rusticana* in a light and surprisingly graceful tenor. This performance was greeted by the other first class passengers with roars of appreciation, recognition that for the duration of the crossing the ship had been a universe hinged entirely to Paul Mantilini's command.

This mysterious and consuming presence only heightened Esko's eagerness to get back to New York. It was hot, the September morning they cruised through the Narrows, past Sandy Hook, and entered the wide, soupy, slow-moving waters of the harbor. Esko thought at once of the previous summer, when families had lain out on balconies and the throttled air of Central Park had been filled with people sleeping outdoors, when the whole of the city had seemed to be melting like the chunk of ice that disappeared in his palm even as it failed to cool it, and the sweltering sluggish heat had been unmoved by the sorrowing voices of a million electric fans. All through that inferno of a summer Esko had worked as never before, the rising waves of heat from the sidewalk stimulating rather than dulling his powers and concentration, and

now his heart thrilled as the ship, a skyscraper recumbent on the ocean, surrounded by puttering tugs and pluming fireboats, nudged its way through the
thickness of the air. For a moment Esko had the fanciful idea that the ship
would run aground and plant itself in the forest of towers growing out of the
haze of lower Manhattan, stone-clad, steel-strutted, glass-encrusted, titanic
and romantic buildings that were even now beginning their dance in front of
his eyes, the Woolworth gliding eastward while the Singer slid south and all
the other tall ones began to pick up the rhythm, changing places in this millionaires' waltz of perspective, almost seeming to kiss and graze hands as the
ship was moved carefully up the Hudson.

Arriving in New York was, as always, wonderful, and for a moment he forgot his worries. As a boy he'd grown up among frozen lakes. Now this majestic gaggle of crowding steel and stone was his home.

Architecture never lies. It invariably expresses both its own era and the
character of the men who build it and Esko knew that this was a restless,
showy architecture, the architecture of an age and a city that felt they need
never stop going, that there wasn't a "too far." The glorious skyline would
look completely different a year from now. At the turn of the century a thirty-
story skyscraper in New York had evoked a forty-story skyscraper in Chicago.
Now a sixty-story skyscraper in New York evoked a seventy-story skyscraper
across the street. It was an era enthralled with the reckless pursuit of its own
seemingly limitless possibilities. Why not one hundred stories? One hundred
fifty stories? The answer to the question, How high can you build it? soared
daily upward like the stock market. For the architect these were giddy, dangerous, and perhaps heroic times, and for a moment Esko pictured himself in
one of Manhattan's downtown canyons where light made angles in the depths
of the shadows. He was in a suit, boldly hatless, striding along, a man of the
world, a man of this splendid new world, a man both talented and, in some
proud Finnish way, accomplished and urbane, a man successfully fighting a
sense of himself as doomed—a romantic, stupid, and possibly self-fulfilling
notion, but one that was driven inside him like a nail that had wormed itself
deep into the heart of a tree.

The ship did not run aground; it failed to rear itself up and become the
French Line's ostentatious addition to Wall Street. Architecturally speaking,
this would anyway have made less of a splash than some schemes Esko knew
were now in hand; and so the tugs did their busy work, guiding the liner to a
pier teeming with welcomers. All around Esko people were jammed up at the

rails, yelling and waving to loved ones on the dock; others strutted and fussed, bossing porters who hurried from below bearing suitcases and trunks festooned with labels. The frenzy of the scene was heightened when, down on the pier, a New York police sergeant came bulling through the crowd, a middle-aged man with a gut who began shouting in a mechanical voice through a mega-phone, commanding people to stand aside while an army of uniforms pressed forward at his back.

Esko caught a glimpse of Paul Mantilini, aloof and disdainful on the far side of the deck, seemingly deserted by his entourage. "They've caught up with him after all," said a voice at Esko's side, one of the other first-class pas-sengers. Esko shook his head, knowing better. That vision of himself as a worldly butterfly seemed to melt and dissolve in the heat. The beer-bellied sergeant and his cohorts weren't waiting for Mantilini. They were waiting for him. They'd always been waiting.

PART ONE

Myth

I

It began with news of an elevator, in 1901 an instrument unknown, unheard of, undreamed of in the tiny Finnish village where Esko grew up, as close to the Arctic Circle as to the capital Helsinki. At that time, at the beginning of the fresh century, the village was almost untouched by the modern world, by a future that would, in a few years, sweep aside a way of life unchanged for hundreds. In 1901, when Esko was eleven, the village boasted no railroad and one telephone, which resided, crownlike, atop a narrow throne of solid oak in the study of the vicarage, the only house with electricity for fifty miles. Armies of spruce and pine creaked with snow during the frozen, infinitely long winter, trees that towered above a narrow, deeply rutted track that led into and out of the tiny village of Pyhajarvi. The track ran past a small general store that smelled of leather and mildewed potatoes and burlap. It weaved its way among four graveyards lit at Christmas time with ice lanterns, thousands of ice lanterns, one beacon for each departed soul, flickering bravely in the northern dark. But the track did not run between the sparse scattering of farms set among forests so dense, wild, and uncharted that strangers required a guide to show them the way from one farm to another. There was a lake, twenty miles long, frozen eight months of the year, and you had to be a local to find it among the trees. There were bears, wolves, and mountainous warm-smelling ant heaps where a booted foot might sink up to the thigh. It was a world of poverty, famine, frequent suicide, a world where most recalled how it was to have to eat bread made from pine bark. Despite this there was no complaint, indeed little dialogue at all, except when coaxed from gruff throats by vodka. The villagers had wary eyes and faces that aged quickly in this place where the ownership of land and winter were the most pressing realities: land that was miserable to work even if it belonged to you, and it almost certainly didn't. The villagers cared little for history or events in the world beyond. They were foxy, hard, and sly—fatalists who for the most part smiled and shook their heads at displays of hope or statements of ideals, these being considered the province of fools and very dangerous men. Esko's father, Timo Vaananen, was known to be one such dangerous man.

This severe place had its hothead—Timo—as well as a building of true magnificence. Viewed from afar, the old wooden church seemed to have two towers, both painted red ochre, one peeping over the shoulder of the other like a parent. Moving closer, you saw that the two towers belonged to two different buildings: there was the church itself, with a twenty-four-cornered ground plan in the shape of a crucifix and a steeply pitched roof giving rise to a dome like an onion; and there was the bell tower, strangely taller and more slender, elegant, with a steep shingle roof and a needlelike spire shooting out of the bell compartment. In years past Esko had climbed the stairs and the narrow ladder that led to the top of the tower with his friends, so they could play hide and seek among the ropes and bells, and with his mother, so they could stand together and admire the midnight sun as it dipped toward the lake and then, at once, miraculously, began to rise again. By the summer of 1901, however, his life had taken a different turn, and he didn't go to the bell tower anymore. When he did happen to notice it, it seemed ominous to him, a warning, saying don't stray, don't go too far.

When they finished supper on that June night Esko cleared and washed the dishes, anxiously hoping to be done and escape, to flee before his father was ready to begin. No such luck: Timo was brisk and determined, decisive as ever. He put a book with a pebbled brown cover on the table, then a glass, then a bottle of schnapps, which he uncorked with a pop and placed beside the glass. Then Timo nudged the glass. Then he poured the schnapps, knocked it back, slopped in another shot, and one more, and commanded Esko to sit. "Now we learn," he said.

Timo Vaananen's mission was to teach Esko everything. At the village school, where Timo was one of the two teachers, this wasn't so bad. In school, at least, learning did not involve slaps. There was safety in numbers, and surrounded by the other kids, his head always deep in a book, Esko had only to pretend to negotiate the laws of geometry, algebra, trigonometry, the triumphs and sadnesses of Finnish history, the subtleties of Swedish, Finnish, and, because it was now the law, Russian, and the dirgelike chanting rhythms of "Kalevala," the national epic poem. "Kalevala" had Vainamoinen, the poet, the sorcerer who creates the world and defeats his enemies through the power of song; it had Aino, a beautiful maiden who spurns him; it had Lemminkainen, a fellow who lies and kidnaps and plays tricks; it had the doomed and sad Kullervo. Esko looked at "Kalevala" and saw a world that was familiar to the one he knew. In 1901, a time of simmering rebellion and nationalistic fervor, there were those who preached that the poem was also the literally true account of Finland in times gone by, an idea that appealed to little Esko, and one that appalled Timo, who preferred his history tinged a different color.

At night, at home, now that school was out, there was no pretense of scientific or scholarly rigor. Timo came on full and furious. Sometimes he stared silently at Esko for minutes on end, daring him to give a wrong answer. Sometimes he leaped to his feet, reciting, not "Kalevala," but the revolutionary verse of a man named Maksim Gorky. Sometimes, as the hours droned by, and the bottle of schnapps emptied, silence and drunken despair stole into the room, and Esko, sitting on his hands, would feel as though he were in a dark cave, as though his insides were being scooped out and flooded with hot rage. He remembered the days when his father had been playful, dashing; now he came to life only when teaching or lecturing, describing with fierce excitement how the socialists, and *only* the socialists, would rise together and strike to free Finland from the cruel hand of that crowned black sheep, Czar Nicholas II.

"We will continue where we left off last night," Timo said. He was tall and slender, with fair hair and piercing blue eyes—still a handsome man. "We will learn more about Ferdinand Lassalle. Tell me, Esko. Who was Ferdinand Lassalle?"

Esko spoke slowly and softly, with difficulty. "He was a German socialist, Father. He was born on April 11, 1825, Father. He was an only son, Father. Like Karl Marx, he was gifted and adored by his father, Father."

Timo stared at him for a few moments. "Are you presuming to mock me?"

A butterfly took wing in Esko's belly. "No." He reached out and turned the schnapps bottle smartly.

Timo stopped. "Why did you do that?"

"Because," said Esko, daring to meet his father's eye, yearning to say that it was because he hated it, that he was afraid when his father was drunk; but there was something else. Less than a year before, Esko had been trapped and badly burned in the fire that had razed their previous house to the ground. Now, at eleven, he was big for his age, a tall, lean boy with a scar that began at the base of his neck and climbed the left side of his face like a tree. Livid aubergine-colored branches shot up over his chin. The skin was burned so tight it was hard to move his mouth. Words crept out in a shy mumble. What remained of his left ear was bloodless and twisted, a broken white shell whose color was a shocking contrast. His hair, which had been burned entirely away, was an outlaw mop, growing back in spikes and unruly tufts.

More than this: he'd lost the sight of his left eye. The mess that remained in the socket was now covered with a leather patch, already frayed because he couldn't stop his hand moving toward it. Sometimes the wound itched; sometimes it felt as thought it were on fire; sometimes ants seemed to be burrowing in there. And yet, as if in compensation, or fiendishly rejoicing in the loss of its partner, the vision in his right eye had become clearer, sharper, and shifting patterns on the kitchen drapes as the sun shone through them seemed to demand his opinion. Objects taunted and goaded him if they weren't arranged right.

Esko swallowed hard and forced the words out. "It's the way you always do it, Father. You have your glass here and the bottle here so the light shines through the glass from the window and falls across the page of the book. But the bottle has to be turned this way otherwise the label throws a red shadow. Do you see?"

Timo glanced at Esko, then down at the table. He poured himself another schnapps. "The god Odin tore his eye from his head in exchange for a cup full of water from the very fountain of wisdom. Do you think it's happened to you, Esko?"

Esko's face was on fire again.

"He wore a broad-brimmed hat he pulled down over one eye and he hung for nine days and nine nights on a gallows of his own making, sacrificed himself because he sought also the wisdom of the dead. Is that your intention?"

Esko said nothing.

"Is it?" said Timo fiercely.

"No, Father."

"Good."

Timo told him how Lassalle had fallen in with Karl Marx and then fallen out again, over money, over a personal loan—much to the secret glee of Marx's other disciple, Friedrich Engels.

"Sometimes our friends are also our enemies, Esko, even if they don't intend to be. Remember that," he said.

Timo told how the German leader Bismarck had puffed cigar smoke into Lassalle's face. "Power is arrogance, Esko, and sometimes their own arrogance is what we must use to destroy the powerful. Remember that," he said.

Timo poured another shot of schnapps. "How did a political man, a man who sought to change the world," he said, prefacing the tale of Lassalle's fatal love affair, of how he'd been shot in the belly in a duel, of how he'd died howling, "how did he allow himself to be dragged into a duel with a dandy who knew his way around a pistol much better than he? It was over a *woman*, Esko, it was over a solid rebellious head of red hair."

He lurched forward, taking the schnapps bottle by the neck and not bothering with the glass this time.

"They can kill you, Esko. Your face might turn out to be a blessing after all. Remember that. Especially remember that."

Just then there was a knock at the door. His father rose, and soon Esko was hearing the cynical, amused tones of Kalliokoski, the village priest, talking quite calmly as he came into the kitchen, talking about Old Adam, the mark and sign of original sin, the horny Satan of Hell, who itched and tickled within the ribs of certain families, condemning them to lives of madness, rebellion, and sorrow.

"A house without God in its barn is indeed prey to any storm that comes across the lake," he was saying.

Kalliokoski, pulling the door shut behind him, was tall, thin, with small ears that stuck out, stiff black hair, and a neat, courtierlike beard. Nearly everything about him was black: eyes like bright black buttons that peeped out from within deep sockets, black boots, a black suit with a frock coat that Esko had never seen him not wearing.

Timo filled a short glass from the nearly empty bottle of schnapps and Kalliokoski tossed it back, frowning and smacking his lips, as if it were a duty.

"I brought the newspaper," Kalliokoski said.

Timo lowered his head, saying nothing. Since Kalliokoski had officiated at his wedding to Julie, and had subsequently baptised Esko, dunking the

boy—who had been silent, stoic, showing a ferocious curiosity in the pro-
ceedings—in the icy shallows of the lake, he supposed this gave Kalliokoski
the right to try to interfere.

"See how the world progresses," Kalliokoski went on, pointing to three
columns of newsprint beneath a grainy diagram. "In Helsingfors, in one of the
buildings there, they have made an electric box that can climb up in the sky.
It is called an elevator. It is a cage for carrying things or people up, up, up."

Kalliokoski smiled and Timo raised the bottle directly to his lips so that
the schnapps went down, down, down. Esko meanwhile gazed at the diagram, touching it, rubbing it, so that he brought away an elevator smudge
on a finger, which he then raised to his mouth, finding his tongue flooded
with a flavor of metal, of lead, of something like blood, which he quite
enjoyed.

"You see, Timo," Kalliokoski said. "History is being made, in Helsingfors."

"History will find us here soon enough. It is by no means necessary to
search it out in . . . *Helsingfors*," he said with a wink to Esko, mocking
Kalliokoski's snooty use of the Swedish name for the capital. Timo, not
unreasonably, thought that Finns should speak Finnish if they really wanted
to be Finns.

Esko leaned forward as if he wished to insert his entire body into the very
text of the newspaper, *Hufvudstadsbladet*.

"Esko, you look ill; are you all right?" Timo said. "Do you wish to go to
bed?"

Esko pressed his scarred cheek against the ink of the diagram and
glanced up at his father. He whispered: "The elevator, Father. What does it
mean?"

Timo turned an unhealthy color. "Mean?" said Timo. "It doesn't mean
anything. Karl Marx *means*. Marcus Aurelius *means*. Objects don't mean.
They don't live or have dreams. They merely are."

Esko remembered how cold he'd felt being choked and stuffed with facts
about the life and miserable death of Ferdinand Lassalle. Now he felt warm.
Hot, actually. Excited. This thing, the elevator, offered something else. He
didn't know what. It stimulated the imagination. It was mysterious.

"Yes, Father, I understand, but the elevator has an . . ." He struggled for
the word. "It has an *implication*."

"Which is?"

Esko felt a chill again.

"Yes?"

Esko searched inside himself; there was something that meant something here, but it was locked away, frozen. "I don't know, Father," he said.

"The implication is plain enough," said Kalliokoski, picking at a spot of dried grease on his coat lapel, an unseemly scab that yielded to the attack of a beautifully manicured fingernail. "The boy is fascinated by Helsingfors. He must go to Helsingfors. Look, Timo, you and I both know what's going on, what's happening in the district, but we won't talk about that. Let's talk about this. We both know that you're not a wealthy man. But that's not the issue here. The church will pay. I mean it. Really. The church will pay. Gladly."

There was an awful silence. Beating up and down against the narrow oblong of the kitchen window, a moth tried to escape into the yard, aiming itself at the waning light of the nighttime sun. Timo said, "Esko, you will go to your room," he said. "And you, sir, I bid you good night."

Esko didn't move for a second. He sat quite still, staring down at the gouged surface of the table. His chest was hot and tight; he prayed with his eyes wide open. Dear God, he said to himself, the words ringing fluently in his head as nowhere else, if you're there, please make him leave the newspaper, please make him leave the newspaper.

"Good night," said Esko, looking at neither his father Kalliokoski nor his father as he stood up.

"Good night, Esko. God bless," said Kalliokoski, getting ready to go himself, but not before *Hufvudstadsbladet* was taken up, folded, then dropped slyly beneath the table.

2

The Vaananens had suffered the most humiliating of all possible Finnish falls from grace. They'd lost Finnish land; worse than that, they'd tried to give Finnish land away. Small wonder, the Pyhajarvi gossips said, that Finnish fate had thenceforth stirred sour things into the family soup. Those villagers inclined to a more Christian doctrine took a different view: the

Vaananens had unwisely tempted the God by spurning His blessings, they noted, and He had responded by inviting the Vaananens to sleep out the rest of their years on beds of nails. However you looked at it, whether blind fate or the stern ever-watchful gaze of the Lutheran God was to blame, there'd been a lot of bad luck, and bad luck, in Finland as elsewhere, was always a secret cause for celebration—so long as it wasn't happening to you. The Vaananens were well known throughout the district, their history much discussed.

Timo's father, the grandfather Esko never met, had been the village priest before Kalliokoski, a tall and delicate man with three sons, a small number in Finland at that time, when families tended to run into the double digits. Lauri, the eldest boy, and the strongest, the brightest, had seemed destined for great things but then, after completing his studies at the University of Turku, on the threshold of a career in the law, he shot himself. There was talk of a girl, of sadness and failure in love; the whole truth never came out. Lauri's father, Timo's father, always a man of deep reserve, ran away from life, as if every road was suddenly too demanding, every room too crowded. Putting aside his priest's robes, he neither spoke nor ate nor drank; he simply faded away, blaming himself, dying without a whimper.

Timo's other brother Juhani took his portion of the inheritance and bought a small farm in the village, while Timo, the youngest, became a teacher and a journalist in Tampere, where he was soon known as The Firebrand. When Juhani left for America at the beginning of the nineties, never to be heard from again, Timo came back to the village and took over the farm. From now on, he declared, he would run it according to socialist principles—an idea met with silence and even stares of astonished amusement by the peasants themselves, and with outright hostility by the local estate owners, seeing in Timo precisely the sort of terrorist—someone wanting something better—who was already causing so much blood and trouble across the border in Russia. It was still a time when any kind of change in the arrangement of wealth seemed to the rich unimaginable; Finland would somehow rid herself of Russia and become free, while they went on being fat and indeed getting fatter. They didn't see that the world was about to change forever. Few did, but Timo was one of these. In his way, he was a visionary.

Things were bad at the farm from the start. Cows were struck by disease. The worst summer on record cut crops by half. People went hungry, and when Timo's horse died, one of the local estate managers teasingly said he would lend him his children's pet, an offer that Timo accepted, and so from then on he was seen bouncing through the snow on a very small donkey with huge, sad eyes. "You look like Don Quixote. Or is it Sancho Panza?" said Kalliokoski, who had taken up his appointment as the new priest.

Timo, forced to start teaching at the school, now found some of the villagers smirking behind his back. They despised him for the hope he'd held out, and it was into this atmosphere of struggle and disappointment that he welcomed a bride. Julie Agren was a distant cousin, so distant that Timo had never met her. Her father was an officer in the Royal Swedish Army who lost a fortune gambling, and then, like Lauri, took his own life. This turn of events left Julie's mother, a one-time belle of Stockholm, with four unmarried daughters on her hands, and it made her entirely reconceive her picture of the Vaananens. Prior to this they had been the Finnish country bumpkins, quite beyond the pale. Now, she suddenly remembered, the father of the family had been a priest, and one of the boys had been to university, somewhere. Wasn't there land?

Julie Agren was sent by ferry to Vaasa, and thence north and east to the village, a five-day journey across rough roads and through the great Finnish forests. She arrived in midwinter, bringing with her a padlocked trunk and nine leather suitcases, the only remaining evidence of her family's wealth, alighting from the carriage with a tentative step and the nervous, sparkling smile of a girl hoping to make a good impression—only to find that she'd stepped into drifting snow three feet deep. Timo and Kalliokoski jumped forward to haul her out.

Timo was twenty-two when they married, Julie only seventeen. She miscarried her first child, and a second, and Esko was born two years later in 1890. The pregancy was difficult, the birth premature, but Esko was from the start a strong and healthy child, and his first memories of his mother were of a woman who shone and sparkled. Julie painted, she read, she learned to smoke and loved to laugh. She studied the Bible with Kalliokoski and took Esko boating on the lake.

Esko was eight years old when, on February 15, 1899, Czar Nicholas II announced that the Russian police would have authority within the Grand Duchy of Finland, that higher taxes would be paid, that ill-word spoken of the Czar would be punishable, as in Russia, with imprisonment and even death. The Russians were out to milk the Finns, which roused anger and anxiety and accusations of betrayal throughout the land, even in the remotest country-side, even in Pyhajarvi where the villagers were usually oblivious to all but the subject of their own bellies and the prospect of the next vodka bottle. They said Czarist agents were everywhere. Mail was opened and read. There was a twenty-four-hour store in Helsinki to supply infiltrators and provocateurs with disguises at any time. Finland was drawn into the half-lunatic world of the Romanov twilight and Julie became obsessed with the notion that the vil-lagers were watching her, checking on her, chattering about her. This struck Timo as entirely possible, though not for the reasons Julie imagined: after all, she was young, beautiful, a stranger they didn't understand and perhaps feared and envied.

Julie was not to be comforted. Her mind meandered deep in some unknown forest. "They're following me about now. There's a short and pock-marked man with hair like a carrot who's making notes." She nodded quickly up and down. "It's true. There's another with a telescope. I saw him take out a knife and slice a wart off his hand, just like that." She shivered, saying she was afraid to leave the house. For hours she would pace the loft where they slept in summer. She painted pictures that no one could understand, which was when Kalliokoski came to tell Timo some of the villagers were saying she was possessed by the devil. She cracked a plate and carved at her wrists. She complained of headaches; she couldn't sleep and always needed company, saying that her blood was melted lead, or that her brain weighed a thousand pounds, or that the air in the house was growing tight around her throat. One night she came into the kitchen clutching her head and crying that her brain was on fire. She stripped naked in the kitchen, drew about herself an oblong of scarlet paint, and announced that this, like the house itself, like the village, was her coffin. She was afraid she'd hurt herself again, or all of them, she said, unless Timo did something now.

That night, with Esko on his back, Timo walked three miles through the summer night to the doctor in the village. The doctor came with them at once to the house, and when they arrived they found Julie covered in a mess of paint and blood; she'd smeared herself in oils, then rolled in broken glass. Timo would always remember his wife's look of confusion and betrayal when he signed the papers and the men arrived in a cart from Kuopio to take her, and there was a moment when he almost gave in, faced by her imploring glance.

Julie returned a few weeks later, but she seemed far away, quiet and smiling, almost dazed, as if a door had slammed shut, leaving her outside herself. There were black rings around her eyes. They'd shaved her head, and thereafter she kept her hair short.

Even as a young child Esko understood that his mother loved him and that she wasn't well. He found that he could soothe the edges of her temper, lessen her anxiety easier than his father, and from then on he adopted a protective attitude toward her. "My little brother, Esko," she called him, when they were in the boat on the lake, or walking in the forest, or making ice lanterns in the snow, and his heart burst with pride. He wanted to look after her forever and when she began to cry he circled her waist with his arms and kissed the tears from her cheek. She taught him to skate and to draw, and these were the fondest, most peaceful memories of his childhood, for when she was on the ice, or when she had a pencil in her hand, he felt a stillness and calm confidence emanating from her—the result of the aptitude she possessed in both these areas, skills she made it the business of her love to pass on to him. She gave him a swooning heart and a belief in himself that was ferociously resilient—a romantic and dangerous birthright.

*   *   *

On that night in 1901, when Kalliokoski dropped the copy of *Hufvud-stadsbladet* beneath the chair in the kitchen, Esko went to his room and didn't bother to lie down. He stood by the window, peering through the tiny, flawed panes into the yard at the back of the house. The yard sloped down past the chicken run to a looming red barn and a line of birch trees whose silver trunks glimmered like ghosts. It was after midnight, and the yard, the village, the whole rest of the world, seemed to be asleep, either dead or dreaming, embalmed in this gorgeous blanket of thick midsummer light. Deep silence—not even a sound from the dogs.

Winter had stayed late this year. There'd been skating and skiing on the ice until mid-May when at last the sun had gobbled up the snow and spring crashed in like a riot, rousing the frozen earth: in the cemeteries, grass shot knee-high above the graves; in the school yard the trees were splashed with sudden green; in the forests black swarms of mosquitoes attacked the head, shrieking like anarchists; and on the farms the men took their girlfriends to the lake, or tried to get them tipsy so they could sneak a kiss and more beneath the boughs of the sickly sweet bird-cherry. A hot sun warmed the lake's chill, tempting age-old pike to show their snouts at the surface. Spring wasn't a season; it was an explosion, an act of violence.

Through the bedroom wall Esko heard his father's drunken snore, a wavering rumble that rose to a crescendo of almost choirlike fluting and then fell away again. Esko both loved his father and was very much afraid of him. He seemed to be angry so much of the time, especially when they were alone together. It was when Esko was by himself that his heart cried out for his mother: her loss was an ache that never went away, as though some big part of him were still burned and bleeding. The world outside felt raw, changed too. The forest, the lake, the village, the church; everything seemed different— scary, chaotic, formless. She'd been his weather, his landscape, and he believed he could still get her back, if he could prove he loved her enough. "Kalevala" had plenty of stories where the dead turned out not to be dead at all. After Lemminkainen was chopped to pieces his mother went to the river of death, Tuonela, dredged the river, collecting now some hand, now some head, now a backbone, now various other scraps, and brought him back to life. She made her son, shaping him, forming him just the way he used to be. And then she anointed him with ointments and song so that he rose from death as if it had been merely sleep.

Esko was bursting with secrets and hopes and fears he couldn't tell any-body about and he would happily go to Tuonela to bring back his mother if someone would show him the way. The letters and drawings that he'd laid on top of his mother's grave in the past obviously had not succeeded.

Turning from the window, he lit a candle and sat down at the desk he'd made in the corner, two planks of polished pine nailed to the upended halves of a cut water barrel; he sharpened a pencil, drew the paper toward him, quickly sketched his mother's face, and then began to write in a hand that scratched and trembled at first but was soon rushing across the paper.

> They say "Kalevala" is all true, that it is a factual account of the old history of our country. Father tells me this is a dangerous lie, and I think he may be correct, for in 'Kalevala,' when someone wants to heal a wound, if they've been stabbed by a sword or hit by an arrow and bitten by a snake, they sing about the origins of the sword, or the arrow, or the snake, they sing the offending thing out of existence. It was

the lake that drowned you, and I've learned about the origins of all our lakes. They were formed when the year-round ice to the north reached all the way down here but began to melt and dragged itself back across the scalp of the earth, leaving the lakes and the boulders and rocks that are scattered all around. The lake is kept full by rainwater, and the rain falls when the clouds are too bloated to hold it, and the clouds form according to changing temperatures in the air. I have danced around the lake at midnight and sung this song, but still you have not come back.

A few nights ago I dreamed about you, Mother. We were flying together in the sky, as if we were born upward like a shooting firework. I was pleased to have the dream, which made me feel close to you. I miss you, Mother, and think of you every day. I believe that Father misses you too.

A wind rattled the glass in the narrow window, the candle wobbled in a draft from the door, and Esko wondered if some spirit was chiding or warning him. Really, he didn't think his father missed his mother at all. From deep within the forest came a shotgun's flat crack. Someone was hunting by the lake, or firing at a crow feasting on strawberries in the midnight sun.

I'm sorry I haven't written to you in a while, and I hope you haven't completely lost interest in me, but Father has been keeping me busy. I've been working hard at my studies and we've been traveling to meetings as always.

Esko coughed and hurried on, for here too he'd written an untruth, or the shadow of one. His father wasn't keeping him busy. The meetings, in this last month, had been infrequent, as if Timo were worried or in hiding. Esko had been ashamed to write because in recent weeks his mother's features had been blurry in his mind and how could he view this blot of memory other than as a terrible failure of his love? Then, tonight, when Kalliokoski had been fussing about with *Hufvudstadsbladet*, the vision of her face had risen before him, restoring the most precious of treasures.

You once said that you would be with me in my difficult
times, or when something big and important was happening.
Tonight Iosip Kalliokoski came to the house and he brought
with him the newspaper as he always does, the one in
Swedish that he and you used to read together, the one Father
doesn't like. There was an article in the newspaper, Mother,
an article about something called an elevator, something
absolutely extraordinary, I know that.

He paused for a moment, drawing a neat line with his ruler under the
word *know*.

I can't describe how I feel. This thing, the elevator, troubles
me. It must mean something, even though Father assures me
it can have no meaning. Mother, I need your help. Explain
this mystery to me, if you can, or tell me what to do. I promise that I'll write again soon. Your son, Esko.

Now, as he folded the paper and laid aside his pencil, another picture of
his mother came to mind. They'd been on the lake when a pair of cranes flew
over the boat and one of them let out a sad cry. "I've never seen them fly so
low before," his mother had said. "They're leaving me." She leaned over the
boat to scoop up a mouthful of water. "Oh God, I drowned my dress," she
said, showing him her soaked sleeve, drops falling from it, laughing; then her
eyes went back to following the cranes. She'd had a passion for birds, looking
at birds, sketching them. She gave them human personalities, as if they were
characters in the village. Some of her birds were calm and happy, even conquering, filled with dreams and spirit; others were melancholy, sad.

Having pushed the letter into an envelope, having sealed it with a shy
kiss, he heard her voice, teasing him: "In Stockholm I knew a boy who read
all the time and he became a Baptist minister. Shall I lose you to religion,
Esko? Will you desert me for the church? Or for politics, like your father.
Come, let's sit together, we'll draw. See that man going into the stable, the
one who's come to talk about socialism with your father—doesn't he look so
sad and typical, with his bent fingers and flattened nose, his face that looks
like a badly abused potato, still screwing up its eyes and smiling. He's one of
the farmworkers, of course, and your father doesn't realize that he'll always be

far more interested in cows than the communist collective. In fact he's not very interesting at all, is he? Let's draw him like he was a prophet. Quite mad." His mother had believed that she saw deep into the essence of people and things. Where his father spoke of materialism and the inevitable process of history, she pulled inside herself Ukko, the god of the air, and Tapio, god of the trees. She'd told Esko about ghosts and spirits, trolls who hoarded gold in the mists of the forest and cursed your fate. Her smile had flickered off and on like a troubled candle.

Esko took a deep breath and the sound of it made him realize the house had grown still. Even his father's snoring had stopped. Everything was calm, though the room seemed hot and muggy, as though the air were pressing on the sides of his head.

He thought: storm's coming.

In summer, storms arrived like this, without warning, speeding across the lake. Sometimes, standing at the shore, you heard the rain before you saw it, as if the lake were a sheet of tin that was being flicked with grain and pounded.

Through the flawed windowpane Esko saw that the sky was dark. The birch trees on the other side of the barn were tossing their heads angrily. The first drop of rain struck the window like in ingot, and Esko jumped. A fork of lightning divided the sky; through the lightning's dazzle came thunder and a few more fat drops, and then all at once rain was falling in rods, filling the air like smoke, bouncing off the roof of the barn, spattering the sill, hammering the house so hard Esko wondered whether the ceiling was going to cave in.

He shivered with terror and delight, for he knew that his mother was within the storm. She was the booming thunder. She was the rain that had turned the window into a dribbling lens. She was the wind that blew open the bedroom door and flattened the candle on the makeshift desk.

Pieces of her are everywhere, Esko thought, she's come back; and suddenly he knew what to do about *Hufvudstadsbladet*, knew as clearly as if she'd whispered the words in his ear. He unsheathed his *puukko*, his short-bladed knife, and poked his face into the room next door, where his father was slumbering through it all, spread-eagled on the bed with his mouth wide open, having removed neither clothes nor boots. His blond hair, limp with sweat, shone like the halo on a sick angel.

Esko rarely came into this room. In the dim light he could still make out the piles of books and papers lying everywhere in neat stacks, an order that existed nowhere else in his father's life. The shotgun in the corner was a single-barreled affair from Helsinki. On top of a cupboard a black revolver pointed its open mouth at Esko's head. The tall stove in the corner gave off a smell of pine and warm metal, mingling with the stink of sweat and schnapps that seemed to exude from every pore of his father's body and that made Esko want to hit him or even stab him. Why weren't things straightforward anymore, the way they'd once been? He crept forward, grasped his father's stubbled, saliva-speckled chin, and pushed shut his mouth. Timo grunted, snuffled, rolled over, and the snoring began again, jousting with the storm.

Hufvudstadsbladet was where Kalliokoski had left it, folded neatly beneath the kitchen table. It was the work of a few moments to secure it, light another candle, and climb the steep stairs to the attic, where he was struck in the face by oppressive, stifling heat, where, only inches above his head, rain drilled at the roof, where long beams of naked pine ran the length of the house, and where he crept through heaps of boxes and old wood tools, bumping into cobwebs as he struggled toward a narrow slit of gray, the window at the far end. Heart racing faster, he lit the candle and smoothed the billowing pages of *Hufvudstadsbladet* on the floor. He pushed his good eye close so he could read for himself the story about the magic box that went up in the sky.

> An electric elevator, the first in Finland, has been installed in the new Diktonius Building on Aleksandersgaten in Helsingfors. "The elevator carries up to nine passengers at a time and moves smoothly at the touch of a lever," says Leonid Mimmelmann, managing director of the Diktonius department store, which will occupy the building. "Our operators will thus carry our customers both nearer to heaven and to more of our goods, which are of such excellent value and quality. The total travel of the elevator cage is twenty-five meters, and safety is ensured by a sealed air cushion at the bottom of the shaft. Sliding doors of great strength, and automatic in action, are the only openings."

There was a picture of Mr. Leonid Mimmelmann, a pale smooth-faced man of indeterminate age who wore a bowler hat; in Esko's opinion, Mr. Mimmelmann was far too dull looking a fellow to be associated with an event as important as the elevator; but below his picture there was a diagram, a cross section of the building that showed the precious nut of the elevator within it, complete with its system of pulleys and cables.

His heart socked like a piston and he leaned his eye closer, until it was within an inch of the newsprint, as if magnetized by the elevator.

He sliced the story from *Hufvudstadsbladet*, using the unsheathed blade of his *puukko*.

"Esko, what are you doing?"

Esko lifted his head, his glance traveling up to a stern face that in the dim midnight light made no answer to his smile. "Nothing, Father."

"What's that? What are you reading?"

Esko stood up, brushing dust from the knees of his pants, an old pair of his father's, far too big, turned up at the ankle and looped to his waist with a belt of wide leather. He was trying to come up with a plan.

"Nothing," he said, raising his eye, struggling with the word.

"Nothing? Then why hide it so fast? If it's really nothing then I won't be able to see what it is. Will I?"

Esko was rocking to and fro, concentrating. He knew that if his father saw the story before he himself had discovered its secret then the power of that secret, whatever it was, would vanish. This was private, something his father should have no part of.

The floor creaked beneath Timo's advancing feet. "You're making me repeat myself. What's going on here? You're hiding something behind your back. What is it?"

Esko shut his eye, his mind questing here and there, searching for words, for the spell that would will his father away.

"*Show me,*" his father said coldly, as if to warn that he'd given Esko life and he could take it away again. Timo ran a hand through his hair; his tone became gentler. "It can't be so bad or important, but I want to know the truth."

Esko, tucking the newspaper clipping into the belt at the back of his pants, realized that the dusty air of the attic was cooler, quieter. There was no more hammering on the roof. The storm had passed and Esko felt a calm penetrate his mind, left there by his mother. He spoke, and the words came out for once with ease, as if he were speaking in a dream. "My mother isn't dead after all," he said, and he truly thought his father would be thrilled by this information. "She was here. She was outside in the storm."

Timo blinked, his face glossy with sweat.

"What's this rubbish about your mother?"

"It's not rubbish, Father. She came back in the storm."

Esko felt the blow without even seeing it. His head clattered. He was lifted from his feet and fell on the floor with a thump, watching the *Hufvud-stadsbladet* article, shaken loose from his pants, waft away like a butterfly.

"Did you like that?" said Timo, and spit flew from his mouth, striking Esko in the face. Timo's face was heavy and red with rage. "Do you want some more?"

"No."

Esko's face stung, his belly heaved. The blow had forced tears into his eye and yet he was determined not to sob.

"Then don't lie to me," said Timo in a hushed voice. Esko thought that his father looked like a giant. All the same, he couldn't lie. And, perhaps too, he wanted to needle and provoke.

"I'm not," said Esko, working his aching jaw. "Mother was here."

Timo raised his hand again and this time it was bunched into a fist. Esko ran. He ran without thinking, pushing past his father and taking a tumble down the vertiginous attic stairs. Regained his balance and ran out of the house, even though he wore no shoes. Ran out of the yard, down the track, into the gloomy, dripping forest. Ran until he was lost and his feet were bleeding.

3

Esko was at the shore to meet the boats that came scudding across the lake to find him. He noted with shame and a little fear the broad shoulders of his father, wielding the oars in the lead boat, and, behind him, the watchful face of Kalliokoski, which carried a smile Esko didn't quite understand, tight with pride and expectation. Esko sighed, prepared to accept without complaint whatever punishment would be his due. He'd already decided that he would forget all about the elevator, if only he could be friends with his father. He was nervous, but proud too, because he'd looked after himself for two entire nights in the wilderness. He'd come to regard this island as his own, a place where he'd grown up a little, and where he'd learned that it was foolish and dangerous to irritate adults with difficult, imponderable questions. He'd never mention elevators. He'd make it his business to try never even to think about them. Perhaps one day he'd see an elevator for himself, but until then the machine would be erased from his mind.

The boats were closer now, and Esko already heard the talk and the relieved laughter of the men, and water splashing as the oars dipped in and out. He looked around for the last time. Two red squirrels chased each other down the branch of a swaying spruce. The sky was stuck all over with scraps of cloud like cotton. The sun glistened atop the quick, low waves and shone through the wings of a butterfly. On the shore there was the rotting hulk of a boat. He made a promise that one day he'd come back and see the boat again, to remind himself of the adventure.

At first the adults seemed in awe of what he'd done, though there wasn't much to it. He'd carved a pair of crude clogs from driftwood because he'd run from the house with no shoes on his feet. He'd fashioned a lean-to from stones and branches, which he'd cut and pruned with his *puukko*. He'd slept on a many-layered mattress of birch leaves.

"We saw your signal. We saw the fire," his father said.

"I lit the fire to cook my fish," said Esko in a low, steady voice.

Timo Vaananen did a strange little dance on the beach, waving his arms and kicking his boots in the air. Then he stopped, embarrassed by his own performance, and took a deep breath. "Oh my. Oh my, oh my. A true Finn, my son's a true Finn," he said. "So he could cook his fish—how do you like that?" Esko felt himself clutched tight in a clumsy hug. "Where's the boat? Did you make yourself a boat then, eh?"

"I borrowed a boat."

"*Borrowed* a boat?"

"It belongs to Turkkila."

The big men in the search party were laughing because Turkkila was a drunk who probably didn't remember even that he *had* a boat, and the smooth side of Esko's face burned with pride; he was happy to be accepted as the comrade of these men.

"Are we going home, Father?"

Timo flicked his straight fair hair out of his eyes and stared at the toe of his boot. He made a small motion, a nervous bob of the head, a puzzled gesture of rage and almost, it seemed, resignation and surrender.

He turned away.

It was Kalliokoski's authoritative voice that spoke, with smooth, polished authority, a clipped aria of triumph. "Yes, we're going back," he said.

Esko was settled in one boat with Kalliokoski; he saw his father, alone, in one of the others. Timo had his back to him. Timo raised the oars, turned about, and began to row to the distant shore. "Dad, you're heading the wrong way. The village is the other way!" Esko shouted, but his father ignored him, keeping his face down, working the oars. "Dad, Dad!" Esko called, frightened now, trying to jump out of the boat. Kalliokoski clamped his arms across Esko's chest, holding him back. "Dad!"

"Your father is going away," said Kalliokoski. "You are coming to live with me and Mrs. Kalliokoski for a while, Esko."

Esko struggled silently with this information. "I don't understand."

"And then you will go to study in Helsingfors. It will be a fine time. We must prepare ourselves," said Kalliokoski, signaling to the other men to get the boat underway. "Your father has asked me to look after you. To make sure you study and better yourself and do well. You will become a lawyer, and perhaps a politician. Certainly a distinguished man."

Esko turned his head, Kalliokoski's words washing over him, as he watched the other boat, with the diminishing figure of his father in it, slip around the back of the island and disappear, leaving the lake smooth and flat for a moment before a breeze came, raising cold ridges that looked like iron.

*   *   *

As the weeks went by, the children in the village tortured Esko with rumors about his father's disappearance. Timo Vaananen was rotting in jail, they said. He was begging in the streets of Vaasa. He'd fled to the east with a Mongolian whore. He lay in an Ostrobothnian ditch with his throat cut, food for rats and mosquitoes. Esko made no answer to the taunts, nor did he complain, even to Kalliokoski. He wandered from room to room in the vicarage, staring at all of the clocks, trying to steer a path between them, feeling that their intricate, whirring mechanisms were somehow malignant and meant him harm; and once, when he knew he was alone, he waited for the grandfather clock in the parlor to spring to life and attack him. He moved closer to it, opened the glass, and, having removed the patch from his eye, pressed close so that the sharp arrow at the end of the minute hand punctured the flesh of the still healing socket and drew blood. Just as he blamed himself for his mother's death, he believed that it was his fault that his father had hit him and no longer wanted to live with him. The fact that he wasn't interested in having his father come back only made him feel more guilty. He didn't talk about this to anybody. He built his own castle of solitude and drew up the drawbridge.

"Esko, are you not happy here?" said Kalliokoski late one afternoon. They were in the vicarage kitchen, where a large kettle stood on the range. All day long beggars had been coming in to spoon brown soup from wooden cups on the kitchen table. Sometimes Esko had imagined that he saw his father; at other times that he *was* his father, filled with stony rage, about to strike the beggar. Each time the image disappeared from his mind as quickly as it had flashed there, and he felt even more restless and uncomfortable with himself than before.

"You never smile or run about," Kalliokoski continued, stirring the soup kettle with a wooden spoon. "I've even heard that on several occasions you have failed to attend morning prayers at the school. Is this true? Is this the behavior of a boy who hopes and expects to continue his education in the capital?"

Kalliokoski smiled as he stirred, trying to coax Esko along, but Esko said nothing, staring at his feet, wondering about the boys he would be likely to meet in Helsinki. They would come from the best families. They would live in beautiful mansions high on a hill overlooking the harbor.

"Is it true?"

Esko said nothing.

Kalliokoski's smile tightened. "You have not been attending prayers?"

Esko moved his head; he had not.

"Why?"

"I don't believe in God," he said without thinking, almost startling himself. Jesus had vanished from inside his head. It had happened suddenly, unexpectedly. Jesus had been there, for sure, when he'd been willing Kalliokoski to leave behind the copy of *Hufvudstadsbladet*. Now Jesus, a certainty that had been inside him, unquestioned all this time, had slipped away. "God's dead, isn't He?"

"Esko, that's blasphemy and it's not true," said Kalliokoski, stopping as if he'd been hit. He quickly reached out to touch a beggar he'd just given a cup of soup, and then pulled back, realizing the beggar's head was alive with lice. He swallowed hard. "When did it occur, this failure of belief?"

Esko's silence was defiant.

"You're telling the truth?"

A nod.

"It's dispiriting," said Kalliokoski, staring into the brown soup. Then he looked up, quick as a bird. "Esko, do you understand why your father left the village?"

Esko's hand went to his eye, to the patch, and then his fingers slipped down over the stiffness of his scarred cheek. "The elevator," he said in a low mumble.

"What's that?"

"The elevator," Esko repeated. This time the word came out loud and he moved his feet, waiting for something terrible to happen.

One of the men in the soup line was staring at him. It was Turkkila, thin and dark and shaggy, like a lean dog with too much hair. His pink cheeks and crushed strawberry nose proclaimed that he was, as usual, very much the worse for vodka. A sudden gleam had appeared in his bloodshot eyes, puzzling Esko for the moment, for what could Turkkila know about elevators? Then, blushing, Esko realized that Turkkila couldn't possibly know anything. Turkkila was embarrassed, that was all, because, strictly speaking, he shouldn't have been in line for soup. He wasn't a beggar, but a gravedigger, not a good job exactly, but a secure one, and now he apparently thought Esko was going to rat on him. Esko couldn't get used to the respect and deference with which many of the men in the village treated him now that he was a member of the priest's household. His father would have hated the idea.

Kalliokoski stirred the soup and ladled another bowlful, his bearded face tight with concentration. "You're talking about the article in *Hufvudstadsbladet*?"

Esko felt his mouth fill again with the taste of metal and newsprint, the taste that was almost like blood. He remembered how he'd pressed his cheek so close to the grainy diagram of the elevator, how his excited breath had seemed to urge the picture into motion, as if his imagination itself could bring the elevator to life and make it soar upward off the page.

"What happened that night after I left you and your father?" said Kalliokoski.

Esko's hand moved again to the patch over his eye.

"I stole the article from the newspaper."

"Yes, that is bad."

"My father hit me."

"You caused a lot of trouble, you know," said Kalliokoski, nodding as if he understood everything now. His smile was warm. "We had to organize a search party."

Esko blushed with remembered shame and looked up to find Turkkila still staring at him. Turkkila had only one tooth in his mouth, a sorry yellow incisor that as he smiled hung over his grooved lower lip like a fang. Esko looked quickly away, seeking the friendlier face of Kalliokoski.

"Finland wants to be free. The question is—how? Do you know Bongman?"

Turkkila grinned, turning his head to one side so that brown soup leaked past that one tooth, dribbling into his beard.

"I'm not talking to you, you idiot," said Kalliokoski in the same mild, controlled voice. "I'm talking to my friend Esko. Be off with you," he said, and brandished the tin ladle like a weapon. Turkkila smiled, shuffling away with his steaming cup of soup.

"Yes, I know Bongman," said Esko. Bongman was the church pastor, a serious, round, fleshy person; he labored in the church office, ordering about Turkkila and the bell ringers.

"There are those, like Bongman, who believe that independence will be achieved merely by the worship of all things nationalistic and the quoting of the "Kalevala" at all times and in all places."

Esko's hand shot out, nudging one of the soup cups so that it sat in a circle with the others.

"Why did you do that?" said Kalliokoski sharply.

"It's perfect now," said Esko.

"Just so," Kalliokoski said with a puzzled frown, looking at the cups drawn up in so artful a pattern on the table. He regarded Esko seriously for a moment, saying nothing. Then he went on: "Your father has other ideas. More in tune with the real world, probably, and much more dangerous."

"He's a Red," said Esko simply.

"Quite. And just now knew that he was likely to be arrested. He'd gone too far, you see, and so he had to go away."

Turkkila muttered and mumbled. "Go away, he tells me, have soup, now go away. What a bloody carry on. Come for soup, get insulted. That's life, innit. Next thing he'll be trying to sell me the idea that the earth is a sphere."

"Not you, I'm not talking to you," said Kalliokoski with an exasperated sigh and a flash of impatience in his dark eyes. "I'm talking to the boy."

"Is he saying I might as well not exist? Isn't he a lovely bloke?" said Turkkila, shrugging his shoulders, appealing to Esko.

"My good man, I'm not about to engage with you in a discussion of philosophy. Thank Our Lord that your belly will be full today."

Turkkila stood up straight, revealing that beneath his worn and ragged coat he wore no shirt and his wiry body was matted with yellowish and reddish hair. For a moment old Turkkila looked a little dangerous, like a wolf. "Me own father's dead now. Went swimming at the bottom of the lake, oh, it's many years since. But when I were young I used to live with him in a house wot had a kitchen almost as big as this one. The Devil were in that kitchen. He'd come out at night, he would, and try to snatch boys and their mothers."

"This is outrageous," said Kalliokoski, moving out from behind the kitchen range. "Turkkila, is that you? It *is* you. Have you gone quite mad?"

"Little Esko Vaananen. A good boy, a clever boy, a sad boy who sees things and has been to the river of death and will go twice more before he sinks in it," said Turkkila. "Beware of iron, boy, beware of steel. Above all, beware of them el . . . them el . . . them wotdoyamacallems . . . them elderberries."

Turkkila plucked a battered black hat from his pocket and tried to position it atop his head; but he was so drunk it was as if his hand no longer remembered the length of his body and he had to reach again and again with the flapping felt. When at last he succeeded, and the hat was perched like a rebellious crow, he said, "Elderberries," and turned, walking to the door with a wobbling delicacy.

"Terrifying, truly terrifying," said Kalliokoski, and briskly shook his head, dismissing Turkkila from his mind so he could go back to doling out soup to less truculent supplicants. "Your father did what he did for his own reasons, which have nothing to do with you or elevators or *Hufvudstadsbladet*. Nor is it for you to blame yourself or him. Do you understand? The God in whom you say you no longer believe will take care of that."

Esko wanted to be reassured and for a little while he was. Later that night he stood at the window in his bedroom in the vicarage and looked out toward the lake, a gray, ruffled, endless expanse, surrounded by trees that were now only silhouettes in the mist and gloom. If he shut his eyes for a moment it was easy to imagine that the trees weren't trees at all, but cowled monks, holy men lost in the forest, and suddenly he was bothered by the memory of Turkkila, who had seemed to know something he didn't, who had seemed to see right through him, into his mind, into his guts, and even beyond, to the spinning things that drove and controlled him. Standing there on that summer night, Esko thought for the first time about his future. What might it hold, and why had Turkkila told him to beware of elevators?

4

Months went by with no word from Timo. It was early September, at which time each year a fair came to the village for the harvest festival, and Esko was locked in his room. Arrayed on the bed in front of him were the new clothes Kalliokoski demanded that he put on. Esko was perched on the floor with his knees drawn up to his chin, fuming, dreaming of how one day he would defeat Kalliokoski in some great battle. Perhaps he would smite Kalliokoski with an ax, he considered, as the peasant Lalli had killed the English bishop Henry on the ice at Koylio Lake many centuries ago. But that would be very bloody, he thought, and, besides, he would have to go outside to get the ax. Chewing on his knee, he came up with the solution. He would wear the clothes and go to the fair, but without Kalliokoski.

Five minutes later his long body was nipped inside a belted jacket of itching tweed, his legs clad in tweed trousers that fell like armor to the calf where they met socks of thick black wool and his feet protesting inside boots that pinched. On his head he wore a cap of the same absurd tweed. He looked, not rich or privileged, but crazy. He swung open the bedroom window, lifted himself out onto the sill, and suddenly found himself skidding down the steep, shingled roof until at the last moment his fingers caught the lip of the gutter, from which he hung, tight boots kicking. He dropped to the ground. Miraculously, no part of his nutty tweed uniform seemed to be torn or scuffed. He set the tweed cap at an angle over one eye and ran, out of the vicarage gates, through the graveyard where late summer roses lay beneath iron crosses and black marble tombstones and a powerful aroma of black currants came to him on the wind that ripped through the trees. He was free for the rest of the afternoon and evening. He hoped no one he knew saw him in these clothes, but then he realized that this didn't matter: the village boys laughed at his face anyway, or turned away altogether, which was even worse. The tweed would give them something new to go at, something he could laugh at; it *was* funny.

The fair was held in a meadow between the church and Kivimaa's place, the richest farm in the neighborhood, where great stacks of corded birch formed a barrier of wood between the two barns, tall structures with angled uprights and chinks left between the crossbeams so that the sun peeped through. In the center of the meadow itself a wide empty circle of grass had been scythed, while the grass beyond was uncut, chest high. Esko slowed to a saunter, wiped his forehead and tried to appear casual, moving between the stalls and flapping tents, among the horse traders who swaggered with their thumbs hooked in their belts and the village boys wearing peaked caps and derby hats that seemed too big, handed down from their fathers. He was about to congratulate himself that no one seemed to recognize him when suddenly he saw Bongman's Son approaching.

Bongman's Son was older than Esko by a year, and his height had made a sudden spurt, as if his body were determined to escape, not only from the clothes that tried to contain it, but its general surroundings. His face was more acne than face and the villagers tended to stare at him, muttering and chewing sagaciously on their pipes. Where Bongman senior was fat, Bongman's Son was lean, indeed almost impossibly thin, as though he could step through the eye of a needle and enter the kingdom of heaven without any trouble at all. Not that Bongman's Son appeared to hold any interest in the hereafter. He more or less lived in the forest, where he claimed to know magicians who were teaching him how to hunt and how to hypnotize bears. In the days when they used to run together, before Esko's accident, Esko had seen him catch a duck, wring its neck with a casual, almost delicate flick of the wrist, as if he were shaking loose a towel, and then slit its throat for good measure. "It's Scarface and he's wearing silly clothes," said Bongman's Son, and without thought Esko slipped into the nearest tent, ran through to the other side, wriggled under the canvas, and shot around to the front just in time to see the boots of Bongman's Son wriggling on the ground at the far side, taking the same route that he had himself only moments before. So Esko passed into the tent for a second time and caught his breath, letting his eyes grow accustomed to the dimness before moving to the darkest corner, where he waited until he was satisfied that his trick had worked.

The tent flapped and billowed, as if at war with the light; from time to time the canvas would appear to have won, and would subside with a happy sigh, and the defeated light would grow dim inside the tent; then the enraged canvas would shake and threaten to fly away, lifting at the edges, bursting at the top, as the wind allowed its ally light to run rampage through the space. Esko was amazed that no one else seemed to be concerned about this life-and-death struggle. They stood about, or lounged on the ground, or sat on benches, laughing, whispering, waiting for a different sort of show to begin. At last a man in a threadbare suit appeared with a straw hat pushed back high on his forehead. He smiled, coughed, and introduced another man who came on with skittles and juggled. It was nothing much, Esko thought, not so fine a spectacle as the game of space and light that the canvas itself was providing, but then it was the turn of a group of men in black boots, black smocks, and with black hoods over their heads, lumbering and dancing like bears. One of them spun around, roaring beneath his hood so that Esko saw the crude felt of a mask suck into the man's mouth, at which time he lurched forward suddenly, appearing to strike directly at Esko, and Esko had to force himself not to jump. Instead he managed a smile, though his heart pounded. Next, a daguerrotypist set up his equipment and invited volunteers. A Russian soldier stepped forward with his friend, a female dwarf whose head didn't even reach the bottom of the broad leather belt of his uniform. The daguerrotypist smiled, fussed the pair into position, and then retreated behind his box, which was on stilts, and covered his head with a blanket. He held up a long instrument that flashed and went immediately dark even as it popped and blinded. The audience gasped and, when they'd finished blinking, stared at the daguerrotypist who busily thanked the soldier and the dwarf and threw his eyes nervously around, searching for the next volunteer.

Esko squirmed, dreading that the daguerrotypist would conclude his scan of the audience and, a hunter having singled out the most vulnerable of the herd, prey on him. Which is precisely what happened. The daguerrotypist stepped forward, arm shooting out. "There's a likely looking young fellow," he said with a grin, and the rest of the audience turned toward Esko, joining in the merriment. "Step forward, young man," he said, and before Esko knew what was happening eager hands were guiding him to the front. "Come on, don't be shy."

It was too late now to try to make a run for it. He looked to see if by chance one of the bear dancers had left behind a hood that he could grab and pull over his head. There was nothing, so Esko stood up straight, tugged the thorny tweed lapels of his suit, and faced the crowd. Suddenly the light in the tent seemed thin and terribly bright, and he wondered whether the spotty face of Bongman's Son was about to burst into the tent, thus completing the humiliation.

But something strange happened. Bongman's Son did not appear. No one laughed. The daguerrotypist, whose puffy, bearded face was fixed in a grin, tugged at Esko's arms, pushed Esko's legs a little farther apart, turned Esko's chin first to the left, then to the right. The audience, it seemed to Esko, watched in a way that was not scornful or amused, but fascinated, even fearful and awed. The daguerrotypist's gun banged, and Esko's good eye went dark, as if its light had been whipped away into that flashing, smoking sulphur.

Afterward, outside, Esko saw that the beautiful afternoon was already, as the sky darkened, turning into a beautiful evening. A rising moon was slashed in two by a long, thin line of scarlet cloud. The air was filled with the smell of black currant and hot birch, and the farmhands who had been harvesting all day were trooping in from the fields. The fair was busy now, and Esko pushed between adult legs, running between the booths and stalls. There was a woman selling red earthenware pots; after that, a man working puppets on sticks; after that, a table with glasses of fresh milk and strawberry juice laid out on it, and Esko heard the clink of coins falling together; after that, a man from Kuopio who would sketch your portrait for a mark. Esko stood beside his easel for a while, watching him work. Bongman's Son was nowhere to be seen.

A red-faced, white-whiskered old man held open the flap to the biggest of the tents. People flocked toward him, smiling and laughing, and Esko gathered that there was going to be a dance. The old man was short, had on a long black coat, and was himself grinning in a complacent way, as if he were the best dancer that had ever been known.

"I dance," said Esko by way of introduction. "My mother taught me. In the kitchen." Filled with a strange confidence, he smiled at the old man and went beneath the flap into the tent, which had been decorated with branches and saplings so that it smelled like the forest. It was gloomy like the forest too, the only light coming from a burning oil lamp, a single eye, which stared precariously down, suspended from the crown of the tent. Soon the lamp was moving, swinging in time to a hundred thumping feet, and Esko was dodging, running, scampering this way and that in the hot, crowded atmosphere, gleeful with raised, indistinct voices, dangerous with kicking shoes and boots. The men who were dancing kept hoisting the women up in the air, and when either of them got tired, the man would sit down with the woman in his lap and they would drink and laugh while the other dancers gyrated around them. At the far end Esko saw the musicians, a pianist, a blind man on the pipes, and a man and a woman with violins stamping their feet and swaying in time.

The crowd parted for a moment and a young girl came across the tent with a smile on her face and a small mirror hanging from her wrist. As two other boys stepped in front of her, barring her way, trying to ask her to dance, she held up the mirror to their faces, as if warding off evil spirits, and Esko saw that her smile was proud and headstrong, superior rather than friendly. The two boys fell back, vanishing into the crowd, and Esko's heart almost failed him when he saw where she was looking next. Her hair fell down her back in a single, braided plait. She wore a dress of black velvet and her throat was gripped tight by a string of pearls. Her gray-green eyes had a sly, mischievous look; they went up at the corners when she smiled. She was smiling at Esko now, as—he thought—an empress might at one of her subjects. He was waiting for the mirror, but she never showed it to him. Instead, in a clear voice he would never, till the end of his days, forget, she said these words:

"What happened to your face?"

"I was burned. Why do you speak in Swedish? Don't you know Finnish?" he said. Only then, as he realized how oddly and easily the words had popped out, did he blush.

"A coarse language for beasts and clodhoppers, but of course I know it," the girl said proudly. Her hair was like a soft rope, which, as she moved her body, tossed from side to side. "I can speak in Swedish, Russian, German, and English too." She counted her expertise on the fingers of her left hand. "We just returned from Paris. I learned a lot of French there, although in the streets they speak many languages. In the Boulevard du Temple, there's a fair that goes on and on, not like this scrubby thing. There are tumblers, jugglers, acrobats, performing fleas, a dog that can sing. Elephants! Tigers! There are beggars with monkeys on their shoulders and men dressed up as Turks in blue blouses selling sweets so lovely and perfumed you can smell them a mile away. Paris! And the streets are *not* paved in gold. That's only a silly story, but perhaps you believe it. You probably do, don't you? You probably think you can pick up money like leaves that have fallen from the trees."

"I don't think any such thing," said Esko, quickly trying to order exactly what he did think. Paris! His mother had talked about Paris, and the poets and painters who lived there. "My mother was once in Paris."

"Really?" she said with a bored shrug, regarding the musicians, the rope of her hair brushing across the bare white skin of her back. "Do you dance?"

"Are you talking to me?" said Esko.

"Who else would I be talking to?" she said, turning back to him with her startling, mischievous eyes.

"Yes, I do, I dance."

"Come on, then," she said, and held up her hands to be taken. "This place is so funny and poor. Why do you live here? Your clothes are so stiff and new. Don't you know you shouldn't wear clothes that look so new?"

Esko didn't feel himself required to answer, because, having taken her hands, he was staring at his feet and realizing with panic that he couldn't remember a single step his mother had taught him. His head fumed until he thought it would burst and at last he shut his eye and pushed blindly off with his left foot, grabbing her tight so she had no choice but to follow.

"That violinist, the woman—she really plays rather well, don't you agree?"

Esko was impressed that she spoke like an adult, a person of infinite sophistication, someone who'd seen and known the world, and he wondered how he could make himself sound more mature, but he was still too busy watching his own feet, hoping he wouldn't kick her in the shins, calling up the memory of how, on a summer night, he and his mother would wheel and wheel around the yard of their old house, the one that had been destroyed in the fire; he was too busy trying to dance well, better than well, to be able to try to hazard an answer.

"Did it hurt when your face burned?" she asked.

Looking at her now, as the musicians passed behind her cool features in a blur, he had the impression for a moment that the two of them weren't moving. And yet they were: amazingly, they were still dancing—his feet galloped, thumping the cut turf of the meadow, and her soft hair brushed his fingers where they lay against the heat of her back.

"Yes. It hurt," he said. His blind eye began to itch.

"Do you think anything else ever again could hurt so much?"

"I don't know; I don't think so." The music had stopped now and they slowed to a halt in front of the entrance to the tent, through which Esko caught a glimpse of the moon, a whiff of the warm night outside.

"Do you think I could hurt you so much?"

"No."

She slapped Esko's face with all the strength she had.

"What do you think now?"

"I think you're a very mean person," said Esko, who had somehow managed to stay on his feet. He was aware that around them some of the farmworkers were laughing, saying that wedded bliss did indeed start young.

"Not really," she said.

She took his hands and tenderly kissed them both.

"You're quite strong, aren't you?" she said. "But there's more than one way to be hurt, you know. Will you dance with me again?"

The violins scratched and then moaned into song, a melancholy call to the feet. Esko allowed himself to hold her again, one hand circling her waist, the other touching her hair and the skin of her back. He didn't know where to look as they stepped, paused, and spun.

The crowd seemed to be thinning out. The music sounded higher, louder, and the lamp no longer swayed and rocked above their heads with such violence. Their shadows against the side of the tent followed them in a stately way, and the earth no longer trembled as if in fear of a hundred dancing feet. Esko felt himself to be floating, no longer sure whether it was happiness he was feeling or a pressure around the heart that would soon squeeze the life out of him.

All at once the music stopped. The man in front of them, dressed in a wadded, greasy jerkin, took the hand of his partner and marched right out of the tent. "Where are they going? Don't they know this is too early for a ball to finish? How strange and funny this place is," said the girl, glancing about, and then she cried, "Papa!" and flew into the embrace of a man who stood at the entrance to the tent. He was a handsome man, thirty or so, clean shaven, gray suited, with—Esko saw in alarm—Kalliokoski trailing behind him, while everyone else seemed to be heading in the other direction. The villagers who had been dancing trooped out, nodding or tipping their hats at Kalliokoski, but pointedly ignoring the newcomer, the girl's father. One or two even spat on the ground. The musicians packed up their instruments and sneaked away at the back. Soon Esko realized that he was alone. The lamp above his head was quite still. He decided to brave it out and stepped forward as he'd been taught by his mother, confidently, but with due modesty, hands clasped behind his back.

"Why this is a hideous child," said the girl's father, speaking in Swedish in an excited and vengeful way. "And this is just the sort of thing I was talking about. Obviously there's an awful lot of such deformity in these remote rural areas. Nothing romantic in that, eh? Nothing to write a poem or a symphony about. Just God's will and nothing to be done about it except keep all Finland's unfortunate children safe under the Czar's extremely wide and beneficent imperial umbrella." He laughed and flicked his sleeve, pleased with himself and his joke. "You get my drift, Kalliokoski? It's quite plain to the eye, what? Who is this boy? Does he have a father?"

The man's face beamed with the utmost malevolence, as if this apparition of hideousness had been placed in front of him by God for the sole purpose of provoking just such an observation; then Esko watched as that nasty smile turned, almost mechanically, into a frown, as if the man were puzzled about why, his brilliant remarks now having been made, the Almighty had failed to oblige him further by making Esko vanish on the spot.

The girl, meanwhile, was whispering to her father in Russian, words that Esko was able to catch. "This is my friend, father. He's not deformed. His face was burned."

The man said with a tolerant smile: "Really! You know this creature? My dear Katerina, you never cease to astonish me."

"His name is . . ."

"My name is Esko Vaananen," said Esko, speaking in Russian himself.

"You know Russian?" said the girl, Katerina, surprised.

"A little," said Esko.

"Really!" said the man, arching an eyebrow.

"We were dancing," said Katerina.

The man repeated, "Really! Really! In this place? Really! How absolutely, how utterly and absolutely extraordinary. Kalliokoski, do you know this boy?"

"I do," said Kalliokoski uneasily. "He is an orphan, and I have made his education my own responsibility. An intelligent and remarkable child, despite his manner."

"Really! Then I suppose I too must make his acquaintance. Otherwise I'll be the odd man out, eh what?" The man held forward a hand, which Esko realized he was expected to shake, English fashion. And as he did, as he felt the other's fingers close around his, in a surprisingly tight, too tight grip, Esko was aware that the man was regarding him in a quite different way now, still coldly, but with an undisguised directness, as if his gaze were a dagger that could penetrate the core of another's mind. Esko wanted to get out of the way of that dagger.

"My name is Stepan Malysheva," he said. "Delighted, I'm sure!"

5

Drifting clouds smudged the moon, and a frosty wind from the lake cut and whistled through the forest. Most of the stalls were packed away now and people were flocking to some attraction at the edge of the meadow, between the dance tent and the dirt track that ran through the village. Esko pushed his hands into his pockets and kicked at a stone. My boots pinch and I'm tired, he thought, so why do I feel so happy? He knew why. From his pocket he drew the little mirror that Katerina had given him. "It's a magic mirror," she'd said. "If you look in it long enough it will show you who you really are." It was the mirror that had been hanging from her wrist, the one she'd flashed in the faces of the other boys. The mirror was small, and fitted easily in Esko's hand. He ran his fingers softly over the wavelike designs of thick silver that surrounded and protected the glass. It was a gorgeous gift.

Voices were raised in excitement at the edge of the meadow, and Esko carefully returned the mirror to his pocket and ducked into the crowd to learn what the attraction was. On this night of wonderful happenings, here was another one: an automobile, the very first, as far as Esko knew, that had ever been seen in the district, though rumors of these fabulous machines had reached the ears of most of the villagers, only to be dismissed as outlandish and improbable lies. "A carriage that runs without horses? They're trying to fool us again," Turkkila the gravedigger had said. But now here was proof that the dangerous new century had indeed begun: a gleaming, polished, hard and angular automobile, clearly an expensive automobile, with huge, and, at the moment, unlit, lamps for eyes, and a pointed snout of predatory appearance, giving Esko the impression that perhaps the black-clad and goggled chauffeur who stood behind the wheel was there, not only to guard this beast and drive it, but to prevent it unexpectedly springing to life and gobbling up anyone standing too close before it roared down the road of the future. The villagers wisely kept their distance, remarking upon the smell of soft, expensive leather that wafted from the automobile's open interior, the boxes that were piled high at the back, perhaps filled with treasure, and a second pair of lamps that lifted themselves like chrome flowers on stalks out of the running boards that arched high over the spoked wheels.

Esko understood at once that the automobile belonged to Katerina's father, that the chauffeur worked for him, that they had driven from a great distance to the village, and would immediately be moving on. His mind filled with the idea that he might snatch Katerina and steal her away, positioning himself behind the stiff, upright steering wheel, while she sat at his side or reclined in the back against the leather cushions. She wouldn't protest, even though she'd slapped his face, because she'd kissed him, danced with him, twice, and stood up for him against her father. She'd given him the mirror. Perhaps she even loved him, he thought; he was certain that he loved her and would never love anyone else. His heart ached and his face burned with shame when he thought of how rude the villagers had been and what she must have felt.

The black-uniformed chauffeur eased the goggles over his eyes and fiddled with them. Leaping down from the running boards, squatting in front of the predatory snout with a big grin, he began the next part of the show, taking hold of the crank, leaning into it with all his weight, and then spinning it with a wild flourish. The motor burst to life even as he launched himself upright and ran back around the side, vaulting the running board so that he could once again take command of the steering wheel. Beams of light shot from the lamps, slicing and making brilliant the night. The villagers gasped. Turkkila, the gravedigger, caught in the glare, covered his eyes and howled, then fainted. The automobile pulsed and chugged, vibrating on its wheels, spluttering and heaving like an enraged animal.

From the boos and hisses and catcalls Esko gathered that Stepan Malysheva must have appeared, which meant that Katerina couldn't be far behind. Esko began to work his way through the crowd, wondering why the villagers—so difficult to stir to feeling about almost anything, apart from vodka, seemed to hate Malysheva so. He must be an official of some sort, Esko thought, or perhaps a spy.

Suddenly Esko found himself dazzled, as Turkkila had been, caught within a fierce incandescent glow, the automobile's headlamps. Moths swirled about his head, beating with their wings against his scalp and cheeks. He raised his hand to shield his eye.

"Katerina!" he called.

It was then that a strange thing happened. He thought it a strange thing at the time, and he would think it even stranger in the years to come. As he turned his eyes away from the awful light, seeking the comforting darkness of the forest and the lake beyond, he thought he heard a voice. It was Katerina's voice saying, quite clearly: *run the boy down.* Suddenly the ground shook and shuddered under him, his feet were whipped away, he was hurtling through the air, and then he was flat on his face in the dirt with something heavy lying on top of him. When he found his feet again, struggling to regain the breath that had been squashed out of him, he saw what the something heavy had been. It had been Bongman's Son, who stood now at the edge of the meadow, cracking his knuckles, and with a smile bending the acne on his cheeks.

"Scarface got his new clothes banged up and dirty," he said. "His snotty pals tried to run him over."

"You're lying."

Bongman's Son, having knocked Esko down once to save him, now a second time did so in anger, and Esko found himself in the dirt again, on his back this time, with Bongman's Son sitting on his chest and aiming a few casual blows at his face. "You're no fun. You don't even want to fight. Want to play?"

"Not really," said Esko.

"You're useless," said Bongman's Son in a tone of disgust.

"What's going on here?" said another voice, the voice of authority, Kalliokoski's voice. "Esko, is this boy bothering you?"

"No," said Esko, spitting out a thin trickle of blood.

"Then why—excuse my asking—is he sitting on your chest?"

As a few of the other villagers clustered around, Turkkila, the gravedigger, acted out a confused version of what, confusingly, had occurred. He was already turning the incident into a story, as he did with every village event and disaster. He told of a fiendish modern machine, and blinding lights, and a carriageman all in black, surely an agent of the devil because the devil himself then arrived on the scene, accompanied by a young girl so pretty she could only be the daughter of Satan. The devil and devil's own daughter in the devil's machine had thundered off, without thought to the fact that they were going to run the boy down. Then, suddenly, amazingly, *wondrously*, Turkkila said, Bongman's Son had appeared and saved the day, most likely rescuing not only Esko Vaananen, the elderberry boy, but perhaps the whole village from the clutches of the devil and his infernal machine.

"Oh shut up with that nonsense," said Kalliokoski, dismissing Turkkila and the rest of the drunken troop, who shambled away into the night, the excited murmur of their voices drifting through the tunnels of pine. Kalliokoski hauled Bongman's Son off Esko's chest, cuffed him about the side of the head, and dismissed him too.

"That boy will come to a bad end," said Kalliokoski, helping Esko to his feet. "Oh, Esko. Your clothes!"

Esko's spanking new tweed was now much of it a disgrace: the jacket was filthy, with pieces of straw hanging from the arms; the pants were ripped at the knee on either leg; the cap had been lost somewhere along the way. He spat more blood.

Kalliokoski sighed, disappointed rather than angry. "What a night," he said, shaking his head.

Esko stared down at his new boots, scuffed at the toe and stained with grass—his dancing boots, he thought with a smile.

"You should cry, if you want to. Do you want to?"

Esko shook his head, very much wanting to, and felt Kalliokoski touch his hair.

"Esko, I know what it is to know that you will never have something you want very badly. It's sad, but it's life. Let's go home."

"I'll walk by myself."

"Your mother preferred to walk by herself, Esko. It's lonely."

Esko allowed his eye to rise no higher than the gleaming gold watch chain that was strung across Kalliokoski's lean belly. His hand went to the mirror in his pocket—still safe.

"All right Esko—but come home quickly."

Esko was irritated by the repetition of that word, *home*, and wanted to say that he had none, but instead he turned and ran across the meadow, where the tent was now being taken down by the same sour-faced gypsies who had put it up, into the silence of the forest, where he picked his way expertly among the trees until he came to the shore of the lake.

He went to the water's edge and sniffed the heady tang of the reeds. He watched the small black waves crossing and recrossing the familiar, expressionless expanse of water. He walked out onto a landing stage, lay face downward, looked down at the black surface of the lake only a few inches below, and thought of the girl he'd met, whose waist he'd held, whose hair he'd smelled, whose lips had touched his skin. He thought again of those moments when the automobile had surged toward him. Katerina hadn't said, "Run him down." Her words, he was sure now, must have been, "You'll run him down." She'd been trying to warn and command the fiendish chauffeur, not goading him on. Esko smiled, angling the mirror she'd given him to the surface of the water. On the other shore a light came on in a house, shining across the lake like a beacon, and he held up the mirror to that too.

The eye of the moon was completely blotted out by clouds, a mist had risen, and the endless lines of birch in the forest seemed like ghosts. He ran back to the vicarage, holding his breath, daring the ghosts to step forward, dreading that they would, and it came to him with childish confidence that one day he would woo and win Katerina, he would marry her as his father had his mother, and they would have children, and they would live happily, and then, remembering his scarred face, he fell again into despair. He wondered how he could ever make himself beautiful enough to deserve anything so beautiful as Katerina.

6

The promise of summer was broken. The lake turned gray, warning of the ice to come. Snow, the first snow of winter, fell through the gray light in big fumbling flakes that seemed impossibly white and soft, reluctant to leave the haven of the sky. This beautiful, eerie scene presaged months of dark. Esko was in his room at the vicarage, staring out the window, when there was a rap on the door and Kalliokoski hurried in without waiting for a reply, bringing with him a chill freshness and the smell of snow.

"Good morning, Esko," said Kalliokoski, and nodded, taking a moment to compose himself. His beard and hair sparkled with melting flakes. "Esko, I'm afraid I must ask you something unpleasant. Have you seen your father?"

The question required no lie. Even so, Esko found himself flushing with shame. The socket of his blind eye burned as though someone had struck a match inside it. "No," he said.

"I see," said Kalliokoski, sitting on the edge of the bed, sighing, fingers playing in his neat beard, as though this were very bad news indeed. "Esko, I regret to report that there has been an outrage—in Runni."

"In Runni?" said Esko, suddenly afraid, wondering if his father's body had been found, if Timo was really dead; but what would he have been doing in Runni, a spa favored by rich Swedes and Russians?

Kalliokoski cleared his throat. "Esko, do you remember the night of the harvest festival? The night of the fair?"

Esko nodded tentatively.

"Do you remember the Russian gentleman? The man with the automobile, the one our discriminating village folk took such an objection to."

"He had a daughter. She was beautiful," said Esko.

"That's right. Did you also gather that he is the new governor of our province, appointed by the Czar himself?"

Esko shook his head. He had gathered no such thing.

"Three nights ago the new governor was in Runni when a man burst into his room and tried to shoot him. Now, our new governor was already aware that his appointment was not exactly the cause for celebration in the district. He was sleeping with a revolver under his pillow and was able to defend himself. The governor was wounded in the shoulder but is bragging that he winged the other fellow."

"And Katerina?" said Esko, suddenly alarmed.

"Katerina? Oh, the daughter. Yes, of course. She was in a room down the corridor. She's fine."

"So. Isn't everything all right?" said Esko, struggling to grasp why Kalliokoski was telling him this.

Kalliokoski stood up from the bed, came to the window, and took Esko by the shoulders, bringing his face so close that Esko saw the strong black and gray points of the stubble above his beard and the pink skin on the end of his nose, still open-pored from the cold. "Not really. You see, Esko. The authorities are asking themselves whether your father had anything to do with this outrage."

"My father?"

"So of course it's extremely important—*extremely* important—that you should tell me if he tries to communicate with you in any way. So we can clear this matter up. Otherwise I will be in a lot of trouble and so will you. Esko, do you understand?"

Esko bobbed his head.

"Yes, I think you do," said Kalliokoski. He stood up straight and let Esko's shoulders go, his gaze moving toward a picture that hung over the bed.

It was a painting that had been done by Esko's mother, one of the few things that had survived the fire and the only one that Esko still possessed, a scene of the lake at dawn, with calm blue waters and quiet miles of waiting sky.

"I was with her when she painted that," said Kalliokoski, coughing and ducking his head. "I admired her very much, and I like to think that she'd be happy that I'm looking after you now. She was a good woman. I'm sure she'd want you to tell me everything. You will tell me everything, won't you?" said Kalliokoski.

When Kalliokoski was gone Esko sat down at his makeshift desk and tried to draw, but his eye was hurting and he couldn't concentrate, so he laid aside his pencil and stole downstairs, creeping softly on stockinged feet. He was slipping past the door to the study when, from inside, he heard one side of a conversation, the voice of Kalliokoski, speaking on the telephone, first to the switchboard operator, then to someone at the other end, perhaps—Esko thought—to Katerina's father. "Yes . . . yes . . . The hotel in Runni . . . Yes, yes . . . Good morning sir, you are feeling well, I trust. . . . Just so, just so. . . . Vaananen? . . . Possibly . . . Yes, sir. . . . I agree. . . . No, absolutely not. . . . The boy, I believe . . . Yes, yes. . . . Vaananen must be caught and brought to justice. . . . Oh, I agree. . . . Of course, of course. . . . Undoubtedly, yes, what was that, sir? He *will* be caught. . . . The Czar requires it. . . . Absolutely. . . . We are together on that, sir. . . . Ha, ha, ha! . . ."

Esko had heard enough. He moved like a thief through the parlor, through the dining room, through the kitchen, past the various clocks. Outside he fully expected to find a police officer, a Russian soldier, an agent in disguise, or quite possibly all three, waiting to snap handcuffs on his wrists; there was no one.

A week passed, by which time the snow, falling thicker, had filled the insides of the boats by the lake and covered the steeply pitched roof of the vicarage. Esko was walking on the track when a man started up from the graves at the side of the church porch.

"Psst! Esko. Get yourself over here."

It was a raw afternoon, almost dark, and in the falling snow Esko didn't at first recognize the man, who was dressed in black and whose breath puffed out in clouds.

"Esko, it's all right, don't run. It's me."

Esko moved closer, peering into the dim light, not daring to believe his eyes.

"Little Esko, come here. Let me get a look at you. Come here, come quick. Don't make any noise. No one must know I'm here."

"Dad, is that really you?"

"Of course. Be quiet now. Come closer. Come."

Esko joined Timo in the shadows at the side of the porch; son and father fell against each other in an awkward embrace.

"Good," said Timo in a low voice. "You look well, Esko. Really. Such fine clothes. Quite the gentleman."

"You too, Father," said Esko, and it was true; Timo wore a dark coat of thick wool over an immaculate gray suit and his boots had a high polish. His hair was cut shorter, slick with brilliantine, and smelled of perfume. He exuded an easy confidence. He looked as though he'd been sent to a factory and turned on a lathe.

"Father, where have you been?"

"Doing important work, son, very important work. As you see, I'm quite the fellow these days. I'm showing an important visitor around our Finnish countryside. I want you to meet him. He's over in the bell tower. We must go there now, quickly."

"What man, father?"

Timo's face puckered—a quick, impatient frown. Then he smiled again. "You'll see," Timo said, and as they moved past the snow-covered graves toward the gate at the side of the church he drew his coat tight at the collar and leaned his head close to Esko's good ear. "Now, Esko, I'm playing a sort of game with this man. He doesn't know that my name is Timo Vaananen. He thinks my name is Ernst Offermans. You don't have to say anything—just don't say the wrong thing. Is that clear?"

Esko stopped. His father was sounding like the stern schoolteacher again, about to spout forth a cataract of tedious information about Ferdinand Lassalle.

"Esko," Timo said in an impatient voice. "Don't dawdle. I haven't much time. You want to meet this man? Believe me as I'm your father. You do want to meet him."

Quickly Timo pushed open the creaking doors to the bell tower but there was no one inside.

"I'm up here," a voice called in Swedish from high in the rafters.

"I might have known it," Timo muttered, glancing at the narrow wooden ladder that led up the side wall of the bell tower. He raised his head and called out: "Herr Lazarus! Are you coming down?"

"Lord, no," came a voice in Swedish. "It's wonderful up here."

Timo sighed, turning his blue eyes toward his son with an unexpected tenderness. "Esko, I do want you to meet this man. It's important. Do you think you can manage it?"

Esko realized that he was pleased to see his father again, even if he was slightly alarmed by his new appearance and different smell; as if these changes signaled whole other undreamed-of strangenesses. "Of course, Father," he said, and he led the way up the ladder, climbing rung after rung, surprising even himself with the jaunty nervelessness of his ascent through a spider's web of crossbeams and trusses.

At the top a strong arm grabbed him and then thumped him down on his feet as if he were cargo. Esko found himself looking at a big man with a fleshy face and a birthmark on his right cheek. The man wore a fur hat and a fur coat brilliant with diamonds of melting snow. "Here he is. It seems that our young hero has a head for heights as well as a heart for machines that rise in the sky," he said, letting go Esko's arm and ruffling the top of his head. Around his throat the man wore a gray silk scarf that was stabbed in the heart by a pin with a big pearl on the end of it. His fists were like hammers and he had a wrestler's powerful hunched shoulders.

"My name is Joseph Lazarus," he said. "And you, I take it, are the young man that Herr Offermans has told me about, the young fellow who thinks elevators must mean something. Herr Otis would be delighted. As I am, delighted to meet you."

This "delighted" seemed to Esko so worldly, addressed to him as an adult. He didn't know whether he was being teased.

"Truly, the elevator is a wonderful invention. Otis was an extraordinary fellow."

"You met him? You met Elisha Graves Otis?"

In the months following his father's departure Esko had gathered as much information as possible about the elevator—not that, in the village, such information was easy to come by. Kalliokoski had translated an article he found in an English encyclopedia. It seemed that following the installation of these machines in buildings in the great American city of Chicago, there had been a series of disasters, not because the elevators themselves had malfunctioned, or plummeted to the bottom of their shafts, but because people's hearts had not been strong enough to withstand the sheer excitement of shooting up and down inside them. Otis himself had guaranteed the safety of his invention with a personal test, standing inside an elevator car with an egg in either hand and then commanding his engineers to cut the cable. The elevator had plunged six stories, free fall, before coming softly to rest, with neither Otis nor even the eggshells in any way cracked or the worse for wear, protected by the air cushion at the bottom of the shaft.

"You met Otis?"

"I did, when I was a boy of about your age," said Lazarus with an easy grin. "He's dead now, of course, though in recent years I have been privileged to install many of his machines."

Install? Esko wondered what that meant exactly. An elevator, as pictured in the pages of *Hufvudstadsbladet*, seemed to be clanking and whirring inside his head, scratching at the top of his skull.

"But what does it mean? What does an elevator mean?"

Lazarus threw back his head, roaring with laughter, and Esko felt his scarred face begin to blush. "I'm not laughing at you. *Ach*, of *course* I am," Lazarus said, scratching at the birthmark on his cheek. "The meaning of the elevator? I think it means that people no longer have to walk up lots of stairs. This bell tower, for instance, could use an elevator, though such talk is sacrilege, and indeed it would be a shame to spoil the tower in any way. It is very fine work, by Jacob Rijfs if I am not mistaken. Weatherboards painted red not only to preserve them but to create the illusion of a bare brick wall. The face of the Lutheran God. An uncompromising fellow. Do you believe in God? Excuse me, I don't even know your name."

"It's Lauri," said Timo, who had joined them on the platform. "His name is Lauri."

"A fine name indeed," said Lazarus warmly. "Do you believe in God, Lauri?"

Esko glanced through the open arch at the north side of the tower: beyond were the frosted tops of birch and spruce, and then distant snow-covered meadows. He shook his head.

"It's all right. It means only that perhaps you shouldn't build churches."

Timo burst in, "Herr Lazarus himself is going to build a bridge in Iisalmi. It will bring the railway to the village. And after that everything will start to change. It will be like a miracle. A scientific and historical and inevitable miracle."

"I really don't care for such talk, Herr Offermans. The last miracle I worked on nearly killed me. The only miracle is that I'm still here to talk about it."

"What happened?" said Esko, gazing at Lazarus with awe and admiration.

"Go on, tell the boy," said Timo.

"I must begin by mentioning that I am a German."

"And we must learn to forgive Herr Lazarus for that," said Timo. "After all, Karl Marx was German too. And Beethoven. And Goethe."

"Thank you, Herr Offermans," said Lazarus, bringing his heels together with a theatrical and vain little click. "I was building a bridge for the kaiser in Africa."

"Africa!" exclaimed Esko, his jaw drooping.

"There is indeed such a place, hard though it might be to believe on a Finnish day like today," said Lazarus, drawing his fur coat tight around his shoulders. "I spent five years building a bridge across a river. For thirty-three months of that time there was a drought, which killed a lot of people and almost killed me too. I was very sick. Then there was something else."

"What?" said Esko, watching, fascinated.

"Imagine this," said Lazarus, lifting his arms as if he were framing a picture. He described how, during those months of drought, the river was little more than a lazy stream running across a bed of dazzling white sand between two towers of red brick that rose higher and higher at either end.

"The natives warned me that the river was sometimes an angry god, and that I should be thankful because it was sleeping. Thankful! Frankly I thought I had enough on my plate."

They had to contend with grueling heat, with sunstroke, with malaria, with cholera, and with various other fevers, not to mention the professional disasters, the errors and miscalculations that killed his laborers and riveters by the dozen, even as they swarmed about the latticework and iron girders with their hammers and their burning firepots.

"Then one afternoon I received a telegram. The monsoon had arrived and the river was already in flood upstream. I was warned I had only fifteen hours. The disaster arrived in four. Wind. Rain that was steady at first, then a torrent, then rain such as I've never seen and hope never to see again. Rain like perhaps Noah saw. Racing water licked the throats of the towers. Soon it covered them entirely. The river lifted like a snake, an enormous anaconda that had swallowed an elephant and kept getting bigger and bigger, and spread itself to the horizon. My shantytowns were swept away. My overhead crane toppled and swam off. Very inconsiderate. Two thousand donkeys drowned. A legion of donkeys. More than three hundred men were lost. More than one hundred women and children. But somehow, by some fluke, some *miracle*, when the flood subsided my towers were still standing. So instead of disgrace and ruin I was handed a medal by the kaiser himself. *Ach*, it almost made me believe in God again."

Timo said, "No miracle. You built your towers well, my friend."

"I'm sure I did," said Lazarus, thoughtfully fingering his cheek. "But better men than I have made better things and watched nature sweep them aside. They never recovered, you know. They became broken, sad. I was lucky. Perhaps I will always be lucky. What do you think, young Lauri? Will I be fortunate with my bridge on the ice? Or is it only the sort of dream Napoleon had about Moscow?"

Esko had been listening in amazement, as if indeed this were a heroic tale from "Kalevala." In his mind he saw the boiling river. He pictured himself atop those proud towers of red brick, withstanding the flood's assault.

"You're an engineer?"

"That's right. And also an architect. I design things."

"What does that mean?"

Lazarus laughed again.

"Another good question, though a little easier to answer than the other about the elevator. It means the bridge came out of my head."

For more than a minute Esko considered this extraordinary notion.

From below came the sudden sounds of someone banging and clattering, then falling over and cursing, then breathing heavily and muttering to himself as he climbed the ladder, inching up to join them among the bells in the topmost portion of the tower.

"Hair falling out, teeth rotting, house in a bad state, too many children and another on the way, too much work, striving, always striving, too much pitching hay, that's the problem, done in me back, done in me head, and now two graves to dig in the snow. People don't stop dying, do they? Oh no, not likely."

A pair of long, wiry hands poked through the hole at the top of the ladder, then a black hat, and finally the outraged face of Turkkila, pink-cheeked, nose like a punnet of strawberries splattered against a window, fanglike tooth worrying at his blistered lower lip. He hauled himself to his feet.

"Vodka, you see, is like a brother. He's got his faults—oh yes. Sometimes I even hate him. But he's a family member nonetheless. Won't be ignored or denied. Ah, that's the way," he said, drawing a long clear bottle from his pocket, taking a swig, and smacking his lips as the liquor flowed down his throat and lit his belly with a fraternal glow.

"Brotherhood to all men." Suddenly he spotted Esko and his eyes grew wide. "Bloody hell, little Esko Vaananen, the elderberry boy! What are you doing here?" Turkkila was trying to stand still, but he seemed to have the bottoms of a rocking chair for feet; he swayed to and fro, squinting with suspicion as his bloodshot eyes now noticed and tried to absorb the spectacle of Joseph Lazarus. "And who's this with you in the fur coat? A gentleman, looks like. Excuse me, sir."

Turkkila spoke in Finnish, and Esko saw that Lazarus didn't understand. Turkkila himself gathered that something was amiss and, undeterred, set about communicating in a more direct way, hopping up and down, making shoveling motions and then pulling ones, indicating that he was not only a gravedigger, but a bell ringer too. He gestured to Esko and Lazarus to follow him around the platform to the other side, pointing up at the empty circles of chiming iron that hung asleep in the rafters.

Duties as guide fulfilled, Turkkila uncorked the vodka again and then glowered with suspicion, as if he thought Lazarus might be expecting to get some, only to grin once more when Lazarus reached inside his lustrous fur coat and produced a flask of thin silver. "Ah, the gent's a soul after me own heart. Steal it from me friends, hide it from me wife, brew it meself," he went on, touching his crushed button of a nose, breathing heady alcoholic fumes at Lazarus. "Get down on all fours and suck the vodka-flavored snow should I happen to spill some. Hidden vodka in church pews, in coffins, even in an artificial limb. Always keep your own supply. It's essential."

Timo, meanwhile, stepped silently across the platform behind Turkkila's back, on the other side of the bells. Gesturing to Esko to follow, he disappeared down the ladder.

For a moment Esko didn't know what to do. Lazarus and Turkkila were happily furthering their acquaintance through alcohol, so he raised his hand in thanks and farewell, received a grin back from Lazarus, and then made his way confidently back down the steps to find his father waiting for him at the bottom of the tower.

"I've saved something for you," Timo said, and drew a leather wallet from inside his coat. Inside it was an article from a newspaper, from *Hufvudstads-bladet*.

"Thank you, Father," said Esko, spreading open the article. It was the one about the elevator.

"Don't mention it," said Timo stiffly. His head, so clear about revolvers and despots, was whirled into a sinkhole when confronted with his son. Esko was tall and fair-haired; he smiled sometimes like a reckless, buoyant angel; he was stubborn and passionate and persistent; his right eye was blue and piercing; he had only to turn around to make you fear for his safety in the world. "Son," Timo said. "Esko, forgive me, please. For everything."

Esko looked up, his face beginning to burn. He didn't know whether it was from shame or anger. "Yes, Father," he said, though he hesitated, folding the article carefully and putting it away in his pocket. An eleven-year-old boy doesn't quite know how to forgive. "I was worried about you, Father. Iosip— Mr. Kalliokoski—said that you were hurt. He said you'd been shot."

"Why would he say that?" said Timo, pushing back a lick of hair.

"He said that you tried to shoot the new governor of the province. Maly-sheva. He said Malysheva shot you back." Esko saw his father's eyes reeling from this and he hastened to fill a silence that threatened to become awful. "I'm happy to see that you're well."

"He's alive?"

"Oh yes, Father. So everything's all right."

"He's *alive?*" Timo lifted his hands to his head and staggered. "I put three bullets into him. How can that be?"

Esko shook his head, sharing his father's confusion. "I don't know, Father. But everything's all right, isn't it?"

"Are you lying, Esko? You're lying, aren't you. My God!" he said, trying to pull back his hand even in the instant he raised it.

It was already too late. Esko ran, ran across the creaking floor of the bell tower, ran toward the heavy plank doors through which light was peeping, burst out into the dazzling, freezing white of the snow.

"Esko!"

Esko ran.

"Esko!"

Esko ran, panting breath puffing out in front, feet leaving crisp prints behind.

7

Turkkila didn't mean to betray Esko—he couldn't help himself. He was talking with Manda Virtanen, the wife of the storekeeper, and the story of his encounter with the mysterious stranger in the bell tower just slipped out, like vodka glugging from a bottle:

"He were a lovely bloke. A man of real distinction, you could tell it by looking at him. But not stuck up. Now that wasn't the remarkable thing about it. No, ma'am. Now I'll not deny that I'd had a drop. I'd spoken with my brother all right, but I weren't *really* drunk. Not like—well you knows how I can be after meeting the brother," said Turkkila, sniffing and getting into the tale. "Thing was. I was coming down the bell tower when who should I see but that one-eyed scamp Esko Vaananen running away into the snow like his life depended on it. That's funny, I said to meself. And then it came to me, weird like. Another voice, calling out, 'Esko! Esko!' A heartbreaking voice. And you know who it belonged to, Mrs. V? It were the voice of old Red Timo himself. I ain't joking. It were Timo's voice as honest as I'm standing—sitting—here in front of you. What do you think, Mrs. V? Am I mad or wot?"

Manda Virtanen was a good Finn but ambitious to win favor; she packed off her husband to tell Kalliokoski, who was soon kop-kop-kopping on the door to Esko's room. Esko said nothing: nothing when Kalliokoski cajoled, nothing when Kalliokoski commanded, nothing when Kalliokoski thundered, still nothing when Kalliokoski shook his head, sighing, and warned that Esko was jeopardizing his future, Helsingfors, everything they were working so hard together for. He said nothing when Kalliokoski was out of the house and Mrs. Kalliokoski without hesitation slapped his face and said he was a wicked, ungrateful boy. Esko understood the seriousness of the situation but maintained his silence even when Kalliokoski took him by sleigh to Iisalmi and marched him into the office of the local police captain, a jaunty fellow in a gray uniform who cracked pine nuts between his teeth and said, "I admire your pluck, young man, but you'd better tell me where your father is."

Esko could have answered, quite truthfully, that he didn't know where his father was, but he said nothing, not wanting to put Timo in more trouble than he was in already.

"Beat the boy," the police captain advised, and cracked another nut.

Afterward, in the sleigh, Kalliokoski was sad and resigned rather than angry. "I'm not going to beat you, Esko," he said, throwing a bearskin rug over them both, telling the driver to take it carefully, though it was a clear frosty day, and the road was easy, with no snow falling. He was silent for a long time while the sleigh jingled and hissed smoothly along on its runners. He said suddenly: "He'd betray you, you know. He let your mother down and he did the same to you. He'd sing his song to the police captain without thinking twice about it. Just so you know my thoughts about the man you're protecting."

Aged eleven, Esko couldn't begin to penetrate the reality of these events. He knew that everything had started with the elevator, and so he told himself that if he could discover the secret of the elevator his father would never come back and hit him again. If he could discover the secret of the elevator, he would one day be happy with Katerina. If he could discover the secret of the elevator, no one would laugh at his scars; he would be free from the scorn of men like Malysheva; he would indeed find a way to be loved and admired by men like Joseph Lazarus. He would heal himself and make everything well. If he could discover the secret of the elevator.

He pinned the article in *Hufvudstadsbladet* on the wall next to the picture that his mother had painted of the lake; then he moved the elevator article to another wall facing a mirror; then he put a second mirror opposite the first so that if he stood between them he could see both himself and the diagram of the elevator reflected to infinity. Meanwhile, as far as the human world was concerned, he had nothing to do with it. He ventured neither to the village nor to the church; if he went out he walked alone through the forest to the lake. He piled silence and solitude on top of himself. If he were to speak, it would have only been to see if anyone else had heard about Joseph Lazarus and the proposed railway bridge in Iisalmi.

The nights grew long. The early snows of September quickly succumbed to dismal October, followed in turn by the driving blizzards, the big freeze of November and December. Deep snow among thick firs. Skis scraping along. The screech of sleigh runners and short days that fled into the dark. Immense stars. Ice crept from the shallow edges of the lake toward the center, not in cakes or patches, but in one unified, slowly advancing sheet. Then there was a cold, absolutely still night and the task was done. The new ice, the iron ice, was clear, gray, and had no cracks or bumps. Its very smoothness was a temptation.

Early one morning a surprising visitor was found in the vicarage porch entrance, hands clasped behind his back, hopping from foot to foot, as if being this close to God made him fretful and nervous. It was Bongman's Son, a pair of skates dangling from his pimpled neck, asking Kalliokoski if Esko would come out to play.

Esko heard this, and then Kalliokoski's footsteps approaching his room. "I don't know why that boy imagines you'd be interested. I know the two of you used to be friends but, frankly, given the different paths your lives are taking, any further connection seems wholly inappropriate," said Kalliokoski, nervous about letting Esko out of his sight, as if at any moment he might be sneaking away to a secret meeting with Timo. "Besides, isn't it a very long time since you were on the ice?"

"I haven't skated since my mother died."

"Quite. You'll be horribly out of practice. I'll tell the miscreant you're busy."

Esko went, of course, defying Kalliokoski as he always would, running through the snow with Bongman's Son, whose first gesture of renewed friendship was to try to clonk him on the head with a skate. Esko ducked, avoiding the whizzing blade.

"Well then, Scarface," said Bongman's Son, "you used to be faster than me on the ice. But if I beat you to the end of the lake and back today you'll have to stand still while I hit you. Agreed?"

"That's not fair," said Esko.

"In that case I'll hit you even if you do win—what do you say to that?" said Bongman's Son, pawing at his cheek with a long, unwashed hand.

"What's in this for me?"

"Look—if you do agree, and if you do win, then you don't get hit," said Bongman's Son with dogged, Kullervo-like logic.

It was still dark when they got to the lake. The ice looked bluish and gave off a ghostly glow, as if in freezing it had swallowed the light of a million stars.

In places, the wind had brushed the ice clean. Elsewhere the snow settled in drifts; waves, ridges, and ripples pushed up, and great swelling banks. In the distance Esko saw a bobbing light, a lantern from which sparks shot out like fireworks—a fisherman was skating out toward an ice hole to gather his nets.

Esko sat himself on a rock and quickly began to pull on his skates. Hearing movement behind him in the forest, he turned and saw a figure, stumbling, muttering, shaking, clapping his hands against his shoulders, and staggering toward the lake. It was Turkkila the gravedigger, or rather, Turkkila the ex-gravedigger, for Turkkila had lost his job after the bell tower incident. He wore his felt hat with its battered, once swaggering, brim, no coat, and his strawberry nose was blue with cold.

"Elderberry boy, young Vaananen. Glad to see you," he said, but he was talking like a husk of the old Turkkila, as if the energy and mischief had been sucked out of him. "You were always a regular little chap and I got you into all sorts of trouble blabbing with me big mouth, and your dad too. He were always straight with me, were Timo, tried to treat me decent." He drew his sleeve under his nose, sniffing. Turkkila wasn't quite himself. "That's life, innit. You try, you don't know, you do your best, but you let down yourself and others. Useless born, useless I grew, useless with work and useless without."

"You're not useless, Turkkila."

He brightened at once. "Kind of you to say so, elderberry boy, very kind. You remember what I said now. Beware of steel, beware of iron." He stamped his foot angrily on the ice. "Beware of elevators. There, I found it, that word that were bothering me. *Elevator*. Now, then, elderberry boy, what is an elevator when it's at home? Can you eat it? Will it keep you warm? Can you snuggle up to it at night like a lively little one?"

Turkkila's crafty eyes slid toward the lake, where the fisherman was on his way back from the ice hole now. The spark-showering lantern swayed high over his head and he dragged behind him a sledge on which there was a basket, filled with fish glinting in the dark.

"There's a man wot's been lucky. Maybe he'll share a little of his luck. How you say to that, elderberry boy? A little fish, and a meeting with the brother, and yours truly will be set up nicely. Remember me. Remember steel, iron. Remember elevators. Remember wood. You stick with wood, elderberry boy. Wood's wot will look after you."

"He's crazy," said Esko, as Turkkila made his way off, stumbling and slithering across the ice.

Bongman's Son frowned, a rare adjustment in his normally stoic, pock-marked face. "He's told me a thing or two about bears and the forest, has old Turkkila. My dad, he says there's a man been coming from Helsinki propos-ing to write down old Turkkila's stories in a book."

"Let's skate," said Esko, suddenly eager. Before his accident he had been a crack skater, the best in the village, and now, pushing off on one foot, nerv-ous at first, but soon shifting his weight from one leg to the other rhythmically and without effort, as if his gliding feet were directed, not by muscle, but by his mind alone, he found that his skill was still there, undiminished and even increased. It seemed strange, almost unfair to the memory of his dead mother, but he could skate even better than before.

So, as a contest, the race with Bongman's Son was no contest, as Bong-man's Son had perhaps known all along. By the time Esko reached the center of the lake he was already so far ahead he wondered whether he'd been tricked, whether the whole skating scheme had been devised by Kalliokoski as a way to get him out of the vicarage and talking to somebody. He doubted it. It didn't matter, for he was exhilarated with the beauty of the scene and the freshness of the arctic air in his lungs. Gathering his strength, he rested his hands on his knees for a moment and, still whizzing along, looked up to see the northern lights flashing and shining above his head. The lights fluttered and played, gathering in arcs and circles that danced and grew brighter, chas-ing each other across the huge dome of the sky, rippling from heaven to earth, shooting back, quivering and shaking before they were at last snuffed out, only to light up again in some fresh and astonishing configuration.

The rush of his breathing and the rhythmic scrape of the skates soon car-ried Esko to the far end of the lake, where he turned and swept back toward a dense crown of birches and pine trees that rose ahead of him—one of the islands. There was an old boat on the shore that Esko recognized with a burst of pleasure. This was his island, the place he'd hidden out from his father. "I'm here, Esko's back," he shouted, raising his fists in the air. He shrugged, feeling foolish. "Esko Vaananen! Esko has come back to claim his kingdom."

His words disappeared into a silence that seemed to enclose the whole of Finland. It was so quiet Esko imagined he heard the noise of the single snowflake that fell and sparkled against the side of the boat, and he thought of the way the sound could deceive you at the lake in winter. Sometimes the ice boomed like thunder, as if the entire frozen thickness might split in two. A gunshot three yards to your left might be borne away, whipped in the opposite

direction by the wind; but when the atmosphere was thick and cold, sometimes a conversation carried a mile or more from the other side of the lake.
The cold air hovering above the ice trapped and amplified sound like water.
To prove the point his mother had once walked three hundred yards away
from him and read a poem. She said afterward she spoke only in a whisper
but Esko heard each word clear as chiming crystal:

> Not much time until we reach the grave,
> Living, like flames in a furnace then let us burn,
> Higher, higher, the fire springing up,
> Dirt stays below, the spirit shoots at heaven.

Esko had dashed into her arms. "Esko, my little sweetheart," she'd said,
hugging and kissing him, and afterward, as they skated home, hand in hand,
Esko had imagined that he would be this completely happy always.

Pain stabbed at his ruined left eye. Lifting the worn leather patch, he
rubbed cool snow into the scarred, tender flesh of the socket. As he did so, he
shut his good right one, and when he opened it again the scene around him
on the island seemed subtly different. A twisted juniper tree sparkled, its every
twig and branch encased in ice. There was no wind, no sound anywhere, and
then a creak as the snow, cooling perhaps only a degree or two, expanded and
found a higher place to settle in the boat. He felt anxious, not calm, suddenly
expecting something. He felt almost afraid, as he had when Katerina had
come toward him, swinging the mirror from her wrist. He wondered where
she was now. Kalliokoski had mentioned nothing further about the shooting
incident at Runni. He didn't even know whether the Malysheva family was
still in Finland. Perhaps they'd already gone back to Petersburg, and Esko
grew sad at the idea that Katerina might be so far away.

A whiff of spruce came on the breeze, then everything was still again.
The thick, dark light was porous, as if it were hanging over the lake, a shroud
sodden with a million tiny drops of water. He shivered and stamped his feet.
If he stayed much longer, they'd find him frozen solid this time.

He looked back down the lake, in the direction from which Bongman's
Son should be approaching; but he was so far behind there was no sign of
him. Esko glanced the other way, toward the village, trying to make out the
two red ocher towers of the church in the dimness. He didn't see them.

He saw something, however.

Esko blinked, wondering if it was the northern lights again, but when he opened his eye the elevator was still there, Mr. Otis's invention rising in the December dark and, around it, being given substance by the elevator's ascent, story after story of a building.

Now he didn't look away. The building rose higher than a house, higher than the church towers, higher than a pyramid, higher than any structure he had ever seen or read about in a newspaper or a history book.

He didn't dare turn his eye. He saw the base in granite. He saw the shaft in stone and a glimmering spire, glass. The stories were stacked one after the other around the shaft—perfect, symmetrical, beautiful.

He saw at last that this was what the elevator meant. A building could endlessly reproduce itself. Something that seemed impossible really could exist.

In later years this is how Esko would view the story. At the edge of a frozen lake, sometime before dawn, in the tiny village where he grew up at the turn of the century in Finland, he envisioned his future. He saw a skyscraper.

PART TWO

History

I

Late one afternoon toward the end of October 1917 the young architect Esko Vaananen rode down in the elevator of the Diktonius Building, thanked Karl, the operator who opened the steel gates (by then Karl was a familiar presence in his life, almost a friend), and went out into the canyon of Aleksanterinkatu Street, wrapping a wool scarf tight around his mouth, walking confidently, his stride long and loping. Sleighs and sleds swept by on their runners against a background of dazzling whiteness. The temperature was ten below, the atmosphere dark and sparkling with this fresh snow that seemed to betoken inner harmony and promise. Anything seemed possible, Esko thought—even the creation of a new Finland without conflict, even the building of a skyscraper.

At twenty-seven, the hatless Esko was tall, powerfully built, with one blue eye and a patch over the other; his hair was an outlaw mop of reddish blond. Running between his thick eyebrows was a vertical wrinkle, the sign of too many frowns perhaps, but also of a bold and persevering man whose somber mask hid too much hope. His laugh was infectious and charming, but heard infrequently in the Helsinki bars and cafés. He'd made it his business to know languages; though he was known as a man of few words, he could speak fluent French now, not only Finnish and Swedish, and he'd added a fair knowledge of English to his smattering of Russian. Even so, he felt words dammed up inside him, plugged down deep. He wondered if they'd burst out one day. He half-hoped they would.

Under one arm he held a drafting case. The hand of that same arm was in his coat pocket, fingering a certain silver mirror that he carried with him everywhere like a talisman, while the tails of that coat, which was black, flapped behind him, big as sails. He seemed to be looking at the ground as he walked, lost in his thoughts, though he negotiated his path through the crowded street nimbly and expertly, with surprising athleticism for a big man, glancing up occasionally with rapt concentration, pausing to stare at buildings as if he saw something magical in them, as if they were characters in a drama enacted for him alone. Thus a scowl was directed at the Pohjola Insurance Building, a squat stone castle guarded by monstrous stone trolls with fingers in their stone ears and their stone tongues hanging out, while a smile went toward the Lundqvist, sleek and large-windowed, seeming to float through the snow. The one hunkered, toadlike; the other swept the eye along. The first was the ugly Finnish past, the second a pointer toward a lighter and lovelier existence.

Esko hopped aboard a trolley car, his eye glancing at the folded newspaper of a woman hanging from the strap next to him. News from Petrograd (as Petersburg had been renamed) took up the front page, telling of strikes, mutinies, corpses in the gutter. Every day brought news of some new horror from Russia, the promise of uncertainty Esko turned his mind against, just the way he ignored now the perfumed charms of the woman whose newspaper he'd been glancing at. He had no time for politics and, with his wrecked appearance, no suspicion that the pursuit of romance could be successful. Architecture was his ambition, his dream, and his life, all of his life; it didn't occur to him that with the pure love he put into a single drawing he might seduce an entire regiment of women.

Caressing the mirror in his pocket, securing the drafting case tight beneath his arm, he hopped off the trolley car, walked briskly up to the top of the hill, and pushed open an iron gate leading toward an imposing villa with a pillared entranceway where a gas lantern glowed and hissed over a sturdy black door that had a highly polished brass knocker.

"Esko Vaananen. For Mr. Diktonius," he said, when a servant opened the door.

He waited for a minute or two in the marbled hallway and then the servant came back, saying, "This way, sir. Mr. Diktonius will see you in the library," and beckoning him into a wide, low, dimly lit, and comfortable room, lined from floor to ceiling with leather-bound books, spines stamped in gold. A globe stood in one corner with brass claws for feet. A stove glowed in another. As the door closed softly behind him Esko saw a man rising from behind a leather-topped desk at the far end of the room.

"You must be Vaananen. I'm Alexander Diktonius," the man said briskly, advancing to meet him, fingering the curling end of his moustache. He was plump, bright eyed, with a squarish, jowly face. He pushed his hands into his pockets, not proposing to offer one of them to Esko. "Show me what you have. Here, lay it out on the sofa."

Esko unlaced and flipped open his drafting case; ignoring the first drawing that his fingers touched, he chose instead the second, and carefully placed it on the warm, buttoned, brown leather of the sofa.

A Diktonius hand, removed from a Diktonius pocket, began nervously pulling once again at the Diktonius moustache. "This design is for an office building, is it not?"

"Yes, sir, it is," Esko said.

"It's a skyscraper—straight-fronted, fashioned largely in glass."

"Quite right, sir."

There was a long silence, interrupted only by the sound of Diktonius clicking his teeth. "I see," he said. "I was under the impression I asked for a country villa."

"I know," Esko said, his hand moving back toward the drafting case, producing another drawing. "And here it is."

"This is what I asked for," Diktonius said in a neutral way, examining this new piece of drafting paper. "It's Oskari Bromberg's work, isn't it? I recognize the draftsmanship."

"Yes, sir, it's Oskari's hand," said Esko, who for these last three years had been employed as draftsman and junior architect by Henrik Arnefelt and Oskari Bromberg, two of the most prestigious older architects in Finland. They specialized in sturdy office buildings (like the Pohjola) and villas in the style of art nouveau, or *jugend* as it was known up here in the north. They were the leaders of the Finnish stone-troll movement.

"And the *pilvenpiirtaja*, the skyscraper—your own work?"

"Yes, sir."

"Why show it to me?"

"Because you're the richest man in Finland," Esko said. This was true. The son of a sailor, once apprenticed to a carpenter, Alexander Diktonius now owned shipyards in Helsinki and Stockholm, umbrella factories in Geneva and the Finnish city of Tampere, and one of the biggest dairy farms in Europe. He was worth millions in butter alone. "Because, years ago, you caused to be built both the Diktonius and the Lundqvist, architecturally the two most advanced buildings in Helsinki. Because you have met Frank Lloyd Wright in America and Adolf Loos in Vienna. Because your friend is an opera singer and sometimes you buy every ticket in the opera house so she will perform Verdi for you alone. Because, sir, you are a romantic with modern tastes. As am I, but I can't afford to build a *pilvenpiirtaja*."

"Have you built *anything*?" Diktonius asked, eyebrows arching expressively above his sharp, shining eyes.

"Not yet."

With the skyscraper drawing in his hand Diktonius moved behind his desk, sat down, clicked on a lamp. "You don't think our situation a little too volatile to be contemplating such a project?" he said.

Since February, and the fall of the Romanovs in Russia, Left had been disagreeing with Right in Finland, Red with White, and factions within either side had been squabbling among themselves about how best to negotiate the path to independence. Finland was no longer under the authority of the Czar, because the Czar no longer had any authority. But who *was* to rule? The question was of little interest to Esko. For him the future was not about statehood, or ideology, but excellence, filled with architectural wonder. It was a future that would learn the lesson of his beloved elevator, leaping endlessly upward, invading the sky, reshaping the age-old horizontal line of the earth's surface. Accordingly he never broke his routine. He rose early in his small, neat apartment, worked, went to the office, worked, returned home in the evening, made himself coffee, ate bread with sausage, drank a beer or glass of vodka (only one), and worked and worked until he fell asleep on his arms at the drafting board, where he always kept the silver mirror in front of him.

Writing in a checkbook now, Diktonius looked up from the desk, and Esko answered: 'I think to build a skyscraper would be a bold gesture of national confidence in these circumstances," he said, knowing that although it was very necessary to want to create a building that would have extraordinary effects, would be a concentrated experience, a poem, a beautiful thing, it was also as well to remember that someone like Diktonius had to slap down an awful lot of hard cash in order for this to happen. Small wonder that architecture tended not to be a young man's profession. Experience was necessary, expertise, to say nothing of Machiavellian skills in dealing with investors and governments and clients on the one hand and contractors on the other. Architecture was an awkward combination of mathematics, money, design, and religion. "Finland needs a new architecture—without stone gnomes and stone pine cones," he said.

"As it happens—I agree," Diktonius said, walking toward Esko, waving his hand to dry the ink on the check that he now folded and gave to Esko. "But tell Bromberg I still require my stone villa." He viewed the hint of disappointment in Esko's face, smiling. "Walk with me awhile," he said, ringing the bell for his coat. "Leave your design with me to look at later. All right?"

"By all means."

Outside, swaddled in fur, and with an astrakhan hat atilt on his head, Dikotonius clapped his hands together in the stillness as they walked down the hill toward the Esplanade Park. "My favorite weather. The whole city holds its breath," he said. "Now then, Vaananen. Tell me about yourself. Who's your father?"

"I no longer know my father," Esko said.

"And your mother?"

"She died."

"What do you do for fun? What did you do last night, eh? See a couple of girls, perhaps."

Diktonius was, famously, a man of pleasure. "I'm afraid I must disappoint you," Esko said. "I translated an article by Walter Gropius. It was about American grain silos."

Diktonous stopped now and threw his square-set jaw toward the stars in the sky, roaring with laughter. "Yes, I can believe that one day you *will* build a *pilvenpiirtaja*."

"Why not now? Let's do it now," Esko said.

"I'll have to think about that," Diktonius said.

"But you *will* think about it?"

"You're a determined young man, aren't you? No wonder Bromberg doesn't let you out too often," he said, giving Esko a sideways smile. "I'll think about it."

Esko was humming with pleasure, therefore, as they came into the Senate Square where the blue and gold cupola of the cathedral stood out against the glowing snow; but then a man ran by, striking his shoulder, nearly knocking him off his feet. "Hey! Watch where you're going, will you?"

Gunshots rang out, two of them, one after the other, and Esko looked quickly at Diktonius, who stood upright and quite still, either very calm or else shocked with fear. Esko felt his own heart slamming against his chest. In front of them a man lay in the snow, blood pouring from his mouth and from the side of his head, as if from a pair of taps. The man wore high, polished boots, and the gold braided uniform of the Russian navy. A bone-handled blade, a *puukko*, was thrust into his chest for good measure. He raised himself on an elbow, blood running from the side of his mouth, and then his eyes went dim and he slumped back down in the snow, frozen cloudberries spilling from the packet he'd been holding in his hand.

Kneeling down, Esko closed the man's eyes. "Godspeed," he said, and looked around for Diktonius, who was nowhere to be seen. He'd fled; and gradually Esko came to recognize that all around him people were running and shouting, yelling warnings, or just yelling. Shaken, he stood, turning away from the dead man and walking swiftly toward Mariankatu Street, up the hill toward a stone building with a turret of gleaming tile.

Oskari Bromberg and Henrik Arnefelt were up on the third floor in the big office they shared. Esko shivered when he saw the long fire crackling with dancing flame in the grate. He stood quite still by the door, his senses gulping down the dark wood, the brass lamps, the framed renderings, the intricate ivory inlay on the desks, the atmosphere snug and secure as a cabin in a boat. Henrik stood, tall and thin and stiff, in front of a drafting board, an expression of fierce concentration on his face, shading with a pencil the edge of a design. Oskari leaned with his elbow against the mantel of the fire, teeth chewing ruminatively at his lower lip. In his other hand he held a book and licked his thumb, idly turning the page. On seeing Esko he snapped shut the book.

"How did it go?" he said, expecting the answer that it had gone very well indeed, because things usually did in the world of Oskari Bromberg.

For a moment Esko couldn't think what he was talking about.

"The meeting," said Oskari with ironically exaggerated patience. "You went to see Diktonius. Did he give us any more money?"

"It went fine," Esko said, reaching into his pocket.

"Excellent! Excellent!" Oskari said, suddenly radiating energy like a dynamo, inspecting the zeros on the check. "Why, Esko, whatever's the matter. You're pale as a ghost."

"I just saw a man shot in the street. He died in front of me."

"What?" said Henrik, turning from his drafting board, hooking a thumb behind the lapel of his heathery tweed jacket, his calm sense of power offended. "Who?"

"A Russian officer."

"My God," Henrik said, jaw falling, his thin face stretched so long it seemed his eyes were popping out. "Oskari. Fetch the boy a brandy—for God's sake."

Later that night, as he was walking back alone to his apartment, Esko was greeted with the incredible information. "Glorious news, comrade!" a voice shouted, and a bare hand pressed a broadsheet into his hand.

In Russia the Bolsheviks had seized power and a Soviet government had been formed. A newspaper account told of the storming of the Winter Palace and a worldwide upheaval that had been set underway:

> There was a moment of silence; then three rifle shots shattered the quiet. We stood speechless, awaiting a return volley. But the only sound was the crunching of broken glass spread like a carpet over the cobblestones. The windows of the Winter Palace had been broken into bits, and then suddenly a sailor emerged from the back, saying that it was all over: the enemy had surrendered. We picked our way across the square, climbing the barricade erected that afternoon by the defenders of the Palace, and followed the conquering sailors and Red Guards into a mammoth building of dingy red stucco. At the end of one corridor was a large, ornate room, with gilded cornices and enormous crystal chandeliers. On both sides of the parquet floor lay rows of dirty mattresses and blankets upon which the defenders had been sleeping. Everywhere was a litter of cigarette butts, scraps of bread, and empty bottles with expensive French labels. The walls were covered with huge canvases in massive gilt frames—historical battle scenes: *12 October 1812* and *6 November 1812*. The canvases were faded and torn, memen-

tos of long-ago imperial victories. This was no imperial victory, but a revolution of all the people, a call to arms as a superb new dawn rose over Russia.

Esko shivered when he saw the name at the bottom of this account—Timo Vaananen, the first that Esko had heard of his father in more than sixteen years.

2

In the following days a hundred Red lanterns were hoisted and a hundred more Russian officers were killed, some hunted down in the streets and shot, others thrown into the harbor. Esko saw some wag put up a sign at the office: OFFICERS' SWIMMING SCHOOL. The Reds decided that businessmen and landowners were fair game, and started killing them too, and Esko learned that Alexander Diktonius had indeed fled, not only from the Senate Square, but all the way out of Finland; he'd run to Sweden and announced in the pages of *Hufvudstadbladet* that he was transferring his business center of operations to Stockholm. Good-bye stone-gnomed country villa, good-bye any chance of a modernistic *pilvenpiirtaja*, Esko thought ruefully; I'll have to find myself another millionaire.

But then he went to a meeting to hear a speech by one of the leaders of the Bolshevik Revolution. Despite his apparent heroism, and his meteoric rise from obscurity to fame and power, the man was unimpressive, ill at ease. His face was dominated by a drooping walrus mustache; his face was gray and showed marks of smallpox; and he spoke in a dull, colorless voice that belied the majesty of his accomplishment.

"Full freedom to shape their own lives is given to the Finns as well as to the other peoples of Russia," he said, and it was some moments before the audience understood the meaning of his words. Suddenly there were wild cheers. People tossed their caps in the air and punched their arms, applauding the words of the man Esko would later learn was Joseph Stalin. "If you want our aid, you'll get it—from hands outstretched in friendship," Stalin went on, his voice echoing in the rafters of the hall with an almost unreal ring, a dummy controlled by some secret ventriloquist. Gripping the edge of the reading stand, he let his dull eyes travel over the crowd as he stood there, waiting, apparently oblivious to the ovation, which lasted several minutes. When it finished, he said, "Forward to the new socialist order!" Again a roar of appreciation.

Other speakers followed. A delegate for the textile workers in Tampere called for action against the mill owners. A Russian sailor regaled them with memories of the rebellion of the Russian fleet. A woman raised her fist and spoke of the role she and her female comrades expected to play.

And then Esko saw his father step forward. Timo was bigger, even more daunting and impressive than he remembered. He'd put on weight, but still looked fit and strong. He was clean shaven, with a wide mouth and a heavy chin. He was dressed in good, well-fitting clothes and fine boots. His hair was long and had turned completely white. His great mouth, seeming to smile, spread wide, and he said nothing, waiting for the wild applause to die down. He was quite evidently very well known in these circles.

"Friends, comrades, we live in momentous times," he quietly began. "We are poised on the brink of a great change in our history. As Comrade Stalin has said—Finland is *free!*" The last word was spoken in a voice like thunder, and Timo turned his face up to where the arc lamps burned brightly, high in the ceiling of the enormous hall. He waited for the overwhelming roar to subside. "But free for whom? For the rich? For the speculators? For those who make fortunes denying you the bread you would put in your mouths. I say *no!*" He bent forward slightly, taking the reading stand in his hands as though he would pick it up and hurl it to the end of the hall. Esko saw a thousand faces staring at Timo in admiration. "Finland must be free for all the people. On earth, here, in our country, we will build a kingdom more bright than any heaven has to offer and for which it will be a glory to die, if we have to. If blood must spill, so be it. Let blood flow! You have been treated like dogs for too long. Now is the time to bite back. In these circumstances you must remember the words of the great French revolutionary Danton. Only boldness will do. Boldness! You must strike now and strike first and strike without fear. Finland is yours for the taking. Seize her, for she is your right! We will be cruel, and we *will* be bloody!"

There was a wild excitement and cheering, unlike anything Esko had ever heard in Finland. "Death to the rich!" shrieked a young man at Esko's side, face shining. A grizzled old man was yelling at the top of his voice: "The Revolution! The Revolution!" Men stepped forward and manhandled Timo off the platform, lofting him high on their shoulders while more cheers rattled the windows. Timo's expression was determined, almost venomous; yet he seemed quite aware of his own power, and delighted in it.

From his father's face, and from the reaction of the crowd, Esko had a sudden, chilling glimpse into the future and his own prospects. Finland was hell-bent on civil war. Finland was going to be dragged into the madness that had consumed the rest of Europe these last three years. Finland was about to plunge itself into a conflict in which, having no care as to which side would win, Esko had no desire to participate. He viewed the complacency of the Whites and the extremism of the Reds with equal mistrust. In Timo's face, in Stalin's face, in the faces of the yelling crowd around him, he saw the expressions of men prepared to fight any fight, to endure any hardship in order that they might achieve their great hopes and illusions, complete the fantastic rewriting of history on which they were embarked. Things were wrong in Finland, plenty, Esko knew, but this wasn't the way forward.

Outside, snow was streaming down from the black, windless sky, snow falling so thick and fast he could scarcely see two feet in front of his face while behind him the hall still echoed with cheers and yells and voices singing, no longer the "Marseillaise," the freedom hymn, but the "Internationale." The Communist anthem was being chanted and an alien air was abroad in Finland. Chaos was coming. The buildings that he'd dreamed of, the buildings that had sprung from his imagination into the pages of his sketchbook would never exist in Helsinki, not anytime soon. For years there would be no building. And so, no need for architects.

Next morning Esko went straight to a shipping office. The dusty premises were dominated by a pendulum clock that ticked loudly, slowly on the wall. The man behind the desk, the shipping clerk, was in his twenties, about Esko's own age. "America?" he said in a sullen voice, not removing his eyes from his ledger. "There are no ships to America."

"There must be," said Esko, trying to laugh this nonsense aside.

The clerk looked up. His high wooden stool creaked. "I tell you there are no ships from Helsinki at this time." He scratched at his nose with the stubby end of a pen.

"I know that," Esko said calmly. He wasn't going to be put off. "What about from Stockholm?"

"No ships from Stockholm to New York at this time." The clerk grinned with gloomy triumph. "Haven't you heard? There's a war on."

Esko let this go. "Stockholm to Liverpool?"

The clerk refused to meet Esko's eye. He scratched at his ledger with the pen. An involuntary grunt conceded the point.

"I can get from Stockholm to Liverpool?"

"It's possible."

"And from Liverpool to New York?"

The clerk sighed, pointing out the folly of traveling at this particular time. President Woodrow Wilson had brought America into the European war. The kaiser's U-boats patrolled the shipping lanes of the Atlantic.

"I want a ticket."

"It will be expensive." The clerk rammed a grubby nail up his nostril.

"I'll travel steerage," said Esko in a calm, determined voice. "I have the money."

"Remember the *Lusitania*," the clerk said, inspecting what he'd found in his nostril, wiping it on the underside of his stool, and then slamming shut his ledger with a self-satisfied smirk. "Went down in less than ten minutes. Twelve hundred people drowned. Dying horribly. You'll probably die too."

"Listen, friend," said Esko, taking the clerk firmly by the lapel. "The U-boat, I understand, is much like the Finnish bear. He doesn't care for the winter. And I don't much care whether I risk drowning or not. I'm going to America. And you're going to give me the ticket. Fourth class, one way."

This was a long spontaneous speech for Esko in those days, but something about leaving the Old World behind left him in an expansive mood.

"Are we clear?"

The clerk thrust out his jaw. He scrunched up his nose.

"The ticket," Esko said. "Write it now."

The clerk sighed. He cleared his throat. But he went to work with his pen.

Afterward Esko strode through the snow toward the Hotel Kamp where, at this early hour of the morning, he knew he'd find Oskari Bromberg holding court with some of his bohemian chums, and indeed there Oskari was, at his usual table, beneath an oil painting of three dashing and handsome young Finnish intellectuals who seemed to be thinking about art and, most likely, death. Oskari was laughing, breaking a croissant between his fingers. He yawned, tired but ebullient. On either side of him was a beautiful young woman, and Oskari's head kept bobbing between the two women, as if he couldn't decide to bite at them, or the jammy croissant. Esko recognized one of the women. She had her flaming red hair done up in a bun and was an actress at the Swedish theater. He'd seen her in something by Ibsen.

"Esko!" cried Oskari. "Sit down, for God's sake. You've got that horrible look about you, as though you're bursting with energy. You're fidgety as a cat and you're making me nervous. Or maybe I'm the cat, the naughty cat. *Miaow!* Ladies, what do you say? Is Oskari a bad tom? Esko, sit, sit!"

Esko pulled up a chair.

"Coffee."

"No, thanks."

"Brandy?"

Esko demurred; Oskari shrugged.

"I can see you've got something on your mind, young Esko."

"Oskari—I'm leaving for America."

"America? *Really?*" said Oskari, looking from one woman to the other with wide eyes, waggling his eyebrows and inviting them to join in the fun. "How extraordinary. And whatever do you think you'll find there?"

"Opportunity."

Oskari laughed out loud. He plucked a leather cigar case from his top pocket and offered it around the table.

"I'm serious."

"I know, Esko, you usually are. You also happen to be wrong."

Esko leaned forward across the table. "There's going to be a civil war, Oskari. It will put an end to building in Finland for years. I have to build—now. Something big. Something grand."

"Oh, of course, how foolish of me. I see how it will go. You will arrive in America. You will of course find it very easy to arrange a meeting with some supremely wealthy man and he will of course give you a check for however many millions you desire."

"I'm ready."

"Listen, Esko. Seriously. You're the most talented draftsman I know, no doubt about it. Your designs are bold, new. You're also a little—how shall I put it? Naive." Oskari puffed on his cigar. "You have a *grand* future here. We've been grooming you for it, Henrik and I."

Esko knew it was a bad sign when Oskari began showering the compliments.

"I can't stay," said Esko with passion. "If I do, I'll be nothing as an architect."

"Oh dear," said Oskari, dabbing ash from his cigar. He sighed, leaning back, rolling his eyes at the ceiling. "Very well, Esko. We will have a serious discussion about this, a *very* serious discussion. But not today, please. Pretty please. Let's make it tomorrow. I'm an older man than you, though obviously not wiser, and as you can see, today I'm already very tired." He stroked the arms of the women on either side of him. "Quite spent in fact."

"Good-bye, Oskari," said Esko, turning angrily to go.

"Excuse me," said one of the young women, the redhead, the actress Esko had recognized.

Esko stopped, smiling. "Yes?"

She shot the question like a bullet. "Sir, are you a coward?"

Esko started, stung. For a moment he wanted to protest—if you were a man, he wanted to say, I'd hit you, or challenge you; but instead he swallowed the insult, for he knew it not to be true. He wasn't leaving to avoid the war, or because he disliked the snobbery Oskari represented, or the tyranny his father was so carelessly prepared to inflict to get whatever it was he was fighting for, or because he was afraid of dying. He'd been haunted by glimpses of the Manhattan skyline he'd caught in motion picture newsreels, a thrilling jumble of buildings, mighty towers with smaller buildings all around, dwindling like dice. He'd dreamed of creating some such landscape in Helsinki. Well, that wasn't going to be allowed to happen, and he was left with only one possible choice. He'd made it, was acting on it. He wanted to build a skyscraper, so he'd go to New York where they grew populous as trees.

"A coward?" he said in a soft voice, proud and thoughtful. "No, madam, I don't believe so."

The next morning he arrived early at work, relishing the prospect of a fight. What can they do, he said to himself, put me in chains? Neither Oskari nor Henrik were in their office; the fire was out. Damn it, Esko said to himself, where are they?

Hands thrust in pockets, he patrolled the chilly room. On the wall there was a framed rendering of one of Arnefelt & Bromberg's more recent efforts, an apartment building on Museokatu Street, behind the National Museum, paid for by a man who made a few million in timber speculation, or herring. The rendering was lovely work, in a way, characteristic of Oskari's style when he actually willed himself to sit down in front of a drafting board; and yet it was a sketch that might have been made twenty years ago, that paid homage to H. H. Richardson, to Norman Shaw, to a generation of architects who had worked in monumental stone. Standing beneath one of the oil lamps that hung from the ceiling, Esko saw clearly how he himself was grabbing for something different and he rehearsed everything that he found wrong, even faintly ridiculous, about the design: it was leaden and heavy; it seemed to have been dumped on the ground rather than growing out of it; it was pompous. In front of it, Esko felt the oppressive weight of the commitment to a useless past behind Oskari's refinement. It was people like him who'd put Finland in a rut. There'd be a civil war and then Finland would most likely go back to being in the same rut. Esko shook his head, amazed that he'd never seen this quite so clearly before. He should be in America already. He'd studied in Paris. He'd traveled through Germany, Italy, France, England, Scotland. He was the third most powerful architect in easily the most prestigious firm in Helsinki and in the past when he'd looked back to his roots, to the village, he'd always thought that he'd traveled a long way. Now he realized he was just beginning.

Esko was shocked from this reverie by the banging of the office door.

Henrik shook snow from his umbrella, hung his coat, and flopped down in front of his drafting board. This in itself was completely out of character. Henrik liked to stand up straight when working. Usually he was strict, forbidding, endlessly upright and firm; now his hands were shaking; his long face looked terrible, caved in.

"Henrik, are you all right?"

Henrik lowered his head. "Good morning, Esko," he said, distraught. "I suppose you know this means you'll be getting a partnership. At least that much will come out of it."

"I'm going to America and that's that," said Esko, not about to be bribed. "I'm sorry Henrik—my mind is set."

"America?" said Henrik, puzzlement in his bloodshot eyes now, and not only distress. "I don't understand."

"I can't accept your offer."

A trolley car hurried by outside, hissing and clattering. Henrik sagged, slumped in the chair as if his bones had been sucked away.

Esko was nonplussed; he'd been hoping Henrik would see this more fairly. "You and Oskari have been good to me—I know that and I thank you for it."

Henrik shook his head. "So much work to do. The new city plan, for instance—we must get on with it. It's more vital than ever."

Esko was more astonished than angry. Hadn't Henrik heard a word he'd said? "I'm leaving for America. I won't be working in Helsinki anymore."

Just then the outer doors opened and a man burst in, fur hat clasped in his hand, fur coat flying behind—Klaus, Henrik's son, tall, fair, strikingly handsome, with flakes of snow in his luxuriant mustache.

"Father, I came as soon as I could. I'm so terribly sorry. It's frightful, just frightful," Klaus said, feeling for the ends of his mustache with his lower lip. "Esko, how are you bearing up?"

Only now was Esko beginning to grasp that something dreadful had happened.

"You've heard the news, obviously," said Klaus with a puzzled frown.

Esko shook his head.

"Oskari was shot last night. Two Reds murdered him outside his house."

"Oskari—murdered?"

"One grabbed his arm and the other shot him in the face. His wife came to the door to see about the noise. He died in her arms."

3

O f course you must go to America," Klaus said as he and Esko walked down the hill to the harbor. They'd taken Henrik back to his home in a taxi. Now Esko knew what was coming. Klaus, in his impetuous, ironic way, was going to give him a lecture. "Naturally you must. Oskari dead. Murders in the streets. My father probably undergoing a nervous collapse. It's the perfect time to leave. I myself have chosen this moment to fall in love."

Esko couldn't stop thinking about Oskari. He felt such a fool, even though, in the end, the fact of the murder clarified things even further. In Finland the current desire was for one Finn to slit another Finn's throat or shoot him in the face as he died—that's what the Reds did to Oskari. Finland was a small forest where the bears and wolves were about to slaughter each other. His determination to go to America was redoubled.

"This isn't the time," Klaus was saying.

"There's going to be a war."

"That's why it isn't the time." Klaus's breath puffed out in front of him. He stroked his mustache with a gloved hand. "Oh, bloody hell," he said, staring across at the frozen waters of the harbor. Frost sparkled on the masts of a sailing ship locked in the ice. It was two in the afternoon, mid-December, the hour of brief winter light. The air was sharp and clear, their shadows stretching in front of them a hundred yards long, wobbling on the snow and then climbing up the red and yellow brick of the market hall. Klaus gave Esko a nudge. "I'm bloody freezing," he said. "Let's go get a schnapps."

Klaus was roguish, talkative, quite the opposite of his conservative father, whom he resembled only in his striking aristocratic good looks. Klaus mocked both the Czar and the "Kalevala"-loving Finnish nationalists. He mocked the boisterous Germans and the fussy British, and he especially mocked the Bolsheviks. He liked to say that he took nothing seriously, but Esko knew that he took some things very seriously indeed. His writing for instance: Klaus had published poems in the literary periodicals and wrote for the big papers in both Finland and Sweden. He'd sold a film scenario to a producer in Stockholm.

Klaus greeted other pedestrians as they walked toward the market. He raised his hat to the ladies. He narrowed his eyes and made a clownish face at a little boy. He had the knack of making whatever and whomever was around him his home. He seemed comfortable everywhere and was the most natural person Esko had ever met. With the bearing of a Viking, Klaus affected the behavior of a flaneur; he was that rare beast, Esko thought, an openly happy Finn. Esko recognized the danger here; if anyone could persuade him to stay, it was his friend.

"Watch out," Klaus said, throwing his arm across Esko's chest while a hurtling wagon passed in front of them, churning up snow, the din drowning out his voice. "You go around with your head in the clouds, my friend. Good thing too. Always liked you for it."

They'd met in Paris, in a motion picture theater, during a picture called *Seven Footprints to Satan*, a terrible story, as Esko recalled, although back then, when the movie-going experience was still new, there'd been the thrill of being in a theater at all, surrounded in the dark, watching images and people leap from the screen as if they would take possession of him.

"Why do you think we met, you and I?" Klaus said, when they were settled at a table with the schnapps in front of them.

"We laughed at the same moment."

"And then we looked across a row of seats at each other. And do you know why? Because, my friend, we are Finns. We sought each other out in that city of mirrors."

This was how Klaus referred to Paris, because, walking in the street, or in one of the arcades, you were constantly catching sight of yourself. The French positioned mirrors everywhere. It was to do with their delicious vanity and sense of show, Klaus had said. He'd written a little essay about it: "Why the French Are Not Like the Finns."

He said, "Don't you think you should stay and fight for your country?"

"What country?"

"For Finland, for *Suomi.*"

"Come on—both Whites and Reds are full of shit, you know that." Esko felt free with Klaus as with no one else. He didn't understand quite why they'd become friends, what it was that they sought and saw in each other; but the choice had been made, stuck to. Klaus had helped fix the job with Arnefelt & Bromberg. He'd introduced Esko to the gallery crowd, eased the way to professional acceptance. "There's nothing to choose between them."

"Maybe so. But we *have* to choose. Because what happens now is going to shape our future."

"War smashes things. It doesn't build them up."

"This will be a good war—a war against the evil of the Bolsheviks."

"Suit yourself. I won't be fighting in it," said Esko, knocking back his schnapps.

Klaus looked around the hall. A porter went by, lugging an empty crate. There was a beggar in rags, a refined aristocratic lady looking through her glasses at a salmon embedded in flakes of ice on a slab. "These are your people, this is your *home.*"

Esko wondered whether Klaus might know him better than he knew himself. Would he miss Finland? Undoubtedly. He'd be nostalgic for the faces, for the light, for the snow, even for the winter darkness probably. And he had no doubt either that leaving for America would have long-lasting, dramatic consequences. That was surely the point. He was making a statement about himself.

"Architecture is my home."

Klaus blew a raspberry. "Now I know I'm in difficulties. The A word has been invoked. I can't persuade you, can I? Well, then—so be it. Here's to you, Esko." He raised his schnapps. "Good luck, my friend."

"And you know I wish the same for you."

They clicked glasses, and Esko knew Klaus would allow him a little breather before regrouping, returning to the attack.

"Did you see the new Chaplin yet?" Klaus asked, and Esko nodded. "How is it?"

"It's Chaplin, you know," said Esko. "After everything, he carries the girl through a door. The door closes. End of film. It's beautiful. Tell me about your new girl. I thought you said you were in love—you old rogue. Whose heart are you breaking this time?"

"This one's different," said Klaus, fingering his mustache. "We're to be married—she accepted my proposal last night."

Esko grinned, genuinely pleased. "That's wonderful. Congratulations. I'm thrilled," he said, and he reached out and grabbed Klaus in a hug. "Someone got you at last."

"Definitely," Klaus said. "And I've never been so glad to be got."

"How long have you known this paragon?"

"Not long. Long enough. I'm head over heels, Esko. I never imagined I could love like this," Klaus said, shaking his head with a shy smile. "I'd been hoping you'd be our best man. But I suppose that won't be possible, what with your trip to America." He held up his hand, waving away the suggestion that he was trying to arouse guilt. "No, no, don't worry—I won't say another word. You'll always be my best man—even in absentia."

They clinked glasses again and toasted. From the schnapps, the gaslights in the market were already looking bright to Esko's eye.

"I couldn't be more pleased," he said. "I wish you all the happiness in the world. Can I at least meet the lucky lady before I leave?"

"Of course. Saturday night—I'm bringing Katerina to meet Mother and Father. Come too. Help break the ice."

Esko touched his glass to his lips. "Katerina?"

"Katerina Malysheva. She's Russian."

"Is she?" said Esko, his free hand flying to the silver mirror in his pocket; his fingers ran over the glass, checking that it was still all of a piece, and it was—amazing, since it felt as though a bomb had exploded in his heart and pieces of him were flying everywhere.

4

A servant showed him at once into the dining room where, alone, he shoved his hands into his pockets and waited, standing with his back to the heat that pulsed from the blue-tiled stove. Laughter, raised voices came from a distant part of the house and Esko couldn't help but rack himself with the idea that Katerina was up there now, being given the tour by Klaus. He reminded himself that it might not be her, that this Katerina Malysheva need not be his Katerina Malysheva, that Klaus's Katerina Malysheva perhaps bore no relation to the beautiful girl with whom he had danced at the fair all those years ago. It didn't matter, he told himself: he was going to America.

Henrik's villa, built at the turn of the century, utilized every imaginable architectural style at the greatest possible expense and tonight a fine show had been put on. The best silver was out, the finest crystal, in front of chairs of green-stained oak that had high, narrow backs and seats upholstered in red leather. The hanging lamps were almost cubic in shape, with concave sides and opaque glass bottoms that softened and diffused the light. The oak parquet floor was covered with a flame-patterned carpet, and the sweeping curtains were of raw red silk. A grandfather clock kept and controlled the time, its soft tick followed by a loud tock, percussive as an explosion.

The table was set for twelve, with place cards pinned like flags on steepled napkins. Esko had been placed where Oskari had customarily sat, prompting the gloomy thought that Henrik's wife, who didn't like him, hoped he'd be the next to go.

On the table one of the chubby crystal goblets was askew. Squatting down, squinting across the table at eye level, Esko nudged the base of the goblet, moving it a fraction of an inch at a time, until it formed a circle with the others, and so that within that circle there fell another circle, of light shattered and splintered as it passed through the glass.

"Perfect," he said, jumping to his feet with a big grin, pinging the edge of the goblet.

"It's you, then!"

Esko started, his cheeks at once beginning to blush. Her voice was as he remembered, more mature of course, and perhaps softer, but the same: playful, imperious, hers. The voice that had asked him to dance, the voice that had called, "Run him down!"

"Klaus told me just a few minutes ago that he'd invited his friend Esko Vaananen, and I thought, Can it really be the beautiful serious little boy I met all those years ago? And here you are . . ."

Esko's cheeks burned.

She was taller than he'd thought she'd be, younger too. During their previous meeting she'd been so composed and adult and in control that he'd always assumed them to be the same age, with Katerina, if anything, the elder. Now he realized she was still in her early or mid-twenties. She was dressed in a sheath of glimmering black satin. No jewelry adorned her wrists or hands or the swanlike whiteness of her neck. Her thick hair was cropped close to the delicate lines of her skull, like a boy's, and was darker than he remembered. She had the appearance of elegance and money: nonetheless there was something of the wild spirit about her, wounded, emotionally aflame. All Esko could do was gaze at her as she circled the table, trailing her wonderfully graceful, long-fingered hands on the cloth, gently humming a tune. Her face was heart shaped, her eyes shining as she advanced toward him from the shadows, and Esko's blood grew hot, the muscles in his body tightening around every vein and jolting up the charge. He'd thought of Katerina almost every day for the last fifteen years of his life and yet he'd never seriously imagined that they'd ever meet again. He'd seen no conceivable circumstance in which such a dream could become real; now it was happening, and he was sweating, tongue-tied. He stood there, trying to speak and failing, helpless in the face of her vulnerable beauty.

"Aren't you going to say something? Don't you remember me at all? My name is Katerina. Katerina Malysheva," she said.

"I know," he said, voice cracking.

"You do?" She shot him a radiant smile. "Klaus says you're an architect now. You work with his father. What do you think of this house? It's a beautiful home, don't you think?"

Esko couldn't stop his shoulders lifting dismissively, shrugging, and she burst out with laughter.

"That's something else I remember. A boy with a scarred face that was so expressive. Incapable of hiding anything."

Esko blushed again; no one else had ever seen that, only the scars.

"Are you a modern architect then, Mr. Vaananen? I bet you'd like nothing better than to tear down poor old Henrik's house."

Esko smiled, this being the first time anyone had ever referred to his boss as "poor old Henrik" in such a delightfully disrespectful way, a fact that seemed to give him permission to speak. "It's not what I would build myself."

"No? What would be your dream home, Mr. Vaananen?"

"I've never thought."

"Think now. Think for me."

She'd come all the way around the table and stood now directly in front of him, her eyes looking up into his face. Her heady perfume almost overpowered him. It fell on his senses like a weight. "A house?" he said, eye closed.

"What else?"

"Architects build other types of structures."

"No doubt."

"A house for me or a house for you?"

"A house for you."

Her scent brought to mind a summer's day, a meadow dazed by the heat at sunset. It was strange, but he, an architect, had never until this moment conceived that he might design his own home. He didn't quite know where to start. He opened his eye again and her beauty hit him again like a blow. To be coherent now, to think about architecture, was out of the question. He was drunk with her. "You look beautiful," he said. "So much more beautiful than when I saw you in my dreams. And I have dreamed about you. But your hair—"

"I was forced to cut my hair," she said, anger flashing in her eyes, playfulness gone.

"I'm sorry," Esko said. "I've upset you."

"It's nothing," she said. She smiled again, but it was just an attempt at brightness. Something in her mood was changed and she shivered.

"Are you cold?"

"A little."

"I'll get something for your shoulders," he said, about to set off for the door.

"No, Esko—stay," she said. Her hand was on his sleeve, holding him back and squeezing his arm, just as the use of his Christian name sent another jolt through his veins. "Don't bother. I'm fine," she said. A soft tick from the grandfather clock was followed by another of those explosive tocks and the hour began to strike. "The others will be here any second."

Her eyes searched his face in the most direct way; her gaze was so penetrating that he'd have stepped back, but her strong grip held him.

He wondered what she was looking for.

"You were such a fearless little boy. You had every reason to be afraid and yet you were brave."

"I didn't feel brave."

"You were. I gave you a mirror. Do you remember?"

"I've had it with me always. It's in my pocket now," he said, but then the door opened, propelling her away.

Klaus came in, smiling at Katerina, glancing back and guiding his mother solicitously by the elbow. Klaus's mother's face lit up when she saw Katerina (whose face wouldn't? thought Esko), but it was with an expression of withering distaste that she turned to him, two scornful eyes and a razor of a nose pinched within a steely gray helmet of hair. Esko never had been able to figure out what he'd done to make her dislike him so.

"Why Mr. Vaananen, you're here too. And I've never seen you so smart," she said, sizing him up and down, as if measuring him for a coffin. "Do you and Katerina know each other?"

"Oh Mother, don't be so preposterous," said Klaus. "How could they know each other? You know Katerina only arrived from Petrograd a week ago." He turned to Esko. "I must say, you do look rather splendid. You didn't buy the monkey suit just for tonight?"

"For the boat," Esko said, this being what he'd told himself while he'd been dithering with his checkbook in the Diktonius Building that afternoon. I'm not doing this for her, he'd said to himself; that would be quite absurd, he'd said to himself, since I don't even know that it will *be* her. Several times he'd almost returned the suit to the rack. He really didn't believe in such vanity. He'd bought the suit anyway. For the boat.

"Darling," said Klaus, taking Katerina's hands and kissing her on the lips. "This is my friend from Paris—Esko Vaananen."

"Of course," said Katerina, offering her hand to Esko as though they'd never met before, as though they'd been standing in the room together without uttering a word. "Mr. Vaananen—I'm delighted to meet you."

"Now old Esko is a man of many parts," Klaus said, gathering Katerina back into his arms and grinning down at her. "He can be silent, awkward, and a little priggish, a great high-minded bear of a fellow, and very shy. On the other hand he loves the motion pictures and is capable sometimes of a weird spontaneous charm. So watch out. No one has ever accused him of being a good dresser before. Indeed, Esko is known to be a disaster in a suit."

"I'm sure Mr. Vaananen has talents none of us can begin to guess at," Katerina said with a gracious smile.

Embarrassed, Esko contemplated the shine on his shoes and throughout dinner scarcely said or heard a word. He smiled, drank, nodded, while Henrik held forth about the latest developments on the political front, about the Red threat and the murder of a Swedish broker, about dear old Oskari. Katerina was seated next to the smoothly adoring Klaus and Esko hardly dared look at her; when he did raise his eye he found that she was looking at Klaus, or Klaus's mother. She too took little part in the conversation and he wondered what had happened to change her mood. Surely not his remark about her hair. He saw at a glance she wasn't vain; about her beauty she had an almost careless attitude. He couldn't make her out. Yet she seemed to be able to read him like a book.

After dinner she took him aside: "Good night, Mr. Vaananen. It was a pleasure to meet you." She spoke softly, her voice low and husky so the others wouldn't hear. "Come to my apartment tomorrow afternoon. Fabianinkatu Street nineteen. Three o'clock."

5

Later that night there was a gale. It snapped at the masts and funnels of the ships in the harbor. It whistled down the streets and promenades and avenues, uprooting trees and bushes, scattering snowdrifts even as it made new ones. Ornaments toppled from the cornices of buildings, pieces of brick and stone exploded in the streets below, leaving great dents in anything—or anyone—unlucky enough to be unprotected. The late morning dawn lit the stricken city with a dripping, feeble light, a pale, corpselike pallor that shrouded the debris. Carriages were overturned; automobiles smashed; a ship had been lifted from its moorings and sent sailing landward, across the cobbles of the Market Square, where it lay on its side, beached.

Esko was awake throughout the night, driven from bed by the racket of the storm, by his recollections of the evening, by the memory of Katerina's face and his dreams of America. He knew things would be difficult there. He knew that he'd be forced to learn the manners of a culture far brisker than his own—to say nothing of conquering a language of which he had only a beginning command. He knew that for a long time he'd be lonely and there'd be no money. Until Katerina's sudden appearance these prospects hadn't worried him. Now he felt somehow changed, weakened, vulnerable to dangers he had long ago forgotten about. Like a conjuror, she'd produced the fluttering bird of his longing for love.

He was ugly; that was another thing he knew. Life rubbed his nose in his ugliness every day. Every day he saw others cross the street so that he would not have to witness how hard, and how unsuccessfully, they fought to suppress their shock. In Paris, under the influence of the flamboyant Klaus, he'd grown a beard and worn a wide-brimmed hat of velvet. But he'd found the disguise humiliating. He didn't want to pretend to be something he wasn't; he'd learned long ago to cope with the revulsion he sometimes inspired, though there were always the nights when he came back to the apartment and had to lie on the bed and close his eye, or sit at the table with his head in his hands, rebuilding the composure that the fleeting distortion of another's face had snatched away. Anger only led to mockery and further unwanted attention, he knew: it piled one ugliness on top of another. Trying to hide provoked inquiry and, always, at the end of it, the same appalled shock in a stranger's face. He'd seen it a hundred times. Yet it was Katerina's response that left him the most defenseless of all; she stripped him of his shell. Without a trace of irony she called him beautiful. Sitting at the table, storm raging outside, he suddenly realized that it was this above all that set Katerina apart from the rest of the world: she looked straight through his face and saw a quality he himself could only dream was there.

He got up, walked across the room, helped himself to a beer. Sitting down again, he uncorked the bottle, pulled the silver mirror from his pocket, and arranged pencils and drawing paper in front of him—a ritual he'd performed a thousand times. With the mirror beside him, he would draw.

He picked up a pencil, sharpening and honing it with his *puukko*. Katerina, the begetter of his ambition, was returned in the flesh, pricking him with life and pain: life—his whole body on fire with the memory of her; pain—he still couldn't conceive how he would ever make anything beautiful enough to deserve someone so beautiful as her. He'd said that he was an architect. This

was true. But what had he done, actually? True, there was the one small factory, a paper mill by a lake near Savonlinna, a commission so modest he
hadn't even presumed to mention it to Diktonius the other day; true, he'd
been with Oskari and Henrik, learning his craft; but still—he wished he was
further along so that he could at least impress her with his professional skill.

His mind swam with the memory of the moment she'd appeared to him
again—a mischievous smile on her face, her emerald gaze, the sound of pinged
crystal hovering in the air like a butterfly spreading its wings between them.

With the pencil he drew a circle, which he cut in two and realized was a
hearth, the heart of a home. Around the hearth he drew a room, leading up
steps to another room, and he realized he was designing a house, not for himself, but for the two of them. Glancing up at the wall, he saw a Japanese print
he'd put there. He wanted this house to have some of that print's elegant
grace and simplicity; yet it must also gather in aspects of Katerina herself. She
was a thin beauty with enormous eyes and something wounded about her; yet
she was hard-headed, commanding, still the mysterious empress of his memory. And so this house, he decided, must be two houses, one thing on the outside, and something quite different within, an austere structure that disclosed
radiant treasures. It would be, like Katerina herself, without fuss, direct and
yet sphinxlike, a contradiction.

We desire beauty, he thought, even though we know it causes pain, for
beauty is hard to create or achieve or even acquire and yet, once glimpsed,
once held, once perceived, it makes you suffer forever. You want to make
things perfect, as perfect as Katerina's almond-shaped eyes, as perfect as the
frozen lake. Nothing less will do.

Esko had little sexual experience. In Paris Klaus had taken him four or
five times to a brothel in Montparnasse. Esko remembered that the girl he saw
had a blackened front tooth and ash blond hair that hung over her forehead
like a curtain. When he asked her how her tooth got that way she shrugged,
saying a man hit her once. She responded to Esko's outrage with a shrug, saying she'd then stabbed the guy in the chest, letting Esko know that she was
well able to take care of herself, a tough and capable girl, but not unkind—
clear, amoral, with a fondness for champagne she didn't insist that Esko buy.
Quite a number of years younger than he, in her late teens, she behaved,
after sex, like a hectoring aunt, anxious that he should get on in the world, so
he could come and see her more often, and afford the champagne. She
never mentioned his face, her assumption being that everybody was ugly—

inside. She was, in her way, a philosopher, a whore with a heart as hard as the Eiffel Tower. Her name had been Catherine, and Klaus was puzzled when Esko stopped going to see her. "She's pretty, she likes you, have some fun," Klaus had said. Esko had shrugged, saying the brothels weren't for him.

He hadn't been consciously aware of holding himself in check all these years, but now, on fire for Katerina, he wondered. Love had been delivered like a truck of bricks, hot from the kiln. The realist in him knew that his feelings were out of all proportion to the amount of time they'd spent together. But wasn't that the way romantic love was supposed to be? A lightning flash. A transforming potion. An obsession that whisked the self away from reality as if it were a balloon, gaily soaring toward the sun. A Parthenon that arose, fully formed. In a way, of course, he'd spent most of his life with Katerina, with his version of her, and now his passion heightened and sharpened and grew hotter with each moment that went by, delicious agony, as if everything he'd previously aimed only at architecture was now beamed at her. His own wakeful awareness sought hers, his mind roaming the storm-blasted Helsinki streets, questing a heart he suspected was somehow torn and wounded like his own, even while his hand stayed on the page, working with a pencil at the design for a home where the two of them might live and love together.

He stood up, stretched. Most of the information he had about Katerina, he realized, came from long ago. Now he needed to know what she thought—about everything and anything, about art, about architecture. What did she think of Brunelleschi, who in the glorious dome of Florence Cathedral had achieved what his contemporaries deemed impossible? What did she think of Louis Sullivan's light, elegant handling of the vertical office building? Of Frank Wright's stupendous interweaving and tiering of interior light and space? Of Lars Sonck's cathedral at Tampere?

He laughed, realizing he had no idea whether she knew anything at all about architecture. He sipped at his beer, threw himself down on the sofa for a moment, and at once sprang back to his feet, returning to the table and his drawing of the house, allowing himself to imagine a very different life for himself, a life in which they would go out and confront and conquer the storm of the world, together.

And then his spirits crashed. He went once more to the window and stood forlorn while a trolley car passed noiselessly at the end of the street. A sleigh went by, the sound from its scraping runners lost in the storm. Who did he think he was trying to fool? Katerina was a woman he barely knew, a beautiful woman who was engaged to be married to his own best friend, and Esko couldn't help but think how much more attractive Klaus must inevitably seem to her. Klaus was easy, witty, brave; Klaus was admired; Klaus knew the opera, was a perfect shot, and had only to read a poem once for it to be inscribed in his memory. He'd been born a crown prince, in Finnish terms, heir to the small, old-fashioned but humane and orderly world that was Henrik's domain. Klaus was the golden boy. He'd sported through the salons of Petrograd and Paris, being brilliant, making love, reading the tarot for bored women of society; yet he'd also roused them to cheers in the lowest of dives. Esko knew; Esko had been there, hanging on Klaus's supremely well-cut social coattails. Klaus had ease and effortless charm—small wonder everyone liked and loved him. Esko liked and loved him too, not that he'd rate himself a snowball in hell's chance as Klaus's romantic rival even if he hated the fellow.

No, it's useless, he said to himself, she'd never choose him over Klaus even if he were stupid enough to give her the chance, which he wouldn't. Why risk the humiliation?

He slumped on the sofa, putting his head in his hands. I won't go to see her, he thought, raking his fingers down his cheeks—what's the point? He shuddered, absolutely ashamed to have allowed himself the romantic and nonsensical and childish idea that she might actually return his love.

He went to the table to destroy the drawing of the house and the foolish hope it represented; but as his hand touched the soft, raglike paper, he realized how strong that hope was. It made him sharpen his pencils again and get back to work. Fabianinkatu Street 19, three o'clock—that meant *something*. It was a glimmer, and he clung to it.

For hours, while the wind howled and rattled at the windows, Esko walked this razor between expectation and despair, teetering now this way, now the other, until at last—at about eleven in the morning—dawn broke and the city was filled with that strange, fog-colored light. The wind fell away, faces of frost began peeking in through the windowpanes, and snow fell in thick, heavy flakes, settling at once. By now Esko was too nervous for any more work. He pulled on a pair of big felt boots, donned his fur hat, and rolled up his drawings of the house, slipping them into a deep pocket inside his coat. Body thrust forward, he was at least able to *walk* with his accustomed air of purpose and determination, as if he was in perfect command of his own destiny, struggling against the snow that drove into his face, into his eye and mouth.

6

Esko's long legs took the steps two at a time, bounding effortlessly despite the long slog through the snow, and when he reached the top he clutched his hat in his hand and tried to calm himself. Sweat prickled at the top of his scalp and on the back of his neck. A pain wormed sharply through the center of his dead eye. His nerves were a tight ball of disquiet. It's impossible, quite impossible. I'd better get the hell out of here. This is mad, he said to himself, facing the green door to Katerina's apartment, but the door opened before he had a chance to move or knock.

"It's you," he said when he saw her, clutching his fur hat to his chest and then stuffing it back on top of his head, about to flee.

"Don't go," she said, smiling, alert to his discomposure. "Who else were you expecting to see? The girl in the moon? I'm afraid she's not available for visits today."

"I must go," he said. His throat was tight, choking. "It's snowing, very hard," he said, and ducked his head.

"Esko, are you all right?"

Faced by her gaze, he felt his wits desert him.

"Katerina—I want you to marry me and come to America."

My God, he thought, where did that come from? For a moment he felt wild, free, light-headed.

"Please, Katerina. Will you marry me?"

Her smile disappeared as if wiped away. She raised a slender, long-fingered hand to her throat, flushed, perhaps even flattered; but then her expression became blank and Esko knew he had to do something.

"I will get down on my knees if you wish. I will—"

"Please, don't," she said, stepping forward and grasping his arm. "Oh, *Esko*," she said. "I'm sorry."

Esko stepped back. In his heart he'd known her answer would be this; he'd steeled himself for it. Yet he'd arrived and blurted out the thing he thought he'd never be able to say; now his hopes were dashed.

"Of course, you're right. It's impossible, it could never be. Excuse me, I must go now."

"You're shivering. Do come in. It's warm."

Esko felt as though he were sinking into the darkness of an icy lake, all the fire and light inside—gone. "Thanks, but I have so much to do. Drawings, packing, preparations." He had no idea what he was saying. "I'm leaving tomorrow."

"Please," Katerina said. She took him by the hand, smiling and trying to draw him inside. "I want to explain."

"You don't have to explain anything. I made a proposal. You refused," he said, neither shaking her hand nor allowing her to budge him. "It was very unreasonable of me to expect you to do otherwise."

"You stubborn man."

"I *am* stubborn," he said, as if this had the quality of revelation. "I'll never feel about anyone the way I feel about you."

The words, again, were a surprise to him.

"That's nonsense," she said.

"It's quite true. Katerina, please don't think I'm going to embarrass you again. You rejected an offer I surprised myself by making. But I'm glad I did."

Katerina was very moved. Her eyes roamed his face but he still wouldn't meet her gaze. He was discomposed, hurt, trying to gather himself. "I need your help," she said.

Slowly Esko wiped his boots against the brushes at the front of the door and then followed her into a dark hallway that smelled of wax and her intoxicating scent, recalling the Diktonius Building where the perfumes glittered like treasure in their bottles of bright glass, arrayed on one of the counters that he usually walked straight by to get to the elevator.

"Here, let me," she said, reaching up to his shoulders and slipping off his coat. Her fingers stopped, brushing over the rolled-up plans of the house he'd designed. "What are these?"

"Nothing," Esko said sadly. "Something I was working on."

Her green eyes questioned him, but he said nothing, sighing inwardly while he tried to shrug off his foolish hopes.

"Listen," she said, glancing at the watch on her wrist. "Any minute now people will be arriving. There's a meeting."

She explained what she wanted; she wanted him to push furniture against the walls.

"I'm the moving man—is that why you asked me here?" he said, feeling angry and cheated now, not that she'd promised him anything.

She looked at him sideways, annoyed herself.

"Of course not," she said.

"Why then?" he said. In the room, there were thick, dark carpets, empty bookshelves hidden in dim recesses, a pair of ottomans draped with red and black chintz. A piano gleamed, keyboard gaping. A gilt clock stood on the mantel above a log fire that suddenly spat. A sharp smell of pine came from the woodpile, mingling with the aroma of cooking fish that insinuated itself from the apartment below.

The room told him nothing. There were no books, no pictures, no clothes or mess. It was as if Katerina had moved in yesterday and was ready to move out tomorrow. Her green eyes had become opaque to him again. Her mystery was inpenetrable.

"Are you going to help me with this or not?" she said, leaning down to grasp one of the ottoman sofas.

Esko felt big and clumsy, not only sad but somehow used; nonetheless he took hold of the other end of the sofa and worked hard for the next fifteen minutes, hefting tables and chairs, rolling the piano beneath the window, shifting ornaments onto the mantel and into corners or onto bookshelves where they would be safe. He worked until he was no longer cold but sweating from the heat of the fire and a space had been cleared in the center of the room. Whereupon Katerina showed him a tray, two bottles of vodka, and a rack of glasses in the kitchen.

"I'm a waiter now?" he said.

"You're promoted," she said, with a wry smile. "Look sharp."

A succession of solemn and sober-suited men came banging up the stairs, wiping their feet on the brushes outside, piling their coats one on top of the other in the tiled lobby, and walking warily into the apartment, where they greeted each other with overeager familiarity, or stood in front of the fire warming their backs, or moved to the window or against a wall, pretending to be fully occupied with important thoughts, or the accuracy of their timepieces, or their diaries.

Esko, circulating with a tray of vodka, recognized the symptoms. Although each of these men assumed himself to be among like-minded colleagues, not one of them was going to give a thing away. This was to be a *political* meeting, and each would be required to put something at risk, his loyalty, his money, perhaps even his life, undesirable eventualities the contemplation of which left some of them jittery, some calm, while others puffed out their chests and sighed, lighting cigars and cigarettes, brimming with self-important courage. They were like peacocks, Esko thought as he dispensed the glasses; their vanity was in the fact of their presence; they'd only come because something big was on the cards.

Katerina was in no way awed. She moved among these men as if she were not only the center of attraction, which she was, but a prime mover in whatever was to follow. She smiled, shaking each of them by the hand, making brief conversation, a flashing glimpse of strength and determination, and moving on, her expression always the same. Even in his sadness Esko studied her and was impressed, all the more so because he sensed a nervousness, a fragility beneath the calm and busy social showmanship. She seemed isolated and frail, and Esko wished he could help, give her a shoulder to rest against, if she needed one. But that wasn't his part to play, he thought with some returning bitterness; he lugged furniture, while the role of comforter and lover belonged to another.

"This is a surprise," a voice said, and Esko turned to be greeted by Klaus's familiar handsomeness. "Esko, what on earth are you doing here?"

Esko, flustered, didn't want to lie. "Katerina asked me to come."

"She did?" said Klaus with a frown. "She didn't say anything."

"Perhaps she forgot," Esko said.

"She tells me everything," Klaus said in an insistent way. His expression was puzzled only for a moment, and then his eyes traveled to the door, where Henrik hurried in, not bothering to take off his coat, with snow on his shoulders and an anxious look on his gaunt face, followed by a calm man in his fifties who refused to be rushed, a man of medium height whose careful and precise, even elegant manner, at once commanded attention. His eyes were deep-set, his hair slicked back, his mustache carefully groomed. He carried himself with the thoughtless arrogance of an aristocrat, straight as a rod, as if he had spent much of his life giving orders from on top of a horse. He looked uneasy in his dark gray suit, and Esko had the sense of a determined, ambitious man, uncomfortable anywhere else but in a uniform.

The room's attention seemed to concentrate on this man, and not all of that attention was free from suspicion, even hostility. Katerina, however, went over and greeted him warmly.

"Who is he?" said Esko.

"Gustaf Mannerheim," said Klaus in a whisper, stroking his mustache so that his hand half covered his mouth. "He just arrived from Petrograd. I think he'll be useful to us."

"Why?"

Klaus said that Mannerheim had been a general in the Imperial Russian Army, and had traveled north from Odessa, a seven-day journey during which his life had been hanging by a hair. "The Reds would kill him in a flash if they knew what he was about," Klaus said.

Esko wondered what help a retired officer of a failed regime could be.

Henrik stepped forward and, with his thumb hooked in the lapel of his somber tweed coat, called for silence. Excited, eyes gleaming, he began: "Gentlemen. I will be blunt and straightforward. A dear friend of mine was recently murdered by the Red butchers. Shot down on the steps of his own home. Shot like a dog." He paused, let the words sink in. "It is clear to me now that unless we act, Finland will not be ours. It will belong to the rabble. An eventuality that—I'm sure you agree—we must not allow ourselves to contemplate. Yet there is nothing more difficult to take in hand, more perilous to conduct, or more uncertain of success, than the introduction of a new order of things." Again, a pause: steam was rising from the shoulders of Henrik's coat, warmed by the fire. "It is time, not for prayers or words. It is time for force. Accordingly I wish to present to you a man already expert in this arena. We must dig deep into our pockets so that he can provide us with an army. I beg you to support him. Baron Carl Gustaf Emil Mannerheim."

Mannerheim, expressionless, held himself straight. He took up position in front of the fire and at once began to speak, in Finnish, though his progress in this language was so halting that after attempting only a few sentences he quickly shifted into a fluent, slightly high-pitched Swedish.

"I have ridden through Galicia and Poland and I have seen the ravages of war. One who has seen them does not bring such misery to his country on purpose. I'm afraid, however, that I bring bad news on two counts. First, because there will be war in Finland. That much is certain. And second, because the Bolsheviks, the Red Guard, will soon seize power in Helsinki."

An outcry ensued, and Mannerheim raised a commanding hand against the roars of denial and disapproval.

"I'm afraid it is so. They will take Helsinki. This cannot be prevented, which means they will control not only the capital but the entire south of the country and thus most of the industrial production. It means that this war must be won quickly, or lost forever."

Esko listened carefully as Mannerheim spoke; and while he appreciated that things of the highest importance were being discussed, they were matters that did not seem personal or urgent to him. Later he would realize that he had been present at a turning point in history, at the first public appearance of a man destined to achieve a measure of greatness and the everlasting gratitude of his country, a man who was about to be transformed by the legend of his own deeds. At the time, however, Esko was consumed with personal pain and disappointment and its consequences, so that he could have left the apartment, intrigued by what he'd heard, but without the course of his life having been changed in a way that would later come to seem fateful. He could have walked away with his determination to go to America and pursue his passion in architecture having been forged again, tempered and made stronger in the hot flame of rejection. Indeed, he was contemplating doing exactly that, when Katerina, who had been standing by the window gazing at the falling snow, came and joined Mannerheim in front of the fire.

7

Esko saw her in profile. Her head was downturned, her graceful neck curved and exposed, and he winced for her, as if he could feel the ax. She began to speak, her voice nervous, unpracticed and hushed; she didn't once change her tone or raise her head; yet the effect on him was of actual life unscrolling in front of his eyes, charged with hurt and pain.

"When I was a child I lived in Finland. My father was governor of Oulu province. This was at the time, I'm sure you remember, when my country was embarked on a course of repression and cruelty against yours. I understood nothing of this at the time. I only knew that men tried to kill my father, that I was more accustomed to guards armed with pistols than to the company of other children. My father actually paid a few children to play with me sometimes, and I was happy when he lost his job and we returned home.

"Let me tell you about my home. My family was very lucky—I don't deny it. Great wealth. Many possessions. A big house and our very own lake. In the Crimea. Another house in Petersburg, of course. Carriages. Gardens. Tennis courts. Yes, it was unrealistic to believe that it could last, especially with the way things have been in Russia these last years. Even my father understood we couldn't live in the high style forever. He labored hard for reform. A political conscience burned in him as it does in most enlightened Russian people.

"I was married a few months before my twenty-first birthday. My husband was rich, the heir to another estate, a tall and elegant young man whose grandfather had known Pushkin. My husband died in Poland in 1914, leading a cavalry charge against a machine gun nest. He galloped ahead and was cut down by bullets, and for a long time after hearing the news, I imagined that my life could hold no greater grief or horror in store."

She paused, raising her head at last, and Esko saw Klaus step forward. He hugged her shoulder with one arm while the other pressed a glass of water into her hand. He gathered her in as if she were a bird he was determined to protect, and his blue eyes glowed with both compassion and possessive pride, playing a role, that of a man of the world who steps forward to save a tragic figure. Katerina drank some of the water, motioning him away.

"I do not doubt the sincerity of the Bolsheviks. Perhaps it's the most terrifying thing about them. They are blinded by the certainty that they are absolutely right. They need world-embracing ideals to accomplish their world-shaking deeds. They believe with all their hearts that their example will be followed throughout the world, that workers and peasants will seize power in nation after nation. Starting right here, in Finland."

The Finnish men protested in unison—no, no, it would never happen in Finland. Katerina merely shrugged, looking at them with the sad knowledge. "We didn't dream it could happen in Russia, either. Who can ever contemplate the idea that their life will be turned upside down and inside out, that they themselves will be subjected to unimaginable terror?

"We were in the country when the Czar abdicated. Things had been bad, but we still didn't believe it. And indeed, on the day we received the news, nothing changed. At the usual time we ate dinner. We played cards and we went to bed, as usual. We heard that there was a revolution. Petersburg was in chaos, we heard. Everything seemed so arbitrary. Yet in Odessa things remained as they had been. Then one night we were riding along in a streetcar and suddenly the streetcar stopped and it was announced it was going no farther. No one knew what to do.

"All through this last summer there was uncertainty. When my father was offered a position in the Kerensky government he decided we would be better off with him in Petersburg. There were areas of the countryside that were unsafe and so we took the train with our suitcases and our sandwiches and our jugs of coffee and we were lucky. We came to our home in the city without incident. This was in August. Even then we none of us imagined that the Bolsheviks would seize power. We didn't know their names—they were dark, fanatical men who had been in hiding or exile most of their lives. What could they know of government? We didn't realize that these were times during which more could happen in fifteen minutes than usually happens in fifteen years. One day one of the older servants put a plate of porridge, cold, in front of me and simply went away. When I went to look for him in the kitchen he was gone. So were the others. We were all terrified.

"Late one night there was a tremendous noise. Big guns. 'The guns of a battleship,' my father said. 'The Germans are invading after all.' But it wasn't the Germans. It was the Bolsheviks shelling the Winter Palace from the cruiser *Aurora* at anchor in the Neva. The Red Guards took the palaces that night, the post offices, the banks, the telephone exchanges, the railway stations, and the power stations. It happened quickly and without much bloodshed, very well planned and efficient, organized by men we'd very much underestimated. Just as they miscalculated the soldiers and workers and peasants who they imagined they were liberating. For the workers and soldiers this wasn't so much about theories and ideals. For them it was something simpler. For them politics meant power, and power meant winning, and winning meant bread and vodka. Especially vodka. For days on end there was an orgy. The streets were filled with men who might or might not have been brutes but were made brutish by drink. The Winter Palace was stormed again—for the spirits and wine in its cellars. Restaurants were smashed. Trains were raided. Houses wrecked.

"We told ourselves that if we stayed inside and kept very quiet while my father organized our escape then we would be safe from these ruffians. We told this to ourselves over and over again." She paused, touching the neck of her narrow black dress and taking a deep breath. "One night my father was out, meeting a young man, a dear friend who believed he could get us all out of Petersburg, to Vyborg, and then to Helsinki. Not so far. A ride of a few hours and we could all breathe again.

"They smashed down the front door and were greeted by my mother, who shot one of them dead with my father's pistol. I was coming down the stairs and saw my mother holding my father's pistol straight out in front of her as if she were afraid of it; but she shot the first man in the chest, shot him dead.

"They took her into the ballroom and spat upon her and held her down and three of them raped her. Then they slit her throat. I stared into the eyes of my mother as her life gushed away. One of them had shoved a rag in my mouth and two others held my eyes open so that I had to see. Others had found the cellar and they were guzzling wine, breaking bottles off at the neck, so that the floor was slippery with wine and blood. My grandmother came out of the small parlor where she'd been hiding and fell, fainted dead away. They put a bullet through her brain. Her body jumped, lying on the floor. I remember thinking, Well, perhaps that was a mercy, at least it was quick. My grandmother—seventy years old. As a young girl she had danced with men who were to be kings. She had survived the deaths of three of her children and the deaths of two husbands. She did not survive the Revolution.

"I myself was raped. I told myself not to resist or to count or even to think about it. I assured myself that somehow these men would be punished. Much later they brought my father in. His face was bruised and bleeding and his hands were tied behind his back. But that wasn't enough. They tormented him. Here she is, they said, a nice little piece, your little girl. Why don't you have her yourself? Come on, Mr. Senator, take her and we might even let you go. We might even give you a bottle of wine. I tried to spit out my gag. I wanted to tell my father that it would be all right, that if he could only get his arms free then perhaps he could free mine and we could at least die fighting. Trying. But something had gone out of him. He couldn't bear to look at me. He was shaking his head and his eyes were filled with horror and shame, and so they spat in his face, laughing and jeering, clubbing him with their bottles. I thought to myself, This can't go on. This can't be allowed. I prayed to God. He didn't listen. No one did. They pushed my father into a chair, put a bottle on top of his head, and then one of them took aim and shot it off. Then it was another bottle and another man taking aim. My father shaking, trying to hold himself still. This one missed. The bullet took my father in the face, killing him, so they propped him back in the chair and went on laughing, drinking, spitting, shooting. Then it was my turn again."

"Katerina, that's enough," said Klaus, stepping forward, trying to gather her in again.

"No, Klaus, it's *not*, it's not nearly enough," she said, and her face for a moment had a startling, savage, wild look that made Klaus start back. She crossed her trembling hands in front of her. "It's men who make this sort of history and the men in this room must know what this sort of history is. Otherwise it will be Finland and Finland's women who will be raped."

She faced them all fearlessly, her eyes calmer now, warning them that they must not stand by.

"Comrade Lenin has called for a war to the death, for the cleansing of all Russian vermin, the erasing of the bed-bug rich. So be it. Now we know that Bolshevism is a fairy tale premised on revenge. But Bolshevism is still weak. It's only at the beginnings of its own story. It can be turned back, destroyed. It can be destroyed here in Finland and then you can march across Lake Ladoga and destroy it in Russia. I've been a soldier on the front line. I've done my part. Now you must do yours. Please. Fight, never give in. Destroy them before they destroy you."

δ

Esko had just said good-bye to Klaus and Henrik, had turned the corner, was waiting for a streetcar. By then it was late in the afternoon and the Esplanade Park was deep in snow, the harbor hidden, veiled by darkness and tumbling flakes. Beneath Vallgren's statue of the mermaid, Esko tried to order his shredded thoughts, shocked, bewildered, outraged by what had happened to Katerina. Images crowded in: a woman with her throat cut; a man shaking with fear, a wine bottle poised ridiculously on top of his head; Katerina herself, her hair shorn, her body ripped. His mouth was dry, his head dizzy with rage. He wanted revenge, for the Reds to suffer.

"Katerina!" he called, for he saw her on the other side of the street, looking this way and that.

She waved, and came toward him, her black coat buttoned to the neck, the collar turned up, nestling her cheeks between diagonals of fur. Snowflakes roosted in her hat and on her shoulders and as he looked into her eyes he was swept away by a great avalanche of tenderness. He could scarcely conceive how badly she'd been hurt, or what it had cost her to tell that story in front of a group of men, most of whom she'd never met, many of whom, stoic Finns, had been reduced to tears. Standing before her now, Esko felt humbled, as if his very humanity had been reduced, called into question. He wanted to gather her in, buoy her up with gentleness and respect, even while a part of him still struggled with the information that she couldn't be his and longed to ask just how things were between her and Klaus.

"Katerina—I . . ."

"Don't say anything," she said quickly. "Take me to the best place in Helsinki."

"What?"

"Your very favorite place, Esko. Where you go to dream your dreams."

"I'm not sure I . . ." He stopped, suddenly understanding her meaning. "There is *one* place."

"Take me there," she said, her eyes bright with a friendly eagerness that seemed all for him.

"Now?" he said,

"Please," she said.

"We'll have to hurry," he said, glancing at his watch. Rainbows shone through the sparkling frost on his eyebrow.

"So let's hurry," she said breathlessly, and took his arm.

In the Esplanade Park lanterns lit a pathway that had been shoveled between walls of snow. The path was narrow, and passersby marked their hurrying progress with disquiet and even alarm, as if they were a pair of revolutionaries who had planted a bomb, or were on their way to plant one. The whole of Helsinki was anxious, looking over its shoulder.

They arrived to find the doors to the Diktonius Building shut and locked, darkness in the windows, and darkness within.

"Damn," Esko said, but then he spotted a familiar face: Karl, the elevator operator. "Wait a moment," he said, and dodged quickly across the narrow snowbound canyon of Aleksanterinkatu Street, returning moments later, jingling keys triumphantly. "We'll need a flashlight. I have one in my apartment. Perhaps you want to wait in a café until I come back. Sip a cognac, maybe."

"I'll come with you," she said without hesitation.

In the crowded rush-hour trolley car they hung from straps, faces close together, bodies brushing against each other as the car lurched and swayed along.

"About the meeting," he began.

Katerina touched a gloved finger to her lips.

"Later," she said. "I have something I need to tell you. In your favorite place."

At his apartment building he tried to make her wait downstairs but she insisted on coming up, inspecting his drawings, touching his books, while he rummaged through his already packed traveling trunk. "Here," he said at last, brandishing the flashlight, disturbed to see her sitting on his bed, smiling at him.

"It's very tidy here," she said. "You live like a monk, Mr. Vaananen." She was teasing him.

"We should go now," he said, swallowing rapidly.

*   *   *

The key turned smoothly in the lock and they passed quickly into the darkened Diktonius Building, the magnificent department store that had for so long been Esko's haven. The air was warm here, drugged with the scents of soaps and perfumes, and Esko's flashlight brought objects to sparkling life: a glass counter, a tray of gems; then the light moved on, giving existence to a mannequin in a suit, a stand filled with umbrellas, a marble staircase, the steel cage of the elevator. Esko felt he was at the entrance to a wonderland, his personal Araby. He led Katerina across the shop floor, reached for the brass latch, and opened the elevator gates.

"We're going up to the roof?" she said, her voice excited, a little uncertain. "Is there an ice garden?"

"Wait and see."

Esko had never brought anyone here before, not even Klaus, and he wondered whether the magic would work now that he was not alone; but when he stepped into the black, walnut-lined, gold-striped, mirror-adorned cubicle, when he felt the floor rock beneath his feet, and when he put his fingers to the handle, its brass warm and welcoming, he felt lifted and at ease, here as nowhere else. Leaning across Katerina, he pulled the steel doors slowly together, and they closed with a reassuring thump, a softness that belied their weight. "Please hold this for a moment," he said, handing Katerina the flashlight while he pulled a box of matches from his pocket and lit the two gas lamps at the back of the car.

Esko took the swaying elevator aloft, stopping midway between the fifth and sixth floors and spreading his arms.

"What?" said Katerina, eyes wide with momentary alarm.

Esko silently cursed himself. The gesture hadn't meant anything; yet his desire for her was out there between them, hanging in the air like perfume, in spite of everything he'd heard from her lips today. He shut his eye, head swimming.

"This is it," he said, eye still clamped shut. "My favorite place. Not the store. The elevator. I come here often, if I'm feeling bad, or even if I'm feeling happy."

He opened his eye again.

"Look. The murals on the ceiling. I painted them myself. One of my forays into the fine arts."

Her look was questioning, intent.

"I asked the management and they let me. Yet somehow I don't think Mr. Picasso is sweating at night, tossing and turning because of his rival Mr. Vaananen in Helsinki. I comfort myself with the assurance that Mr. Picasso isn't interested in designing buildings. I hope."

Katerina undid the buttons of her coat, turning her head to the ceiling. The better the light, the more beautiful she is, he thought. She was beautiful.

"Esko—these are splendid. They're absolutely gorgeous," she said, her eyes sparkling with pleasure and surprise.

Her praise lit a warmth inside him; it gratified him absurdly and almost caused him to shout; it made him shy. "They're not too bad, I suppose. It was a happy time. I would come here when the store was closed. I had to use candles when I was working on the ceiling. The gaslights weren't enough. The wax from the candles splashed on my face. I wasn't worried. What could molten wax do to my looks? Only improve them," he said with a laugh.

Around the central mural Esko had painted four lake-island landscapes. There was one for each season and each brought the spectator in a little closer. The first was the island seen at a distance, in early spring, when the ice was patchy and melting; the second was the island itself, ablaze with green and red and blue in the riot of summer, while the third showed a boat on the shore of the island, sunset, gloomy autumn. In the final scene a black woodpecker drilled at the prow of a snow-filled boat, as if lost, but determined to make a home for himself in the depths of winter.

The island loomed in the deep background of the main mural, a scene in which a blind boy at the edge of a frozen lake was being led away by a wounded angel. The angel's face was blank, expressionless, unreadable, while the boy grinned in ecstasy, or like a fool, and the startled woodpecker took flight above their heads.

"Are you the boy?"

"The symbolism is rather obvious, I'm afraid."

"Out there on the lake there's a woman in a boat. How did she get there when the ice is frozen?"

"You tell me."

"Is that a baby in her arms?"

"The woman's my mother," Esko said, surprised that Katerina had seen a detail that most people noticed, if at all, only when they'd seen the picture seven or eight times.

"And where is she now, your mother?" she said, turning to him with her eyes.

Esko glanced down at her boots. "About what happened today."

"Please, don't."

"Katerina, I must." He forced himself not to move toward her. "I wanted to say something at the time—there were so many people."

"Really, I understand," she said, looking toward the gates of the elevator as if she hoped she could escape through them.

"You shamed me. You shamed us all. I had no idea."

"It doesn't matter," she said, lowering her eyes to her clasped hands.

"It most certainly *does* matter," said Esko with sudden fury.

She glanced up, startled.

"I didn't mean to frighten you," he said in a soft voice. "I'm not angry at you—how could I be? I'm angry at the world. Such things should not be."

The elevator rocked; it creaked and groaned as he pressed his forehead against the coolness of the mirror above the leather bench at the back of the car.

When it became clear that she had nothing further to say on the subject, Esko spoke. "You asked about my mother. That involves a story, if you can bear to hear one." Indeed, it was a story he'd never told before.

"Please," she said.

"I grew up in the far north. Remote. Glory in the summer, months of frozen purgatory in the winter. A hard, beautiful place. I was nine years old when my mother set fire to our house. I didn't realize she'd done it. I didn't realize how dangerous the fire was. I only saw the flames bursting from the windows and I imagined that she was inside. I ran in, thinking I could rescue her. There was no fire in the living room yet, but she wasn't there. Nothing on the stairs. I ran to my mother and father's bedroom and opened the door. After that I remember very little. The heat, crushing my lungs. Flames—a rare, blue light. Something fell. Hence this," he said, making a circle around his face. "In fact the house was empty. She'd gone to the lake and taken out a boat. She filled her skirt with stones she'd taken from the shore and drowned herself. She was a painter, a beautiful painter. They said in the village she was mad."

Esko glanced up at the ceiling of the elevator, remembering the long nights he'd spent shut up here with his paints and brushes. "My father gave me away to the village priest to educate and raise. Perhaps it was for the best. A man named Kalliokoski."

"Do you hate him?"

Esko thought for a moment. "Kalliokoski? No, I don't hate him. I rather like him, actually. He always tried to be decent to me. He's a politician, really, not a priest. One of those people who'll flourish in any environment. Not a bad man."

Katerina was smiling patiently. "I meant your father."

"Of course," said Esko with a wry laugh. Suddenly he remembered that Timo had tried to kill Katerina's father, all those years ago. He didn't even know if she knew that. "For years I thought of him as a madman, a deranged believer, a Columbus—you know? But a Columbus without an America at the end of his journey, without even a boat. Now he's quite likely in Petrograd having supper with Lenin himself."

"Really?"

"A month ago I saw him on the same platform as Stalin himself."

Katerina turned her head.

"My father, not me."

"I know," she said. "Forgive me, but the mention of those names—it's like someone walking over my grave." She paused. "Go on with your story."

"Well—in the end my mother and my father conspired to grant me a great gift. That's the way I see it."

Her head was cocked a little to one side. "How?"

"One morning, out on the ice, not long after my father had given me to Kalliokoski, I understood why this elevator—any elevator—is important. It means a building can be as tall as you like. As tall as you dare to allow it to be.

A skyscraper. The Germans call them *wolkenkratzers*, cloud scratchers. In Finnish the word is *pilvenpiirtaja*—cloud sketcher. I'm going to build one. Every since that moment I've dreamed of it. A building of thirty or forty stories—why not fifty, sixty? Why not one hundred stories, for God's sake? A building flooded with light. Inspired like the great cathedrals were inspired. It's why I became an architect."

She smiled, moving a few steps across the car toward him, her face radiant. "And it's why you're going to America."

Reaching out, his hand uncertain, he stroked her short hair, and quivered inside as she rested her face against his palm. There was more loveliness and grace in the line of her cheek than in the Parthenon, the Pantheon, any architecture built by any master throughout history.

"I'm not going."

Katerina was startled for moment. "Why?"

"You know why."

She slumped, sagging on the leather upholstered bench. "I was afraid you'd say something like that," she said.

"This is no time to be selfish. I realize that now, thanks to you, Katerina. Whatever I want, my big ideas for myself—they can wait."

With trembling hand she took a pack of cigarettes from her coat pocket. "Esko, will you light my cigarette, please?"

"Of course," he said, fumbling in his pocket.

The match flared between their faces, the end of the cigarette crackled and burst into flame, and the elevator car was filled with fragrant Turkish smoke. Katerina lifted a finger to her lip, dabbing away a speck of tobacco. He saw that her glove was frayed at the wrist and in those threads of cotton he seemed to glimpse a whole sad world she'd lost, a way of life turned inside out.

"Have you read Shakespeare, Esko?"

He shook his head.

"There is a play by Shakespeare. His last, a very beautiful play. An island in the sea is ruled by a magician. This island is both wonderful and terrible, depending on who *you* are." She drew on the cigarette, exhaling smoke and glancing at the mural on the ceiling. "This island is both a golden world and a dreadful maze, with two presiding spirits. One is Caliban, a vile, ugly monster, but not without virtue and dignity. He's been enslaved by the magician. The other is Ariel, also the servant of the magician, but such a different spirit.

Sweet and lively. A spirit of the air. He can fly around the world in a moment and turn anything into something else. Dross into gold. Dead men's eyes into pearls."

She drew once more on the cigarette, smoke pluming from her nostrils, and stabbed out the butt in a curlicued ashtray at the side of the bench. She stood up and stepped toward him, peeling off one of her gloves. "Give me your hand. Give it to me, please."

Clumsily Esko held out his paw; Katerina's long, slender fingers tightened and suddenly the gaslights in the elevator car seemed to flicker to the rhythm of some long-dreamed-of music. Esko grinned inside; the touch of her skin made him feel like he was dancing.

"The other night," Katerina was saying, "when I first saw you again, you were squatting on your haunches, squinting and ducking this way and that, making sure the glasses were perfect on Henrik's table. Such a little thing, yet such passion on your face. You want beauty and order and loveliness. These are fine things, wonderful things in themselves. I've always known the Ariel in you, Esko Vaananen. I saw the part of you who longs to be him, all those years ago. And for me that's who you'll always be. A rare and beautiful spirit."

She came closer, gazing up into his face so that he seemed to be swimming in her eyes, smelling her perfume, the sweet tobacco on her breath. Her fingers let go his hand, touching his scarred cheek softly. "This war doesn't concern you. Go to New York."

"You'll come with me?"

"You know I can't," she said, her brow furrowing as she dropped his hand. "I won't. I'm marrying Klaus."

Unconsciously Esko brought the hand she'd held to his lips. "Then I can't go."

"You must," she said in a low voice.

Esko shook his head, heart hammering so hard his whole head seemed to shake, wobbling his vision like an earthquake. "My dream is to build, but if I have visions, if I speak in my sleep, it's only because of you."

She slumped again on the leather bench. With her head in her hands she wept. "I'm a bad woman," she said. "Oh, how I hate to cry. Crying makes me feel weak. I'm a bad, bad woman."

Hesitantly, Esko touched the curve of her shaking back, feeling the bumps on her spine, the warmth of her body beneath the taut fabric of her coat. "You're an angel," he said.

"Don't say that," she said, eyes flashing tigerishly. "You don't know me."
"I think I do."

"I'm going to tell you something now, and I want you to listen carefully.
Klaus came to our house that night. He was the man my father found who
was going to help us get away. Klaus was *my* good angel. Working, organiz-
ing, so that we could all get across the border to Finland. In the end he was
too late. It wasn't his fault. But in the end I was the only one left to be
saved."

She'd taken a lace handkerchief from her pocket to wipe her eyes. The
handkerchief was balled up in her fist. She raised her face, the light from
the gas lamps making glittering rivers of the tears that coursed down her
cheeks.

"Klaus took me out of there. He washed my body. He cleaned my
wounds. He stopped me when I tried to snatch his revolver away and shoot
myself. He brought me here and began to show me that life could go on. He
never tried to force himself on me, or even to kiss me. He was so gentle, as if
we were brother and sister. He treated me with the utmost respect, and a part
of me respects and cherishes and admires him." Her voice was low, but her
eyes burned into Esko fiercely. "But another part of me hates every inch of his
spectacular handsomeness. It's true! How on earth can I explain that? A part
of me hates Klaus, because he saved me, because war means doom and rape
for women and children, because men enjoy the power it brings them,
because something inside me would happily see all men punished, and he is
a man, not a man like that, but *such* a man. Let them all go to bloody war and
kill each other! Am I shocking you, Esko?"

"A little," Esko said, with a faint and bewildered smile that made something snap in Katerina.

She threw herself at him. "Those bastards soiled me," she said, sobbing,
beating at his chest with her fists. "They made me dirty. They cut me, they
abused me." She hit him again, not lightly—great thumps. "They made me
ugly."

"Katerina, Katerina," he said, grabbing her, holding tight her arms. "The
other night you asked about the mirror you gave me. Do you remember?"

Letting her go, he stood back, holding up his hands, his look questioning her, asking her to be calm. Slowly, he drew the silver mirror from his
pocket.

"You told me that this is a magic mirror. If you look in it long enough, you said, you will see who you really are. Look in it now, Katerina," he said, pressing it in her hand. "You're beautiful. You always will be. That's not a gift that someone can take away from you, whatever happens."

Her fingers trembled, holding the mirror, but instead of looking into the glass she came again into his arms, gently this time, leaning her head against his chest. "I'm going to marry Klaus."

"I know."

"And I want you to promise me that you *will* go to America."

He said nothing.

"Esko, you must promise."

He thought for a moment treasuring the weight of her head against his body. "I already have a ticket," he said.

They kissed long, lingeringly, and then Esko rocked the handle and the elevator descended. He walked with Katerina to Fabianinkatu Street. At the door to her apartment she smiled, touched his cheek, and said good-bye. Esko stood for a long time in front of that green door after it had closed. He flew down the stairs and rushed into the darkness and the thickly falling snow, coat flapping open; he was unsure of his direction, unaware of it, neither knowing nor caring, roaming like a sleepwalker, propelled by the thrilling, irregular beat of his heart. When, an hour later, he snapped out of the trance, he found himself at the harbor. A cruel wind flicked bullets of snow. The ice seemed to be creaking and smashing in the dark, and he looked up to see the prow of a ship, an icebreaker. In the night, in the snow, the ship loomed toward him like a building, leaning through the ice, and Esko saw how, during the course of a single day, the geography and structure of his life had changed. America now figured in his life as an absence, not a promise, a part of the design that had been thrillingly erased while his lips still burned with the memory of Katerina's kiss.

9

On the night of April 2, 1918, when the Finnish Civil War had been raging for three months, Mannerheim's White Army stood outside the city of Tampere, poised for victory, ready to attack the biggest remaining Red stronghold. There were untold numbers of Red troops within Tampere, five thousand Whites outside, and the White attack would be from the east. The big problem for them was that Tampere was divided by a river running north and south, connecting the two lakes that straddled the city. The rapids were crossable only by three bridges, which were narrow and easy to defend. Red resistance had been fierce thus far. Therefore Mannerheim had decided to attack in the middle of the night, hoping for surprise. He wanted a big triumph here before the White Finns' German allies landed in the south of the country and began their march on Helsinki. He wanted to prove a point, to be able to say that after all the Finnish Civil War had been won by Finns.

Each man in Esko's company wrote his name and address on a piece of paper that they put in their pockets in case they were killed. They stood in line, receiving two cheese sandwiches and a mug of tea, and then went and waited in another line, the reward this time being 250 bullets and a bayonet to sheath in a scabbard or fix to the end of their rifles. Mannerheim's plan called for them to rush in across the northernmost of the three bridges, to create a force within the middle of Tampere and push out the Reds from the inside. They were prepared for house-to-house fighting, armed with axes and clumsy hand grenades that had an alarming tendency to explode without the pin being pulled. Their objective was St. Matthew's Church, which occupied a commanding position overlooking the railway tracks as they took a sudden turn, sweeping west to run alongside the shore of the lake.

They moved out from the barracks and assembled in five columns, twenty men to a column; they were on the road beside a graveyard, the scene of fighting a few days before. It was a clear, chill night, a full moon had risen, and Esko noted the smashed headstones, jagged as broken teeth, chipped and pockmarked by bullets. The headstones gleamed silver in the moonlight beside splintered coffins and shards of human bone, as if the dead had been ripped from the earth so they could be killed a second time.

Overhead was the whisper and whoosh of shells.

Esko's heart pounded faster. His throat tightened. His buttocks clenched. All right, he said to himself, this is fear. Recognizing the emotion didn't make it any easier to deal with. He blew out air through his lips, bouncing up and down, trying to keep warm. At his side Klaus had produced a tarot pack and was telling a couple of the others their fortunes. Klaus tugged at his mustache. He studied the cards with a serious and somber expression; then suddenly his concentration was transformed to delight, as if he'd received a flashing revelation, some comforting news concerning the inner workings of the cosmos. "You'll fight all day long without a scratch," he told them. "You'll be fine."

The two men beamed, and Esko himself smiled, having seen Klaus do this many times during these last weeks. He wasn't always right; sometimes men died, but the others continued to look to Klaus for hope and energy; he'd taken to soldiering the way he had to everything else in his life, easily, with an impulsive brightness that seemed to transform optimism into an instrument of fate.

Esko didn't care for the army. It was hunger, cold, fear, little sleep and lots of lice; it was disorder and chaos tenuously constrained by the thin membrane of military discipline. And the war was a misfortune, a catastrophe for his country—anyone could see that; but he also had to see it through and see it won. It was a little war compared to the one in France where literally millions were dying, but it had released centuries of dammed-up feeling and resentment, waves of hatred and fratricidal feuding. A little war, but a particularly mean and vicious one. The Reds had bayoneted the rich in their beds; they had hung them from lampposts and buried them alive. Nor were the atrocities only on the Red side. In Huruslahti the Whites had taken twelve hundred Red prisoners. They killed the leaders, but not having enough bullets to kill all the Reds, put them in a long line. Every fifth one was dragged from the line and shot, a process now referred to by many of Esko's colleagues as the Huruslahti lottery. The grim joke reminded them that they at least were still alive, able to drink vodka and feel the ground beneath their feet.

Esko fingered the tight skin where his cheek and neck were scarred. He remembered that he'd been in Tampere as a child. His memory was of a summer day, shortly after the death of his mother. He and his father were on a bridge when they heard a man crying for help, down in the rapids. Timo found a life belt, ran down to the bank, and threw it in; but by then the man was gone, sucked under. The busy rapids were going on with their business, foaming and bubbling as though nothing untoward had occurred. "Where did he go?" Esko had asked, terrified. Timo replied only with a sorrowful shake of the head.

Esko's eye roved toward the graveyard, where the smashed headstones glittered like treasure. He'd heard that Timo was in Tampere himself, in command of an armored train, but rumors about his father were common enough these days. Timo Vaananen was a thorn in Mannerheim's side, a name that haunted the Whites and made them fearful in their beds. Timo Vaananen. Red Timo. Timo the butcher. He was reported in Helsinki, rousing the workers amid a fluttering of banners on the snow-covered steps of the cathedral. He was heard of in Petrograd, in a room heavy with cigarette smoke at the Ministry for Foreign Affairs, negotiating a deal with the Soviet Bolsheviks for grain and arms; he was seen rounding up and shooting White prisoners at the Terijoki railway station. Right now he was evidently in Tampere, exhorting his men never to give up, to fight to the very last drop of their blood, even if Mannerheim shelled Tampere to the ground.

Selin, the company commander, was pacing up and down among the men. They were a ragamuffin lot, on the face of it, almost comically outfitted. Not one of them had a uniform. Yet Mannerheim, in his white fur hat and fur-collared greatcoat, had called them them the best company in the entire White army.

"It won't be easy," Selin was saying. "There are at least five thousand Reds in Tampere. Maybe ten thousand. Maybe even twenty thousand, and only five thousand of us. It's do or die for them now, and they're better organized than we thought."

Selin was short, mild looking, a Finn of Swedish descent with smooth cheeks and slightly protuberant brown eyes. He wore an old coat and a felt hat with a fir branch stuck in it for camouflage.

"Tonight we'll be moving fast, single file. Each of you has a load of heavy gear. I know that. But there'll be no time to stop for stragglers. Anyone who falls behind will most likely get his throat cut. So anyone who doesn't think he can keep up must drop out now."

He didn't stop moving, pacing up and down, looking the men in the eye. As a soldier Selin was cautious and resolute, German trained; Esko also knew him to be a compassionate man.

"I mean it," he was saying. "If you can't move fast enough. If you're sick or wounded, say so. There'll be no disgrace. And from this moment on we won't be carrying any lame ducks."

Klaus took a leap and then a skip. "Quack! Quack!" he said, waddling back and forth. "My pack, sir, it's so heavy, sir, and please, sir, I want to go home."

Up and down the ranks the men laughed and cheered at this clowning— and, just like that, Klaus had settled the issue for them all.

"Good luck, then. Good fighting."

It was 2:45 A.M. In fifteen minutes the signal rocket would go off and they would be running toward a city filled with the enemy.

"I heard from my father today," Klaus said to Esko, serious now. "He sent a package through with one of Mannerheim's spies."

"How are things in Helsinki?" The Reds had taken control there, as Mannerheim had predicted, soon after the beginning of the year. "How's Henrik?" Esko paused. "And Katerina?"

"For her," he said, reaching in his pocket and holding up an envelope. "I want you to make sure she gets this."

Esko glanced uneasily at the envelope. "Make sure yourself," he said, trying to make light of it. "Send it back with the spy."

"I can't do that. He left already," Klaus said. "I want you to do this."

A shell wailed overhead and the two of them glanced up. Already there were fires in Tampere. Sparks and flames climbed up the mill chimney towers; smoke swirled in billowing columns of red; an acrid chemical smell came on the wind, catching at Esko's throat.

"Look, Esko. I'm getting it this time. I won't survive Tampere."

"Klaus—"

"Or maybe it's just another way of touching wood," he said, cuffing Esko on the head. "Of saying to destiny—you keep away from me now. So do me a favor and take the letter. All right?"

He touched the pocket where he kept the tarot pack.

"I thought you always fixed the cards," Esko said.

"Be a good fellow and oblige me."

Esko took the envelope. The paper felt stiff and awkward in his gloved fingers, and he stared uneasily at the familiar name, loved and longed for: Katerina Malysheva. "If I don't get hit myself I'll be giving this back to you tonight and you'll feel like a damned fool," he said, tucking the envelope into his pocket. "If I do get hit, this letter's probably going to be a mess."

The signal rocket screeched, burst, and a cascade of stars came down through the sky. Suddenly the night was loud with cheers, yells, the stomping of boots. Glancing down, Esko was almost surprised to see that his own feet were stomping too. His body shook and the pack on his shoulders bounced up and down. His breath was raspy. With his rifle slanted across his chest he ran toward the cemetery where the dead had been roused from their slumbers.

The attack had begun.

10

They were stealing across the railway tracks when a voice shouted out of the darkness. "You lot! Get over here quick! The White bastards are attacking!" Selin held up his arm and they all froze. They waited, watching each other, but then the voice rose up again. "Hurry! Those White devils are coming."

Esko stared along the tracks, so steely and definite, shooting straight between patches of ice and mottled frozen slush. In the distance he saw a freight car, and then a figure, a man, materialized from the darkness. The man held a pistol in one hand and was waving with the other.

"What are you waiting for? Get over here. They'll be here any minute."

Esko didn't think at all. He made no decision. On a reflex he raised his rifle, trapped the dark figure within the V of the sight and squeezed the trigger. To his shock the man fell.

Then there were more voices, puzzled and angry, even as Esko's mates began raising their rifles around him.

"What's happening?"

"They're Whites."

"What?"

"Shit, they're *Whites*. Let's get the hell out of here."

A volley of shots silenced the shouting. Almost instantly the Reds disappeared back into the shadows.

"They've run," said Selin, peering down the tracks.

In horror Esko watched as the man he'd shot dragged himself up off the tracks, stumbling forward, clutching at his wrecked shoulder. "Aki! Paavo! Antti! Where are you?" he shouted. "Please—I'm hit."

The man was lost, in shock; he didn't know which way to turn, but continued stepping forward. Holm, Selin's second in command, went calmly over with pistol raised. There was a flash, a crack, and Holm came strutting back on his slightly bowed legs, his square face expressionless. He had big hands, deft and used to killing, like a farmer's. A bulge showed over his heart where he carried a copy of the sermons of Martin Luther in his breast pocket.

"One more Red roasting in hell," he said. Holm liked to handle the prisoners. In his ideal world there would be none.

Esko felt sick, but not because of Holm.

"Let's go," said Selin, all business, and then there was no time to feel anything. They plunged down the embankment, leaving the tracks behind them; crouching like cats, they ran, boots skidding, moonlight glittering on the icy road that led them toward the center of the town. Esko glanced at Klaus, jogging along beside him. His eyes were wide, moving rapidly back and forth, ready for anything.

Quick-shifting clouds were banked high against the brightness of the moon. The company moved down the side of the street, hugging the shadows. They crept a few yards, squatted down, waited, crept again. A door banged nosily back and forth. From somewhere behind them came the rattle of a machine gun. Esko felt his bowels tense, but the shooting was far away. Soon Selin raised his arm in silent signal.

The end of the Satakunnankatu Street bridge was closed off with a string of white horses, snorting, trying to paw the air, but their hooves were tied. Behind the horses a pair of machine gun barrels peeped out from sandbags. No Red was to be seen, but they were there, waiting.

Esko opened the collar of his shirt, breathing heavily. The horses were protecting the machine guns from unexpected attack; and when they were killed their corpses would make a stack of bloody flesh over which the attackers would be forced to scramble. Selin and Holm had their heads close together, whispering, figuring out the best way to handle the problem. A shell whistled across and exploded on the far side of the bridge. Behind the bridge there were fires and sparking columns of black smoke. This was going to be even more difficult than they'd thought.

Hooves clattered on the street behind them and a Red officer in a Russian uniform galloped up, leaning forward over the neck of his horse, flicking at the air with his whip. "It's not that dangerous, you cowards," he said. His eyes were bright in the dark. Steam rose from the panting horse. "The White devils are over there. Come on!" He pointed with his whip and it was then that Esko and several of the others raised their rifles and fired.

The officer flew backward off his horse, the horse sagged, crumpling to its knees, emptying its bowels and pumping blood onto the ice, and, even as Esko was transfixed by this spectacle, the machine guns on the bridge opened up, firing beneath the bellies of the tethered horses, and suddenly the air was alive with bullets that sizzled past or ricocheted clickety-clock down the street. Suddenly the man beside Esko was no longer recognizable, pieces of his face torn away. He saw another man jerking and shuddering, caught in a torrent of bullets and then thrown aside like a rag. Esko's first thought was for Klaus. Where the hell was Klaus? Turning, he saw his friend hunched down low, running toward cover on the other side of the street, a sight that freed him from his paralysis, for now he too was running, not trying to dodge or brace himself, but holding his rifle across his chest in a mad dash toward the narrow opening of an alley that seemed to recede the harder he ran, as if his scrambling legs would never reach it. Then Klaus's hand was grabbing his shoulder, yanking him forward, and he was face down in a heap of frozen slush. He hauled himself up to see the dark walls of buildings rising on either side, and his friend's face, pale, close to his.

"Esko, are you all right? Are you wounded? Answer me, man."

Esko nodded, breathless—he wasn't hurt.

"Jesus, this is a mess," Klaus said, squinting down the alley. On the bridge the machine guns were still pattering. Neither of them wanted to think about what might be happening there. "We've got to keep moving. We'll make for the rendezvous."

Selin's instructions had been clear: in the event the company was split up before crossing the bridge they should make their way to a factory that lay to the north, where they would regroup for another attack. But while Esko had a mental picture of the map of Tampere and knew generally where the factory lay, he didn't know where they were *now*. He had no idea. Everything was confused, so fast.

"Do you know where we are?" he said.

"Not really," Klaus said.

"Do you think we can ask directions?"

Klaus burst out laughing, and then covered his mouth, stroking his mustache. He looked up and down the alley again. "Why not? The Reds have been very obliging so far."

The machine guns kept up their conversation from the bridge, pausing and then starting at will. Shells whistled overhead, exploding in the distance. Esko and Klaus slipped down the alley, slowing when they came to the end. Esko glanced up at the narrow space of sky above his head and then quickly poked his head around the corner. The street was empty. Moonlight flashed on cobbles. Across the street were store windows, darkened, like dead eyes. A star shell burst, showing broken ice on the rapids. In the distance, on the other side of the river, the roofs of buildings were floodlit by fires that the shelling had started. Esko saw a man, alone, coming down the street. He raised his finger, motioning to Klaus, pointing out the man.

Klaus whispered, "Not yet, not yet." And then: "Now."

Esko seized the man by the neck and pulled him into the alley. Klaus pinned his arms and they shoved him against the wall. He was a short little fellow wearing a cap that had a red star on it.

"Don't worry, friend," Klaus said. "We just want to ask you a few questions."

"I'm not worried, White asshole."

"We'll let you go," Esko said. "But tell me now—which direction to the Finlayson factory."

"Fuck off," the man said, but his eyes flicked down the alley back the way they'd come.

"It's that way, then?" Esko said.

The man nodded, and Klaus waited no longer. He unsheathed his bayonet and stuck the man in the gut before Esko could protest. From the end of the alley he popped off two shots from his revolver and then they ran, Klaus in front, heading back east for two blocks before looping across on Tuomiokirkonkatu Street, with Esko now getting a good mental picture of the chaos that was in Tampere right then, with large numbers of Reds, suddenly aware that they were under attack, trying to identify the small number of Whites storming in.

The Finlayson factory had a gabled gateway that led to a wide courtyard slick and brilliant with ice. Buildings loomed on all sides, so their footsteps echoed loudly, as if within a cave of brick. At the far corner a slender chimney poked high at the sky, an accusatory warning finger. Esko and Klaus glanced at one another; they'd arrived before any of the others, if indeed there were still any others. Perhaps all the rest of the company had been slaughtered back there at the bridge. This was a possibility they dared not consider.

A ladder of narrow steel ran up one side of the factory chimney and Esko climbed it, gaining a clear view of the rapids, the fires that were spreading throughout Tampere, and the spire of the church that was their objective. An icy breeze made his skin tingle. Back at the Satakunnankatu Bridge the Reds were dragging another machine gun into position. There were fires and it was hard to tell just which direction the rifle shots were coming from, just where the center of the battle actually was. Every now and then a shell landed with a thump.

Esko climbed back down the tower into the quietness of the factory courtyard.

"What's going on?" Klaus said.

Esko shrugged, and they looked at each other, exchanging wry smiles, two men suddenly cut adrift.

"I suppose we'll just have to go and take that church by ourselves," Esko said.

"I suppose so," Klaus said.

Just then a door whacked open against the cobbles.

Esko and Klaus spun, rifles at the ready, and saw a man emerging from a cellar beneath the walls of one of the factory buildings. The man was clad in white, an apparition with his back to them. Ignorant of their presence, he was leaning down to help someone out of the cellar—a woman who tenderly carried a blanketed bundle, her child. He looked like a ghost, Esko now realized, because he was dressed only in his underwear, his spindly legs draining down into a pair of unlaced boots. He was bald, with a beard. He turned, drawing his wife and child toward him with his arm, looking nervously about, beginning to move away from the building. And then he saw Esko and Klaus. At once he was on his knees, holding his hands in the air. "Kill me, please. Kill me, but please, I beg you—my wife and child. They've done nothing. Please, I beg you."

Esko handed Klaus his rifle and went over, showing the man his open hands, telling him not to be afraid. The man's beard was pointy, well cared for. His dark eyes went this way and that. His teeth were clicking together.

"Where's your coat?" Esko said.

"It was taken," the man said reluctantly.

"Who took it?"

The man shook his head, staring at Esko, not daring to answer. He didn't know what side they were on.

The baby had started to cry, and the woman rocked it to and fro. "Shush, my honey, shush."

"It's all right," Esko said, taking the man by the shoulders.

The man looked into Esko's face, for the first time noticing his scars.

"It's all right. We're with Mannerheim and you have a baby. You'll be safe with us. We're waiting for our friends and then we'll be crossing the bridge."

"Really? With Mannerheim." The man's eyes danced with relief and happiness. "With Mannerheim? Did you hear that my darling? Oh, that's marvelous. The workers took my clothes. They locked us in the cellar, that greedy trash," he said, speaking breathlessly. His breath was foul, as if he hadn't eaten for days. Happy popping sounds of relief came from his dried lips. Then he stopped, frowning, and his long bony hand plucked at his beard. "No, no, not the bridge. They've mined it. Oh yes, I saw them taking boxes of explosives beneath the parapet. They'll blow it for sure. You mustn't go that way."

He paused, eyes narrowed and gleaming. "The dam!" he said. "It's the dam for you."

"The dam?"

He nodded eagerly, taking Esko's arm with one hand and waving his other toward the north. There was a low mud dam across the rapids, he said, where they might cross. First they would have to climb to the roof of a small building that looked over the dam. They could jump down from there. It was all part of the factory complex, he told Esko with pride, and then he turned back to his wife. "They're with Mannerheim. Mannerheim! Isn't that marvelous?"

Selin had slipped into the courtyard. His watchful eyes absorbed the scene for a moment, and then he came over, grinning. "Arnefelt, Vaananen. You made it. I thought I'd lost you." The grin vanished. "I lost five of the others. Dead, or as good as."

He raised his arm toward the gabled gateway, and the rest of the company trooped in, survivors, all wearing smiles at the sight of Klaus and Esko, happy to add two more to their number. The losses were fewer than Esko had feared and expected. He realized now that for the last thirty minutes or so, since they'd come under fire at the bridge, he'd been assuming he'd never see any of these men again. Now his spirits soared at the sight of the familiar faces. Klaus was smiling too. They took heart. Everything seemed possible again.

Selin glanced at his watch. "We'll stay here fifteen minutes," he said in his calm and level voice. "Then we try the bridge again."

Holm, meanwhile, was circling the bearded man with his wife and their baby, prowling around them like a predator, caressing the holy book in his breast pocket. "Prisoners," he said, and unholstered his Mauser.

"No," Esko said, stepping in front of the family. Once again he was unaware of having made a decision. But he wasn't going to let Holm harm this family. It had been one thing for Klaus to kill the Red back there at the bridge, necessary—perhaps. This was another matter, and these people needed to be sheltered from the mayhem whirling through Tampere that night; Esko, at least, was quite prepared to disobey a superior officer in order not to give them over to it. He appealed to Selin: "This man has some connection to the factory."

The bearded man nodded, beginning to understand that he wasn't out of the woods yet. "Yes, yes —"

"He gave us some information I think could be useful. Look at his boots, sir. He's wealthy. A White."

"Rubbish," said Holm, his mouth working with pent-up venom. "He stole those boots. They've got no laces in them. For sure he's a filthy Red." He cocked the Mauser. "I've got one bullet for him. Two more for his filthy Red bitch and that mewling Red brat. One more for Vaananen here unless he gets out of the way."

"Sir," Esko said to Selin, ignoring Holm. "Listen to what the fellow has to say. At least do that. He says there's another way to get across the river."

"What way?" said Selin.

The bearded man dropped to his knees again. "Please, kill me," he said, "but not my family."

"Get to your feet, man, for God's sake. Tell me your story. No one's going to shoot you — yet."

The bearded man got back to his feet but his teeth were chattering again. A sharp odor told Esko that he'd lost control of his bowels. "Gather yourself," Esko told him. "Tell the officer your story."

Stammering, the bearded man told Selin about the secret way across the river.

"Lies. All lies," Holm burst in.

"Why would I lie? What could I gain?" the man said, reaching a hand toward Selin's sleeve. "Your soldier here was quite right. See these boots? These are rich man's boots." He wagged a scarecrow leg. "My workers took away the laces when they locked us in the cellar."

"Tell me again about the dam," Selin said, and the man did, while Holm stalked about, hands clasped behind his back, square face thrust forward, expression set, staring at Esko with cheated fury.

The chill of the night made it hard for the men to keep still. Everyone was eager to be on the move, but Selin took a moment to make his decision.

"Very well," he said. "Vaananen and Arnefelt — this was your bright idea. You'll be first across."

They found the dam just where the bearded man had said it would be. They viewed it from the corner of a warehouse whose front wall rose sheer from the rapids. They found a ladder; and then Esko, followed by Klaus, climbed to the top; on their bellies they wormed forward until they reached the edge of the roof, then peered over.

The dam was a mud bank, only about two feet wide but flat on top; it fingered across rapids that were swollen with molten snow and, in the freezing hours before dawn, bobbing with blocks of ice that had broken off and drifted down from the lake. The opposite bank was deep in shadows thrown by another factory building whose brick walls cut sharp outlines beneath the moon. Esko had another clear view of the Satakunnankatu Bridge off to his left; from this angle he saw the Reds waiting behind their machine guns, tiny figures. The horses were all dead now, piled on top of each other at the approach to the bridge, clouds of steam rising from their bodies.

"What do you think?" Esko said to Klaus.

"I like this a lot better than going back there," Klaus said.

"I'll go first," Esko said. "You get the others."

The twelve-foot jump from the flat roof of the warehouse to the end of the dam shook his bones and jolted his jaw—that was the trickiest part, with his clattering kit and the unpredictable grenades; then he walked the dam, not allowing himself to look down into the teeming water, keeping his eye fixed on the approaching darkness of the other side, where he stood and waited, greeting each of the others with a tap on the back as they made it over.

And then they were lucky. Selin was counting heads when Klaus collared a young man in a flat woolen cap. Fear dimmed the bright craftiness of this young man's eyes only for a moment. He at once understood who these soldiers were and began to guess at what they might want and how he might save his own skin, or even advance himself, by helping. He became their guide, leading them toward another factory building through the heating room, through a maze of cellars, up through the office, and then toward a gate that opened onto the street, from which the church was clearly visible, only a few hundred yards away.

After that, both surprise and momentum were on their side. They opposed a large but disorganized enemy, seemingly demoralized and unwilling to fight. Reds appeared in front of their path but vanished at their approach. Victory was within reach, Esko thought; they had will, fury, and a plan that was going their way.

They ran, shooting at anything suspicious and at windows, whether they saw anyone behind them or not. At the corner of Kuninkaankatu Street and

Puuvillatehtaankatu Street Selin shot three rockets to let the rest of the attack force know that they were approaching their objective. As the flares pierced the night, flaring red and green, a horse clattered up pulling a small sleigh with no bells. A Red officer in a Russian uniform lounged in the sleigh, a pink-faced man showing a mouth filled with rotting, broken teeth.

"Why are you running?" he said in a high-pitched voice. "Get back to the other side of the bridge. That's where the fighting is."

"How many guards at the church?" said Selin. "Salmela told me they needed reinforcements."

"They've got five men outside. Plenty. The church isn't under attack," said the Red officer. Then his face went like chalk as Selin grinned. "Shit," he said, his hole of a mouth snapping shut in fear only a moment before Holm stepped forward and shot him in the neck. The horse panicked, bolting away, dragging the officer's body hanging limply over the side, head bouncing up and down off the cobbles like a football.

At Nasijarvenkatu Street they crossed carefully, for the bearded man back in the courtyard had warned them they might find a machine gun there, positioned in the upper story of an apartment building. Instead it was only an old woman who opened her window and shouted, "Fight! Drive off those filthy White bastards," for which she got a bullet from Holm's pistol. When a teenage girl appeared around the corner toting a rifle, Esko grabbed it from her before Holm saw.

"Where should I go?" she said, tears rising in her voice.

"Go home," Esko said, his heart beating faster until she was safely gone, the second child he'd had a hand in saving that night.

At the end of the street they found the church itself, a brooding oblong of stone, squat and dark, with a shadowy tower and a spire rising from out of it, sparkling with frost under the moon. The church faced the cobbles of an open square and was unprotected by any fence or gateway or big guns.

Selin divided the company into three again and they went in from different directions, one group from either side and the third from the center. Esko and Klaus were with Selin, in the frontal attack, shouting, running single file straight at the church doors. Flames flashed from Selin's pistol as he shot two guards struggling with their unwieldy rifles outside. The church doors banged open and a man ran out, trying to jump on a horse that was tethered to an iron stanchion. Selin bagged him too, and, on hearing all these shots, four or five Reds came out and just as quickly disappeared back in, leaving the doors swinging open. Another Red spilled from a window, picked himself up from the cobbles, and limped away, only to be shot in the back by Holm.

Inside the pillared entrance, where the stone flags were carpeted with straw, Esko and Klaus saw nine or ten Reds vanishing up a wide staircase that led to the bell tower.

The two friends looked at one another. Klaus fingered his mustache thoughtfully for a moment before he rushed the stairs, Esko close behind. They reached the first landing without coming under fire, and Esko was about to throw a grenade around the next corner of the stone stairway when a bayonet popped out with a fluttering white shirt impaled on it.

The Reds shuffled back down the steps. They were disheveled, frightened, disheartened, looking sheepish, with dust and straw in their hair. They surrendered, dropping weapons in a heap.

It's over, Esko thought, looking at the defeated faces of the enemy, we've done it. He felt thrilled, elated, and he suddenly realized he was thirsty. He sat down on the floor and drank from his canteen.

It was 5:00 A.M. and still dark.

The attack had taken only two hours.

11

The men felt they had done their share and talked and smoked. Esko explored the building, the beam of his flashlight picking out windows of stained glass, pews of dark oak, chunks of smashed masonry, and a cross, in shadow, at the far end of the nave. Running around the body of the church were finely painted frescoes, biblical scenes—Eve with the apple from the Tree of Knowledge, Abraham with his knife poised over Isaac's throat, Christ throwing bread upon the waters. Some joker had disfigured one of the scenes with graffiti; another was daubed with feces.

A couple of the men stood and prayed, heads bowed, facing the front of the church. Another pissed through a hole in the floor. A shell must have made it. Some couldn't stop talking, their mouths opening and closing, not aware of what they were saying, babbling with relief. No one was triumphant. They were glad to be alive, happy not to be frightened anymore.

Selin began to get them organized. He called Esko outside, to the back of the church, where they found a walled graveyard. The moon was low in the sky now, its golden light on the frozen surface of the lake beyond the gleaming steel of the railway tracks.

Back inside the church, Selin ordered that the prisoners be taken outside and put under guard in the graveyard. Then he and Esko climbed the stone stairs of the tower, winding around and around, rising through smoke and the bitter stench of cordite, until they reached the belfry where a fresh breeze blew through open arches and they had commanding views of the railway tracks and the lake one way, and Tampere, the city itself, the other.

"Damn it," said Selin, for what they saw and heard was not what they had expected.

Something had gone wrong with the rest of the attack.

There was the crackle of small arms fire and the rattle of machine guns—all from the east. There were buildings on fire and a thousand muzzle flashes—all in the east, in the area from which they'd set out a little more than two hours ago.

Elsewhere, it seemed, the Whites had made little headway, had even been pushed back. The thrust of the attack had been slowed and perhaps entirely repulsed. Tampere was firmly in Red control, with the exception of one small part—the church in whose belfry Esko now stood with Selin.

They were cut off.

Selin sagged for a moment. He rubbed his bloodshot eyes, mopping at his forehead with a handkerchief; then he drew himself up. "Go and tell Holm the situation," he said to Esko. "Tell him quietly. I don't want to start a panic. The prisoners must be executed immediately."

Selin caught the flicker of Esko's reaction and his friendly face toughened. "It's an order, Vaananen," he said. "I don't like it any more than you do. But any minute now the Reds are going to realize we're here and there'll be a counterattack. We'd better be ready."

Holm sat on a stone bench in the church porch, watching the door. His eyes didn't waver as Esko approached. His big face didn't move or change. His big hands remained planted on his knees. He might have been made of stone; he listened, intent, until Esko had finished and then he burst into motion, strutting down the aisle of the church like a bull let out of a pen: "Lampi! Akslof! Mykkanen! Nikunen! Kaskivaara! Von Seth! Arnefelt! Come with me! You too, Vaananen."

Two of the men—they were Mykkanen and Kaskivaara—put on a swag-ger, sneering and loading their rifles and their revolvers, while Holm outlined the blunt strategy. "We captured a machine gun, correct? Well—Arnefelt and Akslof, you go grab it. Vaananen and I will get this Red filth lined up against the wall at the back and then—pa! pa! pa!"

Holm mimed gunning down a line of prisoners with the machine gun.

"Then we finish off the survivors. Let's make short work of this, eh? Get it done before they know what's hit them. We've got important work ahead. God's work in Finland."

In the graveyard, with Esko at his side, Holm grinned at the prisoners and started pushing them about, but in a good-natured way. "Come on you scum!" he said, as if this were all a great joke. "We've got some breakfast on the go, if you're interested. I want you lined up nice and neat. Then we'll let you inside so you can eat—but only two at a time. I'm not taking any chances with you fellows. You've given us enough trouble already. Come on, snap to it," he said, going on with his business, shoving and cajoling them against the wall. "Or don't Red bellies get hungry?"

"What's the grub then, eh?" said one of the prisoners, a short, stocky fel-low, bouncing up and down on his heels, slapping his arms against the cold, seizing on what he hoped was Holm's good humor. "Mmm, smells good," he said, raising his nose and comically sniffing the air.

None of the others were interested in this theater. They were exhausted, indifferent; their eyes stared without seeing, and Esko saw that whatever they'd been through in these last days had bludgeoned them to a point where they had no expectations, bad or otherwise. They all looked like old men. A few avoided his glance, looking down sheepishly in shamed and sullen defeat, as if, in having failed, they felt that they'd earned the worst and expected to be treated without mercy. Not one of them appeared to have the spark to try an escape, and Esko wondered how that could be. Would he, one day, find himself on his knees, everything gone, all hope lost, without even the will to raise a fist? Could the intertwining of choice and fate do this to anyone? Or was it the war? His heart went out to these men.

Someone cracked their knuckles, a pair of knuckles the size of hooves, it sounded like, and Esko was aware of the strangest feeling, a sudden bump in his soul, a stirring, a haunting, as if the past were stealing up on him in the shape of the man who'd been lurking in the far corner of the graveyard. It was the tallest, thinnest man he'd ever seen, a man he recognized at once and with inner shivers both of remembered shame and remembered gratitude, an adult grown inevitably from the blueprint of the child he had known. It was Bongman's Son, a giant now, almost seven feet tall, and with fiendish finger-nails and hands the size of shields. His mouth lolled open in a lopsided grin; the grin might have meant insolence, or defiance, or acceptance—it was impossible to say. A thin, scruffy stubble sprouted unconvincingly from his chin, as if almost every ounce of his body's energy had gone elsewhere, into a grab for height. His eyes were patient and watchful. Esko had the sense that nothing those eyes could see would surprise Bongman's Son.

"Get in line, you filthy Reds," said Holm, stepping back and putting his hand to the butt of his holstered pistol, as if wary that this goliath of a man might make a move or rouse his comrades to a dash for freedom. "You too, big man. You look as though you could use a square meal."

"Who do you think you're trying to kid? You're going to murder the lot of us," said Bongman's Son. He turned to Esko with a casual nod. "Hello, Scar-face. So you ended up with this rotten crew." He sighed, rubbing the fuzz on his chin, smiling at the irony of it all. "Fancy that—the son of old Red Timo himself ending up with a bunch of murdering White devils." He lifted his huge head, eyes brightening. "Long time, long time. How you been, anyway?"

"Get into line, you red sonuvabitch," Holm said, still in that awful, play-ful voice. "Stop playing the fool and get some grub."

For a moment Esko thought that Bongman's Son was going to raise one of his huge fists and simply swat Holm out of his life. He seemed to be think-ing about it, and Esko wished that he would; but then he sighed, throwing out his shoulders, and loped off to stand with his colleagues against the grave-yard wall.

"They killed my girlfriend two days ago, so don't you worry, Scarface," said Bongman's Son, calm and unruffled, as if it were clear to him that Esko was the one needing consolation. "I ain't got nothing to live for anyway."

Esko wanted to protest, to tell Bongman's Son that he had everything to live for, that he must never give up hope, but then the idea went out of him. Bongman's Son was going to die. Holm had his revolver out and was prod-ding him into line. Holm was set on his course and would stamp toward it with bovine vigor. There was nothing to be done and yet Esko felt like a cow-ard for doing nothing. He'd saved the family at the Finlayson factory, the girl in the street who'd shown up with the rifle; he could do nothing to help his friend.

He'd seen the murder of prisoners before. He'd been around Holm long enough, after all, but the inhumanity seemed charged and dreadful now. Not pointless—he saw the point: a dead enemy wasn't an enemy who might one day soon have a rifle in his hands and shoot you with it; moreover, the victim's demoralized and fearful family might think twice before complaining about the price of bread or wanting to own land once the fighting was done. It was quite logical in a civil war, a class war; it added up. And yet it was mad, unforgivable. Surely Finns couldn't do this to each other and expect Finland to survive. The whole country would be filled with hate for years.

There were a hundred questions he wanted to ask. Did Bongman's Son still live in the village? Was the old place still the same? How was it there these days when the summer nights were golden and the spreading branches of the bird cherry exhaled such sweet fragrance? Was Turkkila still alive? And what of Bongman's Son himself? What was his job? Who had been his girlfriend? How had he come to be fighting with the Reds? What had he heard of Timo? Did he remember a certain long-ago morning when, in the days of their youth, they had raced on the ice?

A freezing blast of wind came off the lake. Bongman's Son shivered, as if the gust had gone right through him, and Esko sprang forward and rubbed the big man's shoulders and gave him a cigarette.

"Thanks, Scarface," said Bongman's Son. "Don't let them get you down. Not ever. You always did skate like the devil."

Esko felt his throat tighten. He turned to Holm, trying to say that this was all a mistake, that surely they could lock the prisoners in the basement of the church until the fighting was done.

Holm wouldn't let him start. "Now listen to me, Vaananen. If you want the same breakfast as your pal, stay standing where you are. If not, get the hell out of the way. It's all the same to me," he said, strutting down the line of prisoners, poking here and there with the barrel of his pistol. "Red meat or White. You make your choice."

Esko glanced beyond the graveyard wall to the stark frozen flatness of the lake. He met Holm's dull gaze and his hand moved toward his own pistol. Then Klaus's hand was on his shoulder, dragging him back between the gravestones. "Esko's sitting down with us, aren't you, old man?' he said, turning from Esko to Holm, who responded merely with a dull shrug before giving the order to shoot.

The machine gun blazed, raking from right to left, pouring a stream of lead. The men went down like crazy dolls, shaking and flapping, smashed and twisting, lumps of flesh spattering the wall and sailing in the air.

The machine gun stopped, and the gunner snapped open the breech to cool it.

In front of the wall was a new wall of corpses. Not all of them were dead. Some of them were groaning. Esko thought he heard a prayer. One called out faintly for his mother.

Holm thrust himself forward on his squat legs, pistol down at his side. He moved methodically among the bodies, finishing them off, pausing to reload, and then moving on. At last he stood over Bongman's Son. "It's your pal, Vaananen. He seems to want to say something. I don't think he liked the food."

Bongman's Son had raised his head. One-half of his face was pulped and bloody, while the half that Esko still recognized had the most terrifying look of abject patience and understanding. Esko knew he could never understand what Bongman's Son was seeing and feeling at that moment; yet he also promised himself that he must never forget this man whose remaining human features now disappeared, turned to blood and bone as Holm emptied the clip of his Mauser into them.

Soon afterward the Reds brought up their armored train behind the church and the counterattack began. Without support, without food, without water, without word from Mannerheim's command of what was happening or what had gone wrong, Selin's company held the church through the morning and the afternoon, hoping and waiting for reinforcements that never came. Rintala, Voipio, Franck, Nopanen and Von Seth were killed in the first stage of the battle, when a shell from a big cannon on the train burst in the graveyard. By then they'd already moved the machine gun back inside, but Koskelainen took a bullet in the eye while they were setting it up at a window in the tower. A sniper got cocky Mykkanen in the belly and he screamed for almost an hour before finally falling silent. Niiniluoto's face was ripped from his head by a shell that came hurtling through a wall and didn't explode. A Red woman smashed through one of the stained glass windows with two grenades shouting, "For Finland! For Suomi!" before blowing herself to pieces, along with Hilkala, Lahtinen, Glad, and Wallenius. Tervasmaki, trying to escape, jumped through the same hole in the window she'd come in. His shin bones snapped and he was on his hands and knees when the bullets cut him down. A rifle grenade took Kivimies in the chest. Vennola got it with a bayonet when a Red burst through the main doors. The Red was killed at once, but Vennola took a long time die, biting on his knuckles to stop himself from crying. Jutikkala was hit in the groin by a shell splinter, and asked to be put out of his misery. Selin held his hand, kissed him, and shot him in the head. A bomb from a trench mortar whizzed through the roof and got Torngren and Pentti, while Pirinen was crushed when a big shell brought down part of the roof in the west wing.

Through it all, the survivors remained resolute, fighting on, refusing to give in, rousing themselves with determination to answer the fury of the day. And when night came the dozen or so who were able to move issued out of the church at the back, crept down the bank, stole across the railway tracks (where less than one hundred yards away Reds stood guard beside the hissing armored train), and slipped into a kind mist that was rising from the lake. Slushy snow lay ankle deep on the creaking ice and they sloshed and floundered through it, supporting each other, staggering east until they made it back to territory under the control of their White comrades.

News of them preceded their arrival back at the barracks and Mannerheim himself was there, waiting to greet them, astride a white horse, with a white fur hat set rakishly on his head. He shook each of them by the hand, informing them that they were heroes, that their deeds would be an inspiration when battle was resumed in pursuit of the final victory. He cantered into the sparkling icy darkness on his horse, but not before each of the survivors had been presented with a meat sausage, a bottle of vodka, and the chance to sit out the next day's fighting, an option they all, to a man, declined, downing their vodka and cheering, not so much in response to Mannerheim's praise as to the improbable fact of their survival, the realization that blood was, for one more night at least, still coursing through their veins.

Esko cleaned up. He wolfed the sausage, washing it down with hot tea, and threw himself on one of the straw-filled mattresses in the room where he was billeted with Klaus. Esko had found these digs—an old schoolhouse—for the company himself. When had that been? Perhaps less than forty-eight hours ago. It seemed a lifetime.

He lit an oil lantern and set it on the pine boards; he drew the stub of a pencil out of his pocket and began to sketch, because this was his core; even when he was exhausted and confused and downhearted, this was what he knew how to do. He sketched out on the back of an envelope tiny, intricate sketches that were weirder, wilder, than anything he'd ever done, and they came out fast, a whole mass of them, heightened, exaggerated visions, a bout of drawing fever. These buildings would define something new yet celebrate humanity and serve it. They would bring lovely form out of chaos and be bread for the people. The dusty, matted, gummed-up world of Oskari and Henrik's craftsman style would feel the blast of the pure north wind. Hurray for purity! Hurray and again hurray for the fluid, the graceful, the sparkling! Hurray for the light! Against heavy despair he would propose—weightlessness! To deal with gloom and rigid forms—playfulness!

The shaking in his hands was so bad he could no longer hold the pencil. He kept seeing the face of Bongman's Son—not pleading, not begging, not striving, but wearing an expression of sad and stoic acceptance moments before being destroyed by Holm's gun.

"Esko, are you all right?" It was Klaus; Klaus touched him on the shoulder.

"I'm shaking," Esko said. "Look at my hand. I've no control—it's stupid."

"It's fine," said Klaus with an easygoing smile, squeezing Esko's shoulder.

"Oh God, look," Esko said. Flipping over the envelope, he saw the familiar name: Katerina Malysheva. "I've put this rubbish all over your letter. I'm sorry."

"It doesn't matter," said Klaus.

"Here," Esko said, holding up the envelope with a sheepish grin. "I'm sorry it's defaced."

"Thanks," said Klaus, looking at the drawings.

"I said that you'd be taking that thing back."

Klaus tapped the envelope against his cheek, stroking it through his mustache. "About your friend—the guy we had to shoot. Who was he?"

Esko propped himself on his elbow, thinking of Bongman's Son, of Katerina, of an automobile that roared in the dark and left him with dust in his mouth. "I knew him when I was a boy. He was always wild, crazy. He thought every word in 'Kalevala' was true."

"It isn't?" said Klaus, pulling a face. And then, more seriously. "You liked him, didn't you? He was a good friend."

Esko considered this. "More and less than that," he said. "He was a part of me."

Klaus was gazing at the bottle that Esko had placed a few inches from the lantern, so that the lantern's light played through the glass and the liquid it constrained, throwing flickering shadows on the floor. It looked strange, even beautiful; but it was just a bottle.

"You didn't drink your vodka."

"After everything that happened today I wasn't prepared to go along with the general's proposal that we're great heroes. Shining knights for Suomi."

Klaus laughed. "Mannerheim doesn't care about that, you idiot. He wanted us to get drunk so we'd be ready to fight again in the morning."

Klaus drew up a straight-backed chair and slumped down on it. Esko looked at him, surprised by the weariness in his face. He stood up, took the bottle, and handed it to Klaus.

"It is a business," Esko said. "So let's oblige the general and get drunk."

Klaus examined the label on the bottle for a moment. The cork came out with a soothing pop. "Are you my friend, Esko?" he said.

Esko threw himself on the mattress and put his hands behind his head. He thought Klaus was joking. "I hope so," he said.

"I thought I knew you, but after today I'm not so sure. You're a man of passionate and surprising attachments. Do you know that?"

Esko didn't know what to say. There was nothing unfriendly in Klaus's voice. On the contrary—and yet Esko was always taken aback when people were surprised and puzzled by him. It kept happening.

"I think I told you that I heard from my father today," Klaus said.

"You mentioned it."

"And you asked about Katerina."

Klaus handed him the bottle.

"I did?"

"She's in Stockholm now. My father managed to get her out of Helsinki at last." Klaus shook his head, smiling, looking down and twisting the toe of his boot on the floor. "She traveled on forged papers, disguised as an opera singer. Apparently she really got into the part. Feathered hat, veil, black dress, two little dogs." He looked up with another smile. "They were Pomeranians, and she had them on a leash. My father had to pretend he was her impresario. I'm sure he hated it. Henrik's no actor."

"And Helsinki was no place for her to be," Esko said. "She's safe now?"

"Quite safe. The whole scheme was her idea. She's a determined girl," he said, taking the bottle back from Esko and fueling himself with more vodka. Klaus wiped his lips. He sucked a last drop of liquor from his mustache and said in an almost tender voice, "You love her, don't you?"

For a moment the whole room seemed to shimmer in the light from the lantern. Esko looked over from the mattress to where Klaus was sitting in the chair, but Klaus had turned away a little; his face was in shadow.

"Why do you say that?"

"Because it's true," said Klaus, his voice firmer.

Esko slumped back, hiding his eye with his sleeve. For weeks he'd thought about telling Klaus. But what would have been the point?

"I danced with her once, at the harvest festival in our village a very long time ago. You should have seen her that night! She was so beautiful, so composed. She carried a little art nouveau mirror on her wrist and she frightened away the other boys as though they were evil spirits. But not me. She never showed the mirror to me. She looked at me in a way that no one else ever has. I never expected to see her again and I didn't. Not until Helsinki. Not until that night at your home."

Esko sat up now, waiting until he'd got Klaus's eye. "I asked her to marry me. I begged her to come with me to America. She refused. She kissed me, once, to make me feel better. But she doesn't care for me. She cares for you. That's all there is to it. That's the truth."

"I see," Klaus said.

"I'm not sure that you do," Esko said. It was as if his and Klaus's customary roles had been reversed. Now he was the effusive, high-spirited one, while his friend was the morose Finn, swilling vodka. "If I were not myself, if I were not clumsy, ugly Esko Vaananen, if I were the handsomest, cleverest, best man in the world, then maybe I'd have a chance with Katerina. But I am myself." There was a fierce pain behind his blind eye, and his hand went there for a moment. "And I'm fine with it, you know. Because you and she, you're going to be very happy. I know it."

"Thanks," said Klaus. He seemed stricken. "Vodka?"

"Sure, why not?" said Esko, taking the bottle. "Buck up now, old friend. You're alive, she's safe. We'll win this war and you'll be with her. What's there to be so glum about?"

"There was something else in my father's letter. Something happened before Katerina went to Stockholm. Something that alarmed my father. Something that made him think she was maybe going crazy. But it's all clear to me now."

"What?" said Esko, concerned now.

"One morning, when Henrik went to collect her from Fabianinkatu

Street, he found her outside in the courtyard with a bunch of kids. It was one of those days when it's so cold and clear you can see particles of ice in the air. They were making a sculpture."

"What's so crazy about making a snowman."

"It wasn't a snowman. It was a tower. She had these kids making a tower from ice and snow. It took all day. It grew twenty feet high. Henrik was also worried that one of the kids might fall and break his neck. They were all blue from the cold. But Katerina kept egging them on, working like a wild thing herself. When Henrik asked Katerina what she was doing, do you know what she said?"

"No," Esko said. "How could I possibly know?" As the light in the lantern flickered, throwing shadows through the vodka bottle that Klaus was going to raise to his lips, he had the feeling that the course of his life was about to shift once again, that what Klaus was about to say would change things forever.

"She said, 'I'm building Mr. Vaananen's skyscraper. I'm building his *pilvenpiirtaja*. I'm building it so that on a freezing morning in Helsinki the sky will know I'm thinking of him. The cloud sketcher.'"

12

Selin told them the tactic for the second attack was the same as before. They would penetrate Tampere's defenses as quickly and as decisively as possible, this time making at once for the dam near the Finlayson factory to cross the rapids.

Klaus waved his rifle in the air. "And if we don't succeed today we'll be back tomorrow. Won't we, guys?" he said, exhorting the others. "Hurray for Selin! Hurray for Mannerheim!"

Klaus waited for the cheering to die down and at once produced his tarot pack. His eyes were eager and too bright. He bounced on his toes, grinning, tugging at his mustache while he examined the cards and told everyone how confident he felt. They'd all make it. They'd take Tampere today for sure. "I'll do it alone if needs be," he said, his face pink and pinched by excitement and the cold.

Esko was worried. He'd tried to carry on talking to Klaus about Katerina but Klaus would have none of it. "Don't worry, Esko, these things happen," he'd said.

"Nothing did happen," Esko had said.

It was coming up on 5:00 A.M., the time for the second attack. Esko's eye was red and burning with exhaustion while he watched Klaus shuffle the cards again. "Tell my fortune," he said. It was an idea that he'd shied away from; Esko was worried by soothsayers, by fortune-tellers, by readings of the runes. Such superstitions offended the order of his mind, not least because in his blood he sensed there might be something in them. He was frightened, now, and for the first time, of Klaus, as if Klaus held his fate in those cards.

"You're going to die," Klaus said simply, and indeed he was holding up the death card, a man hanging from a gibbet, neck snapped by the thickness of a rope. "But not today," he added with a grin. "Don't worry."

The rocket burst over their heads, pluming down stars.

Klaus howled, a blood-curdling yell.

To hell with winning the war, Esko thought: it's my job to make sure that we both remain safe.

And then they were on their way again.

It had been a cold night and the dammed-up waters of the rapids glistened with a thin cape of ice. To his left, Esko saw that the barricade of horses on the bridge had been set on fire, and the sickly sweet stench of burning horse flesh drifted down the waters. As before, Esko led the way, with Klaus close behind. The night was still. The Reds on the bridge weren't looking his way. Tampere was there for the taking.

He was halfway across the dam when a bullet whizzed by his ear. He shouted, but the noise was drowned out by a sudden wild rain of bullets, hissing and kicking at the mud in front of him, heaving up ice in gobbets and spurts. A bullet ripped the cap clear off his head. Bullets came so thick that he blinked, shut his eye, thinking that if only he could get his fists in the air he would be able to bat them away like bees. The air seemed hot, and even as he began to run, racing toward the muzzle flashes that pierced the darkness of the opposite bank, he raised a hand.

Something kicked him in the side. A bang went off in his head and there was a blinding light all around. He felt no pain right then, only a tremendous shock. His entire body became a zigzagging bolt of lightning that he was somehow watching travel through himself, as if he were an egg being cracked in two. To his surprise he realized that he was falling. He wanted to cry out against his legs. This is absurd, he tried to tell them. You can stand up. He felt ridiculous because he watched his rifle slip from his fingers even though he was telling himself, Hold onto it. Don't let that rifle go.

High above, stars were shaking and glinting in the dark sky. As he fell backward Esko had a sense of utter weakness, of being stricken and shriveling away to nothing. It's over now, he said to himself, and then he thought: Hey, I never did get to build my skyscraper. It would have been lovely. Good-bye, *pilvenpiirtaja*. Good-bye, Katerina. Only then did he wonder where Klaus was. Another bomb seemed to go off inside his body, which didn't seem fair at all. There was another flash of lightning and, after that, nothing.

Esko lay in a corner of a field dressing station and was unconscious for more than a day. He woke one time to find a nurse pouring water between his lips but when he tried to raise himself to thank her the room spun and went dark. The next morning he was still alive so he was put on a stretcher and loaded into a truck that was soon bouncing down a sandy road in the forest. The pain of being jolted down the road woke him up and made him scream, though soon he passed out again and came to with a doctor poking a steel instrument into his side. "There you are," said the doctor; he had bristling red hair and a pockmarked face. "You were hit twice. I took the bullet in your shoulder out, and the one down here went in and straight out again. You smacked your head when you fell through the ice. You're lucky you didn't drown." He wiggled the steel instrument again and the nurse approached, sending Esko back down into the darkness with a shot of morphine.

When he next awoke he was on a train, lying on a narrow bunk. He knew he must be a little better because he was feeling thirsty; someone else in the darkened, rattling compartment was smoking, and the fumes made him nauseous. The train slowed to a halt and stopped. Outside, there were voices, shadowy figures hurrying by, an electric light burning in a swirl of snow. A bell rang, there was a whistle and a hiss of steam; the coupling chains clanked and the train jerked forward, pricking him with needles of pain.

Bumping at regular intervals over the joints in the rails, the train rolled out of the station, passing a light at the end of the platform, passing a stone wall that glinted with broken glass, passing a signal box and a locomotive that was drawing into the goods yard amid clouds of steam and showering sparks. Esko shut his eye, concentrating on the slow and even movement of the wheels, the ringing sound they made against the tracks. The train's gentle swaying sent him off to sleep and he didn't wake again until the next station, where no lights glimmered above the blackness of the platform. The train shivered, pulsed, jerked, and began to roll, Esko aware of its every tremor. A nurse came in to check on him and the other man in the compartment. Water was fed between his lips from a steel canteen. He was tended to much like the stove, whose door was opened, whose life was stirred.

And this was how the night went by. Now Esko was shivering with cold; now sweat glued his hair to his forehead and soaked the blanket covering him. The train journeyed south through Finland in sprints and dawdles. The compartment was a constantly changing pattern of shadow and moonlight, washed in fiery red when the nurse came and opened the stove.

He didn't even know whether Tampere had been won or lost. The fact that he was in this train, flat on his back in a narrow and uncomfortable bunk, he took to be a good sign. The other soldier in the compartment was sitting by the stove now, on a straight-backed chair with his face turned toward the heat. "Tell me friend. What happened at Tampere?"

The soldier turned, reaching inside his tunic. A letter was pulled out, and he leaned forward to hand it to Esko. Then the soldier tumbled off his chair, blood gushing from his belly.

Esko jolted awake with the man in the other bunk shouting: "Hey, you! Cut out that racket, won't you? I'm trying to get some sleep."

Esko realized it was a nightmare. No man sat in the corner of the compartment on a chair by the squat stove. "Excuse me," Esko said, and the words sounded strange and hoarse to his ear. "What happened at Tampere? I missed the end of it."

A racket of springs came from above Esko's head. The man who really was there turned in his bunk. "The Red bastards surrendered. We slaughtered them in the thousands," he said in an impatient voice. "Now can I please get some sleep?"

13

The ceiling was thickly covered in whitewash, crisscrossed by dark beams of oak. The casement windows were wide and low and the oak window seats beneath them were pierced with heart-shaped openings. On shelves halfway up the walls stood green pottery vases filled with early spring flowers.

The floors gave off a sunny glow and the noise of streetcars and horses pushed at the windows. Esko slipped in and out of consciousness, receiving these impressions as if from far away, as if in a boat, drifting. His body seemed not to belong to him. He was surprised when something moved in the bed beneath him and then he realized it was his leg or foot, reaching for a cool part of the sheets. He was waiting for the bits of himself to be drawn back together. At last, when he was able to sit up in bed, and a glass was pressed against his lips, the water seemed to run down his throat with the thick consistency of metal. The warm cabbage soup tasted like salt. One of the other fellows in the ward had lost his leg below the right knee and was painfully learning to hop about on crutches. Another, a fellow with black hair, and the thick provincial accent of Oulu province, urinated blood five times a day. His bed bottle was like a detail out of Hieronymus Bosch. There was a man whose face had been scorched by a magnesium flare—he'd lost half his nose.

And Esko himself discovered that he had a whole new anatomical attribute.

"A second belly button. You should be proud. Not everybody's got one of those," said the nurse, smiling broadly, dousing the wound with stinging alcohol.

It seemed that the bullet had passed through his side, leaving behind it a neat hole the size of a large coin. One afternoon the same nurse brought him a patch and fitted it over his blind eye. The elastic felt tight and strange against the back of his bruised scalp. "Now you'll look as good as new. Would you care to see in a mirror?"

She brought him one before Esko had a chance to say otherwise. He was a fright: pale, unshaven, gaunt as a ghoul from "Kalevala."

"Well, then," the nurse said, in her busy and businesslike way. "You're on the mend." With another of those wide smiles she brought a vase to his bedside and arranged the flowers.

The other men in the ward smoked and argued and read the papers and remembered what had happened during the fighting. Old jokes and scenes were reenacted: "went in when the barrage lifted"; "held up by machine guns"; "Red guy came out of a house with his hands up, shot him anyway." Voices rose and fell, the subjects going around and around. Would Mannerheim press on to Petrograd and smash the Bolshies while they were still weak in Russia? The fellow hopping about on his crutches was excited about the idea. The blood-pisser was for caution. The battle had been won, and Finland should gather itself, shelter beneath the cloak of Germany, elect a German king—give the job to the kaiser himself if he'd have it. The two men were playing checkers and the one who had lost his leg restrained himself until he had relinquished the game, too, before exclaiming: "What if the Krauts lose in France? What then, eh?" The blood-pisser told him not to be stupid. The Germans couldn't possibly lose in France; besides, there were German gunboats even now in Helsinki harbor; Finland was already between the sheets with the kaiser.

"These are for you. A man left them. A soldier, an officer, I think," said the nurse. She put down a box on the table beside Esko's bed and made a show of inspecting the contents: books. "You're an architect?" she said.

Up until this moment Esko hadn't really considered the fact that his life was going to go on. It was as if his identity had been obliterated. "I was," he said.

"You *are*," said the nurse, with her wide-lipped smile. "And so am I."

Only now, after all these days, did Esko take in her appearance. Her eyes were drawn tight at the corner, with the hint of a slant, a suggestion of Lapp blood. She wore a white nurse's cap that struggled to hold down a frizzy mane of chestnut hair. There was a sense of calm and irrepressible optimism about her. Her hands were blunt and largish. She was in her early twenties and she wore no ring.

"You seem outraged," she said, teasing. "Do you have such a low opinion of women? There are many female architects in Finland."

"I know," said Esko. The weakness of his voice still surprised him. He cleared his throat. "I studied with some of them. But I don't know you."

"Before the war I worked with my brother in Turku. His name was Anton Harkonen. He was killed."

"I'm sorry," Esko said. He'd heard of Anton Harkonen, a young man of promise, talked about the way people do. "He was a fine architect."

"And so are you, Esko Vaananen. So—you see, I knew you were an architect before I asked the question. I was just drawing you out. I could easily have left the books and gone away. I'm not like that."

"Apparently."

"I'm Anna Harkonen."

"Hello, Anna Harkonen."

The books were from his apartment. Someone had been there and picked them—Esko could only assume it had been Klaus. There was a volume of Ruskin, the big German book on Frank Lloyd Wright, and *Wren's City Churches*, with a gorgeous black and orange design on the binding.

Thanks, Klaus, he said to himself, brightening. He was flipping through them the next day when Selin appeared at the foot of his bed, smiling awkwardly and crushing his shabby cap between his fingers. A badge on his shoulder showed that he'd been promoted to colonel.

"Are they all right?" Selin said, an anxious smile cutting across his round face. "I had to pick them out in a hurry. I had the blazes of a job finding your apartment."

"Didn't Klaus take you there?"

Selin looked down, his fingers tearing at the cap. From his pocket he produced an envelope with the familiar drawings on the back.

Selin said, "When you were shot Klaus pulled you clear of the rapids. He disobeyed my orders to do it. I'd have left you behind, I'm afraid—the attack had to come first. But Klaus went back and hauled you out. After that he fought like a bear. He was killed just before the end. A sniper got him from the roof of a building."

Esko couldn't speak. It hit like a weight—Klaus. Klaus was dead.

Across the ward the others were still arguing politics. Finland was now a cake, set in front of the kaiser for his midmorning snack. Finland was pastry, about to be devoured by the greedy giants of empire. Finland was a pike, gutted even before it had the chance to realize it *was* a pike. The fellows were laughing and bickering as usual. The polished floors gave off their even, golden glow. Outside, in the street, a trolley car clanged its bell and came to a halt with a whir.

"That's impossible," Esko said. "Klaus can't be dead."

"I'm terribly sorry," Selin said, seeing how badly Esko was rocked. "Shall I call the nurse?"

At her desk by the door Anna Harkonen was writing in one of her ledgers. The frames of the tiny eyeglasses she wore for close-work glittered in a shaft of morning sunlight. Her expression was sharp and hopeful.

"No, it's all right," Esko said, shutting his good eye and breathing deep. "I'm all right."

Selin drew up a chair.

"The family were informed by Mannerheim himself. It seems there was a family connection," Selin said. "We all liked him, Esko. Everybody did. He was a splendid fellow."

"Yes, he was."

"I never thought he'd be killed. He seemed invincible."

Esko was remembering one particular night in Paris. He and Klaus were at dinner, at a cheap place up in Montparnasse. While they were eating, Klaus looked over a book by Maupassant. He read a paragraph, put down the book, drank some wine, and exclaimed: "Isn't that something? Wouldn't it be something to be able to write like that? I'd give my soul to be able to write something half that good." Then he picked up the book and began to read again, assuming the voice of each character, doing sound effects, but in a way that was both dramatic and understated, giving this material his most tender attention. In that moment Esko had had no doubts whatsoever that Klaus would indeed write something as good as Maupassant, and maybe better. As always, he'd been swept along by Klaus's confidence and energy. Klaus took everything very seriously, and yet his lightness and playfulness told Esko that such an approach need not be solemn. Klaus had made him feel like a dullard; now that light was gone, and he and Katerina had played a part in snuffing it.

My God, he thought, what must she be feeling.

"There's this; it's yours, I think," Selin said, holding out the envelope. On the back of it and in the margins on the front, Esko saw once more those fantastic sketches, huddles of boxes that burst into vistas flanked by soaring towers. "I found this in the barracks when the battle was over. I knew it must be the property of Esko Vaananen. I see from the address on the front that you've been writing to a lady," Selin went on, aiming for a bright tone. He spun his cap between his fingers. "I thought you were dead too, Esko. I'm glad I was wrong about that, at least."

Esko saw that Selin, shyly, was offering friendship, and he tried to smile, but the attempt was cut off by emotion tightening around his throat like a tourniquet. The ink on the front of the envelope was smudged and blurry, and the paper itself was torn at one corner and streaked with dirt. Yet somehow this letter, this artifact, had survived where Klaus had not, had survived beyond Tampere and the life of the man who wrote it, not just evidence of fate's talent for heartbreaking contrivance, but a message too—here was another part of the past that would never let him go, another barnacle added to his keel as he strove across the lake of life.

That night Esko eased himself off his bed. With difficulty and some pain he struggled into the clothes that Anna Harkonen had placed on his chair, saying they were for when he was well enough to be up and about. Well, said Esko to himself, buttoning the rough cotton of the shirt, pulling on the wool pants and thick socks, I *am* up and about.

He waited until she was on her break and then slipped past her desk, where her charts and pencils and trays of medical instruments and a book she was reading swam within a pool of light. He snuck down the wide oak staircase in his stocking feet, holding to the banister for support, and only when he had reached the marbled lobby did he pull on his boots and the thick weight of the overcoat. He paused for a moment, staring back up the steps down which he'd come. Everything was dim and silent, cocooned. Everyone seemed to be asleep. A hot water pipe gurgled.

He was unprepared for the gusting Baltic wind that nipped at his face and lifted the tails of his coat. The moonless night was dark and still and he took ginger steps down the sloping street that ran down from the hospital until he stood in the deep, damp-scented shadow of the National Museum, waiting for a streetcar that at last came along, swaying and clanking like a galleon. With difficulty he heaved himself aboard.

On the streetcar the light seemed dazzling after the darkness of the shadows. Everyone wore a white armband, a sight that so startled him, it was a moment before he understood these were badges of allegiance, not surrender. The people of Helsinki were letting it be known what side they'd taken in the war. Since the Whites had all but won, everybody now seemed to be a White. Such was human nature. Yet there was no air of celebration. Examining the grim, tired faces, Esko realized he had no clue as to what Helsinki's state of mind might be, no idea, really, of what had happened here while he'd been fighting in the north—terrible things, no doubt. The woman standing next to him wore a felt hat with a ferocious pin stabbed into it. She stared askance at Esko's bandless arm. "Are you a Red?" she asked in a pointed way. Esko just looked at her. For the losers, he began to understand, the terrible things might just be beginning.

He changed at the railway station, where even the statues outside seemed less solid than before, holding their electric globes to their granite bellies a little more tightly, as if afraid they might roll away and shatter, like everything else in Finland. Then he rode another streetcar up into the Eira district, where Henrik's big villa stood, the lines of its little round tower and tapering spire almost dissolved in the misty night sky.

One of the servants, a shy girl he'd known before the war, let him in. She at once bowed and hurried away, and he waited alone in the lofty hall, warming his hands at the stove. A log stirred and rumbled in its belly. From the adjoining dining room he heard the old grandfather clock winding up with a groan and then announcing the quarter hour. He thought of the dinner here that night when he'd met Katerina again. Klaus had teased him about Walter Gropius, he seemed to recall, and Katerina had summoned him to the possibility of love. All that seemed at a point impossibly distant in time. Experience had pushed it back into another era. He fingered Klaus's letter in his coat pocket, checking that it was still there.

Esko waited for more than fifteen minutes. The electric lights mysteriously went off, and then came back on again, and Louise Arnefelt appeared. Her small neat face was pale. She looked drawn and tired and on seeing him she gasped and her hand flew to her throat as if she'd seen a ghost.

"Esko, is that really you?"

For the moment she seemed to have forgotten that she disliked him.

"You're alive? We heard that you'd been killed at Tampere, with . . ." Her voice caught in her throat. She tried to move toward him but was so shaken that her legs crumpled and she had to clutch at a table for support. "Is he . . . is he with you?"

She saw at once from his reaction what the answer was. For a moment the hope of a miracle had risen within her. Now she was flattened again. Her Klaus was gone. As for Esko, she'd thought he was dead too and she didn't much care that he wasn't.

"Louise—I'm sorry."

She couldn't look at him. "Please, don't say anything," she said in her proud, distant voice. "You want to see Henrik? You know where he is."

In the studio the lights were on but both the stove and grate were unlit. Henrik sat in a deep leather armchair in front of a wall of books. Books were piled on either side of the chair. A book sat, unread, in his lap. A pipe hung, unlit, from his lips. His cheeks were mottled and blotchy.

"Henrik, it's me, Esko."

Esko once again had the strange experience of someone looking at him as though he were a creature from beyond the grave.

"I wanted to come and tell you how sorry I am about Klaus. He saved my life."

Henrik took the pipe from his mouth with the careful movements of a man afraid his composure might shatter at any moment. "There's no hope, then?"

"I'm afraid not, Henrik."

"No, of course not," Henrik said. "Mannerheim informed us himself, you know. But we haven't seen the body yet. People have been kind. I've never had so many callers."

"People loved him," Esko said.

Henrik's mind seemed to wander. "There was a man here today from the government. They want me to design a new banknote. What do you think about that, Esko Vaananen?"

"It's an important commission."

"It is, isn't it? They want to put a picture of our new German king on the front. For the new Finland. Klaus would have been pleased."

"He would have been very proud. He admired you very much, Henrik, both as a father and as an architect."

"Thank you, Esko. Will you take some vodka?" Without waiting for a reply Henrik drew himself to his feet, moving in that same fragile way. The world had become a threat to him now and he viewed its every manifestation, including this house, which he had designed himself, as an enemy waiting to trick or hurt him. Nothing had prepared him for the devastating loss of his son. The very diligence and opulence of his surroundings now mocked the values of warmth and beauty they'd once embodied.

"I have this," Esko said, reaching inside his pocket. "Klaus wrote this soon before he was killed. It's for Katerina."

Henrik shrank away. His sharp blue eyes viewed the envelope with suspicion; as if it too meant him harm.

"I think she should have it."

Henrik hooked his thumb under the lapel of his tweed jacket. "I wonder if I might presume on you for a favor. Would you take it to her yourself?"

"In Stockholm?"

"Stockholm?" said Henrik, puzzled. "Lord, no. She's here. In Helsinki. I saw her a week ago. She came back when we heard about you and Klaus."

14

The temperature had dipped and snow fell in big wet flakes that didn't settle but dissolved on Esko's cheeks and left the cobblestones in front of him slick and treacherous as he ran down the hill toward Fabianinkatu and Katerina's apartment. Gas lamps floated and bobbed toward him through the murk, and his boots thumped jarringly, stabbing pain through his side and chest. Soon he was forced to pause, resting with hands on knees; then he began to walk again, picking up the pace until he was obliged once more to rest. He made progress in furious spurts, his eagerness to see Katerina as thrilling and driven as his guilt about Klaus was hobbling and real. He had no idea what they would say to one another; he only knew that they had to talk. He wanted to look at her, to see her eyes, her neck, her lovely hands. It was terrible that Klaus had died, but they were still alive, their futures full of wonderful opportunity, even if they went their separate ways. He supposed that he wanted to tell her that. They would soothe each other, and see. And there was, of course, the matter of the letter. There was no way of knowing what Klaus had written from Tampere. They might be words of comfort, or a curse.

Esko realized what a well of emotion Katerina and the war had opened up in him. Gone were the days when, in the lower depths of his being, far below the frozen surface, the shadows of emotions occasionally stirred like a pike. He'd lived much of his teenage years like that, much of his adult life thus far, it felt like. Now, on this night, with snow melting all around him, he felt fully engaged. Life's sensations crowded in on him, filling him with equal measures of disquiet and exhilaration.

His ascent of the stairwell at Fabianinkatu Street was torture. On each landing he was aware that noise in the apartments on either side stopped, the people inside straining to listen, wondering who this visitor might be, as if the arrival of any stranger were a cause for alarm in Helsinki in these uncertain times.

On reaching Katerina's door he paused, standing in front of the green door, taking a great breath.

He rapped his knuckles against the green paint; no answer; the door gave way to his nudge, however.

"Katerina!"

Almost at once he realized something was very wrong. The apartment was so dark and cold. A tart smell of pine rose from the woodpile by the fire, as before, but when he turned on the electric light he saw that the windows were thrown wide open and the place was wrecked.

Books, yanked from their shelves, lay in heaps on the floor. The stuffing of the chintz ottoman poked out through jagged slashes. Glass crunched beneath his feet. A cabinet had been toppled, the table upended, drawers spilled. Even the piano had been smashed—it was tipped on its nose, like a ship going down.

In the bedroom the scene was more of the same—a broken mirror, gutted pillows, feathers and scattered bits of packing straw rolling and chasing each other in the draft that his entry made. A steamship trunk had been turned over, and its contents lay everywhere: ripped clothes, shoes, a notebook with the pages turned out. The bureau drawers were empty, stripped clean. Perhaps the contents had been bundled up and taken away.

In the grate there were pages of *Hufvudstadsbladet,* twisted together to make fire lighters. Smoothing one of them out, he saw that the newspaper was only four days old. Presumably she'd been here as recently as that.

Esko looked around cautiously, stepping over the mess. Some papers shuffled in the breeze from the window. Crossing the floor to the deep-silled windows, he shivered from the cold and gazed down into the courtyard. It must have been down there, he realized, that Katerina had built the *pilvenpiirtaja* from bricks of ice and snow. All was silent. In a doorway a cigarette drew glowing circles in the darkness.

Going back down the stairs, again taking a pause for breath on every landing, hearing the noise of the apartment house tremble and settle around his presence, he tried to fend off his disheartening feelings of confusion and alarm by making a plan. Tomorrow, he told himself, he would visit the office of every steamship company in Helsinki. If Katerina had taken passage to Stockholm, he would follow and find her; there was a letter in his pocket that must be delivered.

In the courtyard the brick walls of the apartment building rose high, concentrating the darkness. A faint smell of cigarette smoke was trapped there and Esko thought, not only of Katerina's *pilvenpiirtaja,* but for some reason of that long delirious night journey from Tampere, when he'd been lying in the narrow bunk, wounded, drifting in and out of sleep.

Just then a figure materialized from the shadows, a short fellow with a bouncing walk and a fur coat that stretched to his ankles. "Good evening, big man," he said. "You got a cigarette?"

"I don't smoke," Esko said.

"Pity," the short man said with a shrug. He had deep-set eyes that were too close together, crammed either side of a nose that was sharp as a blade. His dark, oddly luxuriant hair struggled to escape from beneath his cap. "What were you doing up there?"

"That's none of your business, my friend," Esko said.

"I'm not your friend and it is my business, so how do you like that?" the man said with a cutting smile. "You know Katerina Malysheva?"

"Do you?"

"She's dead now," the man said in a flat voice.

"What—?" said Esko. Suely he hadn't heard right. He couldn't, wouldn't believe it. "What did you say?"

"I think you know more about this than you're letting on, pal. You a Red? I think you'd better come with us."

Esko's head was swimming. "She's dead?"

"The Reds came three nights ago. Your friends grabbed her and killed her."

"That can't be," said Esko, scarcely aware that three other men had appeared and were stepping forward to take his arms. His lungs felt as though they would burst. It was cold in the courtyard but sweat had started to trickle down his forehead.

The man in the long fur coat hawked, spat. "What's your name, comrade?"

"Esko."

The three men holding him gave him a jolt.

"Esko Vaananen," Esko said. "There must be a mistake."

"You made it," the man said, pushing his cap back on his head. "My, my, Esko Vaananen. That's a very interesting name these days. You wouldn't be related to Timo Vaananen by any chance? He got out of Tampere, that bastard. We're very anxious to meet up with him."

"He's my father," said Esko without thinking. He was numbed, dizzy with shock. "How do you know she's dead?"

The man's sharp little face registered both pleasure and surprise. He stepped back, smiling, as if counting his blessings, then opened his coat and pulled a long-barreled revolver from where it was tucked into the waistband of his pants. "Red Timo's son. My, my. It's our lucky night."

It wasn't the gun that made Esko vomit.

"Scared shitless," the man said, in a smug tone, and his cronies laughed.

"Nothing left in his belly now," one of them said flatly.

"Maybe we'll fix him some *pulla* bread, just like mother makes it," said the man, allowing his fur coat to flap loose, aiming the revolver in the general direction of Esko's heart. "Come with us or I'll blow you open right now."

The four of them manhandled Esko into the street, where the leader held up his hand, signaling to an automobile that rolled toward them, engine snorting. "Get in," the man said, and the car's back door swung open, issuing cigarette smoke and a blast of warm air and the otherwise welcoming smell of leather.

"Where are we going?"

"Never mind that." The barrel of the revolver poked him in the rib. "It's *pulla* time. Let's go and talk about your mother. And especially your father. Let's go somewhere quiet and do that. We haven't got all night."

Esko looked into the man's pointy face. He'd been struggling with the information that Katerina might be dead; only now did he realize that he himself was in danger.

"What exactly do you fellows want with me?"

"Make it easy for yourself, comrade," the man said. "Tell us what we want to know and we'll make it quick."

He fought against the arms holding him, but they were too strong. A hand was on the back of his head, pushing him down, shoving him toward the dark interior of the car. "Let's get this over," the leader was saying, his voice flat with boredom and contempt. "All this talk about food is making me hungry. I could use a bite."

Esko was pushing, straining back, fearful of the inside of that car, with its warm bouquet of leather and cigarette smoke.

"What the bloody hell's going on here? Let that man go at once."

Esko heard the loud, commanding voice behind him. At once the grip on his arms and neck slackened, and he was able to raise his head sufficiently to see the reassuring sight of Selin, in uniform, with his Mauser drawn. Anna Harkonen, the nurse, was with him, a cape clasped at her throat.

Selin whipped the revolver away from the man in the fur coat. Now he had two guns, one in either hand. He looked like a cowboy from a Tom Mix western, Esko thought.

"What's your name?" Selin said.

"Rasa Veikko, sir," the man said grudgingly, noting the badges of White Army rank on Selin's shoulder.

"And just what did you think you were doing with my friend?"

"He's a Red. We were taking him for interrogation."

"Don't be so bloody ridiculous," Selin said. "Esko, what's been happening here?"

Gathering himself, Esko explained the situation.

Anna Harkonen, watching all this with concern, said: "You're still sick, Esko. You should be back in bed."

"I don't give a damn about that," Esko said. "I need to find out what happened to my friend."

"I can help," said Rasa Veikko, eager, almost puppyish now, quickly recovered from the affront involved in the removal of his pistol and his victim. Now this man who only a few minutes earlier had been proposing to blow Esko wide open was busily determined to ingratiate himself. "We're still holding one of the Reds who was here that night," he said, turning back to Esko and Selin. "I'll take you to him. He can tell you the story himself." He coughed, risking a mean little smile. "Of course he may mumble a little. We had to rough him up."

Soon Veikko sat alongside his driver, his arm stretched casually on the back of the bench seat while he turned his ferrety face toward Selin, Anna, and Esko, and the car made quick speed toward the outskirts of the city. "We found this guy and his friend at the railway station. They were trying to get on the train to Viipuri with phony papers. From there they were hoping to make it to Petrograd. I shot one of them right away to let the other know I was serious. Turned out he was quite ready to talk after that," said Veikko with a self-amused smile. "He told us his story."

"Which was?" Esko said.

Veikko coughed. "Perhaps he should tell you himself. That would be best, you know?"

On arriving in front of an anonymous brick building, the car stopped and Veikko jumped out, beckoning them to follow him inside, where they passed several bored guards drinking coffee in the hallway and walked quickly most of the way down a long and narrow corridor with a guard at either end before Veikko turned on his heel and slapped a black iron door with the flat of his hand. The door opened and he drew Esko inside a cell that stank of excrement. A single electric bulb flickered and buzzed in the ceiling behind a grille of steel mesh, filling the airless space with a harsh and glaring light. There was one occupant, a man sitting in an attitude of frozen despair on the edge of a steel bed that folded down from the wall. He was wrapped in a threadbare green overcoat that he held tightly to himself, afraid someone might try to snatch it away; or perhaps there's nothing underneath, Esko thought. The prisoner's bootless stockinged feet rested on the floor, sloshing in a pool of his own urine. His hair was gray, his face bruised and cut to ribbons; his bloodshot, listless eyes gave no sign that he knew they'd come in. He was staring into a little art nouveau mirror that he gripped in both hands as though it were the book of his salvation.

"He's a vain one," said Veikko, and gave the man a brutal kick on the shins. "Aren't you, Matti?"

Esko couldn't take his eye off the mirror. It was an art nouveau mirror, adorned in silver; the silver was worn and bent and speckled with what looked like congealed blood. He knew that if he were to study the back he would see the name and hallmark of the Parisian manufacturer.

"Where did you get that?" Esko said, feeling as though he might faint, dreading the answer, for until this moment he'd almost been able to convince himself that Katerina was still alive, despite what Veikko had said. He'd held onto a hope that now seemed as fragile as beauty itself. "Where did you get that mirror?"

"Come on, answer, you scum," said Veikko, lashing out once more with his boot.

The man was too beaten to notice. He did moan a little, and begged them not to hurt him anymore. His listless eyes remained fixed on the mirror, seeking salvation there. "It came from a rich Russian lady. We loaded her with the others in a truck. Took 'em to the ice. Lined 'em up at the edge of the sea. It was a cold night. Foggy. Then we stepped back and the machine gunner did his stuff."

"And the mirror?" Esko's voice was shaking.

"I took it from her after. She was a pretty lady."

Rasa Veikko was about to strike the man another blow to the head but looked around at the sound, a howl like that of a wolf caught in a trap, that Esko let forth as he quickly turned away and pounded with his fists against the door.

15

In the hospital Esko lay now on his side, now on his back, now on his face, drifting in and out of sleep, weeping quietly, barely speaking even when Nurse Anna Harkonen came to dress his reopened wounds. Three days passed before he would take food or drink. Once he woke up and he was lying on top of a rubber sheet. He'd wet himself. Again and again his mind went over what had happened. He kept seeing Klaus, grinning and handing him the letter at Tampere. He thought of Katerina, and his lips burned with the guilty memory of the kiss they'd shared. His whole world was shamed. If he'd gone to America, he told himself, if only he'd gone to America as she had insisted, then both she and Klaus would be alive now. His would-be nobility had been fraudulent and stupid, a sham. It was as if he'd murdered the two people most precious to him in the world, and now he knew that the disasters he most feared were always doomed to happen.

Figures bustled up and down the ward. It was May 16, 1918, the day of Mannerheim's big victory parade. Fresh flowers stood proud in all the vases and the windows were open to a warm spring breeze. From outside came distant applause and a cheering that grew steadily louder, as if borne by a great, unhastening wave. Lying on his side, Esko heard the brass pomp of a military band, the stately clatter of iron-shod hooves on cobbles. All the other men in the ward crowded to the windows so they could be closer to the intensifying excitement and racket. Cannons fired; peals of ordnance rang out. Cheering and whistling were taken up by every onlooker. Esko turned in his bed, showing the scene his back.

Once again he was surprised by Selin.

"Mind if I sit down?"

Selin was in a proper uniform. His fair hair was newly barbered and he was in a smart gray tunic, the chest emblazoned with medals, for although it had scarcely seemed so at the time, their holding of the church throughout that long day had proved a turning point in the battle of Tampere.

"What are you doing?" Esko said to him. "This is your time. You should be out there with the parade, celebrating."

"I'd rather be with my friend," said Selin, turning his cap between his fingers. "Besides, right now I'm not sure what all this was for. I just saw a little girl handing daisies to German machine-gun crews. Victory is complicated and I don't pretend to know what I think." He shrugged. "I'm glad it's over. Except it isn't really over. The fighting's done and now we're killing more Reds than ever."

All over Helsinki, Selin told him, there were scenes like the one they'd witnessed the other night. The victorious Whites were hunting down the Reds. Some killings were orchestrated by hasty tribunals. Others were ad hoc affairs, simply the settling of old scores. Mannerheim himself had appealed for the killings to stop—to no avail.

"It doesn't matter if you're a Red or not. Just the suspicion is enough," Selin said. "You were lucky the other night."

"I wish I hadn't been."

"Don't say that," said Selin with a frown.

Only now did Selin pull up the chair and sit. He had a knapsack with him; from it he produced a bottle of vodka and two tumblers of thick glass. "Will you have a drink?"

Esko shrugged. Outside, the horses and the military band were yet closer, filling the spring air with the clamor of drums and trumpets.

"Not to victory. To absent friends," Selin said.

"Absent friends," said Esko. He scowled at the thick, oily taste of the vodka.

Selin splashed more into his glass. "Anna tells me you'll be up and about in no time," he said, raising his voice to compete with the brass.

"Anna?"

"The nurse. Anna Harkonen. She says you're strong as an ox,"

Esko's eye fell on the architecture books on his nightstand. He seemed now to remember asking Anna Harkonen to take them away. Obviously she hadn't done it. He would have ripped them up himself but he didn't have the strength.

"This is a beautiful book," Selin said, picking up the Wren, inspecting the ornate *jugend* lettering on the spine.

"It was designed by an Englishman. Arthur Mackmurdo. He also helped build the Savoy Hotel in London. Not that you or I are ever likely to stay there."

"These are wonderful churches," Selin said, going on through the book.

"Wren was commissioned to do them after the great fire of London. It was in sixteen hundred and sixty-something. He wanted to rebuild the whole city. They wouldn't let him."

"What wouldn't I give to be able to do something like that? But I'm a dull man. A farmer. When all's said and done that's all I am. I fought this war so I can go back to shoveling shit in peace," Selin said with a smile and a shrug. "More vodka?"

Esko flicked his eyebrow. "A little."

"Are you religious, Esko?"

"No," Esko said too quickly, taken aback. "Not anymore."

"It's funny, but I still am," Selin said. "I believe in God." Shaking his head, he regarded his blunt hands. "God exists. His Son suffered and died for me."

Selin raised his eyes to the ceiling, disquieted and surprised by the idea of his continuing faith. He looked at his feet, shuffling his boots in embarrassment, and then his gaze searched out the Wren book.

"If I were an architect, like you, I'd build a church. I would, Esko. That's what I'd do. A different church. Something to show that we haven't forgotten even though we mean to go on in a new way," Selin said. "It's important to remember, isn't it?"

"Yes, I suppose it is," Esko said. Outside, the noise was dwindling as the big parade passed into the distance. The other men in the ward were moving away from the windows, back toward their beds, chattering to each other in low voices. The light was hazy and thick, a northern light, a spring light whose soft tones of welcome foretold the abundant summer light that was to come, a light that played gently across the floor and on the whiteness of the sheets on his bed. It was a mysterious and yet a soothing light, filled with promise and life, contrary to his mood, and yet something in him warmed to it. For the first time in days he felt more cheerful.

Selin was saying, "When I was a child I would ask my mother, 'What is God? Where is He? Is He a toy? Is He a cow?' "

Esko grunted; he liked this idea of the childish Selin's cud-chewing Almighty.

"I thought that if I looked hard enough on the farm I'd find Him. But I never did. So I gave up on that idea. And then one day my father and I made models of all the planets. From clay. We squeezed the gray clay between our fingers, rolling it on a big white table in my father's office. We got some string and hung the planets from the ceiling in my bedroom. I thought I was in God's house then."

Selin smiled shyly, spinning his cap, and said he'd grown up with a very old-fashioned idea. "I believed that God would help me find patience, would teach me to endure. That He would always be by my side. During the fighting we saw things so bad it didn't seem possible that God would allow them. But God did. At Tampere I was very afraid and I asked Him to be with me. To protect me. And do you know what, Esko? I never felt Him there. Not for a moment. I mean to say—how much further does He have to go to prove to me that He doesn't exist? He showed me Tampere. He introduced me to Holm. And that came on top of a lifetime of freezing cold churches and gloomy Finnish pastors droning on and on. Yet still I believe."

Selin shook his head. "It's a stubborn business, this faith," he said in a wondering voice. "What do you think?"

Esko didn't know what to think, but he was moved by Selin's confession. "I willed my faith away when I was about eleven years old," he said.

"Do you think you could will it back again?"

"I don't want to. God's gone for me and He can stay that way," Esko said.

"You've perked up. Are you hungry?"

"A little. The vodka's gone to my head."

"I'll see what I can grab," Selin said.

While Selin was gone Esko picked up the Mackmurdo book, idly turning the pages, looking at Wren's London churches one after the other. There was something striking about their simplicity; they were, unlike his great cathedral of St. Paul, quite humble designs, the product of a man whose instincts were concrete and worldly, practical, not only visionary, and perhaps not religious at all. And yet they were moving, serene, and orderly counterpoint to the tempestuous times of plague, fire, and revolution that Wren had witnessed. He'd lived at the end of one era and the beginning of another. Out of space and light he'd spanned the two.

Selin was coming back now, bearing two white plates loaded with food. He was looking over his shoulder toward Anna Harkonen, saying something that Esko couldn't catch. A warm breeze came through the open windows, ruffling the drapes, sending shadows dancing on the floor of polished pine, making patterns with an effortless fluency no human hand could presume to emulate. In that moment something in Esko reconciled. A process began. The icy shell of his melancholy began to crack and shiver away, revealing the resilient idealism that demanded something new now; he saw that out of Selin's friendship and the terrible debt he owed the memory of Klaus and Katerina he too must make a bridge. He had a glimmer, a notion. He saw a pure white space, clean and spare and cool, not smashed by light, but healed by light, bathed in light's gentleness. He saw a cross on a wall with another cross behind it, a shadow cross, the shadow of what God left behind when God was gone, the continued need for joy and beauty, a commitment to hope where there appeared to be none, and to grace in spite of everything.

16

Selin's father, a landowner, ran one of the biggest and most prosperous estates in Ostrobothnia, and two months later Esko was at the heart of it, hands clasped behind his back, leaning forward, striding slowly to the top of a low hill speckled with granite boulders. It was a hot summer day. A falcon hovered high in the sky. The shouts of children came from a distant straw-berry field. His nostrils were filled with the smell of blackcurrants and grass and the earth that was slowly cooking beneath the sun.

Esko stopped, turned, looked back toward the barn at the distant end of the meadow; it was a fine barn, built in the old Finnish style, with chinks between the horizontal logs that let in wind and light; it was in a fine location, well protected and with good drainage; it was an admirable barn in every way, red and sturdy and with years of use in it yet; it was going to have to go, for it lay on the precise spot where he knew he must build the church.

Under the shade of his wide straw hat Esko's face was humorous and determined. He doffed the hat, sipped cool water from a bottle that he'd brought with him, and smoothed his hair with the attitude of a man satisfied to have come to terms with a problem. He rubbed his side, where the bullet had passed through; the wound had healed now, but it ached and itched sometimes, especially when the weather was about to change. His body had become a barometer.

Esko turned his face to the sun, its warmth making him shudder with pleasure; he put his hat back on, took another gulp of water, and sat down, opening his sketch pad. He began to draw, his hand scratching and swirling across the paper. Now that he'd finally decided on the site, everything else came easily, in a breath, in a burst, as if the church already existed in his mind and the unearthing of this one last detail opened a door to reveal it.

The space *within* the building would be its primary reality, not the exte-rior. The altar, he saw, must be a simple white oblong struck by light. Behind it would hang a cross and, behind the cross, recessed into the wall to a depth of three or four inches, would be the shape of a cross, a cross of exactly the same dimensions, the shadow cross. In front of the altar, and level with it, would stand pews of white pine, leading back toward tall doors of oak. The walls would be plain, whitewashed; the white floors would be of concrete. The ceiling would be barrel-vaulted, with openings for light cut out of it at unpredictable intervals throughout its height and curve. Thus, during each day, as the sun moved above the open Ostrobothnian plain, there would be a constant rotation of light and shadow. The light within the space would never be still; it would shift and dance, from brilliance to shadow, and back again. When the sun went down, and throughout the win-ter, interior light would come from deep-hanging lamps of glass and copper; the barrel ceiling would reside in mysterious dark, with perhaps the stars and the northern lights flashing through, while the space below would be warm, welcoming.

Esko was trying for something bold. Hitherto churches had developed since Roman times in many different ways but according to one architectural law that had been universally applied: a church always had two naves crossing each other at right angles, forming a cross. Esko was ignoring that, using the cross motif in an entirely different and original way. This in itself would make his church striking, modern; some might even call it ungodly, just on principle. He knew he had to counter that possible charge by really making sure that this was a holy and a peaceful place. After all, whatever its architectural pretensions, it would still be a church, and people would be bringing the most religious and most wounded parts of themselves here; accordingly it should evoke both what was unknowable, eternal, those lofty ideas to which man aspires in his dreams, and what was real, intimate, the drama of changing fortune and destiny with which every human being struggles every day.

He recalled a drizzly November afternoon in Paris when he and Klaus had crossed the Pont Neuf to the Île de la Cité. With Victor Hugo's *Notre Dame* in hand they had approached the great Gothic cathedral, Esko intent on architectural inspiration, Klaus determined to locate the terrible word, *ananke*, fate, that Hugo had seen scratched on one of the stones of the cathedral and that had inspired him to write his novel. They were both young men, eager to leave a mark on the world, and Notre Dame duly dazzled and seduced them with its glory, and then tripped them up. For Klaus found that *ananke* winked at him from a thousand stones, written there by a thousand previous pilgrims; and Esko saw a building that was inimitable, the labor not only of the architects who had designed it and the stonemasons and carpenters who had crafted it by hand, but the colossal work of an entire nation and era. It had taken the whole of France to produce Notre Dame, all of the Middle Ages.

Esko sipped at his water. He fanned his scarred face with his wide straw hat, looking across the meadow toward the barn that would have to be pulled down, reminding himself that Notre Dame was nothing less than a cosmic symphony; what Finland needed from Esko Vaananen, right then, was one pure note, clear as struck crystal. It was what Esko Vaananen needed too. Forget *ananke*; fate was how you wrote it. He would make his church, his way, a memorial to those he'd lost, and a solace to others.

Anna Harkonen came from Helsinki to help. When they spoke on the telephone in Selin's study, Esko told her this really wasn't necessary. She wouldn't have any of it.

"Whether you like it or not," she said in her calm, no-nonsense way. "Meet me at the station in two days."

They rode back to the manor house in Selin's rattling troika. First thing, Esko took Anna and showed her the proposed site. He outlined the plan for her, showed her some of his sketches, and told her that he thought the church should be done in reinforced concrete. The unexpected curve and swing of the barrel-vault ceiling would utilize the possibilities of this new material. It would be, to the best of his knowledge, the first such structure in Finland.

"The trouble is," Esko told her, "I don't know if there's anyone in Finland who can handle specifications like this."

"I'll find out," Anna said. "If there isn't now, there soon will be."

Anna moved into one of the guest rooms at the manor house. She booted Selin out of his study and took the room over, laying out Esko's plans, ordering materials, and orchestrating their arrival. The plan was to build the house the following summer, in 1919, starting at the end of April as soon as the snows were gone.

Together with Selin, Esko built a small cabin from hand-hewn logs for use as a studio. His strength was coming back. He was able to chop some of the logs himself. He tried to pour all his faith into the future and every ounce of optimism that he could muster into the fine piece of craft he believed this church could be.

The winter was harsh that year. The snows came early and drifted deep. In October the Finnish Parliament offered a job to Friedrich Karl, the nephew of the German kaiser. The job was that of the king of Finland and Friedrich Karl was quite happy to accept it; but then in November the Germans lost the war to the Allies in France, and no German was about to become a king anywhere. So Finland was forced to fend for itself, a new nation, a small fish trying to negotiate its path through the murky waters of international politics and diplomacy, where big dramas continued to be played out. In Russia, the Soviet Union now, they had their own civil war brewing. Many Finnish Reds had fled there. Many Finnish Whites were itching for another fight, anxious to grab back from the Russians the remote forests and lakes that were the landscape of "Kalevala." Finland was still in ferment, deciding what it was going to be. Envoys sped to England and America. A new constitution was hastily drawn up. Henrik Arnefelt was commissioned to design a whole new batch of banknotes. Esko worked and drank and read about these matters in *Hufvudstadsbladet* and played cards with Selin and Anna, holding on to the little peace that he'd made. He wasn't interested in consciously trying to identify himself with the times in some political way; he'd had enough of that.

Esko and Selin signed no contract, and Esko refused to discuss the matter of a fee. The Selin estate paid for the materials, which, come the spring, started arriving from Oulu. While the earth groaned and turned to mud from the quantities of ice and snow that were melting into it, Esko supervised the destruction of the old barn and the clearing of the site. As construction began he made a little speech, both Selin and Anna having assured him that this was a good idea. He remembered the slick way that Oskari Bromberg and Henrik Arnefelt handled such situations. Seeing the faces of the crofters and peasants in front of him, men whose lives had been unforgiving even before the war, he felt more inclined to grasp each of them by the hand than pontificate from on high. So he ducked his head and said briefly he hoped that together they might build something fine.

Anna found a contractor who poured and prefabricated the concrete to Esko's careful and detailed specifications. The elements of the walls and roof arrived in three trucks one July afternoon when the horseflies were stinging and a warm breeze swayed the sea of honeyed flowers in the meadow. Sticking up from the flatbed trucks, big and white as sails, those various pieces of concrete looked like pieces from some strange puzzle, which in a way they were.

The foundations had already been prepared, and so Esko took a deep breath and briskly ordered the slotting of the walls and bellied roof into position, the work being done by men with ropes and ladders, a perfect melding of old and new. In less than three hours the basic structure was joined, and, but for the detailing, a church had been built.

Afterward Esko noticed something strange. One by one the workers looked up at the white concrete shell of the exterior and disappeared inside; side by side, Esko and Anna followed them.

Esko knew that he'd planned the church carefully, appropriately ambitious in his aims and yet respectful, conscious that he was making a permanent change in the landscape; he knew also that there were few things you could guarantee about a building, except that it wouldn't be perfect. Yet in this instance the effect of the design was even more dramatic and wonderful than he'd envisioned in his most optimistic moments. The wind helped, changing the sky with each passing moment, constantly adjusting the light that filtered down through the deep-set and irregularly positioned windows in the barrel ceiling. Spangles and coins of light danced across the concrete floor and the concrete wall. At the far end, behind the altar, the shadow cross flared with light, was extinguished, flared again. The whole interior of the space of the church flickered and changed constantly, as if the light were a more palpable and dominating presence than the concrete itself, a physical manifestation of the certainty that life will die and be reborn every second.

Anna nudged Esko in the ribs, pointing out to him one of the younger workmen. He was tall and big boned; he held his cloth cap in his hands and he was staring up at this pouring spectacle of light, his face a part of it, ablaze with a sort of ecstasy.

"Esko," Anna said admiringly. "You must be so proud."

During the next weeks they flung plaster at the inside walls and lightly smoothed it, leaving an unfinished, handmade surface that they painted with thick whitewash. The concrete floor was painted, rubbed with steel wool, painted again. The windows were fitted; carefully, mindful not to overdo it, Esko and Anna began to layer the church with more symbols. Above the entrance, the shadow-cross motif was repeated like an echo. Esko designed a frieze, to be executed in sandstone, that would stretch around the church's interior back wall. The frieze was a triptych, three scenes: the first was from "Kalevala," and showed Vainamoinen singing a tree into existence; the second was a wartime episode—a man on his knees, about to be shot; the third showed Christ's spirit ascending to heaven. A stonemason came from Vaasa to work on these, an old man with a lean face like sculptured granite; he had a patience and a devotion to craft that Esko came to revere. He was a perfectionist, that old man, and a drinker too.

At the end of those warm nights, when the sun dipped beneath the tree-tops, Esko and Anna and Selin and all the workers would sit down together and eat dinner with beer and vodka at a long table while a mist began to obscure the silvery birch trunks and steal into the hollows of the meadow. Drunk, they would retire to the sauna, refreshing themselves in the coolness of the lake, where low-flying duck skimmed the waters, and the reflections of sun and moon together rippled on the surface. It was a wonderful time, a long, hot and luxuriant summer, constantly refreshed by downpours and thunderstorms that were as brief as they were sudden.

Esko and Anna were together a lot of the time. As a draftsman she was skilled, patient, and sure. She was good with money and knew how to handle contractors. In Turku her father was a lawyer so she had an eye for that side of things. She made with her own hands the hanging lamps for the inside of the church; so smooth and efficient was she with all manner of machinery that she even undertook to teach Esko how to drive, laughing with delight as he learned how to change gears and use gas and brake to negotiate Selin's chunky Renault down the dried-mud track from the front of the manor house to the meadow. A confidence, a skeptical obstinacy, a good humor propelled her past every problem. On site she was always in control, steady and funny with the men, standing with hands on hips, rolled-up plans under her arm, the captain of a ship she somehow knew would never go off course. Without even thinking about it, Esko came to rely on her; she was the steadying keel on which the project rode to swift completion.

For Anna herself there was already more at stake than a shared passion for architecture. She never asked about the war or about Katerina directly. She'd been there that night in the jail where the Red prisoners were being held and she knew there was a story, a woman, a tragedy that Esko never talked about and from which he was recovering, slowly. She didn't mind. Tactful, sensitive, Anna knew when to step forward and when to leave alone; she was quite prepared to wait, for a long time if need be, for however long it took, for she was already in love with this brusque, tender man who had such noble visions and such an ache in his heart. Esko wasn't easy, but he was never knowingly unkind, and being around him was never dull. The intensity of his personality saw to that; it ran in flashes of electric light and dark, like a Finnish summer storm. He was the one for her.

Late one August night she and Esko were walking in the forest. The church was all but done. It was a Saturday, and the rest of the men, who had just been paid, were off chasing girls in the village, or fishing and making bonfires by the lake, or drinking and playing cards, telling each other improbable yarns about their adventures with wolves and bears. It was a perfect night. It was twilight, still warm. A woodpecker drilled away somewhere nearby. The enticing and childhood-familiar smell of warm spruce wafted from the trees all around them. Ancient anthills dotted the forest floor, big as boulders. A full moon peered through the treetops, hanging in haze like an orange speared and bleeding in the sky. Their feet meandered down an ill-defined path through the lightly rising mist until they reached the edge of the lake. Little wavelets rolled by like scrolls of silver.

Esko seemed suddenly sad.

"Everything can turn out for the best, you know," Anna said. "It really can. It will. Look at the church you've made."

Esko turned to her with a smile. He'd been wondering about what might be next for him, now that the church was completed. He really had no idea. Just looking at Anna's face assured him that something would turn up. Her irrepressible optimism rubbed off on him.

"The church we've made together," he said.

She blushed then, and turned her head away.

"Anna, what's the matter?"

"Nothing."

"Are you crying?"

"Being silly."

"Anna, don't, please."

He reached for her hand but she wouldn't let him take it.

Esko smiled sadly. He was inexperienced with women; he lived with his head in the clouds a lot of the time; but he was no fool, and he saw a kind of pain with which he was only too familiar echoed in Anna's Lappish eyes. The sympathy and regard and tenderness he felt toward her grappled with his reluctance to talk; he feared any serious emotional dialogue between the two of them would swiftly turn his mind down toward a dark tunnel of memory and loss.

Reaching down, he retrieved a slender piece of birch bark from where it gleamed on the shore. He brushed dirt from the bark, knocked it into the shape of a boat. "Here," he said, holding it out to her.

"Oh, Esko," she said, a little exasperated. "I know you regard me as a good friend, and I value that more than I know how to tell you. But I hope one day you'll think of me in another way."

Now her hand did grab his.

"I know this makes you uncomfortable and you don't want to talk about it but I'm going to anyway. If you need help, or advice, or a hand to hold, or lips to kiss—here I am." She squeezed his hand, her eyes flashing in the moonlight. "I want you to know that. I'm always here. All of me—for you."

17

A letter was sent to the bishop of Vaasa, one Iosip Kalliokoski, inviting him to consecrate the Church of the Shadow Cross on New Year's Eve, 1919. "I know him," Esko told Anna, even though he hadn't been in touch with Kalliokoski for years. "He'll come." Meanwhile Selin asked Esko to design a summer cottage down by the lake. And the merchant who ran the local store decided he needed a new building with a forecourt gas station, realizing that the automobile was the coming thing. These modest offers were very good for an architect in Finland at the time, during the postwar lull. Anna took care of the contracts, brisk and competent as always.

"We seem to be partners," she told him.

Summer gave way to autumn, to darkness and the dismal rains of November, a time of year (the flowering of spring, oddly, being the other) when lots of Finns began to think about taking a one-way dip in the lake. It was a hard month for Esko and he was glad when winter proper set in. Snow creaked in the branches, skis and sleigh runners skittered on the tracks outside, and the clear stillness of the Arctic sky was pricked by a million twinkling stars. The ground froze hard but smelled fresh. Esko used this time to clear the clutter in his soul. He walked, read a lot, and, although building was of course impossible, went on working in his little log cabin studio, where a Primus stove toasted the front of his legs. When his back became too numb he would turn his chair around and grill that side too.

Kalliokoski arrived early in the afternoon, about two o'clock, just as the briefly risen sun was starting to sink once more. In the church Esko was watching the play of winter light through the deep-set windows, and then the heavy doors swung open and banged shut quickly.

"Esko, my old friend, my dearest protégé."

The voice was familiar, as Esko had anticipated, and welcome, which came as more of a surprise, and he began to stride toward Kalliokoski with hand outstretched. "Iosip," he called. "It's wonderful to see you."

Kalliokoski had the same quick dapper neatness of demeanor, the same smart black garb, but he seemed more like an owl these days than a peacock.

The beard was gone, making his head look rounder, his eyes bigger. He'd aged well, acquiring new dignity and confidence with his authority, and he set off briskly down the nave toward Esko, smiling and offering his own hand. But then he stopped, as if he were unable to do otherwise, the building demanding—and commanding—his attention. He slid into a pew, his eyes drawn up to the vaulted ceiling. He gasped.

"Esko—you've amazed me," he said after a minute or so. He smiled again, but now his face seemed to have been scrubbed, as if the building had cleansed and refreshed him. "You've stunned me. It's perfect, wonderful. I was against your becoming an architect, as you know. I favored the law, or banking. All these years I've asked myself, Did he do the right thing? Is he an architect *really*? Should I have kicked up more of a fuss? And now you've created a shrine that's beyond my powers of description. From the outside, I wasn't sure. Impressive, I thought to myself—but I wondered if it was too much the beacon, too much the white marker. The interior explains everything. It's holy. It really is."

Esko was remembering the first time he told Kalliokoski that he wanted to be an architect. He'd been fourteen years old, a student at the Lyceum. He'd been reading everything about buildings he could get his hands on. When the other boys were at the playing fields or massing tin soldiers into great armies he was studying photographs of skyscrapers by Louis Sullivan. "You're chasing windmills like your father," Kalliokoski had said, and had bitten his tongue, knowing that Esko would go his own way, as always. All these years had passed, with Esko never understanding quite what, if anything, it was that Kalliokoski wanted, or why the older man seemed to feel such deep affection for him. After all, he'd not been an easy child—silent, stubborn. Now he felt gratified by Kalliokoski's praise, humbled by it.

"Thank you."

"No, thank *you*, Esko Vaananen." Kalliokoski sighed, scratching his smooth-shaven chin, his dark eyes far away. "Your mother would have loved this." He brightened, adopting his more customarily amused and ironic tone. "I'm a bishop now. They promoted me."

"I heard. Congratulations."

"Oh, not necessary," Kalliokoski said, raising his hand and shrugging it off. "The church turns out to be a race like everything else. And I've always been a good runner."

Esko smiled, sitting beside Kalliokoski on the pew.

"It does mean that I have rather a lot of power." He put his head on one side, making fun of himself a little. "I rather like that."

"How will you use it?"

"Gently, I hope," he said. For a moment he was plunged into more somber thought. "I hear your father's back in Petrograd now. Before that he was in England, and then Murmansk with a small army. He hasn't given up. A few months ago he crossed the border and spoke at Mantyniemi."

Esko was thinking of the armored train that the Reds had brought up behind the church at Tampere. Had his father really been in command of it? Had he himself escaped from right in front of his father's nose? "What did he say?"

"The usual. That the Reds killed in the war and those still dying in the prison camps are good Finns."

"He's right, for once."

"I agree—in principle," said Kalliokoski. "Though at the moment it's scarcely a popular view. I know a lot of men who would kill your father, even if he happened to be in this church."

"That's not very likely."

"Thankfully," said Kalliokoski, showing his teeth in a neat grin. "Then there are those who Timo himself would like to murder or to have murdered. It's certain that I'm on that list. You too, perhaps."

Kalliokoski rolled his eyes, smiling; he looked toward the end of the church where the cross with the shadow cross behind it was shining like a beacon.

"I'm glad at least you've found a place for God in your life."

"Not God, exactly."

"I believe I understand," said Kalliokoski. "The war changed everything, didn't it? Including our relationship with the Almighty."

"Don't tell me you've become an unbeliever—you're a bishop now."

"That's true. But a God who can let man devise wars like ours is no candidate for the Salvation Army. The church needs to think again about how best it can serve Him—and the people."

*   *   *

The local landowners were there, along with their wives, the various church officials, and even the local artist, a smiling fellow with a big mustache who specialized in Finnish winter landscape scenes. They sat in an anxious circle on straight-backed chairs in Selin's father's living room, trying to make small talk with coffee cups balanced on their knees. It was, in its combination of desperate formality and the strangled quest for social connection, a very awkward and very Finnish scene. Someone made a remark about the coffee, and there was a pause. "Looks like snow tonight," said someone else, and the ensuing silence was broken by the sound of mouths busily munching biscuits. Esko was about ready to scream, and then the workers who'd helped build the church filed in. They yanked the caps from their heads, nervously shook Kalliokoski by the hand, and then stood by the window. Esko winked at the old stonemason who was having an even harder time than he was himself with one of those wretchedly tiny cups.

It was left to Anna to break the ice. She came in from the kitchen bearing a punch bowl brimming with spiced red wine. Once some of this pungent-smelling brew had been consumed things began to warm up a little. Esko saw that Anna had decided she and Kalliokoski were to be friends. She kept filling his glass, quizzing him about being a bishop, and insisting that he tell her all about Esko's bad habits as a little boy. "Oh, there were many to be sure," Kalliokoski said, arching an eyebrow. They discussed economics, the buildings of Eliel Saarinen, the civil war in Russia, and the raising of the church and how its design fitted in the general scheme of contemporary architecture. And as he listened to all this, Esko suddenly realized what Anna was doing. She was working his corner, a performance intended to benefit his career. She was doing it out of love for him, and he was moved.

Kalliokoski then cleared his throat and addressed the room at large. He seemed quite at ease doing this, sitting, knees pressed together, with a biscuit in one hand and a glass of fragrant hot punch in the other.

"The war was a terrible thing for the Church," he said. "We found ourselves pulled two ways. On the one hand we are of the people, for the people. On the other we must support and rely upon the stability of the state, for the state is the forest at whose center the true oak of the Church must stand."

Kalliokoski sipped his wine and continued. "We've all heard the stories. That the church condoned and even organized the killing of Reds. That in some cases it was the priests themselves who loaded a pistol, pressed the barrel to the heads of their countrymen and countrywomen, and spilled their brains."

A profound silence fell over the room, which contained both Whites and some workers who'd undoubtedly been on the Red side, though they kept that fact to themselves these days. Kalliokoski, who now wore a raffish smile, as if pleased to have gained everybody's attention at last, had raised a subject that was forbidden. It was in the very nature of civil war, he said, that each side should accuse the other of unspeakable atrocities. It had been thus in America, in England, in the ancient conflict between the Greek states. "Perhaps it's inevitable, even necessary. I don't know. I really don't. What I do know, however, is that the Reds are broken in Finland and that to carry on torturing them and slashing them with bayonets and starving them and shooting them is like burning a boat even as it's sinking in the lake. We're a divided country now. It's the Church's duty, all our duties, to mend that divide and bring all Finns together."

He sipped at his wine and smiled. "Thinking about this, I've made a proposal to the Senate. The Church will pay for the building of twenty new churches, a systematic program throughout the nation. Two churches in Helsinki, two in Tampere, two in Turku, and one church each in fourteen of our smaller towns. These churches will symbolize Our Lord and His teaching in a different way. They won't be grand. Indeed they mustn't be. But they must be beautiful. Uplifting. Wondrous. They will be the people's churches. They will be modern. Architecturally, I had no idea what this might mean." He looked around the room, his gaze finally settling on Esko. "Until today."

Later they all sat down to dinner and, as midnight approached, put on their coats and walked quickly through the snow to the church, which Kalliokoski blessed and consecrated before greeting the new year, the new decade, the 1920s. Esko and Anna were together in the last pew at the back. She whispered in his ear, asking what Kalliokoski had meant about the churches, and Esko whispered back, telling her to be quiet, that he hadn't the faintest idea.

In front of them the shadow cross rose above the heads of the congregation, a symbol whose meaning was as ambiguous as its beauty was haunting. With so many people in the church, coughing and shuffling, filling the space with their human rumble, Esko found himself counting off the mundane things he'd got right: the roof didn't leak, the doors closed, the heating system worked. The church, whatever its other merits, was an excellent piece of engineering. But in his heart he knew it was something more; with the luxury of a few minutes to look around, not having to worry about who was doing what or which of the fellows had been at the vodka, and with the chance now to see how the building actually worked when a church service was in

progress, he knew that he'd created a pure and thoughtful space, perh
even an inspiring one. It was a lovely feeling.

"You seem pretty well, Esko," said Kalliokoski afterward. "I'm glad."

They were walking back to the manor house together, breath billowing in
front of them, feet crunching through the hard, glittery crust of the snow.

"Have you ever thought of being married?"

"Does the institution make for better architects?" Esko asked, trying to
make light of it.

Kalliokoski looked at him sharply. "Anna is good for you."

"I couldn't have built the church without her."

"Marry her." A mittened hand tappped Esko lightly on the arm. "You're a
lucky man, if she'll have you. She's what you need." Kalliokoski said this as if
it were the easiest and most natural thing. Then, much to Esko's relief, he
changed the subject. "And now to this other matter. Twenty churches. Build
them. Build them all."

"You're serious?"

"I'm very serious. The job needs to be done and you're the man for it."

Without realizing it Esko had stopped in his tracks. "It's a huge project,"
he said, daunted but thrilled: such an opportunity might be offered to only
one architect in every generation, if that.

"Build as many as you can," Kallikoski was saying. "Supervise the rest.
The Church can help you with everything you need. We have the resources.
Believe me, no one else in Finland does."

The lights of the manor house were spangling ahead of Esko in the freezing crystal air. "I'll have to think about it."

"Don't think too long. And say yes," said Kalliokoski, thumping his mittens
together. "Now let's get in out of the cold. I need a brandy. A great big one."

Esko was pulling off his boots in the kitchen when Anna came and stood
right in front of him.

"Well?"

"Well what," he said, and received a thump on his chest for his pains.

"Don't play dim. Does he want us to build them?"

"He does."

Selin, who at that moment came into the kitchen for the key to the cellar,
saw the curious sight of two architects starting up to dance the polka.

"About time," he said, eyeing them with a smile. "Now come and help
me get some more booze."

Those next two years were full. Having completed Selin's summer cottage and the local merchant's gas station, Esko and Anna set off for Europe, for Italy, to make a study of Tuscan hillside churches. On their return they ventured to western Finland and to the remotest stretches of Karelia in the east, seeing for themselves the wooden churches that were a feature of those districts. Some were almost seven hundred years old, and even though they'd been battered by the weather, riddled with bullets, attacked with axes, subjected to most of the conceivable indignities that history could throw their way, their beauty was still extraordinary, because they were so simple. Some were onion domed, built during the years of Russian rule. Others, the older ones—and it was these that Esko preferred—had no such details, their exteriors and interiors dominated by bare timber. The surfaces of the vaulted ceilings were usually white, with a silky patina, and the atmosphere they contained was soft and intimate, the floorboards worn and shaped by the curve of time and the weight of generations of human feet. The sturdy pews had panels and high, gently profiled ends. Sometimes the pulpits were decorated with wooden carvings, added presumably by members of the congregation, images that mixed Christian iconography with the ancient code of the shamans. There was a sense of real use about these buildings, Esko thought, of a religion that had evolved to suit the needs of its congregation, a religion whose purpose was not blind rule but the discovery of whatever spark of God lay within the heart of man; and the goal he set himself was to find a contemporary vernacular equivalent.

As he worked and traveled Esko felt himself begin to heal, and more than heal: a weight of tragedy and disappointment that he had imagined would press down on him forever simply fell away and he knew that Kalliokoski had spoken the truth—Anna was right for him. Together they designed and built three more churches. It was a productive and uplifting time, one of his best times. The first church was in Turku, the old capital of Finland, on the west coast; the two others were in Tampere, one in the center of the city, the other on the site of the church that had been destroyed in the day-long battle. He didn't do away altogether with those charred and broken ruins; rather he incorporated what was left, so that the new building rose out of the old like a phoenix, the flame of the future joined with the weight of the past.

Esko was proud of the two Tampere churches, and writers in *Hufvud-stadsbladet* and *Helsingin Sanomat* proclaimed them the "finest examples of the new architecture anywhere in the country." He didn't know about that, but he felt his powers growing with each new design. Still, the Church of the Shadow Cross was special to him, and it was there that he and Anna were married in a quick and simple ceremony conducted by Kalliokoski, with Selin shy and bashful as best man. Afterward the newlyweds traveled alone by train to Helsinki, hurtling through the night in each other's arms, checking into the gilded splendor of the Hotel Kamp on Esplanade, where, on having shown them to their suite, the bellboy sped off, coattails flying, merrily clinking the unreasonably big tip Esko had given him.

"Nice digs, Mrs. Vaananen," Esko said, taking Anna into his arms in front of the unlit fire.

"Big bed," said Anna, who in her brisk and direct way had already made sure that she and Esko had slept together many times; what began one night on blankets thrown on the ground in a Karelian hut had become a habit and a pleasure enjoyed by them both.

A knock came on the door and a maid bustled in, lighting the kindling in the grate, standing by until the fire caught, and then adding pine logs that quickly fired and spat, sending forth waves of heat.

Esko's hand shot to his cheek; he felt a stab of toothache.

"Poor darling!" Anna said, stroking the pang away.

Esko smiled at her familiar touch. The edges of her fingers were cool and a little rough. When young, Anna had been a tomboy, insisting on working in the fields with the farmhands; she'd been the sort of girl you'd go steal a horse with.

"Is that better?"

"Much."

They decided not to leave their suite for dinner, instead ordering salmon and champagne from room service. Thinking of that first night in Karelia, they pulled down linens, pillows, and blankets from the four-poster and picnicked and made a bed in front of the fire, allowing themselves to fall asleep only at three in the morning, bodies aglow, warmed by the dying embers.

The next day was spent on errands in Helsinki. The workload on the churches project was now so big they needed a third architect, and Anna went to see her old professor, Frosterus, at the Polytechnic, asking him if he knew of any likely prospects among his recent graduates. Esko, meanwhile, put on his coat and, leaning forward, aimed himself across the snowdrifts of Esplanad Park toward the offices of the National Board of Antiquities, where he went through records concerning the building of some of the wooden churches in Karelia. Here was a contemporary account, from 1496, of the building of the church at Saloinen, near Raahe:

> Whoever saw or heard the like? The Lord of the Manor, Sten Sture the Elder, his wife of noble birth, their children, their proud heads bowed, harnessed like beasts of burden to carts, bringing wine, corn, oil, lime, stones, timbers, and other things needful for the church and the sustaining of the life of those who were building it. And though more than a hundred people are there, deep silence reigns, no word is heard, not even a whisper. Nothing can stop them. The church climbs higher and higher by the hour. When more pilgrims reach the church they want to help build, they form a camp and light a fire and watch and sing psalms the whole night through. On every cart, candles and lamps are lit.

The Saloinen church had been built on an island soon after the razing of the entire locality by Russian brigands. Thousands of Finns were slaughtered, or raped, or taken into captivity, and in the story of how they replied, more than four hundred years ago, by building a church on an island, a structure that would serve as fortress and place of worship both, he found a model for what he was about in 1921, a story that moved him in the same way as his discovery that the cathedral at Chartres had been designed by a genius whose name had never even been recorded, let alone remembered. Architecture was about the building, not the architect. Esko Vaananen was nothing special, and to be a good citizen he should regard as sacrosanct everything to do with the community, everything that he shared with the many and if possible with all. His churches were a recognition of that, he now saw.

He arrived back at the hotel before Anna. He cleaned the grate and lit the fire himself, not bothering to ring for the maid. Having washed his hands and face, he picked up pencil and paper to draw, sketching the scene from the hotel window: a clear, snowbound night, lights from the harbor twinkling in the distance, halos of frosty air that seemed to ache around a glimmering gas lamp in Esplanade Park. There was something sad and lost about that lonely lamp, Esko thought, as if it knew it was about to go out at any moment.

He completed the sketch and picked up a book—Vasari's *Lives of the Artists*—a gift from Anna, who came back at six-fifteen, kissing him on the lips and handing him a small dark brown bottle.

"Oil of cloves," she explained. "For your toothache."

"Thanks," he said.

Anna was busily moving around, taking off her hat, gloves, and coat, warming her hands at the fire. "You lit this. Good boy," she said. "I was talking to an American in the lobby. A nice old woman with a voice like a foghorn. She gave me this." She held up a copy of a magazine, *Vanity Fair*. "You really must take a look at this, Esko. Americans—they're so extraordinary. They seem to think you can buy and sell anything. Even souls."

The cover of the magazine was lovely, a small masterpiece of elegant design. It showed an oval-faced beauty in an evening gown by Worth. Orchids drooped from her waist; a band of fierce red silk was wrapped tight around her head; her mouth was a modish bow.

Something told Esko he shouldn't look any further; and yet he wanted to look. Riffling the pages, he couldn't help but admire the layout. *Vanity Fair* was obviously able to afford the best. There were essays by Noël Coward and Jean Cocteau, poems entitled "On Drink," "On Insomnia," "On Driving Too Fast." There were articles about playwrights, about song-and-dance men, about the miracle of Chaplin. There was a piece strangely entitled "Cravats and Character—How to Know People by Their Neckwear," and there were advertisments for suits, for soaps, for soups, for tie clips, for teeth you admire in women, "clean and pearly, free from dingy film"; mostly there were advertisments for automobiles, splendid automobiles by Lincoln, by Rolls-Royce, by Wills-Sanye Claire, by Fiat and Isotta-Fraschini, by Bugatti and Reo.

It was a magazine that wore spats. A story about the Bolshevik Revolution was festooned with references to debutante dinners. It told the fashionable what to say and how to spend; presumably they were so busy they couldn't decide these things for themselves. Even to Esko's Finnish eye *Vanity Fair* looked like tremendous fun. Never mind the mysteries of the human soul; it had elegance and spark.

Near the front he found four pages of photographs. The photographs were of skyscrapers. These skyscraper photographs were taken from unusual vantage points. The usual way was to position the camera in middistance straight in front of the building—snap! But these photographs were very different.

The buildings were familiar to Esko; they were the Woolworth, the Flatiron, the Singer, the Equitable—all in New York. He'd seen them photographed a hundred times before, but never like this; these images made the buildings soar out of the pages and assault the eye; they were oblique, low angled, as if the photographer had lain down on the street with his head pressed against the bases of the buildings, camera aimed straight up, reporting on their hum and energy and the thrilling, dangerous feelings of vertigo they induced. They were utterly uncustomary photographs—to understand some of them, Esko had to hold the magazine over his head and turn it; they were bold and magnificent, driving upward, giving an impression of breathtaking height. They turned the skyscrapers into living, breathing, forceful things. Beauties. Monsters. Of course they spoke to him very personally. They took him back to the ice, to his childhood vision. They made the hairs on the back of his neck stand on end and he stared at them for a very long time.

"Esko, what's the matter? Are you dizzy?" Anna was asking.

"A little. It's all right," he said.

But then he turned to the table of contents and saw that he'd been wrong in so lightly assuming that these extraordinary photographs had been taken by a man. For there, in the front of *Vanity Fair*, it said: "Pp. 46–48—The Tall Building Artistically Considered. Photographs by Kate Malysheva."

PART THREE
Quest

I

The offices of *Vanity Fair* were on West Forty-seventh Street, just off Fifth Avenue in Manhattan, in New York City, in America. In one room Esko glimpsed a man snoozing on a sofa, as if sleeping off a heavy lunch—except that it was the middle of the morning. In another room two men were down on the floor rolling dice, facing each other on their hands and knees, yelling like dogs. A paper dart flew through the air, whistled over the reception desk, and skidded at his feet. Two telephones, ignored, rang with unnerving insistence. A typewriter hammered, briefly. A woman stood on top of a desk, squinting back over her shoulder to see whether the seams in her stockings were straight, a fetching spectacle casually ignored by the other photographers, artists, writers, the legions of somebodies and has-beens and wanna-bes who kept up such a steady clamor for attention and admission. Every now and then a staff member would appear, a low wooden gate to the side of reception would be opened, and some lucky pilgrim would gain the grail.

The guardian of this scene, its Cerberus, was a formidable, bespectacled, gray-haired woman in her late forties who disliked Esko from the start. "You still here?" she said, her smile as insincere as her teeth were horsey. He'd been sitting in the reception area two hours.

"Still here," he said.

She sniffed.

"Not going anywhere," he said, when several more minutes had gone by and her glance flashed in his direction once more. The lunch hour came, the lunch hour went. The afternoon progressed and Esko needed to pee very badly. Still he sat. He stood. He paced. He kept treating the receptionist to different aspects of his wrecked face, and at last she buckled, getting on the phone with an expression of vengeful hatred. Several minutes later one of the editors came out, an unemotional man with a carnation in his buttonhole. His meticulous gray suit matched his silvering hair. His expression did not suggest that he regarded Esko with disdain. It suggested he regarded Esko as a creation hitherto unheard of outside the novels of one of his contributors, Mr. H. G. Wells. With exaggerated patience he told Esko that it was magazine policy never to give out information about contributors.

"You'd be better off putting an advertisement in a personals column. We don't *have* a personals column," he said, his frosty grandeur expressing even more forcibly than his words the idea that such a thing was far below the blue-book goals of his extraordinarily successful magazine, the publisher of, not only Wells, but Somerset Maugham, Cocteau of course, John Galsworthy, and a rather promising poet named T. S. Eliot.

Esko, undismayed, came back the next day. The receptionist, shooting him an officious look over her horn rims, said nothing to him but at once picked up a phone and asked for the police. Esko was thinking that he'd better go and rethink his plan of attack but just then the gate to the side of reception banged open and he was being inspected by the young woman who'd been straightening her stockings the day before. She was small and dark-haired, very pretty, and she wore a lipstick whose fierce red shade embodied some riotous, reckless fact about the twentieth century that Esko had yet to grasp.

She lit a cigarette, pluming smoke through those red, red lips, her fearless, curious gaze not once wavering. "You really know Kate?" she said at last.

"I know *a* Katerina Malysheva. I need to find out if this is the same person. Will you help me?" The words, as he said them, sounded faintly absurd, but New York was having this effect. He'd been off the boat less than thirty-six hours; in that time he'd found New York disorienting, overwhelming, a thrilling cyclone of a town. The sheer size and momentum and racket and crammed-togetherness of the place made him feel like a peasant, and here he was, at a loss, facing this collected, assured, short, sophisticated young woman in a black coat with a sumptuous fur collar. She was probably ten years his junior and yet her hardboiled stare assured him she knew sensual and moral worlds he'd never dreamed of. She was modern, and not in the way that Kalliokoski wanted his churches. She was definitely a Ziegfeld kind of a girl.

"So," she said, breathing out more smoke. "What's she like? You know her so well—bang me out a description."

Esko blinked, taken back to that afternoon in the offices of Arnefelt & Bromberg when Klaus had first introduced the subject of his new fiancée. Now, as then, there was always the possibility that two entirely different women were being discussed, that this Kate Malysheva was not his Katerina, that he'd come to New York on a wild goose chase. As to what Katerina was like, to describe her in words—he wasn't sure he was equal to the task. She was tall, dark; she had small, agile hands, a firm light step, a long neck, light, nimble movements. Her hair had been short the last time he'd seen her. What was she *like?* She was passionate, restless, insecure. She was determined and inventive. She had the reckless nonchalance of an aristocrat. She was the mirror that freed him to believe in the possibility of anything. She was the inspiration of his best dreams; she was the voice that called, "Run him down." She was white skinned, thin boned, with straight eyebrows and green eyes that sometimes looked blue.

She was supposed to be dead.

Esko realized he couldn't begin to try to explain this to the tough little number standing in front of him, impatiently tapping one of her galoshes. Instead he drew a pad from his pocket and dashed off a quick sketch.

"So you do know her," the woman said. "Well, well. She's in California."

"In *California?*" said Esko. His heart sank. "Where in California?"

"Haven't a clue. It's a big state. It's a big country—or so I keep hearing. Kate comes and Kate goes—she's a law unto herself."

At least now there were no doubts. It was her. "Do you know anything about those photographs she took—of the skyscrapers?"

"Sure. I wrote the captions. I was with her a lot of the time. She likes skyscrapers. Calls them 'cloudsketchers.' Ain't that cute?"

Esko felt elated, fortified. "When will she be back?"

"No idea," the woman said, cigarette hanging from her lips. I'm Marion Bennett by the way," she said, offering the tops of her fingers in a limp handshake.

"Esko Vaananen."

"Say again?"

He spelled it out for her. "Did she leave an address, a telephone number?"

"No. Wouldn't give it to you even if she had."

Esko began to see this wasn't going to be as easy as he'd thought. "Will you tell her I was here—if you talk to her?"

"*If* I talk to her."

"Will you?"

"Sure thing. Good-bye," said Marion Bennett, turning on her heel and showing him her back with flippant finality, a young woman very sure of herself, entirely comfortable in the hard and glittery world where she moved.

Esko had put himself up at the Plaza, a hotel famous even in Finland, a venue that made the gracious old Kamp in Helsinki seem like a shoe box for a dowager. Here was style! Everyone seemed so young, so rich. In Finland, at least millionaires had the good grace to carry canes and resemble walruses. In the Plaza the beautiful people swept this way and that, voices shrill and unable to contain themselves. There was brittle laughter, the rise and fall of conversation, an atmosphere of luxury and bustle. Bells chimed on the onyx-topped desk of the concierge. Pianos and string quartets and jazz orchestras struck up tunes of fevered energy and poignant sadness, alternately stunning the air, then haunting it like Chanel No. 5. Ice rattled against glass. Money spoke to money across the marbled spaces. Men slipped flasks of whisky from their pockets and instructed waiters on the making of cocktails with extraordinary names: Freaky Sidecar, Wall Street Slammer, Rich Boy's Sling. Esko wasn't sure he heard the names right. Everything in the Plaza seemed at once so fantastical and yet so perfect, inevitable. Helsinki was a chill planet on the distant edge of things. New York was the sun.

It was February 1922. In Greenwich Village, an illicit whisky still, operated by a janitor in a basement of East Twenty-sixth Street, had blown sky high, removing several tons of Manhattan masonry and numerous souls to boot. An influenza epidemic was subsiding, but people were still nervous about traveling by subway, just as at that moment they were wary of bootleggers, not because these fine entrepreneurs flouted the Volstead Act prohibiting the manufacture, sale, and transportation of liquor but because the hooch they peddled was often bad, poisoned, the wrong stuff. Those guys had better look to someone to get their act together! The throng wanted its nightcap, needed it, had to have it. Esko was agog, too drunk on the atmosphere to need a drink. What were his early impressions? The air was so dry it seemed electric. Door handles gave him shocks. Carpets fizzed beneath his feet and stuck to them. Up and down the avenues the extreme cold drilled into his chest and blinded his eye, the wind somehow crueler than Helsinki's because less predictable. All the people he passed looked isolated from the rest of the human race, millions of separate souls, each a busy gambler in the American game of success. New York was hell, an Italian waiter told him with pride. It seemed unkempt and unshorn, ecstatic, material, jazzy, pleasure driven, its energy constantly threatening to burst apart the grid the city planners had so sensibly imposed to try to restrain it. No one seemed to care what anyone else did. The city was a moral holiday where cash was king and flip irony de rigeur. Its insularity was as deep as its buildings were tall. No one knew anything of Finland, though he overheard a couple of radicals purring at the mention of Lenin, Stalin, and Trotsky, perhaps believing these charming fellows to be the latest brand of cologne or motor car. This was in the offices of *Vanity Fair*. Esko kept going back, braving Cerberus at reception, flushing out Marion Bennett, two, three, four times a day, obsessed, until at last she told him that while she was charmed by his persistence and wished some husky brute would pursue her the same way, he'd really better lay off, be patient, wait for Katerina to come back to the city, which no doubt she'd do when she was good and ready.

"Be a good little soldier and run along now," Marion Bennett said, sending Esko's spirits into a dive, for he'd thought the boundaries of this trip would be simple: either the photographer would or wouldn't be Katerina; either she would or wouldn't want him. Now he was in limbo, with his money running out.

That day back in Helsinki, when he'd seen the photographs in *Vanity Fair*, Esko told Anna the full story of Katerina, and Klaus, and the *pilvenpiirtaja*. She took it well, level and calm as always, listening with a frank sympathy that soon became practical. "We must find out if it's really her," she said, and they set about doing that; but the wires they sent to *Vanity Fair* went unanswered; a visit to Henrik Arnefelt produced no further new information, and so they agreed that Esko must book passage to New York. "You know I want you," Anna said calmly. "But you must decide if you really want me. I don't want to live with a man who's not there. And you haven't been, Esko, not since you saw those pictures."

Prior to his departure they walked through the snow in Esplanade Park. It was a clear morning, bitter and cold. Anna was telling him about someone she went to school with, a girl whose father had spent a year in New York, when suddenly she broke down, bursting into tears. "I'll never see you again," she said. "I know it. Oh Esko, please don't go." In front of Vallgren's lovely

mermaid Esko took her in his arms, feeling lost and tearful himself, not knowing what to say, for the reality was that if there was a chance Katerina was alive
he could never be entirely Anna's. She was a cherished part of his life now, as
habitual and familiar as his clothes; yet he'd never longed for her, never
dreamed of her, never lain awake unable to sleep because of her. She'd
arrived in his life like a charm, like good luck, like a change in the weather, a
healing force he at once appreciated and in time came to revere and, yes, to
love. He knew her habits inside out: the neat quick way she ate, the no-
nonsense posture she assumed while doing business, her inward stillness
when listening to music, the tuneful hum that passed between her pursed lips
as she drew, the way she curled her body around his at night and sometimes
moaned while sleeping. She held no surprises for him, and that was fine.
He'd had quite enough surprises, thank you. She was a good woman, and he
knew her love for him was unreserved, unconditional, unquenchable. He
thanked his stars every day for her calming presence in his life. He felt cen-
tered with her, as though he'd found peace. But she wasn't Katerina; she had
no connection to that ache inside he now realized hadn't gone away at all;
she wasn't quite a part of him; she wasn't bound up with a need, a longing, a
keen loss he knew could be recovered if he dreamed big enough, worked
hard enough, risked enough, ran fast enough, was a good and bold enough
man; she didn't burn him like fire and ice. To see Katerina walk across the
room toward him was to watch everything and everyone in the world fade and
die a little.

One morning, four days after his arrival in New York, two wires awaited
him in his pigeon hole behind the front desk of the Plaza.

The first ran: "Are you insane? stop You have wife, career, responsibilities
stop Await/expect imminent return to Finland, country of your birth and
future stop Yours, Kalliokoski."

The second, gentler in tone, stabbed Esko like a *puukko* in the heart: "I
miss you stop Please come home stop All my love stop Your Anna."

Esko pushed the wires into the deep pockets of his overcoat. Wandering out
of the lobby, down the steps, past the doorman in his little sentry box, heading
south, he knew that he'd come to a crossroads. One way was Finland, a steady
and useful future, and Anna; the other way was—what exactly? In the street,
melting ice mingled with horse droppings in the gutter. The odor of gasoline
turning to carbon was already competing with the rich stench of the dung. A
black Model-T rattled by, followed by a man heaving a cart loaded to toppling

with junk and furniture. An empty liquor bottle stood sentinel where a drunk lay sleeping it off on a bench. The clamor of a riveting gun made Esko's nerves stand upright like hairs on end. In the cross streets the slush was being hosed away from the groaning trucks of the street-cleaning department. People charged and dodged, swarming out of a subway entrance above which a sign warned, DANGER. It was a little before 9:00 A.M. and New York had a face like a hangover.

Hands in pockets, he went down Broadway, passing signs for Coca-Cola, for Camel cigarettes, for a politician named Charles Gurgenhatter, for Maxwell House Coffee—Good to the Last Drop. Acres of neon looking listlessly down, as if disappointed by the morning and the slush, waiting for the mystery, the life-giving charge of light that would be theirs once more when darkness fell and a switch was thrown. A streetcar clanked by. Automobiles honked and parked. Looking down the canyon of a cross street he saw a girdered box through which an elevated train thundered. People hurried past him on the sidewalk, sparing no glance even for his face and its hideous imperfections. New York was oblivious to Esko Vaananen; here he was nothing.

He walked for almost an hour, head down, dodging through the crowds, until at last his eye was caught by a building, and he found himself looking up and up, rooted to the sidewalk, swaying with vertigo beneath a building so tall it seemed it must sway over and topple on top of him. Stepping back, narrowly avoiding being squashed by a truck that blew by with an operatic blare of its horn, he realized he was looking at the Woolworth Building, still the tallest skyscraper in the city, the so-called Cathedral of Commerce, dignified without being pompous, so elegant it made him smile. Before the war he'd studied plans of the 792-foot-tall building. He knew that during a workday it housed more than fourteen thousand workers and had in its belly generators that could light up the whole of Finland. Yet the urgency of these facts struck him only now. The Woolworth was a gorgeous beast, soaring from a lot no bigger than a stingy piece of pie. It was mad and wonderful that a man had designed such a thing and caused it to be made. He moved close to the building and, pressing his ear to the cold, gritty stone, listened. There was a rumbling, a pulsing, as if a dragon were sleeping inside, and for the first time he received a glimmer of how difficult, really, it would be to build one of these things. And yet he was thrilled. "My name is Esko Vaananen," he said, by way of introduction, and was embarrassed to see that he'd been observed by a passerby, but the man gave him barely a look, as if the sight of men pressing their ears to the flanks of skyscrapers, talking to them, was a commonplace in New York City.

In the lobby there was a churchlike dimness. Gargoyles glowered at him from the ceiling and from friezes on the walls. Closer inspection revealed that the gargoyles weren't sticking out their tongues or making devilish faces, as they did on the cathedrals of Paris and Chartres or on the front of the Pohjola Building on Aleksanterinkatu Street in Helsinki; these gargoyles were counting their money, separating their wealth into lots of little heaps of stone dollars. The floor was marbled, spotless, gleaming beneath the mysterious light of lamps hanging like lonely beacons from the lofty ceiling. The effect was as if a bank had been turned into a place of worship.

Esko rode the elevator sixty-five floors to the observation deck, where an icy salt breeze smote his face and lifted his hair. Up here he was startled to realize that Manhattan, like Helsinki, was framed and surrounded by water. Unlike Helsinki, however, Manhattan was narrow, a slender spur broken off the earth. To the north a locomotive belched smoke, proceeding toward the New Jersey shore. To the west the steel rump of a liner passed the Statue of Liberty as it dwindled toward the Atlantic. To the south lay the tower-jumbled point of the island and the gulchlike streets of the financial district. To the east sharp winter sunlight splashed over the Brooklyn Bridge, where cars scuttled to and fro like glinting scarabs. The scene was all geometry, angles, stone, breathtaking, and he had a clear view of each of the city's big skyscrapers, rising up like the Woolworth's rivalrous and defeated siblings: the Metropolitan Life, so like an Italian campanile; the monolithic Equitable, sending down a forked shadow that blotted out two entire city blocks; the Singer, with its oddly bulbous dome perched atop a virile shaft; the Flatiron, twinkling at him with a thousand flirty eyes. The spectacle was so magnificent, so tempting and astonishing in its promise, that he wouldn't have been surprised if Satan had appeared, as he had to Jesus on the mountaintop, offering him all this, if only he would pledge his soul.

No such bargain was in the offing. Lucifer did not appear, sidling out of the Woolworth elevator, sauntering onto the observation deck disguised as a Wall Street broker complete with homburg and dashing cane. Instead Esko realized that he hadn't come to New York only for Katerina. She'd called him here with skyscrapers, and a skyscraper, *his* skyscraper was going to make him stay, here in this city where he had no reputation, no contacts, and nothing to live on but his wits and ambition. He believed that he had no illusions concerning the difficulty of what he was undertaking. He knew far better now the problems of beginning life anew in a strange and faraway land.

Later that afternoon he walked into the telegraph office at the Plaza and drafted a wire to Kalliokoski, apologizing, resigning from the churches project and recommending that Anna be appointed chief architect in his place; then he leaned over a desk, blotting out the babble of people chattering on the phones all around him, ignoring the two stock tickers that chattered like a pair of excitedly mating woodpeckers, and picked up a pen.

Dearest Anna,

I'm sitting at a table in the Plaza Hotel, cracking open my chest to try to find the words to put in this letter, my heart aching because I know I'm going to hurt you, my sweet Anna. You'll cry. You'll curse me. I feel guilty, but not ashamed, because I don't know what else to do. You see, I've discovered that the woman who took the skyscraper photographs is indeed the Katerina Malysheva I once knew. I haven't been able to talk to her. She's not in New York. No one knows exactly where she is. Or when she'll be back. And I have no idea whether she'll want me when she does arrive. But I love this woman, Anna. It's as if my life were a theorem that only exists to prove this love, a structure that has no meaning without it. My love for her is love to the death, and so long as I thought that she was dead, I believed I could love you, be a faithful husband. But that's all done with. It's not to be. Katerina is alive and I know what I must do. Call it Fate. God's will. My character. I've known her since I was a little boy and although I know her nothing like so well as you—indeed I scarcely know her at all. She's always been bound up for me with who I am and what I dream I might be.

None of this is fair to you. You've brought me only sweetness and goodness and light, and, believe me, I do know what I'm missing and how much this will hurt you. I can't be fair, so I'm trying to be honest. You must forget me—please. You must proceed with your life as though I no longer exist. I know that happiness will seek you out because happiness knows on which side his bread is buttered. Be lucky. Be happy. Live your life.

Esko

*P.S. I've written to Kalliokoski and instructed him to offer you
the position in charge of the churches project. Please accept
the job—you'll do it superbly. I'll always treasure my memories
of you, our walks and the work we did. You're the most purely
good person I know.*

The paper trembled as he sealed the envelope, which he stamped and
dropped into the mail slot. Then he walked out of the Plaza and sought out
the nearest construction site, calling to the first man he saw, a young man
with a flat cap perched on his head. "What are you building?"

"A hotel," said the man, strutting over. He had close-cropped gingery hair
and a brawny handsomeness he was clearly proud of. "Fifteen stories."

"I'm looking for work."

"You are, are you? What's your name, fella?"

Esko was sad, but he also had a thrilling sense of adventure about to
begin. "Offermans," he said. "Esko Offermans."

2

One hundred fifty feet in the air, Esko leaned back a little against the light
breeze that ballooned his shirt. Gunnar raised his arm, showing that he
was ready, and plucked a rivet from the coals with a pair of long, ungainly
tongs; then, with a smooth, underarm motion, he tossed the rivet. Esko saw the
button of red hot steel catch the light as it flew up toward him, dragging flames
behind it like a rocket before landing *plunk* in his can. His own tongs were
smaller and easier to wield than Gunnar's. He pulled out the rivet, tapped it
against the steel beam, shaking away dirt and cinders, and then plunged the
rivet into one of the holes at the junction point of two steel beams. Bo then
stepped forward on the platform and held the still malleable rivet with a
wrenchlike bar, ready for Cristof who smashed it into place with a riveting gun
that trailed an air hose behind it. Sparks spat as the metals fused together and
Esko turned to see another rivet already hurtling toward his can: *plunk!*

It was four months later, the middle of a New York summer, and Esko was working on the high steel, swaying above the scorched expanse of Central Park, teamed with three Swedes in a riveting gang. He was the catcher and sticker-in; Bo was the holder, or bucker-up. The two of them stood on one side of a plank scaffold, twelve feet wide, ten feet long, that was suspended by ropes from the crosswise steel beam where they were working. Cristof, the riveter, stood on the other side of the scaffold, ready with his gun. The steel beams themselves were for the moment held in place by temporary bolts and guy wires that had been put there by the raising gangs. It was the riveters' job to remove the temporary bolts and fix the permanent ones in place. It was the most dangerous work on site. Men who wanted to do it were rare and men who could do it were even rarer. Esko's step was sure on the planks and the narrow steel beams, and, to his surprise, he had learned to tolerate the incredible heights. The noise of the riveting gun shook his chest and went through him but he'd got used to that. He told himself there was no better way to learn about steel frame, skyscraper, construction. This was true, but he now knew there was more to it. The work required a concentration, a nonchalance, a certain kind of contained manliness that was helping him discover and define his new self, the Esko who could exist and hopefully flourish in America.

Twenty feet below, on more wooden planks, Gunnar stood in front of his coal-burning forge. A lean and narrow-faced man, wearing as usual a sad and harried look, Gunnar was their gang's leader. He stood up straight and narrow as a bayonet, brandishing his tongs, plucking a rivet from the burning forge. Then another red hot mushroom was on its way.

Plunk!

"Did I tell you about my new girlfriend yet?" said Bo, who had pulled out the temporary bolt and was scratching his wiry red hair while Esko went to work with his tongs, pushing in the glowing rivet until its flat head was flush with the steel beam. It was handsome Bo who Esko had first met on the site back in February. He was a ladies' man. "She's Italian," he said.

"I thought you were seeing some little nigger hat-check pixie up in Harlem," said Cristof, kneeling on the other side of the beam with his riveting gun, watching Esko step aside and Bo move in to brace the rivet with his steel bar, which had a mushroom-shaped hollow on the end of it.

"Turned out she had a boyfriend. He wanted to fight. I thought, 'What's the point?' Plenty of fish in the sea."

"Fucking Romeo Bo," said Cristof, and then Esko's chest shook with the racket of the gun. The din subsided. "What a fucking operator. You fuck the nigger?"

"Only twice," said Bo.

Beneath them Gunnar frowned. Married, unhappily married, he didn't like this talk about sex. Lofting his arm, he signaled that the next rivet was ready.

Plunk!

On they went, repeating the same procedure again and again, tight and controlled, to a dancelike rhythm, until they had riveted up every bolt hole they could reach. Then it was time to move the plank scaffold. Esko tucked the tongs into his broad leather belt, watched while Bo hoisted himself onto the steel beam they'd been working on. Esko followed suit, and now he was a little more than a hundred and fifty feet above the ground, with thin air on one side of him and, on the other, the inside of the building where—to judge by the rumble—trucks were delivering an avalanche of stone at ground level. Esko strolled along the two-foot-wide beam, pausing so Cristof could hand him up the riveting gun.

Cristof did so, carefully; he was a big, truculent man, bearded and bull-like. He belched, hoisting his weight up onto the beam. "So tell me about this Italian, little Bo. You fuck *her* yet?"

"She ain't like that. She's sweet. Pure, you know," said Bo, wonder-struck at the idea of the currently unattainable object of his desire. "I'm thinking I'll maybe marry this one."

"Yeah, yeah. Sure you think that," said Cristof, standing up on the beam, surprisingly nimble, and taking back the gun from Esko. "That's the promise you make—until you fuck her, am I right?"

"*Cristof*," said Gunnar, in his stern Lutheran tongue.

"Yeah, Cristof, don't talk about her that way. I'm serious."

"Sure you are. Like I said, Bo, the fucking operator."

Esko and Bo unlooped the thick ropes that had been holding the plank scaffold and inched down to the other end of the beam, where they began to knot the ropes once more, still within range of Gunnar's forge. The work required much precision and little thought; or rather, the thinking had better be done beforehand. In this, Esko saw, riveting was typical of the whole process of steel construction. Each piece of the jigsaw arrived punch-holed and cut to measure from the mills in Pennsylvania, marked with chalk or paint, indicating where on the frame it was to go. If the truck was late, or broke down, or got held up because the driver took a wrong turn and the crust of a midtown street crumbled like toffee beneath the weight of all that steel, the frame ceased to rise. There was no margin for error. Building a skyscraper was like a battle. Plans could and did go wrong but it was best to have one.

"This Italian pixie you're operating on, little Bo. Tell me more about her," said Cristof, checking the knots on the thick rope, setting the scaffold so that it was hanging plumb, three feet or so below the beam. "Does she singa da opera? Where'd you meet her?"

"With the Mantilinis—she's their sister."

"With the fucking Mantilinis?" Cristof said, his voice rising incredulously.

"The Mantilinis?" said Gunnar, looking up from his forge. Even he was surprised.

The Mantilinis were riveters too. Like a majority of the gangs, they'd been hired as a team, had trained as a team, and always worked as a team. They had the additional advantage of being brothers, so each really knew the moves of the others. With smooth skin, dark eyes, and long handsome faces, they looked like a daredevil circus act; and indeed they were fearless in their work. No one seemed to make any attempt to give them their individual names. They were simply the Mantilinis. Their father, a lobster fisherman, had drowned off Staten Island some years before; they lived with their mother. That was all Esko knew, but there was something magical about them, he thought.

"The fucking *Mantilinis*," Cristof said, knotting his fingers through his beard, glaring at handsome Bo with a fury that may even have been real. "Isn't it enough that they get the fucking bonus every fucking month?"

"They're better workers than we are," Esko said.

"That's right," concurred Bo.

"True enough," said Gunnar, implacably fair.

"Because they take more fucking risks," Cristof said. He belched, kneeling down on the beam and attending to the other knot. "What about you, one eye, Mr. fucking Finnish mystery man, Mr. Esko Offermans. You got a woman on the side?"

Esko shrugged, glancing down at his right boot, beneath which glimmered the burnished waters of the lake in Central Park. There was no word from Katerina, though he'd been checking in with Marion Bennett every week and had written her three letters care of *Vanity Fair*. She was still in California, the big state, the dream state. Meanwhile he had in his pocket a letter from Anna, telling him the latest from Helsinki.

"No, Cristof," he said. "No woman on the side. One in front and one behind."

3

He'd taken a loft on Harrison Street because the rent was cheap and the light was good. The loft smelled of lanolin from the wool that had once been stored there. In those hot summer months the stones of the building gave off a whiff like a memory. He'd furnished the place simply with a bed, a desk, an armchair, two lamps. He slept with the windows open, unused to the heat, and woke very early with the bustle of the city already rising to greet him: the rattling carts, the clanging streetcars on Broadway, the hoots of the big ships on the Hudson. He washed, dressed, and walked uptown to a roomy diner on the west side of Sixth Avenue where he got along well with the countermen and waitresses. It was part of his solitary routine. The diner had a row of wobbly seated stools and it had a row of booths. Eating there was another aspect of Esko's slowly starting to feel that he belonged to the city. He was comfortable in that diner, reading, watching, sipping coffee, allowing the early tide of the New York day to wash by. There weren't many people around at that time, so everybody said hello and was polite. It was a fine thing to sit by the window and watch the big city getting started before going to work.

Esko was there with his newspaper and his book, his hair still wet from the shower, early on the morning of June 17, 1922. It was a humid morning with the threat of heat later. As usual, Esko didn't bother to glance at the menu; as usual he ordered eggs with bacon, toast, and coffee, which came to him steaming in a thick, white mug. Folding his copy of the *New York World*, setting it on the table next to his mug, he scanned the front page: Trotsky, Stalin, and Zinovyev had been appointed to rule in the Soviet Union while Lenin recovered from his illness; experts from Cambridge University had been called to the Valley of the Kings in Egypt, where it was thought that strange hieroglyphs found outside what was believed to be the tomb of King

Tutankhamen might warn of a curse in the event that the tomb was opened; in Illinois thirty men had been killed in a riot outside a coal mine. Thirty men! America was as volatile as Europe right now, class war as much a reality here as there.

A waitress came with a refill for his coffee. Through the window from his booth Esko saw an ice man setting up his cart on the corner. During the months he'd been in New York he'd yet to make a single drawing. An ocean—no, a frontier—had been crossed; and in his time off he studied English, studied buildings, read newspapers and novels, went to galleries and to the motion pictures, eagerly trying to absorb the idiom, a sense of the place, before turning his hand back to design. The churches he'd built back in Finland were fine work, no doubt about it, and very modern into the bargain, but they could no more exist in New York than the ice man outside could set up business in the remote northern forests of Finland.

Now there's an idea, he thought. If I don't make it as a skyscraper architect in Manhattan I can always go home and sell ice to the Finns.

"You're laughing at yourself," said a friendly, companionable voice. "Don't do that too much in public. People will get the idea that you're either crazy or so rich you don't have anything to worry about."

Looking up, Esko saw two of the Mantilini brothers. Both were dressed in boots and faded blue overalls and they had flat caps on their heads. It was the younger of the two who was doing the talking. He spoke softly, so that Esko had to lean toward him to catch what he said. He managed to seem pleasantly shy, despite having interrupted Esko at breakfast. He had a ravishing, razorblade smile and perfect white teeth. His hair was thick and very black. The impression was at once of softness and charm and a shocking energy.

"I'm Paul Mantilini. This is my brother Steffano. Mind if we join you?" he said, sitting down anyway and grabbing a piece of toast so that he could immediately start to butter it.

"Be my guest," said Esko in a level voice, not quite sure whether he was amused or not.

"Thanks," said Paul Mantilini with a flash of his teeth, choosing to take Esko's response as a courtesy. Esko put his age at about twenty, though there was a wariness, a watchfulness about his eyes that made him seem older. His leg bounced beneath the table and Esko recalled that he'd been in trouble a while back, this Paul Mantilini. There'd been a police charge, reform school, and his brothers had brought him to work on the steel to keep his nose clean.

With no seeming effort he treated Esko as though Esko were several years his junior. His face was smooth, almost too handsome, until he smiled; the smile was the crack that let out the wildness, the intimation of a spirit that would stop at nothing—a hugely attractive spirit, a tragic spirit almost.

The waitress stopped by again with her pot of coffee. "Thanks, I'll take a cup," Mantilini said, impeccably polite. "Nothing else, though, thank you. We ate already." His leg went on bouncing. He said to Esko: "I'll cut right to it. My brothers and me, we're worried about your friend Bo and our sister." He leaned back, intent on the sugar, lifting a spoonful and stirring it into his coffee, then another spoonful. "Let me explain. My mother, she has me and my brothers. All these boys. Only one daughter. Teresa's special."

"She is a *child*," said Steffano, enunciating each word with emphatic, though heavily accented, clarity. He was much older than his brother; it was he, who, on the high steel, operated the forge. Scars from the coals had been branded onto his fingers and forearms.

"She's sixteen years old," Paul Mantilini said.

"Talk to Bo about it."

"Bo won't listen. Bo's not a listener. He ain't got good ears, that Bo. I've tried."

Esko smiled. "What do you expect me to do?"

"You're an older guy. Bo respects you."

Esko said nothing; this was news to him.

"What is it with you, anyway? How come you're working the steel?"

"I like it."

"Been in this country long?" Paul Mantilini jingled the coins in his pocket.

"Not long. I'm an architect."

The coins fell silent. "Is that a fact?" he said with real delight, his face open with a frank and genuine pleasure, as if to say there was no predicting the things people got up to in this crazy world.

"Your friend," Steffano said, interrupting in his slow voice, each word a bullet of warning. "He must *honor* our sister."

"My brother's polite," Paul Mantilini said, with another of his flashing, cutting smiles, his leg restlessly banging up and down again. "Tell Bo that if he doesn't, I'll slit his throat."

Such was Esko's first dealing with Paul Mantilini and his family; the second came later that same day, that same morning, after they'd walked uptown together and punched in. Esko didn't get a chance to talk to Bo before the

Klaxon hooted, and he was glad, needing time to consider what to say. Everything Esko knew about Bo suggested that the Mantilinis had every right to be worried about their sister. He was a nice enough kid, but dim, and horny as a goat. So what was he supposed to do about it? In Finland the situation might resolve itself by the men carving at each other with *puukkos*, then going out to get drunk and concluding, ridiculously, that the sister was most likely no good, and anyway we all lived in a fallen world. He knew that the Italians took matters of honor more seriously, and he was both amused and a little shocked by Paul Mantilini having come to him. I'm thirty-three years old; I must look like a crazy uncle to these guys, he thought.

The raising of the hotel's basic structure was almost done. Another week and the steel frame would be complete, and the steel workers—the raising gangs, the riveters—would move on to another building. Through that June morning the derrick cranes hoisted steel, columns were plumbed up, and beams connected with the temporary bolts and wires, ready for the riveters to move in. Gunnar was for some reason happy that day. He got a rhythm going, and the rivets flew from his tongs, unwavering missiles of steel that streaked into Esko's old paint can with Esko barely having to move it. Gunnar's economy of effort flowed through into Esko and Bo, and even the spurts from Cristof's riveting gun seemed shorter, bursts that only panicked Esko's bones a little. They completed all the rivets around the junction of two beams, moved the scaffold, nearly two hundred feet up now, and got to work again, a process they repeated twice within three hours, fifty rivets to the hour, good going. They were in a groove, with Esko, Bo, and Cristof up on the unguarded steel of the fourteenth story; below them, on the thirteenth story, was Gunnar, plucking hot rivets from his forge; below him, the twelfth story was entirely covered with a temporary wood floor, littered with tools, bags of concrete, cement mixers, teakettles, cutting torches, and rods of steel.

It was coming up on noon, and Esko was thinking how easily the process of tall building could be improved if each part of it were simplified and broken down, streamlined, made as smooth as the way he and the Swedes were working now. Skyscrapers should be built in the way that Ford assembled cars—a production line, everything thought out, the same job done over and over again—for in the end, skyscrapers were very simple, just the same floor plan replicated endlessly.

Another rivet flew from Gunnar's tongs, whistling and trailing flame. Esko didn't have to move his can an inch.

Plunk!

With his tongs he pulled out the rivet, tapped it against the beam so that cinders shook loose in a scintillating shower, eased it into the bolt hole, and then stood aside for Bo, feeling the sweat on his back turn cold. Glancing to his right, he saw the Mantilinis, high on the web of steel at the side of the building, framed against a sky that had suddenly lowered itself like an awning. For a moment everything was still. A purple silence petrified the branches of the trees in Central Park. The distant Wall Street skyscrapers stood upright like hairs on end. It was as if every stone and particle of matter on the whole of Manhattan had suddenly acquired a nerve and was waiting. Lightning forked the sky high out over the ocean.

Cristof's gun slammed in the rivet, and at once another was hurtling from Gunnar's tongs, its tail of flame brighter and more distinct.

Plunk!

Esko went to work with his tongs, and when he looked south the next time, glancing over at the tip of Manhattan, he saw black and gray clouds standing from end to end of the sky like a rampart. Against this dark, unbroken wall rose swirling, puffed-up streaks of white vapor. As near as Ellis Island the rain had already begun, although where they were now standing the only signs of this disturbance were the cooling of the air, the strange stillness. A single bolt of lightning descended upon the Woolworth Building. A storm was on the way, a big one.

"Hey, Offermans! Wake up!"

Gunnar was shouting.

Esko realized he hadn't even been aware of Cristof's gun that time.

Now another rivet was on the way, and Gunnar's aim was off because he'd been made to wait. Esko lunged with the can.

Plunk!

Bad weather was the worst enemy on the high steel; bad weather was the only thing they were afraid of. A breeze that felt soothing at street level might be an unruly gust up here. A gust could be treacherous; a gale didn't bear thinking about. Had it been Esko's choice he would have had everybody off the building right then. It wasn't his choice. He wasn't in charge.

"Offermans!"

He set up the rivet for Bo, and Cristof did his bit with the shuddering gun; then another rivet was on its way, tossed a little harder this time by the angry Gunnar.

Plunk!

From the corner of his eye Esko glimpsed Petroski, the site foreman, leaning out over the corner of the building, looking out through a pair of binoculars. Petroski was paunchy and dark-haired, a weasel of a guy from Warsaw; he took pleasure in pushing the men too hard and wasn't easily rattled. He was regarding the coming squall and talking into a field telephone.

What the hell is there to have a conversation about? Esko thought. This storm was coming the way they did across the lake in Finland, fast and unforgiving as a train.

Plunk!

Esko stood up straight on the scaffold. Petroski wasn't watching through binoculars anymore. He was nowhere to be seen and the sky had grown darker still. All around, the riveting guns of the other gangs were banging and hammering, and Esko realized he was going to have to make the decision himself, to break the rhythm of work before it was too late. Carefully he lowered the tin can to the scaffold, the glowing rivet still nestling inside it.

"Get down," he commanded Bo. "We're through for the day."

"What's that?"

Just then the scaffold swayed in a gust of wind and Bo's cap flew off, spinning down long depths of air toward the grass and trees of Central Park, where figures were already starting to scurry and dodge.

"That's it," Esko said. "We're done. Storm's coming."

He gestured south toward the swelling banks of cloud.

"Good," said Cristof, never unhappy about quitting work.

Esko tucked the handle of the tin can into his belt. Raising himself onto the crosswise beam, he accepted the riveting gun from Cristof, threw it across his shoulder like a rifle, and walked with sure step toward the upright, which he clasped tight, swinging himself around, his boot reaching for the first of the little steps fixed into the steel with temporary bolts so they could clamber up and down. Soon he was facing Gunnar as he passed the forge set up on the planks on the thirteenth story. Gunnar's gaunt face was aghast.

"What's the matter? Have you gone crazy?"

"I'd get down, if I were you. There's a storm brewing."

"Everybody else is still working."

Esko didn't have to glance around to know that this was true. Even as the sky turned blacker and the wind's random gusts grew more frequent, everyone else on the frame was still at it.

"Get back to work," Gunnar said, the stern leader in him unable to prevent a spasm of rage. "Right now. Otherwise you're fired, Offermans."

Only then did the building's Klaxon hoot, three long blasts, sounding the general retreat.

"Happy now?"

"You came down *before*."

"Oh shut up, Gunnar," called Cristof, his boot nudging at Esko's head as they made their way down to the firm floor of the twelfth story and safety.

"We were going so well," Gunnar said, huffing and muttering away.

Damned Swedes, Esko thought, they think they still rule the world.

"Yes," Cristof said. "And now we'll be able to go well tomorrow—thanks to Esko."

Men moved all around them, securing tools, lashing down the air compressors, the cement mixers, the bundles of steel that had such a sinister gleam in the dimness, then hurrying toward the hoists. We've been up here much too long, Esko thought, and as if to prove the point a gust rocked him on his feet, swirling dust and debris around his knees. Thunder pealed through the wind, calling up echoes from the crosstown canyons. Still the storm hadn't reached them, though it was dark as dusk now. Lightning flashed, filling in every corner of the steel frame with a startling blue light, so that each individual rivet sprang out as if photographed.

Even now not everyone was off the two unprotected levels of the frame.

Four men remained: the Mantilinis, going on as if there were no storm, no danger, as if nothing were happening, as if they were simply lobbing a baseball during lunch break. It was Steffano, Esko saw, who was manning the forge; with his tongs he took a burning rivet from the coals and lobbed it upward; one of his brothers caught it in his can, and then Paul Mantilini, the bucker-up, held it fast in the bolt hole while the fourth brother wielded his riveting gun, level-pegging with the coming thunder.

They're mad, thought Esko; but he also understood that there was something completely magnificent about their bravado and skill.

All the other men were shouting, calling to them.

"Get down!"

"There's a storm!"

"Clear the steel!"

"Get the hell down!"

Even Gunnar's imperturbable Swedish singsong joined the chorus. "All right, all right, you crazy Italians. You've proved your point."

"They're fucking idiots," said Cristof, but he was laughing, as if to say, yes, those Mantilinis, those crazy wops, they really had something.

Steffano turned away from his forge, glancing toward the onlookers, bobbing his head in a graceful little bow, and then holding up his forefinger, indicating one more rivet.

"Get down!" Bo was shouting.

"Get down!"

"Get down!"

The last rivet went flying on its way, aimed dead center at the catcher's can and Esko, though at this distance he couldn't hear it, imagined the sound . . . *plunk!*

Paul Mantilini darted across the scaffold, holding the rivet steady, while his brother moved in with the gun.

Like gladiators, they had triumphed, and all around him Esko saw the other men start to hoot and holler, to clap and shout and cheer, roaring their approval.

The brother with the riveting gun stood up straight, brandishing the gun above his head, shaking it, overalls billowing, the dark curls of his hair tossed by the wind, profiled against the blackness of the sky as though a human exclamation mark could be a hero.

Then he was gone.

"What? What happened?" said Gunnar, breaking a stunned silence.

Nobody even saw the body fall. That mark against the sky had simply vanished, as if rubbed out.

"Did he fall? Is he safe? Where is he?"

The forge tipped over, thrown by the wind, and red hot coals spilled over Steffano's legs and boots. His overalls caught fire, and he began a crazy little dance, jittering up and down, beating at the flames with his hands. Then the wind came again, and he too was falling, but inside the building, dropping down two stories and landing in front of their eyes with a noise like a pig dropped in a sack.

Rain struck. In those first moments the drops hammered singly against the frame, pinging the steel, heavy as ingots; but then the rain increased instantaneously with a hissing, rushing sound, and it was as if whole, continuous, massive volumes of water had suddenly been released from the sky and were pouring down so that the entire frame of the building groaned and throbbed under the weight of the attack. The wooden floor on which he was standing shook beneath Esko's boots even as it turned into a rink in front of his eye. The thunder was scarcely audible through the water. The worst, the incredible was happening. The plank scaffolding where Paul Mantilini was perched with the one remaining brother, the catcher, jerked crazily, attacked by a flurry of rain, and another of them was gone.

Esko didn't think or plan. There was no time to feel brave or afraid. Suddenly he was running, splashing through the rain that already ran deep on the wooden floor, slowing before he reached the edge, stepping carefully, not looking down even as the wind and rain struck him like a double blow, hugging the upright steel beam that was slick with wet and smelled like rust, swinging himself around, feeling for the first steel plate with his boot and starting to climb, face pressed sideways by the angled assault of the storm.

And then Esko stopped, alarmed by a movement in the air: he saw a seagull, tossed in by the wind, wheel toward him, and then sideslip, bearing down toward the shaking heads of the trees in the park.

Breathing deep, he moved again, hand over hand, reaching for the next step to grab onto, water splashing on his head as if from a spout, plastering his hair to his forehead while he pressed his body close to the steel. He climbed thirty feet through the rain this way, boots slipping, now pausing, now starting, passing Steffano's spilled, hissing forge, at last reaching the crossbeam where the three other Mantlinis had been working, squirming onto it, and then, like an eel, on his belly, inching along, buffeted by the wind, hammered by the rain, until he saw the plank scaffold, swaying three feet beneath him. His heart stopped, queasy, for no one was on the scaffold; but then he saw, through misting flurries of rain, a pair of legs, dangling and kicking, a pair of hands gripping the edge of the outermost plank, and a face pale as death with a pair of eyes looking up at him like dots on dice. It was Paul Mantilini, desperately holding on.

This time Esko paused a moment. Should I jump from here, try to grab him? Stupid, he thought, we'd both die. Instead, easing himself over the beam, he planted one foot on either side of the central plank, steadying the scaffold, still holding onto the steel while the wind drove the rain like arrows into his upright body. Then he ducked beneath the beam and jumped forward, timing immaculate, his big hand closing around the other's wrist; for what seemed like an eternity the scaffold swung to and fro while he held onto what he'd caught, his shoulder a slow scream of pain as the arm was slowly wrenched from its socket, until he grabbed Mantilini's other wrist and was at last able to haul him back onto the planks. The two men linked their arms. They breathed in unison. Together they got to their knees and grasped the steel beam above them, clutching it like drowning men in the ocean will cling to the edge of a lifeboat. They waited, soaked and gasping, until the sky began to lighten and slowly the storm abated.

"Steffano—is he alive?" said Mantilini, knowing for sure that his two other brothers couldn't have survived.

"I don't know," Esko said.

"Shit." Mantilini smacked his forehead against the steam beam. "Shit, shit," he said, his voice flat, banging harder so that blood mingled with the rain coursing down his face. "Shit."

"Easy," Esko said, resting his hand on the other's sopping sleeve.

"Fuck you. My brothers just died. Fuck you!"

Esko's hand gripped tighter. "Whether you like it or not."

The rain stopped, the wind subsided, and, with the black storm clouds moving slowly away, the two men dropped to their knees on the scaffold. The air was still surprisingly humid.

"I owe you my life," he said, more a growl than a vote of thanks.

"Don't mention it," said Esko. Looking down into the building he saw some of the other men milling around the prone figure of Steffano. Petroski was there, shouting, raising his arm and calling for a stretcher. "That little Polish *asshole*," Esko said, the spurt of rage shocking him as much as the impulsive American usage. And then he began to weep. Tears came unbidden, welling from deep inside. He covered his eye, his whole body shaking, with delayed fear, with release from tension, with the stirring of painful memories of those he'd been unable to save: Klaus, Bongman's Son, his mother. What a mess, what a ruin. "I saw the storm coming," he said. "I should have done something sooner. Maybe your brother, the one who was up here with you, maybe I could . . ."

"Are you crazy? Do you realize what you did coming up here to get me like that?"

"It wasn't *enough*," Esko said.

Mantilini was watching Esko in a different way now, with eyes narrow, judging him, assessing him. His gaze was cool, almost terrifyingly controlled, and something passed between the two men, a shared depth of feeling, passion, that they were careful to mask and struggled to constrain.

That cold gaze fell on the *puukko* at Esko's belt. "May I see?" he said, and before Esko knew what was happening, the blade was unsheathed in Mantilini's hand. "What is this?"

"A *puukko*. A Finnish knife. My father's gift to me."

Mantilini was nodding, inspecting the gleaming steel, and Esko felt a twinge of alarm, remembering his threat to cut Bo's throat.

With a quick motion Mantilini drew the knife across his own palm, watching thoughtfully, and for several seconds, as blood bloomed from the gash; then, quick as the previous action had been slow, he took Esko's hand in an iron grip, pushed in the point of the knife and drew it across.

Esko's hand ignited with pain; he tried to pull it back, but Mantilini wasn't letting go.

"Are you crazy?" Esko shouted.

"You ever need something, anything, you come to me," Mantilini said, pressing his hand against Esko's, rubbing them together so that the wounds grazed and drops of their comingled blood splashed fatly on the scaffold. "You're my brother now."

4

Some six weeks after the storm, in mid-August, Esko looked up Sixth Avenue and saw the air wobbling, wavering like a solid substance above the tarmac that oozed and sucked at his shoes. He'd never believed there could be such heat: ferocious, blinding, merciless, like being in a sauna with no cool lake to jump into, heat that offered no relief even at nightfall. Businessmen staggered by, sagging pillars of flesh, melting, crammed tight into cruel suits. Esko himself wore smoked glasses, a sleeveless cotton shirt, and light cotton pants; he was already dripping. A streetcar came up with a roar like an enraged beast. The black hood of a parked Chrysler was scalding to the touch. Beneath the elevated a train crashing overhead made kaleidoscopic, ever-changing patterns, slicing and dicing this filthy world and raining down hot cinders upon it. A sign said, RIDE ON THE OPEN AIR, and Esko gave a rueful look. There *was* no air. Manhattan was a steaming rag shoved down his throat, and it stank, of rotting fish, of maggoty meat, of dissolving fruit, of harbor bilge that carried with it the odor of some unspeakable decay.

He walked on, across to Seventh, seeking refuge, as every afternoon, in the cool shadows of Pennsylvania Station, passing along one of the grand arcades and walking down into the vast murmurous echo of the waiting room. Soaring fifteen stories high, vaulted, muraled, designed a decade or so earlier by Charles McKim (partner of the murdered Stanford White), the place was filled now with the breeze and rustling flutter of several hundred people fanning themselves, with fans, with magazines, with folded newspapers, with empty paper bags, with theater programs, with their hands and their train tickets if they had nothing bigger. Esko circled this space, so constructed, so generous, so civil, such a contrast to the burning waste of the avenue outside. He gazed at the enormous windows, through which great beams of moted light fell aslant on the marbled floor, and it seemed to him that McKim had understood that arrivals and departures were matters of mystical import, even for the young men in their skimmers, the women office workers in their hipless summer dresses, who were merely hurrying to and fro between the city and New Jersey; even they, every day, were filled with the bouncing hopes of their own story, and the few minutes they spent here would bolster them with the reminder that they too were creatures of infinite possibility; for Pennsylvania Station, even on a day like this, the filthiest and meanest of New York summer days, enclosed the harsh reality of the world as it was with a wonderful sense of how the world could be. Esko had been coming here every afternoon for more than a month now, ever since he discovered the place.

He was no longer working with the riveters. Gunnar and Cristof had taken off for California, for Los Angeles, where they'd heard a new city hall was going up. Bo had lost his nerve, or—as he put it—come to his senses, had in any event been burned by that terrible day, and had quit the high steel for good. He'd become pally with Paul Mantilini and was now engaged to the sister, Teresa. Esko hadn't seen or heard anything of any of them since the funeral, which had taken place at a cemetery high on a hill in Queens, the distant towers of Manhattan visible through the haze. Neither the construction company nor the hotel's financiers sent a human representative, though Petroski did arrange for a wreath in honor of the two dead brothers (Steffano having survived, with a smashed hip, both legs broken, and the possibility that he might never walk again), a wreath in the shape of a rivet, a round and imposing floral rivet that quite dominated the other tributes. Paul Mantilini had taken that wreath and sent it sailing through the air, saying he wanted no reminder of the manner of his brothers' deaths.

Esko's hand was itching. The scar did that when the weather was hot, and it had been scorching every day since. At the funeral Mantilini had made no reference to his stunt with the *puukko*, to their supposed blood-brotherliness, and Esko had been relieved. The gesture had been violent and melodramatic, even if understandable, and it was best forgotten, he thought; but that was the rational side of him talking, because he knew he'd always remember that moment when their eyes had locked up there on the scaffold and he'd seen something of himself reflected: an odd singlemindedness, a passion, a willingness to do whatever was required. He felt a little wary of Paul Mantilini and the idea that there might now be some inevitable connection between them, because he thought that perhaps Mantilini was a very dangerous young man. He thought that Mantilini would probably understand the Finnish idea of *sisu*, for he did indeed have the air of a man who was capable of anything.

There was also the alarming idea that Mantilini possessed some dark secret about America that he himself was not prepared to contemplate. For, despite the accident on the steel, despite his failure to make contact thus far with Katerina, despite his lack of funds (once again chronic), even despite the heat, Esko remained buoyant about New York and his prospects there. He truly believed that somehow, somewhere down the line, he really would do this unlikely thing—*he would build a skyscraper*. He knew it as surely as now, approaching the newsstand to buy a notebook, he knew the brand (Ticonderoga) of the pencil he was drawing out of the breast pocket of his shirt so that he could sketch some details of Mr. McKim's masterpiece, a building that, it seemed, had at last freed his hand to draw in New York. Optimism was America's national chemical, its opiate; he seemed to have ingested some of it.

On paying for the notebook Esko turned away from the newsstand, and his eye was caught by a tall, corpulent man, dressed in white, standing at the top of the stairs beneath the four-sided station clock. The man, who was bearded, frowned a little and glanced at his watch, not bothering with the clock, even though it was directly above his head. He began moving down the stairs with a restrained swagger, lazily kicking one foot in front of the other, a black drafting portfolio dangling from his left hand.

That man, Esko, thought, is Joseph Lazarus. Not, *that man reminds me of someone I met as a child*; nor, *that fellow is really rather like the engineer my father brought to the bell tower in the village.* It was knowledge, certainty. It was Lazarus, and as he approached, Esko saw that he'd grown heavier, ruddy in the face. His hair and his neat, spadelike beard were jet-black, gleaming black, too black, as if dyed. There was something vehement, almost coercive about his appearance, willing all these bustling New Yorkers to get out of his way. He must be sixty, Esko thought, but he was still a very handsome and impressive man, and his aging eyes were perhaps even sharper and more driven than before.

Lazarus transferred the portfolio to his right hand and looked again at his watch. He shrugged, theatrically, and shook his head.

He's waiting for someone and they're late and it'll be trouble for them, Esko said to himself. He remembered the wonderful story that Lazarus had told about building the bridge in German East Africa, that inspiring story. He thought too of the proposed bridge in Iisalmi, never built. What was the story there? Swept back in time, he even remembered the gray silk cravat Lazarus had worn. It had been stabbed through the heart by a pin clustered with pearls and diamonds. And then there'd been the ankle-length fur coat, glistening with jewels of melting snow. Lazarus had appeared clad in treasure. Esko shivered.

"Young man! Yes, you! You, young man!" The voice sounded like machine-gun fire. "You! You're staring at me! Do I know you?"

"You're Joseph Lazarus," Esko said, rushing forward and offering his hand.

"I am Lazarus," the other said, clicking his heels together and folding his hands together behind his back, bowing stiffly. He spoke English with a thick German accent, wielding this adopted language like a prop or weapon. "And you are?"

"Esko Offermans," he said, surprising himself by continuing to use the alias he'd all but forgotten in these last weeks.

"Offermans?" Those thick black eyebrows bunched together, frowning. "Do I know that name?"

"We met. A long time ago, in Finland. I was just a boy at the time."

"In Finland?" Lazarus snorted. "*Ach*, a benighted country. Moss and swamp. Black forests. Ice. Peasants huddling in huts. Wretched place."

"My father brought me to meet you. At the top of the bell tower in a church. You told me a story about a bridge you'd built in Africa. That story's stayed with me all my life."

Lazarus thumbed the fine linen of his suit lapel. His dark eyes shone, flattered.

"I'm an architect because of you," Esko said. Inheritance, chance, lots of different causes had made him what he was, but Lazarus was a part of it. "You started me on the way."

"You're an architect? Offermans, you say?" Lazarus was curious now. Rubbing his beard, narrowing his eyes, he searched back in his memory. "Of course, *ja, ja,* now I remember your father. The crazy fellow, the radical. Supposed to be my guide. How could I forget? He tried to murder someone. I lost a commission because of him and got out of that crazy country as fast as I could."

"He cost you a commission? How was that?"

"I was going to build a bridge in . . . what was the name of the place?"

"Iisalmi?"

"Never thought I'd hear that name again," Lazarus said, laughing. "You know what I remember about Iisalmi? Reindeer. Reindeer stew. Reindeer soup. Reindeer steak. Pudding of reindeer. The Finns ate so much reindeer I'm surprised there were any of the poor creatures left at Christmas to pull poor Santa's sleigh. The menus were hell." He showed his teeth, much brighter even than his white suit—false, presumably. "That lunatic was your father? And you're an architect, you say? Well, well. What have you done?"

"Three churches. In Finland. Before the war I was with Arnefelt and Bromberg."

"Bromberg died," Lazarus said with a casual pounce. "Didn't he?"

Evidently the career progress of any potential rival was important to him, even in benighted Finland.

"He was shot."

"He's designing *jugend* villas in heaven now, or the other place, the one with the lousy menus," Lazarus said with a merry flash of his brilliant teeth, gaze arrested by offending smut on his suit. "And in New York? What have you built here?"

"Nothing," said Esko, smiling himself now, refusing to be daunted.

"Nothing?" Lazarus studied him for a moment before his eyes lit, not with pleasure, but with glee really; he'd just found something very funny cavorting in the waiting room of his memory. "This is amazing. It is. *Amazing.* Because now I know who you are. Exactly. You are the little boy with the scars who asked about elevators." He laughed with wicked gusto. "You wanted to know what they meant. Did you even find out?"

"They mean a building can endlessly reproduce itself," Esko said with a smile, prepared to join in the mockery of his own childhood earnestness. "They make the skyscraper possible."

This tickled Lazarus still further. "And now, don't tell me—you are going to build one! The tallest and most beautiful in New York."

"That's right."

"Ha! You Offermans guys. You are all lunatics. Dreamers."

But his voice changed when he saw that Esko's face didn't.

"You're serious?"

"Very."

Lazarus sighed, not unhappily, anticipating the defeat he was sure Esko would come to know, because such was the business of life. "Good luck," he said, and clumsily raised the hand that was holding the portfolio to take another look at his watch. "Where is that fellow? I have a train to catch. Good-bye, Herr Offermans. Good luck with your *wolkenkratzer*. What do you call them in Finland?"

"*Pilvenpiirtaja.*"

"How could I forget? Good-bye, good-bye."

Esko watched the broad back of that white suit weave through the crowd toward the stairs, and it was just beginning to dawn on him that he'd been brushed off when Lazarus span on his heel and came back, moving with the easy confidence of a gunboat approaching an unprotected enemy position.

He stopped, evidently weighing something. "Maybe I too am a lunatic," he said at last. "Who knows? But I have this crazy hunch. About you, Esko Offermans. I will give you a chance. We will make a joint entry. Split the prize money if we win."

"Prize money?" said Esko, baffled.

"The *Gazette* contest. Haven't you heard about it? They have announced a great competition. For a skyscraper."

5

Lazarus had his offices in a brownstone on Forty-seventh Street, close to *Vanity Fair*. The plaque outside was as immodest as the building itself was unassuming: JOSEPH LAZARUS, ARTIST, ARCHITECT, ENGINEER, & MASTER CRAFTSMAN, it ran, addressing the street in clean script on polished brass.

"If New York has taught me anything," Lazarus said, wheezing a little, catching Esko's eye on the plaque, "it's that you must toot your own horn, as the Americans say. And run a tight ship."

He explained that he thinned out his staff ruthlessly. Draftsmen kept coming and going. Secretaries tended to last only a week. He told Esko this while they entered the building and pressed themselves into an elevator narrow and airless as a coffin. "Our arrangement is just for the competition," he said. "I don't want you to get any ideas."

"Understood," Esko said.

"And my office is nothing special, but I get work. Lots of work," he said, as the elevator began its groaning ascent. "I'm not like one of those Yale or Harvard guys with all their rich old-money contacts. I hate them. After Harry Thaw killed Stanford White they should have given him a machine gun. Encouraged him to kill the whole damn lot. I tell you, Offermans, one of the big lies the Americans tell themselves is that they don't have a system of class and privilege. They do! It's worse than Berlin." He sniffed. "Maybe not so bad as London. But bad enough."

Esko glanced at Lazarus, taken by the energy and fire of a man his age, impressed that even now he was hungry, eager to build. It was the afternoon following their meeting in Pennsylvania Station, another day of hideous New York heat.

Lazarus, sweating profusely, pulled open the doors and led the way out of the elevator on the fourth, and top, floor, pointing out the door that led to his own office, the draftsmen's room, and then showing Esko his own space within the operation, a suffocating windowless room inside which were crammed two steel desks, a Bakelite steel bin, a steel bookcase piled high with dusty volumes of building codes, a wooden swivel chair behind each desk, and a white telephone.

"Don't worry," Lazarus said. "I'll keep checking in with you."

He left Esko with the advertisement for the *Gazette* contest.

$50,000 PRIZE FOR ARCHITECT WHO DESIGNS WORLD'S MOST BEAUTIFUL SKYSCRAPER. The building is not only to be striking and impressive—its practical purpose must be taken into account. It must house all the newspaper's departments, including the printing works. The building is to be a vigorous form, a skyscraper capable of inspiring the readers of the entire universe.

Prosaic detail followed this celestial hyperbole, including a list of conditions, the names of the jury members (none of them familiar to Esko), the location and dimensions of the site, and, particularly, details of the 1916 New York zoning ordinance that regulated building heights through a series of setbacks; the idea was that the skyscraper could proceed directly upward off the lot only to a certain height—then the building must step back to admit light to the street. Reading this, Esko realized that this zoning law was a design project as well as a legal requirement. New York skyscrapers would assume the form of Babylonian ziggurats, tiered like cakes.

Esko was leaning back in the swivel chair, feet on the desk, studying all this, when the door opened and a young woman with bright eyes and a sunburned face came in. She gazed at him for a moment, gave him an offhand smile, sat down at the other desk and took from her bag a device that turned out to be a miniature electric fan.

"I'm Esko Offermans. Are you working on the competition too?" Esko said, wondering with vague panic whether Lazarus had been trawling the streets, offering this opportunity to every architect he could find.

"I'm Miss Kott," she said, setting the fan humming with the press of a button. "I'm your secretary."

"Well, Miss Kott, that's fine."

Esko was both a little relieved and a little puzzled; what was he supposed to do with a secretary?

"Miss Kott—are you here to spy on me?"

Miss Kott just smiled, turning her attention to her vermilion fingernails, wafting them in front of the fan.

Over lunch Lazarus had been quite frank, saying that the only reason he was taking Esko aboard was because he himself was too busy, the competition deadline being only two weeks away. "Anyway you've got no chance. Every great architect in the world has been invited to enter," Lazarus had said, goading him with a tone of lofty patronage, sucking at an oyster shell with boisterous lips. Esko had thought, "I'll show *you*," knowing that this was the expected response. Lazarus was clever, manipulative, already applying pressure, putting him on his mettle, wanting to see if he had any stuff. Not that

Esko minded; actually he rather liked the idea; he was going to do something that would knock the socks off Joe Lazarus.

Kicking his feet off the desk, he picked up sketchbook and pencils, slung his jacket over his shoulder, clapped a hat on his head, donned his smoked glasses, and paused at the door to nod at Miss Kott, who was gazing at him over her whirring fan.

"When will you be back?"

"When I'm ready, Miss Kott. When I'm good and ready," Esko said with a genial smile.

The site picked by the *Gazette* was on Forty-second Street, close to the el and the banks of the East River, a bold spot for a company's signature building, and not only a cheap one, an announcement that this entire neighborhood was to be dragged up by its boot straps. In 1922 there was nothing within several city blocks to compete with; the new building would dictate the tone for an entire area that Esko saw as he strolled through it was comprised of boarded-up tenements, run-down antique shops, looming gas tanks, steaming laundries, and shabby tailors' shops, all soot blackened from the nearby breweries and power plants.

No big skyscraper had gone up in New York since the Woolworth, and part of the job here, part of the opportunity, he knew, was to make a building that would truly reflect the new century, the postwar world that was vital, energetic, and disillusioned with the past in a way that seemed as justified as it was frantic and a little desperate. Louis Sullivan, the father of the skyscraper, had a simple dictum: form follows function. For thousands of years engineers and architects had been checked in the quest for height because the walls of a building had to carry its weight. Hence the shape of the pyramids. Hence the tendency of medieval cathedrals to keel over. In the 1870s steel frame construction swept away this problem. Skyscrapers were suddenly possible, waiting only for one further encouragement—Esko's old friend, the electric elevator—to bid them grow. Now the steel bore the weight; thin walls of stone or concrete were simply slotted in as the frame went up, a process Esko had observed firsthand with Mantilini and Bo and the others. The walls were only a suit, not the body, and, like a suit, they could be dressed with as many frills, as much ornamentation, as the architect and client desired. Cass Gilbert, when he did the Woolworth, tailored it as a cathedral, a cathedral of money but a cathedral nonetheless, because that, for him, or more likely for Mr. Woolworth, was what tall meant. Tall = Chartres. Tall = Rheims. The gorgeous Woolworth was a hybrid, ersatz antiquity. The electric air of New York in 1922 called for something new. The world had changed; Esko felt that, he'd seen it. Millions had died in the European war; empires had fallen and a new empire had arisen, here, in America, the land of the automobile, the radio, the camera, the motion picture, the land of the first truly modern city—New York.

Walking, thinking about all this, Esko came to a ramshackle pier where he persuaded a tugboat captain to give him a ride out onto the river. Soon waves were slapping and sliding against the sides of the puttering tug. A pair of gulls screeched and cackled above his head, squabbling over the carcass of a fish, and he absentmindedly rubbed his shoulder, still sore sometimes from where Paul Mantilini had almost wrenched it out of its socket. He stood at the back of the boat, regarding the shore. The distant skyscrapers of lower Manhattan shimmered in the haze. A breeze brought with it the fresh ozone tang, lifting the hat on his head. Sunlight glinted atop one of the gas tanks that looked down upon the waterfront piers. Back there, up close, on the street, he had noticed only how rusty and dilapidated those old gas tanks looked. Now, as the tugboat idled on the deep, slow-moving river waters, it was possible to see the clarity and purity of their original lines. They rose stark and unadorned, wavering in the heat, liberated from surface detail, soaring, with nothing to detract from their supreme and most sublime quality—their form, their height.

He opened his sketchbook and quickly outlined the gas tanks, the factories, the power plant, the slaughterhouse, the brownstones that faced him on the shoreline. Then he drew on top of this gaggle of buildings, envisioning an exclusively vertical style of architecture. He sketched a new skyline, a forest growing tall and proud, as if ugly seeds had grown into mighty, glorious trees. At once he saw that if all the buildings were to rise so very tall, there would necessarily be fewer of them. So he turned the page and went at it again with the pencil, spacing the skyscrapers on a grid, surrounding them with parks, connecting them with raised concrete roadways along which cars would run. The street, with all its confusion and filth and mess, would be eliminated. The cogged angles and junk of this part of New York would be swept away, replaced by immense clear crystals of steel and glass, by an architecture that was in itself a symbol of equality, of humanity, of conflict banished. The whole East River shoreline would be a utopia, a very modernized Venice, a city of arcades, plazas, and bridges, with canals for streets, canals filled not with water but with freely flowing automobile traffic, the sun glistening on the black tops of the cars while the shimmering glass in the buildings reflected back those waving floods of traffic.

Laying down his sketchbook, Esko gripped the tugboat rail and looked back again to the shore, his eye seeing not what was there but what would be. In Italy, in the Renaissance, artists had worked for the popes and the Borgias. He would work for the riveters, for Bo and Gunnar and the memory of the two dead Mantilini brothers, for the secretaries and the young men in skimmers who hurried through Pennsylvania Station, for Klaus and Bongman's Son, for the common man to whom the future must belong. This new Venice would rise in New York like a beacon, a bargain made with the infant century. We can be better, it would say; we can bring beauty into the world.

The tugboat captain noticed his passenger pacing the stern, aflame with concentration and excitement. For at a stroke Esko saw himself the architect of a metropolis within the metropolis, the articulator of a splendid social effort. And why not? He'd been offered twenty churches. Why *not* twenty skyscrapers? For it to begin to happen, all he had to do was design one bold and beautiful one. He had to win the *Gazette* contest, that was all—just beat out every major architect in the world.

Esko slammed his palms together. I'll do it, he said to himself, and he knew just how, for the prize-winning entry had been burning inside his mind since he was eleven years old.

"Miss Kott," he said, when he got back to the office on Forty-seventh Street, "we are going to work!"

But then the door banged open and Lazarus came in, mopping at his forehead with a linen handkerchief. Espying Miss Kott's minature fan, he seized it and held the whirring blades beneath his chin. "Great news," he said, evidently very pleased with himself. "While you have been out walking, Herr Offermans, I have been at work. I've just met with a friend who is on intimate terms with one of the *Gazette* judges. In fact they were in bed together last night."

He turned to Miss Kott with a slow wink. "Excuse me, my dear," he said. "But the point is this—the judge told his friend, *my* friend, something very interesting. A Gothic tower will win the contest. They want a Gothic tower. Something like the Woolworth."

He put the fan back down on Miss Kott's desk. "Where did you get this? It was cheap? I want one," he said, shameless, exuberant, fingering the red suspenders that climbed over his stout belly. "That makes things easier, wouldn't you say? Narrows the field. It's Gothic. It's official. A design like the Woolworth, different, but not too different. It's simple, *ja?*"

Esko was still a moment. "No," he said finally.

Lazarus shot his hands forward. His huge-cuffed silk shirt was of a gallant jade hue. "You want to have a chance to win? You want my office to send in your entry. Then it is *commercial gothic*, my friend. You think you can always control your own work? In Finland, maybe you do just as you like, a bit of this and that on the ice. In New York we live in the real world. In this instance, a world that wants another Notre Dame of the dollar."

Esko stood up, reaching for his hat from the hot metal of the desk. "Then I'll design for someone else," he said.

Lazarus threw up his hands, throwing his eyes to the ceiling. "Miss Kott, it's my fault! I blame myself. I find this man in Pennsylvania Station. I should have known better." He wailed theatrically, operatically, Pagliacci betrayed yet again. "I have given the job to an idiot!"

Esko didn't quit, though he spent the next days in an agony, unable to think or draw. Everything that had been flowing so enthusiastically inside him now stopped and froze. He stared at the blank paper on his desk and it was as though blocks of ice were grinding and creaking inside him, coalescing into a solid mass of frustration.

"The man has no ideals or principles," he protested to Miss Kott. "He doesn't care about building. He just wants the commission, whatever it takes."

Miss Kott sniffed.

"I've met men like him before," he said, which was true. Oskari Bromberg had been like that. Esko also understood that this was the way architectural competitions always worked. Judges had their preferences, often stupid ones; in some way or other the fix was usually in. He wasn't naive, he'd gathered all this during his professional life thus far; but a part of him screamed out against it. "He'd sell his grandmother's soul for a job."

"Probably," said Miss Kott.

What it comes down to is this, Esko thought—how badly do I want to win? The answer was easy; he wanted to win very badly indeed. The twenty skyscrapers had to start with one. At the same time he wasn't prepared to compromise, at least not on Lazarus's terms. So here was the trick: how to take business, the past, the true spirit of America, his own passionate search for form, and spin them together into an irresistible song that would convince the judges they were getting what they wanted, while in fact . . .

A smile passed across his face as he thought of a scene in "Kalevala," of the old magician singing and chanting, making his enemy sink into oozing swamp with the power of his spell, and then raising him out again.

"Miss Kott!" Esko called, and there was a click as she turned off her little electric fan. "I just had an idea. I'm going to give them all a show."

"Fabulous," Miss Kott said with a bored air. "Will it be as good as the ball game?"

"Better, Miss Kott. Much better."

First he and Miss Kott emptied the suffocating, airless office. They took out Esko's desk, his chair, the steel bookcase, the various volumes of building codes, heavy as slabs, stacking everything in the corridor outside. They left only Miss Kott's desk, which they pushed back against the wall, and her chair, and her little fan. Esko even disconnected the phone before sweeping the floor until it was spotless. "I'll be back," he told her.

He returned a little less than an hour later, followed by a procession of workmen, each bearing two buckets of slopping clay.

"What's going on?" Lazarus said, bustling out of his office, thumb hooked behind a red suspender. "What is this? Are you proposing now to start a kindergarten?"

"I realized something this morning," Esko said, rolling up his sleeves and plunging his hands into one of the buckets. "I was thinking about the zoning law and the setbacks." Two handfuls of clay were dumped on the floor, then two more. "You see, Joe, what the setbacks mean is a change in the relationship between the building and the air itself. Do you see?"

"Not quite," Lazarus said in a dry voice.

"The setbacks mean that a tall building must be sculpted, as if the air itself had cut and carved it. Now do you understand. I won't draw the design. I'll shape it."

Lazarus's face confessed that Esko had something.

Esko added four more big handfuls of clay. "There won't be any ornamentation on this building."

Lazarus more or less moaned. "It must be *Gothic*."

"I'll stick to the most fundamental principle of the Gothic tower, and *only* that one. The mass will taper to the top. It'll be Gothic, all right, but my Gothic, not much like the Woolworth." Down on his hands and knees Esko began shaping the clay with his *puukko*. The pale gray clay was wet to the touch but with a pleasant, slightly chalky smell; it sliced easily, like tender flesh. "You still here, Joe?"

"Where's my telephone?"

"In the trash. I'll resume communication with the world when I'm good and ready."

Esko worked day and night, staying until the small hours of the morning when the neon dimmed on Broadway and the lonely lights glowed like lanterns in the tall buildings and the murmurs and hoots and distant echoes of cars and boats crept through the thick and stealthy dark. It was then that Esko could almost believe in the radiant and romantic promise of New York, a Cinderella of a city, not only a place but the dream of everyone who went there.

Slowly, during those next days, Esko's design for the skyscraper began to take form. One morning Miss Kott arrived at the office to find Esko already there, as usual, no longer on his hands and knees, but standing up straight, because the sculpture had already reached chest height. She raised her eyebrows, stepping around the mass of clay to get to her desk, behind which she sheltered with her fan spinning for additional protection in case Esko got it into his head to try anything really crazy.

By now the rising tower of clay had ceased to be a spectacle that provoked only amusement. There was still some hostility, but people were starting to be impressed. The model was like an upward sweeping force, a slender fountain soaring up in clay. Even Lazarus was pleased. "Finland may turn out to have something after all, Miss Kott," he said, scratching his cheek.

Late one night Esko was coming back from the washroom when he noticed the smell of cigarette smoke, sweet, Turkish, and he walked into his office to see a man standing there, quite casually, inspecting the almost completed clay model. The man was handsome, slender, of medium height, smoothly shaven, with a straight narrow nose and a dimple in his chin. His hair was fair, longish, and slicked back. He was in evening dress, but tieless, and a silk scarf was draped around his neck like a shining white noose. His youthful face puckered a little as he took another drag on the cigarette.

"Well now," he said at last. His voice was lazy and cultivated, a drawl that protested against the requirement of having to speak at all. His grayish-blue eyes stayed locked on the model. "Who *are* you?"

"And who are you to barge in here as though you own the place?"

A finger went up to the dimpled chin. A hand slipped into a jacket pocket, coming out again with a cigarette case of slim platinum. "Want one? Suit yourself," he said with a shrug, tapping a cigarette against the case, lighting it, exhaling clouds of smoke, in no hurry. "As a matter of fact I do own this building," he said. His air of superiority was bantering but complete, Esko thought, no doubt put in his mouth at birth, along with the silver spoon. "I own most of the street, now that you mention it."

"Bully for you," Esko said, refusing to be impressed.

The other shrugged, indifferent. "This your work?" he said, cigarette poised in the corner of his mouth, eyes squinting against the smoke.

"It is."

"It's beautiful," he said with no particular emphasis, though Esko got the curious sense that he meant what he said; Esko was pleased, of course.

"For the *Gazette* contest?"

"That's right."

"Might win."

"There's always that chance."

"Joe's been hiding you away, hasn't he? He didn't mention anything about hiring a new architect."

"It's just for the competition—a joint entry."

"Really?" he said, exhaling. "Where are you from?"

"Finland."

"And now you propose to win the *Gazette* competition and rebuild a substantial proportion of the city where I grew up. My father would be most upset."

"I'm sorry about that."

"Don't be. He's dead." With his finger he dabbed a speck of tobacco off his tongue. "I'm Andrew MacCormick, by the way."

"Esko Offermans." The two men stepped around the tall clay model to shake hands. "You know Lazarus?"

"Oh sure, I've known Joe for years," MacCormick said. "He's built a lot of things for me down in Miami. A couple of hotels, a country club, a house or two. Joe pretty much rules the roost down there, not that there's much competition. Anyone tries to poach on his territory Joe says 'Boo!' and they go away. Now New York, that's a different story. He's yet to have quite the same success here."

Esko absorbed this without disappointment, Joe Lazarus's standing in New York being no obstruction to their chances of winning the contest. In fact this information endeared Lazarus to him, if anything. Esko was always on the side of the underdog.

"You're a speculator?"

MacCormick turned his head to the ceiling to avoid blowing smoke on the clay model. "I put money together with ideas to make more money. Is that what a speculator does? Then I guess I am one," he said. When he looked back at Esko it was with a laconic smile. "Joe's very jealous about me, you know. Always afraid I'll defect to some other architect's camp."

"Will you?"

MacCormick laughed, surprised by such directness. "I like loyalty in others so I try to be loyal myself. But then I'm a businessman, and I do like architects."

"You like Joe Lazarus?"

"Well enough. He gets things done. He knows how the world goes. He buys lunches, pours liquor into people, and at the end of the day the job he does is not too shabby. You're different in every way, I bet."

"Is that a compliment?"

"Take it any way you like," MacCormick said. "Good luck in the contest."

6

Esko made a perspective drawing of his design on fine quality drafting paper; he completed the elevations and the longitudinal sections; all these were sent to the *Gazette* offices along with the clay model of the skyscraper in time for the competition deadline. All he had to do then was wait for the results.

During the next two months, throughout the fall of 1922, while Benito Mussolini, Il Duce, came to power in Italy, while the German mark collapsed, sending inflation through the roof and an audience of fifty thousand hurrying to listen to a political upstart named Adolf Hitler, while Tutankhamen's tomb was indeed opened, revealing treasures unheard of, while movie mogul Samuel Goldwyn journeyed to Europe, announcing that he was offering $100,000 to Sigmund Freud, the celebrated doctor of love, for advice on a series of motion pictures dealing with erotic subjects, while King Oliver's Chicago jazz band was joined by a promising young second trumpet named Louis Armstrong (he was discovered playing funerals), the *Gazette* boosted itself and its wisdom in concocting the skyscraper contest by running a series of articles devoted to great architecture through the ages: the Tower of Babel, the Pyramids, the Parthenon, the Coliseum, Notre Dame, St. Peter's in Rome, Thomas Jefferson's mansion at Monticello, the Eiffel Tower in Paris. There being no mention of any building later than that, the inference was clear: the winning entry would be the next to join this line of ultimate architectural prestige.

Esko noticed something odd during this time. The making of the model, the doing of the design, his immersion in it positioned him in the life of the city in a new way. The waitresses in the diner where he still ate breakfast each morning treated him like a regular. The young man behind the desk in the New York public library smiled and greeted him by name. His long hikes throughout the city were guided by a knowledge of the streets that had entered his blood as if through the soles of his shoes. At Lazarus's office, where he continued to work, helping on the design of a hotel down in Miami and throwing in ideas for a number of commissions that Lazarus was hoping to win in New York, he became an accepted and familiar presence, liked because he worked hard and was prepared to help anyone. He was still an outsider but no longer an observer, and because he felt this, because in some way his *Gazette* entry had already fulfilled such an important purpose, had already given him so much, for a long time he didn't even worry at all about the competition itself. The matter was out of his hands, after all, and he was sure that if any useful politicking could be done, then Joe Lazarus was busily doing it. So Esko was calm, until four days before the results were to be announced. Then suddenly, walking through snow on Sixth Avenue, he thought—what if I win? It wasn't the fanfare of trumpets he dreamed of (well, only a little of that), but the thrill he would experience when the first rivet was driven home, and the skyscraper, his skyscraper, began to rise. He thought of telling Katerina, not boastfully, but as if for the first time he could appear to her as a completed person—the real Esko, the full man, ready to receive the full measure of her love. He told himself not to be so stupid, that it didn't matter; the work was the important thing, he *knew* that. Yet he also knew that what the outside world decided did indeed matter, that a judgment was about to be made, perhaps already had been made, that could change his life in some small or perhaps big way. He was a Finn, and as a Finn he took winning and losing very seriously. He at last began to appreciate the romance and drama of the competition itself. A skyscraper would be built, an architect plucked from obscurity and made famous. Why not him? Why not, indeed?

The announcement was scheduled for Friday, December 11. The day before, he took the telephone in his office out from the drawer into which he'd stuffed it, swaddled in towels. He stared at the telephone; he pondered it, willing it to ring.

"You're driving me crazy," Miss Kott told him, filing her nails. "It'll be in the paper tomorrow, along with something about that guy who's going to the chair. So what's the big deal? Go to the movies."

"Miss Kott, you're right," he said. He put on his coat and spent most of the rest of the day and all of the evening surrounded by human tears and human laughter in the glimmering dark, rushing from *The Birth of the Nation* at the Selwyn, to a reissue of *All Night* with Rudolph Valentino at the Loew's, to Rex Ingram's *The Prisoner of Zenda* at the Plaza, and then on to the Rialto to see Buster Keaton emerging from a Manhattan subway kiosk in the middle of a snowy wilderness in *The Frozen North*, and ending with the new Chaplin two-reeler, *Pay Day*, in which Charlie held onto a salami in a lunch wagon as if it were a strap in a subway car. It was after midnight when he emerged from the Rialto, and beneath the awning, he turned up his collar against the real snow that was falling, a bell of excitement ringing in his mind. The morning editions were on the street already.

A gusting wind whistled down Broadway, swirling snow in his face and flapping the thin pages of the *Gazette*. Next to a front page headline proclaiming "Is Boy Crime Wave Our Fault?" he saw "*Gazette* Announces Contest Winners." He leafed anxiously through the paper until he found this:

DESIGN NUMBER 92
BY PETER WINROB
CHICAGO
FIRST PRIZE—$50,000

DESIGN NUMBER 180
BY JOSEPH LAZARUS & ESKO OFFERMANS
NEW YORK
SECOND PRIZE—$30,000

DESIGN NUMBER 22
BY FRITZ HOOSMANS & JAN SCHMIDT
AMSTERDAM, HOLLAND
THIRD PRIZE—$20,000

He read on, not quite sure yet whether the little men bouncing up and down in his stomach were performing a celebratory jig or a sad waltz of despair. He hadn't won, but on the other hand—second prize! Back in Finland architects made whole careers out of coming in second. Something might really come of this.

> There is no precedent for this great contest, which has drawn upon the genius of the old world and the new. The competitive method is adopted in the case of public buildings with increasing frequency, but the new *Gazette* building will be the first privately owned edifice, the design for which was awarded in a prize competition open to the best architects in the world. There has never been such a competition and it is very doubtful that there will be another.
>
> The *Gazette's* desire to erect the most beautiful and distinctive office building in the world is now certain of fulfillment. The response to our invitation was in no way short of magnificent. Three designs received prizes, but there are a dozen or more, any of which, if erected, would easily surpass any skyscraper in New York and compare favorably with the highest achievements in the field of architecture anywhere. Thus our contest has achieved two aims in a most triumphant way: first, to provide the *Gazette* with the greatest building in New York: second, to stimulate architectural genius and bring forth works of beauty. These were the hopes of the *Gazette* and they have been fully realized. The jury's decision was unanimous and, as stated in the entry regulations, cannot be disputed.

Next morning Esko arrived at the brownstone on Forty-seventh Street and found, a little to his surprise, that a celebration was already in progress. On seeing Esko, Joe Lazarus shook up a golden-necked bottle and sprayed some champagne about.

"Wonderful news," he said showing his even teeth, clutching Esko in an embrace. "It is absurd, *naturlich*, about Peter Winrob and a great shame that Harry Thaw never got as far as Chicago. For Winrob should be dead in the ground in reality. He's dead for sure as an architect. I heard from the *Gazette* that they are setting up the exhibition of all the entries. *Komm mitt.*"

Esko was dazzled, amused by Lazarus's energy. "Now?" he said.

"Certainly now. Definitely now. Right now," said Lazarus. Donning an ankle-length coat of sleek fur, jamming on a fur hat, he snatched up a cane and took Esko by the arm even before Esko had time to chink glasses with Miss Kott. Soon they were in a taxi, skidding north through snow and clouds of rising steam, and Esko found himself joining in the excitement, entranced as he had been as a little boy by the explosive energy of this peacock figure, Lazarus.

"You're pleased?" Esko said.

"Very. So should you be, Esko Offermans," Lazarus said, swishing his cane like a sword, laughing. "It's a *beautiful* morning."

"Where are they doing this—the exhibition?"

"At the Plaza."

Esko nodded, wondering why he'd had a premonition that Lazarus would say that. At the Plaza, where he'd stayed on first arriving in New York, they knew him as Esko Vaananen, and while it was unlikely that a doorman or concierge would recognize him and blurt out his name, this was something that had best be cleared up now.

"Look, Joe. There's something crazy I have to tell you. My name isn't Esko Offermans. It's Esko Vaananen."

The taxi rolled to a halt, throbbing in the blizzard in Grand Army Plaza. Beyond Lazarus's face, through the window, Esko saw a barren tree leaning toward the frozen fountain, its branches snapping under the weight of driven snow.

"Have you done something you shouldn't?" Lazarus said, regarding him with a frown. "Are you involved in espionage like your father? You're a Bolshevik, don't tell me."

"Nothing like that. You have my word."

"Then why?"

It was a question Esko had asked himself a number of times during these last months, and he still wasn't sure he knew. It had seemed quite natural, back at the beginning of the year, when Bo had asked him for his name, to say: "Esko Offermans." It had been a way of cutting himself off from the past, of announcing to himself that he was beginning a journey that would also be a transformation.

"I only know that I need my name back now," he said.

Lazarus arched an eyebrow, but then he leaned over and tapped Esko on the knee, climbing into the opportunity to be gracious, seeming to understand Esko's plight better than Esko did himself.

"My dear boy, don't worry," he said expansively. Then he laughed out loud, his eyebrows bunching together in a frown. "I'll have to get used to this. Your real name again, if you please."

"Vaananen. Esko Vaananen."

"Vaa-na-nen?"

"That's right. My apologies—I lied."

"Forget about it. It doesn't matter at all," Lazarus said, pulling off his leather gloves, folding them carefully and pushing them into his coat pocket, watching a muffled doorman who'd been standing in a sentry box beneath the marquee of the Plaza spring forward into the snow, popping open a wide black umbrella in front of him like a thought coming into bloom. "Let us go now and heap scorn on Peter Winrob."

People were busy in the tall, chandeliered ballroom, bringing in the competition entries, fixing them to the walls. With satisfaction Esko noticed his clay model, mounted on a raised stage at the far end of the room along with the first- and third-place entries.

Flat-foot, splay-footed Lazarus was moving in that direction, his voice already beginning to shoot forth missiles of superb scorn.

"Look! Is it not grotesque? It is a design that fifty years ago even the English would have laughed at. Even the English, those architectural nonentities. Tell me, Offer—*Vaananen*. Does this not make your blood boil? Does this not make you wish to spit or to work with your knife, your *puukko* or whatever you call it. Give it to me now. Please, please. *Ach*, it's terrible. The judges should be ashamed. We have been *cheated*."

It was true. Winrob's entry was Gothic gowned, Gothic crowned, plastered with flying buttresses, decorative gargoyles, and false ornamental masonry. It belonged elsewhere, in another time, or in an overheated fiction by Edgar Allan Poe; certainly it didn't belong high in the sky above the jazzy, jiving, tooting, never-resting streets of New York; certainly Esko wasn't being arrogant when he thought his own design better—he was merely being objective.

Lazarus stamped his boot. "The judges were blind men. It is the only way to account for it," he said, glaring at Peter Winrob's entry with anger as precise and violent as a dagger. "Something must be done."

Esko smiled, knowing that Lazarus had a point, knowing too that there was nothing to be done. The competition was over. The judges' decision was bad but final and Finnish stoicism was a more appropriate response than Wagnerian rage, and so, tracing his fingers fondly across the smooth, sculpted clay of his own entry, he walked around, turning his attention to what was being put on the walls, all the other entries, an extraordinary survey of how architects from around the world viewed the skyscraper and its present state of development, a point about which there seemed to be considerable, indeed amazing, areas of difference. There were Beaux Arts wedding cakes, with layers and tiers and curlicues. There were lots more Gothic towers, as if the secret really had been out, most of them of the "Fall of the House of Usher" variety, and two columnar skyscrapers that suggested the perpetrating architects had visited Athens and viewed the Parthenon, but only from afar, and while working at retsina-lubricated leisure. There were two entries that would have been built in glass from the Gropius gang in Germany, beautiful, but statements of some crystalline future ideal rather than practical possibilities at this point in time. There was even a concrete tower with a concrete typewriter on top of it, the architect having taken Sullivan's "form follows function" rule and applied it in a doggedly literal way to what was, after all, the proposed home of a newspaper.

Esko, like Lazarus, was angry that they hadn't won; but he was able to hide it a lot better and to take something too from the inspection of these other entries, which, viewed together, showed a chaotic striving, a puzzled attempt to figure out what architecture should be doing in the modern world. He saw that this was a great time to be in the architectural profession, the moon plump in the sky and begging to be shot for; and he knew now for sure that he was on equal terms with the best. In this hunt that was afoot he was perhaps even ahead of the pack; having come from a little-known country that was very out of the way of things, this made him feel good.

Then he came to the last design.

It was hung down low, at the end of the wall, and as he espied it, he stopped breathing, so struck that he had to turn his eye away before he dared look again, only to find that this second, more careful inspection merely confirmed a feeling of shock that almost at once turned to wonder.

The design was crisp and sharp, cool almost, drawn without ostentation, with smooth horizontal planes that seemed to float, interrupting the verticality of the building without in any way denying it or detracting from it. Having visited the *Gazette* site, Esko knew at once that this design belonged to it, and that his self-congratulation of a moment ago was misplaced. Whoever had done this was way ahead of him. The design seemed to dance; it had arisen from the chrysalis of the present, without any bogus sentiment. It was the future, delicate and lovely as a butterfly.

Esko didn't resent it. On the contrary, it left him as excellent work always did—exhilarated, uplifted. He was affected, moved; the perfection and passion of this work didn't merely take his breath away; it made him want to follow.

And yet this glorious design hadn't finished first, second, or third; it wasn't even decorated with one of the red rosettes indicating honorable mention. In the jury's judgment, it was nowhere, a nothing.

"Who's W. P. Kirby?" Esko said to Lazarus, for that was the name on the card at the bottom of the design. "William P. Kirby, from New York. Who is he?"

"Isn't he dead?" Lazarus said. "*Ja, ja.* I think he is one of the ones Harry Thaw got to."

"Apparently not," said Esko, trying to draw his attention to the design.

Lazarus glanced at it for only a moment. "Not bad," he said, in his quick, clipped way. "Now, Esko. This business about your names. Offermans. Vaananen. It's a little confusing, and I've been thinking. The interviews. I should handle them all I think."

"Interviews?"

"All the press and that tedious so on and so forth."

"You'll deal with the press?"

"It would be better—no?"

"Sure," Esko said, happy to be free of a responsibility he hadn't even considered. "Why not?"

Then he turned back to W. P. Kirby's miracle in pencil, knowing that his whole attitude toward his work was going to have to change.

7

Two days later a letter was published, not in the *Gazette* itself, but in the mighty *New York Times*.

"Architect Attacks 'Phony' Contest," was the headline.

"I write as an architect, as one whose passion is his profession," W. P. Kirby began.

> Now it is in the nature of such affairs as the recent *Gazette* contest that they are contrived and phony and subject to corruption and compromise. I accept that, and while others will no doubt argue that I'm raising my voice now in tones of spite and envy (my own entry having been ignored), let me assure your readers that I do so only from a sense of injustice that has been done and from my convictions regarding some wider, indeed vital, issues that this injustice suggests.
>
> To be blunt: the winning design doesn't belong in this great city of ours. It doesn't belong anywhere, except in a museum. This is dangerous because a new machine—publicity—will carry this design around the world. With no help or suggestion from anybody it will be printed in Dutch and German and English magazines two months from now. Professional people in these countries will imagine that this is the best American architects can do and I hope they get a good laugh out of it. Swift global dissemination of ideas in graphic form is one of the best, and maybe also one of the worst, things that the machine age has done for us. It makes us powerful, but it might also make us lazy, our ideas being so easy to convey, and that's dangerous, because the whole world now looks to America for a lead.
>
> To return to the *Gazette* contest itself. Amid the trash there was one design that stood out: the runner-up, by Joseph

Lazarus (a man whose work I'm familiar with) and Esko Offermans (a name I've never heard). As a loser, this remarkable design deserves to achieve a legendary victory. In many ways, in terms of pure architecture, it doesn't go far enough, but it grapples realistically with the problem of what a skyscraper should be in 1922 and achieves a solution of beauty that would have graced our skyline. It is a single solidarity of concentrated intention—that's what's impressive. It looks like something that has sprung startling and fresh from our own American soil. It looks like it would be pretty happy, soaring up there in the sky, and it would make us happy and New York better too. It's so good that even my admiration feels like insolence. My hat is taken off and duly raised. As Whitman wrote, "I understand the large hearts of heroes, the courage of present times and all times."

Thank you, Lazarus and Offermans, for showing us that we no longer need look to Europe for architecture or anything. America provides us with our tools, our own ideas and materials to work with. We must use them responsibly. We must use them as Washington and Jefferson did, as Whitman did. We were given, or perhaps we took, one whole continent, and now we are about to launch into a second—the clouds. Let's treat it with the energy, and reverence, that we surely owe the discovery of another new world.

Yours, William P. Kirby.

Esko read this in Lazarus's office, where Lazarus was on the telephone, sitting at his desk, leaning forward and barking into the mouthpiece through his beard and his fleshy pink lips. "You read the letter? Of course, it is wonderful what the old man said—and true, you know? My heart breaks, not for myself but for the city of New York. Such an opportunity has been missed. It is a scandal. I think so, *ja, ja*. By all means say that—say that Winrob must be forgotten." He winked at Esko. "Say it in print a mile high! *Gut!*"

Lazarus on the phone was, as Lazarus elsewhere, a theatrical production, an epic and almost maniacal performance. He banged the receiver back onto its cradle, pushed back his chair, and stood. "We must play this carefully," he said, rubbing his hands together. "This association with Kirby must not come too close. There was a scandal a long time ago. A fire in one of his buildings. People died." He drew a finger across his throat. "But he is still admired, still a figure, it seems. *Naturlich*, not like me. Still, a figure."

Esko nodded vaguely, sitting on the windowsill with the *New York Times* in hand, reading the letter one more time, overwhelmed by the idea that something he'd done should prompt such understanding and warmth from a fellow professional. He felt as though he'd been spoken to by a friend, an older man, but a soul mate.

"What else do you know about him?" he said.

"He is on our side," Lazarus said with a shrug. "What else *is* there to know?"

Esko watched Lazarus arranging the pencils and papers on his desk, thinking through the next strategic move without the trace of a smile on his face.

"Do you really think you can shame them into taking away Winrob's prize?"

"No," said Lazarus, looking up sharply, his face wearing the same expression of faraway, almost abstracted, concentration it always did when he was maneuvering toward something important, willing the world to obedience. "But I think I can make sure that everyone knows the true winner came second."

That afternoon Esko took the subway downtown to look at the one Kirby building that so far as he'd been able to establish was still standing on Manhattan. It was close by the seaport, and he almost missed it in the snow—a flat-roofed rectangular building between two taller neighbors, fitting so snugly in its lot that it looked like an exquisitely positioned piece of furniture. Only fifteen stories high, the building had a lightness, a force and power of altitude that seemed to make it soar above its actual space. A delicate terracotta facade rose from a one-story base. There was a corner entry, unusual in a high-rise. The structural columns were fat, solid, those merely dividing the windows slender and lithe. Up top, six sculpture angels supported the cornice with a flourish of their outspread wings, and Esko thought that Kirby must have appreciated that he was reaching toward the divine; he'd made a little joke of the fact, with his angels. The unassuming elegance of this gorgeous little building was quite unlike anything Esko had seen in the city; it didn't brag and bray the way a lot of buildings in Manhattan seemed to; it had an enviable tact, another sort of American quality.

The doorman wore a black uniform with gold braid on the shoulder; he was a small, friendly man in his sixties, with stiff, crinkly silver hair like tin. He showed Esko around inside, where everything was calm, light, and well ordered.

"Who owns this building?" Esko asked the doorman.

"Andrew MacCormick."

"MacCormick?" said Esko.

"That's right," the doorman said, touching his hair. "The rich guy."

*   *   *

Esko saw MacCormick a few days later, at the *Gazette* prize-giving lunch, where he grasped Esko's right hand in both his own. "There's no justice," he said, more serious than Esko had remembered him. "You really should have won."

"Thanks," Esko said, pleased at MacCormick's genuine affection.

"Well, I mean it," MacCormick said, his quick intelligent eyes glancing around the ballroom, decked out now with a score of circular tables, each laid with a white cloth, silver, and crystal. He seemed in a mellow, expectant mood. He was wearing a splendid dove-gray suit with a vest and a silk shirt nipped high at the collar by a tie.

"I wanted to ask you something."

"Shoot," MacCormick said.

Esko explained about Kirby and the building downtown.

"I liked it so I bought it. I do that with lots of things," MacCormick said, his hands thrust casually into his pants pockets. "You and I are probably the only people in New York—the only people who matter—who know it still exists. It's a shame Kirby didn't do more here."

"Why didn't he?"

"People fall off the map, I guess," he said.

Esko thought about this; obviously it could happen—fate provided some people with prickly and inhospitable geography, in life, in love, in career; the thing was to go on, to turn endurance into its own reward; *sisu*, he supposed, if you could manage it.

"It sure is a pretty building. I've kept the top two floors for myself and my wife. I had the idea I might turn the space into a penthouse. Hey," said Mac-Cormick, without much change in the languid tone of his voice, "perhaps you'll design it for me."

Esko had no idea if he was serious.

"That is—if it's not too lowly a commission for the runner-up of the great *Gazette* contest," MacCormick said with an ironic smile.

"Why not get Kirby to do the job himself? Did you see his entry yet?"

They wandered through the tables to look at it, standing there while MacCormick's quick eyes took in the design and then gave Esko a glance.

"Tell me how it worked with Joe," he said. "Who did what?"

"What do you mean?"

"That's what I thought," he said with relaxed charm. "The design's *entirely* yours, isn't it?"

"Joe offered me some good advice."

"You know he's been swanking about all over town allowing people to draw the conclusion that he did all the work?"

Esko shook his head; he didn't quite know this, though in recent days he'd seen a number of newspaper pieces that had referred to the contest, and to his design, while curiously mentioning only the name of Joseph Lazarus.

"I'll tell you something about Joe," MacCormick said. "He built an office building for me before the war. Upstate, in Rochester. It's not a bad little building. Shall I tell you how he got the commission?"

"Please."

"He wrote me a letter more or less saying he'd designed something that had been built by W. P. Kirby in Buffalo. He'd worked as Kirby's right-hand man, he said. Done most of the work behind the scenes, he said."

MacCormick scratched the little cleft in his chin, bearing down on this story with amusement, almost glee.

"He got the commission and later I found out the story was all hooey. He'd never worked with Kirby. He'd never even met Kirby. But by then Joe was doing a good job. On time. Within budget. So I didn't say a goddamned thing." MacCormick shrugged. "Make of this what you like," he said. "I like Joe, and I'll go on doing business with him. But he has the knack of doing ruthless things without losing the ability to think well of himself. It's a useful knack. Don't let him use it against you. Fight your corner."

Esko was thinking about this when, a few minutes later, they sat down for lunch. MacCormick was steered toward the head table, along with Peter Winrob, the judges, the mayor of New York, and various *Gazette* dignitaries. Esko and Lazarus, on the other hand, were at a table in the center of the room, just sufficiently far from the main event to be made aware of the difference between winners and runners-up. Lazarus made his own comment on this arrangement, sailing into the room with his superb fur coat flowing behind him just as the *Gazette* editor, a small and surprisingly young man with a cherubic face, was rising to his feet to make an introductory speech. He paused, noting the disturbance, and Lazarus gave him an ironic bow before turning to the other guests and raising his upturned palms to the level of his shoulders, smiling, suggesting that he was lifting the prize of victory. Only then did he shrug off his coat and sit down, noisily, making sure that he clattered his chair. He turned to Esko with a wink. "These occasions. Too tedious for words, don't you agree?" he said in a loud voice, ignoring the fact that the *Gazette* editor was already droning on in a solemn voice about the architect's duty to society.

It was, as was so much with Lazarus, a theatrical production, an epic performance, well judged and nicely polished, and Esko found himself smiling. So what if he was trying to take some credit for the design? It really didn't matter: they hadn't won, it had been a joint entry after all, and it wasn't even going to be built. People in the office knew he'd been the one who'd done all the work, as did MacCormick. Besides, as far as he was concerned, that little part of his professional history was over; his *Gazette* entry had been a compromise, Gothic *moderne*, a success on its own terms but a limited success, and W. P. Kirby's haunting design had shown him the nature of those limits. Now was the time to push further, to come up with something really special, work moving ever closer to the beauty and purity of his vision on the ice, the beacon that was always turning in his mind; sometimes its light went dim, but it never went away, and it was flashing bright right now. He felt like a man who had beauty locked away like treasure in a secret vault, he just had to discover how to spend it. First, though, he'd find the key.

Just then, cutting through the monotone of the *Gazette* editor's speech, came a ringing sound, a note pure and high, as of a finger struck against crystal, and Esko felt something detonate in his heart. Looking across the room, looking through a forest of heads, looking straight toward the head table, he saw a woman leaning toward the seated figure of Andrew MacCormick with her hand on his shoulder. He couldn't see her face, only the top of her skull, encased in a cloche hat dangling with a thousand delicate glittering fragments of silver, but he knew it was Katerina. He felt her presence like flame, as if each one of those slender shining silver pieces was an arrow of desire shot through his veins; then she raised her eyes and looked right at him. Her eyebrows were plucked thin; they made delicate lines above her eyes, which seemed darker and more soulful, even bigger than before, with longer, thicker lashes. She'd aged, but was at the height of her womanly beauty, approaching thirty now, and somehow transformed. It wasn't just that she was dressed like an American woman of fashion, rich and successful, like a motion picture star. She was thinner, harder, more removed, less vulnerable, composed, complete, refined, diamondlike. She met his glance for a few seconds and then averted her eyes.

Esko pushed back his chair and breathlessly stood. Beside him Lazarus said, "Esko, what are you doing?" Ignoring him, and unaware of the expressions of curiosity, the flashing angry looks that greeted his progress across the room, he rushed to the head table.

"Hello, Esko, it's been a long time," Katerina said, speaking slowly and very quietly, drawling her words in a husky voice. Her accented English was fluent, her manner calm and cheerful—perhaps too cheerful. "You look well. It's wonderful to see you."

"Katerina . . . I . . ." Esko was exploding with happiness. "I'm overcome. I don't know what to say."

"Then say hello," she said; removing a white glove, she stretched a slender hand toward him; there was a ring with a diamond on it on the wedding finger; and her expression was sad for a moment, as if she wished she had other news to give him.

"I gather you kids met each other a long time ago," MacCormick was saying in his easy way. "Esko—I'd like you to meet my wife. Kate MacCormick."

ठ

While in New York MacCormick lived in a suite at the Waldorf-Astoria. Esko went there to look for Katerina; he left messages; he telephoned, he traveled up in the elevator and knocked on the door of the suite—all to no avail. So in the end he decided to sit in the lobby. He waited one whole day, and then another, reading the papers, striking up a rapport with the bellboys. He didn't care if anyone found his presence or behavior strange; it *was* strange. The idea of Katerina—the sight of her, the smell of her—swirled in his mind like fever. He drank whiskey, and ate sandwiches, and drank beer, and nothing stopped the longing. Even when he dozed off for a moment, sitting upright in his chair that faced the elevators, he dreamed of her. Having seen her again, he loved her with an extremity that shocked him—more than his work, more than his life.

It was seven o'clock at night, two days after the *Gazette* prize-giving, when at last he spotted her, coming, not from the elevator, but from the hotel's long interior arcade that ran parallel to Thirty-fourth Street. There was a second surprise: she was with, not MacCormick, but another man, a lean, dark man, with a shock of black hair and dark eyes that looked out sharply from behind thick, wire-rimmed spectacles. His face was handsome, in an intense way, and he was looking with concentration, even adoration, at Katerina, who wore a sleeveless sheath of silver and a silver cloche hat. Her black fur coat was folded over her arm.

Esko started to stand up, but checked himself; instead, feeling slightly ludicrous, he raised his newspaper in front of his face and waited while the two of them, laughing, walked past him and headed through the lobby toward the hotel's spinning doors.

In the street Esko watched them climb into a cab, so he took the next in line, telling the driver to follow. The ride wasn't a long one: ten blocks north, and then across to Broadway, where Esko paid the fare and dodged through the crowds, following Katerina and her friend into the lobby of the Garrick Theater, losing them only when he realized they had tickets already and he would have to buy one.

Bumping knees, muttering, "Excuse me—sorry—excuse me," Esko made his way to his seat just as the lights went down, the curtains swept open, and the play began with a flash of light and a rolling roar like thunder. Onstage there was a storm, the foundering of a ship. Men screamed and cried out, struggling against rain and a wild wind. Sails ripped, timbers crashed, and lightning split the sky. Then: blackness.

Esko looked left and right, staring into the audience in front of him, his eye guided as if by instinct toward the back of Katerina's head. He saw the intense young man lean his head toward her, trying to attract her attention, but she kept her eyes fixed on the stage as gentler lighting came up on a very different scene. A tall old man stood alone, wearing a cloak of star-spangled black in a book-lined room where he was soon joined by his daughter, a beautiful and vibrant young woman innocently fearful for the lives of those lost in the wreck. The old man—a magician, it seemed—assured her that the storm was of his own creation and that all was well. The ship's crew had been delivered, safe, onto his island and into his power. He smiled, rubbing his hands, and summoned his assistant, a spirit who flew across the stage hanging upside down from a trapeze; then the magician's slave, a deformed creature, slithered out from behind a rock, dressed in fur and seaweed, with a club in his hand and a fish that he took out of his mouth so he could curse.

Caliban was the name of the slave, Ariel the singing spirit of the air, and the play, Esko only now realized, was the one that Katerina had described to him in the elevator of the Diktonius Building; it was *The Tempest* by Shakespeare.

Esko peered once more through the forest of heads toward Katerina; her eyes were locked on the stage. What was it that she'd told him in Helsinki? That he was Caliban longing to be Ariel. Wasn't that it? She'd seen in his horrible face the yearning for light and beauty; recognized, as no one else had, that his running up a building to heaven was the act by which he could conjure away his ugliness. And there, in the elevator, things had shifted between the two of them, deepened. For Esko it hadn't been a matter of fantasy and mere longing anymore. In that moment he'd known there were such creatures as soul mates. He believed it still, sitting behind her in this performance of *The Tempest*, even though he'd found her—and lost her again—in but a moment's time. She was married, to a millionaire, to MacCormick, a man he respected and was even coming to like; and she was here tonight with a stranger—a beau, presumably. Esko was disappointed, depressed, even angry; then again, he told himself, what could I have expected? People change, move on. And yet still he hoped, feeling now much less like Ariel than Caliban.

> *Be not afeard. The isle is full of noises,*
> *Sounds and sweet airs, that give delight, and hurt not.*
> *Sometimes a thousand twangling instruments*
> *Will hum about mine ears; and sometimes voices,*
> *That, if I then had wak'd after long sleep,*
> *Will make me sleep again; and then, in dreaming,*
> *The clouds methought would open and show riches*
> *Ready to drop upon me, that, when I wak'd,*
> *I cried to dream again.*

Esko wasn't giving up; he wasn't even waiting for that day when the clouds would open; he was going to carry on climbing up toward them, defiantly Caliban, resolutely Caliban, determinedly Caliban, the entrapped monster who sees the world raw but radiant, reaching for the domain on the other side of the mirror.

And so, when the play was over, he pushed through the swarming top-hatted throng that was borne like a wave past the flashing lights and golden-framed posters in the foyer, calling, "Katerina! Katerina!" He found himself carried out onto the street, where glistening black taxi cabs stood five deep, rattling and belching fumes, beneath Times Square's Niagara of neon. "Katerina!"

Only now did she turn, her glance seeking his. "Esko?"

"Katerina!"

She came toward him, eyes flashing. "Have you been following me?"

"Is this fellow bothering you?" said her companion, the dark-haired young man, taking his hands from his pockets, rolling his shoulders and moving toward Esko with a bantam swagger.

"Robert—it's all right," Katerina said, holding him back, a hand on his sleeve.

Robert stared at her for a moment, and then at Esko. "Are you sure?"

"I'll see you at the restaurant. Go. Please," she said, and, reluctantly, he did, raising his arm for a cab.

Esko waited until Robert was in the back of the Ford and on his way. All around them people were talking about, not the play—who cared about that?—but where to go next. Supper? Jazz? A speak? This party or another? The air was pregnant with electricity, with fur and perfume and the clicking of high heels. Excitement lit up people's faces and made them like lanterns.

He put his arms around Katerina, drawing her close. For a moment she held her face back, but then he was allowed to find her lips. They remained closed, ungiving, with little hint of the tenderness he'd felt outside her apartment on Fabianinkatu. There was just the small tremor of a response. His eye was closed. Intoxicated by her smell, the closeness of her, he tried again. This time there was nothing.

"Please, Esko, don't," she said, pushing him away.

"Do you love him?"

"Robert—no, of course not."

"I meant MacCormick."

She slapped his face, not hard, not playfully either. It was a warning. Undeterred, he said: "Do you?"

"I'm meeting Robert and the others down in the Village," she said, tense with anger. "I have to go."

"I'll come with you."

"It won't do any good."

"I'm coming anyway."

She looked at him for the first time with a sympathy, almost a sorrow in her eyes, and sighed.

In the back of the speeding taxi Esko told himself that he really should try and think out a plan, some sort of a strategy for dealing with her. But he was no good at any of that. He just went right at it.

"I thought you were dead, Katerina. I married."

She stared out into the street. Part of Broadway was being torn up and men were working by the light of flares, sending shadows that played across her face and her long neck.

"I left my wife behind to come here."

"Those damned pictures. Damn you and your *pilvenpiirtaja*, Esko Vaananen," she said, face ablaze with sudden passion. "I thought you were dead too."

"Almost. I was shot crossing a dam at Tampere. Klaus pulled me out. By the time they got me to the dressing station I was frozen to the sledge with my own blood. They say that Klaus cut me free with an axe and carried me to the surgeon's table himself. Then he went back to the fighting. I never saw him again."

"Dear God," she said, voice breaking, covering her ears with gloved hands. Tears started to her eyes. "I won't listen to this. Stop, Esko, please."

He grabbed away one of her hands, forcing her to listen. "Tell me about the skyscraper in the snow. The skyscraper you built with the children."

She looked at him furiously now. "Let go of my hand."

The taxi stopped, and Katerina pulled down her silvery cloche hat and quickly disappeared beneath the awning of the restaurant while Esko paid. Inside he saw her again, heading for the longest table in the place, where a party was waiting. Robert was at once on his feet, waving to her and beckoning, his eyes piercing behind those thick, wire-rimmed spectacles. "Kate!"

"Hello, you customers," Katerina said, all brittle brightness and smiles now. "Shakespeare kept us."

"Oh boy. You must need a drink."

"I *do* need a drink."

Katerina flopped down in a chair next to Robert, who at once threw his arm around her shoulders and started whispering in her ear.

"I see you found her," a woman said, looking at Esko. A cigarette hung, unlit, from her fierce red lips.

"Excuse me?" Esko said, still dazed from the taxi, New York giving him no time to relax, its festive, carnal atmosphere going on and on.

"I'm Marion Bennett. From *Vanity Fair*. You introduced me to a whole new way to play find the lady."

Now it came to him. "Of course—at the magazine. You forwarded my messages. Thank you."

"She's married, you know."

A restaurant matchbook was sitting like a little red cap on the white table-cloth in front of an empty chair. Esko slid into the chair, broke off a match, and lit Marion Bennett's cigarette. He had the impression she'd been waiting for him to do that all along.

"Thanks for mentioning it," he said. "I do now."

"You've got some catching up to do. I'm crocko. Squiffy. Let's call over one of those terrible, handsome waiters and have him whip us up a couple more martinis. As you see, I'm prepared, as every Girl Scout should be."

Marion Bennett had three silver flasks lined up like soldiers on the table. Her eyes were big with makeup and her breath smelled of gin and smoke. Her dress was red. She wore a hat she hadn't taken off. She had a magnificent air of not giving a damn.

"My sister's having a baby," she said, the way she said everything else, like a wisecrack—take it or leave it. "Do you have babies?"

"No."

"Does the ice queen?"

Esko realized he didn't know the answer to that question. "No, I don't think so."

"You're in love with her, aren't you?"

"Yes, I am."

"Wish I knew what she did to men. I'd sell it in very small and very expensive bottles at Bonwit Teller. Did I tell you that I'm drunk?"

"You mentioned it."

"No wonder she landed a big fat money salmon," Marion Bennett said, exhaling smoke. "Will you just look at the way Robert's gawking at her now? That dope with his goo-goo eyes. He's a poet, you know. He writes verse dramas about the myths of ancient Greeks recreating themselves in Hoboken. They're very deep. He thinks she's so mysterious. *Sans merci* but so very *belle*. Have you eaten? What are you going to eat? Of course her photographs are wonderful. I'm afraid even I have to admit that. And now she's got money. Oodles of boodle. Have you encountered the spouse?"

"He's—yes, we're acquainted."

"While we eat you must tell me everything you know. I won't touch anything myself. Food makes fat," she said, sloshing gin from her flask into a cocktail shaker that a waiter had brought along. "Gin, on the other hand, makes woo. They haven't been married long, you know. And she's away a lot of the time. Being an *artiste*. They say he's crazy about her. I guess I would be if I were a guy. I'm not."

"I noticed."

"You *did*," she said, clapping a hand to her mouth. "Now I feel bashful. Do you box?"

"I build."

"You got your scars some other way then."

"In a fire."

"Is that the scoop? Isn't life grand?"

"Sometimes."

"Sez you," she said, without expression, with a sense of sad loneliness despite her crazy energy and glamour. "Have you read Freud?"

"Some."

"He says it's all about sex and that's all right with me. I like to drink and do the James Joyce word."

"What's that?"

"Fuck, silly. In public places. Preferably with a sugar daddy, since the poet who's supposed to be tonight's date is dead set on the empress of all the Russias. I wonder if Mr. MacCormick knows that half the men in New York are in love with her. Maybe he likes the idea. Though he strikes me as the jealous and secretly driven type. Machiavelli in a cloak of charm and honey." She clapped a hand over her mouth again. "Oh Lord. Now I've put my galoshes in it. That Katerina. She's a *very* modern girl."

This, right now, was a little more information about Katerina than Esko wanted to know. Despite the way he'd behaved in the cab, he hadn't expected her to fall into his arms. He also hadn't expected to find her so changed; whereas, even after everything that had happened, he saw himself as doggedly the same, better adjusted (perhaps), more worldly (hopefully), and more focused on those goals that had driven him for almost as long as he could remember: the skyscraper, his *pilvenpiirtaja*, and Katerina, who, at this moment, had her gray-gloved hand laid on Robert the poet's wrist while he whispered something in her ear—probably not about Hoboken. America had acted on her like alchemy. She wore a jeweled armor now.

"What do you write?" he said to Marion Bennett.

"*Write?*" said Marion Bennett. Her black eyebrows shot upward in mock alarm, chiding him for this too blatant changing of the subject.

"Words in the right order, sometimes. Light me another cigarette, Scarface."

"It's been a long time since anyone called me that."

"What happened to the last person who did?"

"He was shot in front of a firing squad."

"You're funny," she said, and saw he wasn't joking. "The war?"

"A war. A small and very nasty one. You've probably never even heard of it. In Finland."

"In Finland? Probably not. No, I probably never heard of it." She peeled back one of her black cotton gloves an inch or two, revealing on her wrist two long dark gashes, healed now. "These weren't made with a toothbrush, kiddo. Life is like being fired from a cannon and they don't even give us a helmet. God used to be the helmet and look what they did to him. As I said—ain't it grand?"

"Sometimes," said Esko, like before, and Marion Bennett gleefully threw back her head, puffing out smoke in a perfect ring.

"You *are* persistent. I'll say that for you. Does she know?" she said, nodding toward Katerina.

"I hope so."

After supper the whole party of about twenty piled into taxis and went to a joint on Third Avenue, a dingy, grimy speakeasy that stank of stale, rotgut beer and dead cigarette ends. Marion Bennett slipped her hand into his, and as his thumb rubbed her leather glove his mind went back to the frayed edges of the glove he'd once seen Katerina wearing, to the sense he'd gained then of all she'd suffered and lost. Looking at her ivory beauty now, seeing her smoke a cigarette and call for another whiskey, watching her run a cool eye over the room as though it were a scene to be photographed, it was hard to imagine that she carried with her any scars from the past; but then he remembered her anger in the cab, and the tears that had welled. She was a living thing in contact with the world; she'd acquired a mask, and he had to believe that it wasn't her heart he was seeing now.

By then it was after midnight. With the speak getting busier by the moment he still couldn't get close to her. Dark figures slouched and jostled flank to flank in the smoke. A fight broke out between two drunks and was quickly smothered by the bouncers with sounds of glass and bones breaking. Marion Bennett, jammed against Esko's chest, passed out and started snoring even though she was still standing up. There was nowhere to sit or put her down and he was still holding her in his arms when the door let in a cold rush of wind from the street. In stepped a red-haired man wearing a hat and a pale trenchcoat over a dark suit. It was Bo, the Swedish riveter.

"Where you've been?" Bo said, slapping Esko on the shoulder. His blue eyes went big at the sight of Marion Bennett. "You've obviously been busy."

"Very funny, Bo. Hear from Gunnar and Cristof?"

Bo shrugged his wide shoulders. "Still out west, so far as I know."

"You didn't go back to the steel?"

"Hell, no."

"So what are you doing these days?"

"Oh—this and that." Bo frowned, thinking hard, and when he did that it was as if you could see inside his head, a piece of jittery machinery. He raised his hat, waving at a man on the other side of the bar who came over and handed him a package that he slid into the pocket of his coat. "More dough, less danger."

"What about the Mantilinis—you still seeing Teresa?"

"We're like family," he said grimly. "Steffano's walking now."

"That's great," Esko said, truly pleased. "And Paul?"

"Don't talk to me about Paul," Bo said. "You know, Esko, you hold a woman like you ain't had no practice. Don't they teach you how in Finland?"

"Not with unconscious ones."

Marion Bennett's head came up with a jerk. "Hey, watch what you're saying, buster." She blew hair out of her eyes and regarded Bo with pop-eyed candor. "Why hello, babe," she said. "You're gorgeous. May I feel your muscles?"

Bo stammered, his face turning deep red like a brick.

"Buy me a drink, Sheikh," said Marion Bennett. "Hey gang!" she shouted. "Something pretty showed up and the night is young."

9

The party went on. They got drunker and drunker and piled into another fleet of cabs, roaring up to Harlem where they staggered down six concrete steps and a pair of bloodshot eyes inspected them through a steel door with a grille. In the basement beyond there was no bandstand though over in one corner six or seven or eight men—all black—with trumpets and saxophones and a piano and a small set of drums were blowing and banging deliriously. Tables with red lamps burning on top of them were shoved against the wall, and couples danced, some black, some white, some black and white, a tangle of whirring legs and jostling knees and bouncing ropes of pearls. The air was thick with smoke. In a small adjoining room a man in a little white jacket splashed liquor from a bottle from Scotland (at least the *label* was from Scotland) into shot glasses. He was a very tall man, skeletally thin, with a face whose pallor suggested he might pass dead away at the sight of the sun. A tough thug leaned against the bar with a fedora jammed on his head and an ominous bulge apparent beneath his jacket. He seemed to know Bo and nodded a solemn greeting. The music stopped, started up again, and a dancer strutted out, half naked, wearing gold toeless pumps and a feather that snaked around her body. Her black body glistened as she swayed to the sighing of the saxophone and shook her ass like a hummingbird. The place stank of bodies and bootleg booze, of an excitement that was instantaneous and dangerous as lightning. Esko wished he could paint this scene, memorize it, unearth the means to render its equivalent in thrilling architecture. A feather tumbled from the dancer's boa and was caught in a hot updraft, spiraling toward the ceiling as a hundred flailing hands reached to grab it. It wasn't Esko's world, but Esko loved the energy, the lawlessness, the abandon, the shock of all this hot jazz.

Bo had brought them here, saying there was a girl he was supposed to meet. Now he couldn't find her. Unworried, he surveyed the scene, unaware that Marion Bennett had already made a decision for both of them. She simply came and stood next to him and put her hand on his pants. Bo stood up ramrod straight, as if he'd been given a jolt; then they were kissing, attacking each other with their lips.

Katerina watched the two of them with absolute concentration, once again as if she were taking a picture, ignoring Robert, the Hoboken troubadour, even though he was leaning close, whispering endlessly in her ear, his fingers brushing her shoulder. She had the power, Esko realized, not just over him, but over many men, whether she wanted it or not. Pain permeated her appeal and was part of it. He wondered about Marion Bennett's hint that she'd already been unfaithful to MacCormick. Could that be true? It really didn't matter. He didn't want her to cheat on MacCormick; he wanted her to leave him.

Esko went over and took her by the arm. "Let's get out of here," he said.

Her cool eyes met his. She'd been drinking all night, like the rest of them, but she didn't seem drunk. "Why?"

"I have something for you," he said. "It belongs to you."

"Give it to me then."

"No. Not here."

*   *   *

In Central Park ice creaked in the trees and their feet crunched through a crisp crust of snow. There was no hum of traffic—only, from the distance, came the low rattle of a train on the el.

"Sit?" Esko said, gesturing to a bench beneath a gas lamp whose halo wavered even as the sound of the distant train fell away. She sat, expectant, as he reached into his coat pocket.

He handed her an envelope, worn and dirty. In the dim light, it took her a moment: on one side the envelope was scrawled with drawings, on the other, her name, written in a chillingly familiar hand. "It's from Klaus," Esko said. "I've had it with me a very long time."

A spasm passed through Katerina's body. She gasped, but she said nothing, staring at the envelope for a long time.

"He made me promise to deliver it if . . ."

She clicked open her purse, pushed in the envelope, snapped the purse shut again. Taking a deep breath, her expression suddenly weary, she said: "Just what exactly do you want from me, Esko?"

"I want us to be together."

There was fight in her eyes. "And what do you see ahead for us? A little place in the country? The pram in the hall and the patter of little feet?"

The collar of her coat was turned up high to her neck. Frost sparkled in her hair as she gazed at the ground. Slowly, she pulled off one of her gloves, finger by finger, and took his hand in hers.

"I'm bad luck, Esko, you should keep away from me," she said.

"I'll take my chances."

She was shaking her head. "It's no good."

"So you'll take pictures of skyscrapers, you'll even build one in the snow from bricks of ice, but you won't be with me, is that it? It's only the notion of me that's beautiful, is that it? Noble little Esko with his big ideals—I'll patronize him a little, he's interesting in a way, but as a lover—well! Is that what you think? Be honest with me, Katerina. Tell me the truth."

Her eyes went skyward for a moment. "The truth? I don't think you want to hear the truth."

"Try me."

"Do you know what I felt when I got your letters, when I first saw you the other day?"

Her fierce look told him he might not enjoy the answer. Still: "Go on."

"Dread. I felt dread."

It was starting to snow. A big flake tumbled dreamily past Esko's face. He felt suddenly as though his soul were in his ungloved hand, numb and blue with cold.

"I saw a door opening that I'd slammed shut. And that I wanted to *stay* shut. I'm not the person I was four years ago."

Beneath her worldliness and composure she was so much the wild and wounded animal in many ways, he thought, sensitive to every impulse around her, suspicious of any attempt to tame or hurt.

"There's no destiny or pattern, Esko. Everything's random. The names of Esko Vaananen and Katerina Malysheva are not written in the stars. Maybe I thought so once, for a moment. Not anymore. Not now."

Esko saw hope here, a route that might take him to the other side. "When was that moment, Katerina?"

"In Helsinki. That morning—the *pilvenpiirtaja* in the snow. I was angry with you when you went to the army, Esko; it wasn't what you should have done." Her eyes traveled around the park. "You should have come here, to

New York." Her gazed was fixed on a distant tree. "And then I heard that you and Klaus had died." She looked down into her lap. "This is it, I thought. There is no more Katerina Malysheva. Her home is gone. Her country is gone. Her friends are gone. She has ceased to exist. I gave my apartment in Helsinki to a woman I knew who'd just got out of Russia. I left."

Esko was thinking about the mirror, the little art nouveau mirror that had hung from her wrist as a little girl, the mirror she'd given him and he'd returned to her; the mirror he'd last seen in the hands of a defeated and dejected Red in a prison cell in Helsinki.

"You left the mirror," he said in a whisper, reaching toward his pocket, fingering the sheath of his *puukko*. Objects: some possessed lives in poignant parallel to those of their owners, shimmering with depths of memory and meaning one moment, only to be turned into inert matter, mere stuff, the next. The mirror Katerina had given him was doubtless still in the world, somewhere in the hands of a bum or beggar, or on the shelf of a store, tarnished or even smashed, stripped of all those previous associations that had been so precious to him.

"I came here, Esko," Katerina said. "And it was hard. I had no plans. I had no money. I had no idea what I might do."

"You met other Russians?"

"They were working as waiters and waitresses in restaurants and cafés. One of them had been a prince. I'm not joking—in Russia he had literally been a prince. That was how much some of us had lost. Now he was clearing plates and so I thought, Why not? If he can bear it, I can too. I worked for almost a year, trying to forget, not thinking, allowing myself to want and expect—nothing."

Not letting Esko interrupt her, she went on, and Esko had the feeling that she'd never mentioned these matters to anyone, not even to MacCormick. She told him of her early months in New York, combining the most trivial details with her most intimate feelings.

"The restaurant was on Broadway. A Frenchman owned it, a sad little man who looked like a vampire but was in fact very kind. He seemed to give everyone a job, anyone who came in the door. I was a waitress, and that was lucky, because of the tips. There was another guy, Eddie, who washed the dishes in the kitchen. He'd been a pianist. He spent all his money on cocaine. One night he slashed his hand on a glass. I went with him and the Frenchman in a cab to Bellevue, blood everywhere. Sixteen stitches. But I never really got to know Eddie. He was crossing Third Avenue when he was hit by a car. Drunk driver. At three o'clock on a Sunday afternoon. Just the week before he'd been telling me, 'It'll all be different one day.' Poor Eddie." She puffed breath, shivering in the cold. "And then, for me, suddenly it *was* different. Things changed. A man came in, an older man, a gentle man. He ordered soup and a glass of champagne and he left a very big tip. He came back the next night, and the night after that. Always ordering the same thing. Eating very slowly. Taking his time as if time was important. He told me that he was a photographer. His darkroom assistant was driving him crazy, he said, and he was looking for a replacement. Would I be interested?"

Her voice was level and calm. These episodes, as she talked about them, were like old snapshots she was thumbing through, as if, Esko thought, she'd willfully laid aside the power to be moved by her own memories and was now, without really thinking about it, giving that job to him. That, at least, was the responsibility he assumed, sitting on the bench, breath fogging out in front of him. He'd keep these memories for Katerina and one day give them back to her, intact, so she could reclaim all her life.

"He had a small studio on Bleecker Street. It was long hours, less money than the restaurant, but I was glad to do it. One day I asked for a raise. He just looked at me and laughed and said no. 'I'll let you take some pictures for yourself, how about that?' he said. And so there I was, the next day, with this big old box camera in my hands, not having a clue what to do. I took pictures of people in line for the Staten Island Ferry. Deserted streets. Storefronts."

"And?"

"I started to feel again. I wasn't trying to do anything clever. Just trying to clear away the clutter between myself and whatever the subject was. Just letting myself feel, *something*—and all a question of when I release the shutter. All in my control. All in my hands."

Esko leaned forward, his elbows on his knees, glancing at her.

"I have a favor to ask you, Esko."

"What's that?"

"Don't try to see me. Don't have anything to do with me. Please."

Esko sat up straight. Someone hurried by, a walker on his way home or to the next party, face smiling at the two of them for a moment from beneath the brim of his hat, and then hurrying into the darkness and the snow. All night long Esko felt that he'd been a barometer, an instrument calibrated to one woman's mood: her briskness, her buried sadness, her brittle brightness, and now, her calm, with its attendant plea. His heart ached for her, even if she was indeed treating him like Caliban, commanding him off her island.

"You'll pack up your things and you'll come to my place," he said. "We'll stay there until we find somewhere bigger. We'll put in a darkroom, a studio, or we'll rent one someplace nearby. You can be away as long and as much as you like. I don't want to keep you prisoner. That's not my idea at all. We'll be together even when we're apart. Katerina—I know I'll never be rich like Mac-Cormick. But we'll always have what we need."

Her head drooped. She wrung her hands together and the sound that came from her lips was something primal, a moan, a creak of misery and pain. "Oh, *Esko*," she said. "Haven't you heard a word I've said?"

"I've listened very carefully. You know that."

"I have Andrew, I have connections, I have money," she said, quick and decisive once more. "Yes, isn't that terrible? Money is freedom and without freedom I'd slit my throat. I grew up with things that were precious to me and they were ripped away and I was tortured and if I have anything to do or say about it then nothing like that is going to happen to me ever again. I can't go through this one more time. I don't have the strength. For the first time since the revolution I feel my life is back in my hands. I'm not about to hand it all back—not even to you."

And Esko returned to his earlier question, not about to give this up. "Do you love him?"

Just then, before Katerina could answer, feet came running, hurrying through the snow, and Bo arrived, drunk, panting, but sure on his feet as ever. "Esko—thank God I found you," he said. Leaning forward, he put his hands on his knees. He'd lost his hat during the course of the night and frost sparkled in his tufty hair. "The woman in the red dress, with the lips. What's her name?"

"Bo, this isn't . . ." Esko said.

"She stuck a fork in some guy's leg," Bo went on, gasping out his story. "There was a fight and some guy was shot in the chest. Not by her."

Instantly they were surrounded by a racket of excited voices, people milling all around with their excited, disjointed versions of what had happened.

"A gun . . ."

". . . called her a . . ."

"An inch deep, I swear to God . . ."

"This guy . . . blood . . ."

"She got out of there," Bo said. "She's a little crazy, that girl. But I like her. I think she liked me too. What do you think, Esko?"

"Look, Bo," Esko said, preoccupied, his eye searching for Katerina's. "Her name's Marion Bennett. She works for a magazine, *Vanity Fair*. Try their offices tomorrow."

Bo ran off, thanking Esko as he disappeared, and Esko turned back to Katerina, but Robert was there, already igniting her cigarette with a lighter big and clunky as a weapon. She didn't seem unhappy about it; quite the reverse—she seemed relieved, rescued by Hoboken.

"Katerina . . ." Esko began.

"Don't worry, Esko. Robert's taking me home. Thanks for a swell evening."

Esko didn't move. He waited until they were all gone and everything was quiet, knowing that Katerina wouldn't come back but not wanting to leave the park either, imagining that he could still smell her perfume, a fragrance that seemed to have been blended only for him; he stared at the snow, remembering that, after he'd first met her as a little boy, all through the following month he'd stood at the window in Kalliokoski's vicarage, for hours, feeling his body falling loose, shaking itself free of the world of reality, waiting for something else to arrive. What he'd been waiting for had been the vision on the ice, the defining moment of his life. And just as he'd never lost sight of that vision, so he'd always felt that he knew exactly who Katerina was. He'd known it then, and he'd still known it in Helsinki in 1918, as if her innermost self glowed inside her with a flame on which his own eye had a unique perspective. He'd never been able to predict whether she'd allow him close to that flame, but he'd always been able to glimpse it. Until now: now it was lost to his sight, and, for all he knew, gone for good.

Snow had the power to hypnotize, Esko knew, and he stood in Central Park for almost an hour, unable to see any of Manhattan's buildings, as if the whole of the island had come under some enchantment and he was all alone while in the gentle darkness the flakes continued to fall without a sound.

10

The next morning he rose early, ate breakfast at the diner as usual, and walked all the way uptown on Broadway, not bothering with the elevator when he arrived at the brownstone on Forty-seventh Street, but instead skipping up the stairs, surprising Lazarus in his office.

"Joe," he began at once. "I know that you've been telling people that my *Gazette* design is yours."

Lazarus looked up warily, his eyes watery and bloodshot. A cup of coffee steamed in front of him on his desk. Pushing back his chair a little, he looked at Esko and blinked, sheepish now that he'd been confronted.

"Frankly, I think it's pathetic, but I don't really give a damn," Esko said. "You and I will always know the truth. You're a tryer, Joe, and I daresay you'll go on trying. I can only speak for myself. As far as I'm concerned you've ceased to exist. I resign."

Esko gathered his things, and said good-bye to Miss Kott. Surprisingly, she rose on her heels and planted a kiss on his cheek. "Good luck, Mr. Vaananen," she said, and Esko stood back, fortified, touched.

"Why, thank you, Miss Kott," he said, determined to go ahead with his plan.

Two hours later he was on the eleventh floor of an undistinguished building that faced the Flatiron, high above the snowdrifts and ruthless winds of Broadway, facing a dark paneled door where a simple plaque announced: W. P. KIRBY—ARCHITECT. The door was shut, and a copy of the *New York Times* lay on the mat, alongside the previous day's edition, which was still uncollected.

Esko knocked crisply. While he waited the elevator clanked and whirred in the shaft behind him; then the door opened slowly and a head peered out.

The man could have been sixty or seventy-five or anywhere in between. His face was lined and gaunt, his gray eyes instantly probing. His close-cropped hair was quite white, only a little longer than the stubble that stood up on his cheeks like the spines on a prickly pear. It was a face sucked at by life, wary of life's blows, evidently having known more than a few; yet it was also a face filled with determination, a noble face swimming with the knowledge of what it meant to have one's every hope dashed and scorched, of what was required to go on. It was a face that Esko revered at once.

"I'm looking for W. P. Kirby," Esko said, sure that this was his man.

"I'm Kirby," the other confirmed at once in an easy, surprisingly casual voice.

The corridor filled with fumes from the previous night's whiskey; or maybe he'd been drinking already this morning, Esko thought. "It's an honor to meet you, sir," he said.

Kirby's surly eyes examined Esko's outheld hand. "Who the hell are you?" he said, rubbing his own palm across the wiry surface of his skull. "I asked you a question, comrade."

"I'm from Finland, not Russia. My name is Esko Vaananen. I'm an architect."

"Good-bye," Kirby said matter-of-factly, and slammed the door.

Esko's knuckles went back to it.

Music started up inside, a piano concerto by Beethoven.

Kirby was playing the gramophone.

"Mr. Kirby," Esko called, raising his voice. "If you please, I must speak to you."

Beethoven got louder.

"You wrote a letter about my *Gazette* design," Esko said, raising his voice yet again.

Beethoven shook the walls.

Kirby's reaction seemed perfectly reasonable to Esko, and he wasn't in the least deterred by it. He stood back, picked up the *New York Times*, and waited. The front page informed him that a woman who'd killed an insurance broker had attempted suicide three times, first with poison disguised as rouge, then by slashing her throat, finally by dashing her head against the wall of the Tombs Prison, demonstrating an incompetence regarding the whole issue of self-removal that as a Finn Esko found endearingly comical. It seemed very clear to him that the murderess wanted to live too much.

He continued to read.

A chauffeur had stolen $75,000 worth of diamonds, two aviators had drowned when their seaplane sank in the Delaware, a man had plunged ten stories to his death during a publicity stunt for the latest Harold Lloyd comedy, and a Finnish statesman, Pehr Svinhufvud, had come to America seeking a loan from the government. A picture of Svinhufvud showed him to be a stout man with a mustache and a Finnish potato face.

Esko wondered what his stolid compatriot made of America, so addicted to excitement, violence, and adventure. "You should try holding up a bank, old man," he said, not even aware that he was speaking. "They'd like you better." Svinhufvud wore a wing collar, a black tie, and a shiny top hat, as if determined to make himself as much like any other politician, and as little like a Finn, as possible. It was easier to copy than to think—hence fashion, Esko thought. Hence men like Joseph Lazarus. And then, as if his mind would now allow him so lightly to dismiss the subject of suicide, he thought for a moment of his mother, defiant, always going her own way; he pictured her in a boat, on the lake, trailing her hand in the water. *And what about you, my little brother, Esko, what will you do? Will you be a priest? Will you be interested in politics like your father? Look—two ducks flying! They mate for life!*

Her death was still like a rend in the rainbow.

Beethoven came to an end; through the door Esko heard Kirby shuffling around, presumably getting up to change the record.

Esko folded the *Times*, throwing it down.

"Mr. Kirby! I require only five minutes of your time. I have a proposition."

"Goddamnit!"

"I saw your *Gazette* design. It put my own to shame."

Something went smash against the other side of the door and Esko flinched—Beethoven, he realized.

"I entered my design under a different name—Esko Offermans."

Kirby's relaxed voice, after a pause, came as a question: "Offermans?"

"That's right," Esko said, speaking to the closed door. "You remember my design?"

"Joe Lazarus pretty much did that design himself," Kirby said. "I read it in the paper."

"Well, now, Mr. Kirby, there's a question—do you believe everything you read in the paper?"

From beyond the door: a grunt.

"It's mine, Mr. Kirby. Lazarus had nothing to do with it."

The door opened, giving Esko's nostrils another strong waft of whiskey and his eye the vision of Kirby's back, white-shirted, walking away from him. "What are you waiting for, goddamnit?" Kirby's shoeless feet were swathed in socks of thick gray wool; a big toe peeped through one of them. "Come in."

"Thank you."

The well-lit room was small, perhaps only twenty feet square. Sheets and blankets lay in disarray on a camp bed that had a downturned book and a whiskey bottle belly-up beside it. Ragged gray flakes of cigar ash dotted the threadbare rug, twitching in the draft, inching toward the stanchions of a cracked and grubby sink.

Esko hadn't known what to expect, but certainly he hadn't expected anything as deadbeat as this.

"Were you born in a barn up there in Finland? Shut the goddamn door behind you."

Esko did as he was told, pushing aside various thick, pie-shaped segments of gramophone record with his toe, and when he turned, Kirby was standing behind a plain oak desk. The polished desk was clean and bare, as if awaiting the arrival of a thought. Behind the desk was the room's only window, a big one, through which Esko saw the Flatiron bearing down through the snow like the prow of an ocean liner. On the wall to the left of the window were various framed drawings.

Esko knew he was being rude, but he couldn't resist. Those drawings pulled him around to the other side of the desk.

They were in pencil on tracing paper. The first three were of houses, low, spreading houses, with rooms running into each other, terraces reaching into the grounds, and roofs that projected like protective wings. They were beautifully proportioned. More than that, they were revolutionary. For centuries architects had designed houses that were nothing more than lots of little boxes crammed into one big one. Sometimes the big box had an interesting form, sometimes not. Kirby had simply driven a train through the box with designs that embraced two concepts, the comfort of shelter and the grandeur of space. They answered two deep-seated compulsions, one seeking rootedness and protection, the other freedom and mobility.

Esko felt humbled, as he had in the Plaza ballroom when his eye first fell on Kirby's *Gazette* design. He was in the presence of a master, perhaps *the* master, who was now living and working, or—more likely—drinking and dying in this poky room, all he could evidently afford in an undistinguished building with a small-windowed view of a very beautiful one. What had happened?

"Do these buildings exist?" Esko asked, unable to keep the astonishment out of his voice. "Were they built?"

"In Chicago," said Kirby gruffly. He pushed paper and pencil in front of Esko's face. "You claim the *Gazette* design is yours. Prove it to me now. Draw something."

"Where?"

"Sit down at the desk."

"I can't do that."

"Hah! Why, goddamnit?"

"It's your desk."

Kirby blinked, unused to such delicacy, treated to the world's bad manners for so long he'd forgotten there was any other kind. "I made that desk myself—a long time ago."

"I know."

"How? How do you know that?"

Esko shrugged.

"Sit," said Kirby, softened.

"If you insist."

"I do."

While Kirby removed himself to the camp bed, easing himself down onto it and struggling into a pair of shoes, fetching forth a dustpan and clearing up the mess, Esko stood over the desk, thought for a minute or two, sat down, and quickly began to draw.

On seeing the result Kirby scratched his head and straightened the belts of his suspenders over his shoulders. "The *Gazette* design *is* your work," he said. "And now Joe Lazarus is just trying to steal it."

"It would seem so."

"It figures. Joe's that sort. You're not worried?"

Esko looked into Kirby's eyes. "No, I'm not," he said.

"Don't tell me. Your attitude probably goes something like this—how much worse it is to have to steal than to be stolen from. Am I right?"

"Something like that."

"*Bull!*" Kirby said in a thunderous voice. "Shall I tell you the first rule of architecture?"

"Please," Esko said dryly.

"*Get the job*. Beg for the job. Swindle for the job. Change the job if needs be. Make that job your life, because it is your life, pal. Never let anyone take the job away. Not for any reason. Ever."

"In this case Joe Lazarus didn't get the job. Neither did I. Peter Winrob did."

Kirby shook his head, as if he knew better. "Give me my chair back, goddamnit."

"Certainly," said Esko, standing.

Kirby didn't sit.

"What did you say your name was?"

"Vaananen."

"Say again?"

"Vaa-na-nen."

"Vaa-na-nen," Kirby repeated. "Now just hang on a minute!" he said, taking himself across the room to a steamship trunk that was behind the door. The lid of the trunk flew open and Kirby crouched down. For a few minutes there was the sound of Kirby, muttering to himself, as he scrabbled through papers. Suddenly he announced, "I'll be damned."

Up on his feet, Kirby was holding a back copy of *Deutsche Werkbund*, one of those magazines he'd referred to in his *Times* letter, a device that like *The Studio* in England and *Architectural Record* in America was speeding design and architectural ideas around the world. "You build this?" he said.

He handed Esko the magazine, pages open to two photographs of the Church of the Shadow Cross. Esko had a distant memory of a photographer appearing at the site but until now he'd never seen the result. The sight of the church warmed him and he thought of the joy of that summer, was reminded that he hadn't heard from Anna for a while.

"Yes, this is my work too."

"Well I'll be damned," Kirby said, staring at Esko for a long time. Then he plunked himself down slowly on his camp bed. "Oh boy," he said, and put his head in his hands. "What do you want from me?" Kirby said, seeming weary and defeated all of a sudden, afraid of the answer he guessed Esko was about to give.

"I want you to teach me how to be an architect."

Esko had known that Kirby would understand, and it was clear that he did.

"Goddamnit," he said in a low emphatic voice, measuring the implications for them both. To be a teacher was no easy thing, especially with such a pupil. "Me? Are you nuts?"

Esko explained that Kirby only had himself to blame. "You were very generous and gracious about my *Gazette* design. From your point of view it must have looked like the best of a bad lot. But you gave the game away. You hinted at something and you were quite right. It didn't go far enough." He searched for words. "Look at the Flatiron. I know you do. You must look at it a hundred times a day. It's why you're here, in this little room, so you can see a building that was radiant for its time and is no less radiant now. Yet if you and I built it now, it would be grotesque, like Winrob's effort for the *Gazette*. There's a rhythm— something in the air. Maybe it's passing from Europe to America. Maybe it's rising from America itself. It's some fact about the here and now, about me and the world out there." He gestured out the window. "If I can grasp it . . . if I can find what's right within me . . ." He stopped, frustrated, scratching his cheek. "I feel like I'm trying to fly without wings. Or like I only have wings sometimes."

Kirby watched sadly from the bed. His arm swept slowly from one corner of the room to the other as he went on, without rancor or bitterness, merely cataloging the facts as he saw them. "A chair, a desk, a steamship trunk. A few pieces of paper with pencil scratchings on them. Is this what you want, Esko Vaananen? Is this how you see the end of your days? Loveless, childless, with the kind of box for a home that you fought against all your days—is this your vision for yourself? Because it's most likely how you'll end up if you follow me."

Kirby looked at Esko with a melancholy knowingness, letting his words sink in. "I'm flattered, my friend, but the truth is that I'm through. All washed up. W. P. Kirby's not even history anymore. They've forgotten about me entirely. I live by bumming money for cigars and whiskey from my friends, and they laugh about it so they don't have to embarrass me by looking at me with pity. I'm a joke."

Esko wanted to grab Kirby and shake him. Instead he went and took one of the designs down from the wall. "Mr. Kirby, now you're the one talking bull." He thrust the drawing of the graceful, well-proportioned house in front of the old man's face. "The man who did this could never, in any circumstances, be a joke."

"Goddamnit," said Kirby, cradling his head as though it were splitting in two. "I haven't built a thing in five years. Not even come close."

"That's about to change."

Piqued, fearful of what Esko might say, but longing to hear it, Kirby looked up, eyes filled with curiosity. "What the hell do you mean by that?"

"I mean that I didn't come empty-handed. I come with a carrot, Mr. Kirby," Esko said, smiling broadly. "I come with a *commission*. And one that will be very meaningful to you."

11

E sko and Kirby walked briskly to the end of Broadway, skirting Battery Park to come upon their target from the seaward side on this chill and blustery morning when it seemed Liberty had better keep hanging onto that torch of hers otherwise the wind would rip it right out of her hand and send it twirling into the heavens. One of the big liners was on the Hudson, smoke stretching behind its funnels like frozen rope. Beneath the watery winter sun, gulls screeched, wheeling this way and that, first diving on the wind and then suddenly held motionless, buffeting against it.

"Are you sure about this?" Kirby said, not nervous, not seeking reassurance, just wanting to know.

"It's like I said," Esko replied. "I'm the one who's being selfish here."

"Then let's go. Let's knock this fellow dead," Kirby said with an actor's flair, face splitting in a bright-eyed grin. "I'm going to have fun." And with that he turned around and marched toward the sheer cliffs of brooding downtown skyscrapers, unbuttoned coat trailing behind him like a banner.

In the two weeks since their first meeting, Esko had seen Kirby revive, the words *commission* and *work* acting on him like a youth-inducing cocktail. Color had returned to his cheeks and a bounce was back in his step. He'd shaved, sworn off drink and, in this rush of renewed health and confidence, had assured Esko that he'd show him a thing or two. Now he had on what he called his clients' uniform, an ostentatiously wide-brimmed hat of black velvet, a hairy tweed suit, and a red and black polka dot bow tie whose setting, slightly askew, made it resemble a pimpled propeller likely to be set spinning at any moment by the unrestrainable motor of his genius. He looked splendid, bohemian, and rather extraordinary: Abraham Lincoln uniquely conjoined with a fin de siècle poet.

"What's he like, this MacCormick?" Kirby said, not breaking his stride, still marching along with his hands in his pockets, head thrown back, chest thrust out. "I know he has power and money. He makes things go. But what's his bottom line. What does he care about really?"

Esko said that MacCormick was affable, knowledgeable, that his perennially youthful expression was hard to read.

"We'd better find out more. Because shall I tell you what the game of architecture is about really? It's about control. At every turn you're fighting against someone who's trying to control you. There's the investor, with his love of the dollar. Well, at least he's easy to understand. The client, with his impossible expectations. The city, with its books of codes and rules. So I need to know—this guy MacCormick, what's his bottom line? Is he, for instance, a tightwad?"

"I doubt that."

"Goddamnit, I'm starting to like him already," Kirby said, giving Esko a little knock of triumph. "Will he interfere?"

"He likes architecture. He understands it."

"Sometimes they're the worst," Kirby said, stopping in his tracks. His suit of fine old cloth had many pockets, like a magician's cape, and from one of them he now produced a leather case filled with cheroots. "Blathering on about arches and finials."

"He's not like that."

"Better not be, goddamnit," he said, setting off again, lit cheroot angled rakishly in his mouth, hurrying toward the elegant skyscraper that he'd designed. "Not been here in years," he said.

"Why did you put the angels on the roof?" said Esko, who'd been meaning to ask.

"Used to believe in them," Kirby said, with just the briefest glance up before he pushed through into the lobby. He went on briskly: "Clever, the guy who gave me the commission. That was back in ninety-two. He was a vain man but a good friend. Paid me well. Dead now."

Kirby stopped in front of the elevator. The sight of the gates seemed to make him reflective. "It's a long time since I've done this. Been on my way to a meeting with a client." He swung open the gate. "I always liked the feeling."

MacCormick was waiting for them when they got out at the top. "Mr. Kirby," he said, smiling that faint, ironical smile of his. "I've been waiting a long time for this."

Esko had been wondering how MacCormick would react to his proposal, his insistence, that he and Kirby take on this job together. Now he saw the two men hesitate, then step toward each other, pausing for a little bow before they shook hands, and there was a moment when he wasn't sure whether this was going to work out.

"It's an honor," MacCormick said.

"I'm looking forward to working together," Kirby said. "The pleasure is mine."

Both of them were acting, Esko saw, assuming roles: one was the well-groomed and relaxed man of the world, his insouciance not quite concealing his power; the other was energized, attentive, the would-be explicator of great mysteries, refusing to adopt a subordinate position.

"Mr. Kirby, I'd like for you to meet my wife. She's the stickler. Boy, it's tough to please her," MacCormick said, unbuttoning his overcoat and pushing a hand into his pants pocket, his voice softer now, wooing Kirby with disclosure. "We were married just six months ago, you see."

"I'd be delighted," Kirby said.

"Kate!" MacCormick called. "Come and say hello to W. P. Kirby. He built this building in the first place—how many years ago?"

"Thirty," said Kirby.

"Kate!"

The three men stood beside the elevator, waiting for Katerina. She appeared through one of the doors at the far end of the corridor and swam into Esko's vision, dressed head to toe in dark fur with her hands pushed inside a muff. He hadn't known for sure that she'd be here; he'd hoped, and now he smiled.

"Hey, you—where'd you get to?" MacCormick said.

"It's cold in there, and a mess," she said, pulling her left hand from the muff and offering it. "Mr. Kirby—I'm delighted."

"The pleasure is mine," Kirby said, sweeping off his hat with a courtly air.

"You know Esko, of course," MacCormick said.

"Of course. Hello, Mr. Vaananen," she said, giving him a cool, wintry smile, straight from the frozen streets of Petersburg.

"I guess we should poke around," MacCormick said. "I told them to try to whip this into shape a little but, like Kate says, it's pretty much a mess. It's been empty up here since I bought the building two years ago. I always had at the back of my mind the idea that I'd like to do something special with it."

They went through a door and Esko understood at once why MacCormick thought so. The top two floors of the building were internally one, surrounded by a gallery and lit by skylights. Parts had been sectioned off, but the main area was on the open plan, cluttered with desks, chairs, adding machines, addressograph machines, tall three-legged stools, speaking tubes, heating ducts, radiators, iron stoves, a printing press. It was indeed a jumble, but the potential was spectacular. The tall windows were gracefully arched, the gallery immediately suggested possibilities, and if you wanted better views of the harbor you probably had to go to the top of the Woolworth to get them.

"Some insurance company had this, and then they moved out and it got filled with all this junk," MacCormick said, poking at an upended typewriter with his toe. "Tell me, Kirby. How do you feel about this? Does it worry you, gutting this space? It's your baby, after all."

"I made this building to be used. Use changes, like everything else. Frankly, I'm pleased the thing is still standing," Kirby said. "Now you tell me something, MacCormick. What made you buy this building?"

"It was cheap," MacCormick said flatly.

Kirby roared with laughter, a gleeful explosion. Then he raised his hat. "Esko and I won't be."

"Heaven forbid," MacCormick said, realizing that in this game it was his turn to laugh now.

Esko only half attended to this banter. The words skated through his mind as he circled the space, exploring, watching Katerina. They hadn't seen each other or been in any contact since that night in the park. He recalled fragments of their conversation that night and realized that she was still most likely angry with him. She had a lot to lose — he appreciated that; and maybe the sad truth was that they couldn't go backward; but, reminding himself of the image he carried of her making the *pilvenpiirtaja* in the snow, he was reassured.

She stood beneath one of the arched windows, her back to him. Her hands, gloved in gray leather, were spread against the window ledge. Down in the harbor the departing liner was surrounded by sailboats. Esko drew his coat around him. There was no heat up here, and the freezing wind seemed to pulsate through the wall. Katerina's head turned for a moment, and the glance she gave him was questioning, almost imploring; *don't do this,* she was saying.

When Esko spoke, it was MacCormick he addressed. "I have an idea about this work," he said. "I want to make it an experiment in total design.

We'll do the furniture, the rugs, the drapes, the cutlery, and the crockery. Even the bathroom fixtures. The whole thing. Not just the penthouse. Everything. It will be extraordinary, a labor of passion and love."

Katerina turned away, facing the window again.

"Goddamnit, Esko, that's a great idea," said Kirby. "Let's do this right. An entire penthouse, springing from the smallest details within it."

"You'll design . . . *everything?*" MacCormick said, frowning slightly. "That's a lot of work."

"Sure is. It's harder to design a first-rate coffeepot than a second-rate building," Kirby said. "The project will be unique. There'll be nothing like it in all of New York. Esko's right—it's a fabulous opportunity."

"Kate—what do you think?"

For a few seconds Katerina didn't react; she didn't speak, she didn't shrug; and when at last she turned, her face was a blank.

MacCormick took off his hat and spun it between his fingers, weighing the degree of trust, as well as the amount of cash that he would likely have to give them. He nodded. "Let's do it."

"Hah!" said Kirby.

"Yes!" MacCormick said, and clapped his hands together. "Spend what you need and don't waste a cent," he said, shrewdness returning immediately. "I want to approve the designs, and before I do, I'll expect a detailed budget. And, gentlemen, you'll stick to that budget—so do your sums right. We want this to be perfect, don't we, honey?"

"Won't this be incredibly expensive?" Katerina said.

"Will it?" said MacCormick.

"Incredibly. Hellishly," Kirby said. "If you want the best."

MacCormick went over to Katerina at the window, sliding his arms beneath her unbuttoned coat. "That's what we want."

Katerina moved away from him a little, a rustle of fur and silk. She smiled, but said nothing, lighting a cigarette.

"I want to show you something. I've always been proud of what I did over here on the gallery," Kirby said, leading MacCormick over to the far corner where the old printing press was standing. "Now I think there's a way we can still use the idea, extend it," he said, guiding the other's attention upward.

Esko and Katerina were left facing each other.

"What's this all about? What's going on? Why are you doing this?" she asked, she whispered, questions tumbling angrily one after the other.

"You know why. Because your husband asked me. Because there's a lot I can learn from Kirby and I need to. And so that when this is finished and you walk in the door for the first time you will know that the walls, the windows, the chairs, the tables, the knives, the spoons, even the bed, every atom of the air in this space will be filled with the passion and regard I have and will always have for you."

Katerina's face flushed while Esko paused, amazed at his urgent fluency.

"I'll never step through that door," she said, touching a glove of gray leather to the pale skin of her throat. "You can't make me, Esko."

"Then I guess it really will be all over between us. But this will still be here." He was silent for a moment. Then he said in a soft voice, "My home for you."

12

Esko helped Kirby move his camp bed, his clothes, and his few personal belongings to the loft on Harrison Street, while the room facing the Flatiron became their office. The two men worked together, ate together, walked together, watched old Keystone Chaplins together at the little Crystal Hall Theater on Fourteenth Street, where the number of days that a Chaplin picture had *not* been playing in the last eight years was precisely five. Late one February afternoon, when blocks of ice drifted down the Hudson and smoke poured out of the city's drains, grates, and ventilator shafts, issuing from the mouths of people in the street as if their bodies were frozen and their souls on fire, Esko told Kirby of his plan for the East River Utopia, his lofty idea for a contemporary Venice, with twenty soaring towers and automobiles removed from the street and running down raised concrete canals.

"What horse shit!" Kirby said, his pale eyes twinkling. "I never heard such bull." They'd just returned to the office. Still wearing his coat, Kirby rubbed his hands in front of the radiator. "You want to launch an attack on decorated architecture? Fine. But don't destroy six hundred acres of New York to do it. The city's not a blank slate anymore. You can't just treat it any way you want."

"And why the hell not?" Esko said, crushed but instructed, a part of his stubborn spirit rising.

"We're not dreamers, because we want what we do to become real. We're not moneymakers or businessmen, though we have to know about business. God knows, we're not poets. We're trying to help people live. With harmony and a little grace. People, land, and building united. It's not easy and our mistakes tend to be permanent. So maybe it's best to aim for one small good thing. End of the first lesson. Now are you going to make the coffee or shall I?"

"I'll do it," he said, thinking that this was what he'd sought Kirby for, even if he hadn't expected him to be quite so dogmatic. What if Kirby was right? Was that all he'd been proposing to do—to rip down a shabby but living neighborhood and replace it with a tomb of concrete?

Kirby was humming happily to himself, seated in his swivel oak chair with his feet on the desk. His spirits, now that they'd been revived, never seemed to shrink. It was as if Esko had given him the one burst of energy he needed. He was, indeed, an old man; but his mental energies didn't flag or let on that he was fighting a battle against his aging body every day. He and Esko would talk, they'd ramble, they'd quarrel about the merits of certain buildings they looked at. Kirby was lively, generous, and wry; he wasn't always gentle, but he was never disrespectful. And he never wavered, now that he'd committed himself to the idea of their working together. Being with him gave Esko a sense of excitement and, in the best possible way, seriousness about what the two of them were trying to do.

Kirby began to talk about the early days of his career, forty years earlier, in the Chicago of the 1880s, when that city really *had* been a blank slate, after the big fire, and the question was—what to do with tall buildings. The technology was all in place: they had the elevators, they had the steel to make the frame, they had no coherent idea of the design. One solution was to make the tall building as though it wasn't tall at all, to wrap two or three floors with heavy embroidery and pile them on top of each other as if making a cake. Another way to go at it was to rummage around for an old building type that could be adapted—the campanile, the classical column, the Gothic cathedral—and then come up with a hybrid, resulting in the same sort of confused cornucopia that Esko had seen in the assembled *Gazette* entries, meaning that the problem wasn't solved even yet.

"Everybody started reading books about architecture, looking at pictures of architecture, instead of just getting out there and doing what was asked for and needed. It was just like Victor Hugo said. The printed word was death to natural growth in building. Suddenly you could pick styles and mix them like candy. And that was what most everyone did, tromping after each other into the past like a flock of sheep. Louis Sullivan was the exception of course. He was a prophet, and for a while it seemed his teaching would win out. But his face didn't fit. He didn't look after himself. And so the aristocratic ass-kissers were easily able to push him down to the bottom of the barrel. Sullivan! The first truly *American* architect. Maybe that's what they were all so afraid of."

He talked about two writers who were never far from his thoughts, Melville and Whitman. The antipodes of the American heart, he called them. Even in death Uncle Walt saw rainbow wonder, the heroic message of the American future. Mad Uncle Herman saw the evil beast panting beneath America's skin. One ran at God's elbow, the other spat in God's face. They were talking about man's architecture, he said.

"Right now I see a lot of Melville in New York, a lot of dancing and drinking and screwing to jazz and generally not giving a goddamn. So maybe we want to offer them some Whitman. Let them know that we've looked down deep and we still believe. Prove that we care and love the world too much. That's the other American extreme," he said.

Kirby sucked his teeth. He sighed. He grunted and ran his hand across the frizzy white hair on top of his head. "We're in the machine age," he went on. "The engineers have taught us to rethink architecture. I applaud that. I was an engineer first myself. But engineers have always made machines for people to kill people and sooner or later an engineer-minded architect will create a machinelike building just for killing. He'll build it because some madman will ask him. Architecture matters. Our choices too."

To Esko, it didn't seem utopian at all to suppose that New York could be made a better place by building one kind of building rather than another. It seemed like an opportunity, a responsibility that left open the question of how they were to proceed with the one commission they had on hand, Katerina and MacCormick's penthouse in Kirby's old building. They'd supervised the demolition of the old interior and removed the junk. They'd agreed that the penthouse should be done in a single untheatrical style. This was, after all, a place where two wealthy people would want to live in the comfort to which they were accustomed. At the same time, it would be inappropriate to turn from views of Manhattan's increasingly Babylonian skyline, of those ocean liners plowing in and out of the harbor, and see a Louis XVI sofa. So they studied the most recent designs and thinking, the prewar houses of Wright and Loos (Esko was amused, and taken, by the latter's essay entitled "Crime and Ornament"—Loos saw something sinister and lascivious in the flowing curves of *jugend*), and two postwar European magazines, *de Stijl* and *L'Esprit Nouveau*, that were championing the new manner of clarified, simplified, boxy concrete architecture. They examined the technical achievement of American trains and boats and airplanes; they looked at reproductions of every abstract and cubist picture they could find, lots of Mondrian and Picasso. Kirby exclaimed his admiration for Saarinen's Helsinki railroad station and Poelzig's weird Grosses Schauspielhaus in Berlin; Esko countered with the long crossing lines and balanced proportions of Wright's Imperial Hotel in Tokyo, which had ridden out the great earthquake of the previous year. They were equally respectful of each other's heritage and tastes, as if determined to unite Europe and America. On Kirby's Victrola they listened not just to Stravinsky and Beethoven, but also to Gershwin and Irving Berlin and Scott Joplin.

Kirby never once referred to the fact that stared him in the face, namely Esko having taken this commission because he was in love with Katerina. In this, Kirby's tact showed itself as impeccable as his impish energy was remarkable, and Esko was allowed to persist in the idea that his passion for Katerina and his architectural quest were intriguingly and not damagingly intertwined. His ideas about this were changing. In any event he saw the penthouse design differently. This wasn't a mad chase, like the skyscraper, but a quieter, softer gesture. He hoped it would have a tenderness to it that she would always appreciate. He was trying to make something lovely, not so that he'd be lovely to her, but for her alone. It was a gift, a rose. If she didn't want it—fine, let her throw it away; if she wanted to live there with Mac-Cormick—so be it, that was her choice. He remembered her eyes as she'd looked across at him up there in the Kirby Building, her intense gaze burning his cheek, asking him not to do this. If this signaled the end of everything between them, then he'd learn to live with that. He told himself now that he was no longer laying siege to her affection—he was simply creating a beautiful home. His thinking wasn't quite straight, but in this he was only human. His analysis of his own motives was perhaps flawed, but then the heart is a dense tangle. I'll never try to see her again, once this job is done, he told himself; but then what he told himself and what he felt were perhaps as different as a penthouse and a skyscraper. Esko was a passionate, awkward man, a good man, always reaching for the butterfly; but butterflies on the wing have an evanescent bloom quite lost once pinned to the lepidopterist's card.

"Today we start," Kirby said.

"Where do we start?"

"Where do you *want* to start?"

Esko grinned at that. "With a coffeepot."

They sat down facing each other on opposite sides of the desk, like hounds ready to slip their leashes, and on that first day they drew one hundred coffeepots without finding *the* coffeepot; on the second day, a hundred more, with the same result. On the third day Kirby looked at something Esko had just done. "That's it, that's the one!" he said, voice rocking with excitement. "You see, Esko—imagination applied to the whole world is nothing compared to imagination applied to a detail."

"What's next?" Esko said.

"A coffee *cup*," Kirby said with a flashing smile of triumph.

After the coffee cup came a saucer, a plate, a bowl, a vase. The kitchen table determined the kitchen chair, in turn providing a motif that played into the larger armchairs and sofas in the living area and the new staircases they determined would lead to the gallery. At first Esko took stubborn pleasure in the mere performance of these exercises but after a while saw with excitement how the design for the penthouse entire was flowing from the tiny droplet of that beginning, the coffeepot, a selection he'd made at random, almost as a joke. The painstaking process gained its own inevitable momentum, the trick being to concentrate on the latest small task at hand, rather than to stand back and gape in terror at the enormous quantities of work still to be done.

Kirby kept himself fresh each day with prodigious amounts of coffee, and by duding himself out in his tweed suits, shirts that he now kept crisply laundered, and debonair bow ties. Esko worked, walked, or stretched out on the floor if his back ached or the old wound in his side was smarting. Sometimes he found himself thinking of Anna, knowing that she would have enjoyed this, wishing that she could meet Kirby. There was a purity to this work that reminded him of the churches, and it occurred to him that in becoming obsessed by this design, by pouring every ounce of his skill and all the love that he felt for Katerina into a creation that would be laid at her feet, he was perhaps purging himself of his desire. And that might indeed be a good thing, a great thing, he thought.

In all, they spent three months on the drawings for the penthouse and its contents, then two more weeks building a model—a long time for such a commission, though Esko felt all the while that he was putting money in the bank, building up resources he could call upon later, gaining a core of certainty about himself and design. He was happy that the phone never rang and there was no one else he and Kirby had to see. They lived in the city like monks, and then the thing was done, and they went back into the world.

MacCormick's office was all the way downtown, off Broadway, only a few blocks west of Kirby's old skyscraper in a building that rose like a mountain— solid, craglike, brooding—above the rolling Hudson and the teeming piers. The lot where the building stood was in the shape of a parallelogram; hence there was a twist between the base of the building and the stubby tower that rose from it. Just looking at the thing gave you vertigo. On that afternoon, late in the summer of 1923, when Esko and Kirby were at last ready to go there, a liner had just come into the pier at the end of the street and was being lashed to its moorings as if restrained by policemen. MacCormick operated from the topmost floor of the building, reached by a rocketing express elevator that served it exclusively. As soon as the elevator doors opened they found them- selves in a rectangular space that was about half the length of a city block. At the room's cardinal points were giant windows with red velvet drapes, open, offering spectacular views of the ocean dusk and of a strange, rosy glow that hovered and pulsed in the haze over the factories on the Jersey shore. The soft torchette lighting was all directed upward at the ceiling, where it bounced off patterns of red mosaic and suffused the room with a soft, almost bloodlike light. The walls were hung with tapestries, richly textured fabrics of yellow and gold. The floor was laid in black and golden tile and the tiles were in turn thrown with sumptuous rugs. The torchettes themselves were of dulled cop- per cast in such a way that they seemed to be melting in the light of their own heat. It was a room designed for a prince, and for great dramatic moments, as if in the far silences of its dim corners hid an audience—watchful fates, or waiting courtiers.

MacCormick was in his shirtsleeves behind a desk at the end of the room. As Esko and Kirby got closer they saw that the desk was five, maybe six yards across; it was vast, and MacCormick was leaning against it with both his hands, listening calmly to an assistant. It was as if they were approaching the throne where the money king reigned. Esko had understood that Mac- Cormick was rich but he'd really had no idea, until this moment, what that might mean. The idea of wealth was abstract. The physical evidence of power in this room was overwhelming, a hand at the throat. A stock ticker chattered beneath its glass dome. Another assistant rushed forward and pressed a pile of papers into MacCormick's hand. MacCormick glanced at them briefly before securing them with a paperweight that was a brick of gold bullion. And only then did he acknowledge Esko and Kirby's presence.

"Gentlemen. What a pleasure and what a surprise," he said in his lazy way, scrunching up his eyes and fingering the little hole in his chin. He selected one of his Turkish cigarettes from an ebony box and snapped shut the lid of the box. "I was beginning to think you'd run out on me."

"Good work takes time, Mr. MacCormick; you know that," said Kirby, unstoppering his sparkle and flamboyance, rising to the occasion with a flourish. "Look what we brought you?" He hefted a bulging portfolio. "May we?"

"Please, go ahead," MacCormick said. "Would you guys like a drink?"

"Is your scotch real?" Kirby said.

"As genuine as the Old Masters on my walls. I buy only the best, you know that."

"Then, sure—I'll take a drink," Kirby said.

"Esko?"

"Thanks," Esko said, helping Kirby unlace the portfolio.

MacCormick spent a long time going over everything, examining each drawing with care, and there were more than a hundred. Sometimes he smiled. Once or twice he sighed. He looked at one particular drawing and shook his head, but it wasn't clear whether this was a thumbs-up or a gesture the other way. Finally he looked up from the desk, and swept his longish hair out of his eyes, blinking at the chattering stock ticker as though it had dragged him back from a world where he'd rather be. "Gentlemen—I'm amazed. I'm bowled over. This is terrific work."

"We know that," Kirby said.

"How much?" MacCormick said, returning to his senses.

Esko had prepared a list with all the figures broken down. It was in his pocket. It mentioned a sum. Kirby now looked MacCormick in the eye and doubled it.

"Fine," MacCormick said, drawing a book of checks toward him. He hesitated, reaching for a pen. "How fast can this be done?"

"We'll need at least a year," Kirby said.

"Ridiculous," said MacCormick, putting the stubby black pen down again. "Kate and I are leaving for Europe soon. The place has to be ready when we get back. Three months."

"Absurd," Kirby said, waving his arm. "Nine."

"Six."

"Agreed."

MacCormick leaned back, clasping his hands behind his head, giving them one of his elusive smiles. Esko knew that six months must have been the period of time he'd had in mind all along.

MacCormick took up the fountain pen, and soon its golden nib was scratching; he waved the check in the air, drying the ink, folded the check, came around the desk, and pushed the check into the top outside pocket of Esko's suit. "I'll look forward to seeing our new home in six months," he said. Then he turned to one of his assistants and it was as if they didn't exist anymore.

Going down in the express elevator Kirby slumped theatrically in the corner like an exhausted old gunslinger and started to laugh. "Esko, we did it, *goddamnit!*" He glanced at the ceiling. "Did he really write the check for the full amount? For what I asked for?"

"It's for the full amount," Esko said.

"You haven't even looked at it."

"No, but I know MacCormick." He also knew that Kirby mistrusted power, display, big business, having seen friends and colleagues damaged, battered, destroyed by what that triumvirate can do, so he showed him the check.

Kirby threw back his head and whooped, an old man letting out an Indian war cry.

That night they celebrated: an evening that began with champagne at Delmonico's and concluded, at 3:00 A.M., with snifters of ancient brandy in the lounge of the Algonquin.

The next day they met with a general contractor and began to assemble an army of artisans and craftsmen. They had control, and they gave Mac-Cormick the best. Everything proceeded smoothly and without a hitch, and the job was completed ahead of schedule.

13

Katerina did indeed summer in Europe with MacCormick, but returned ahead of him and spent several weeks traveling through Yosemite and Arizona taking photographs. By Thanksgiving of that year, 1923, she was back in New York, awaiting the arrival of her husband. One night she and some friends broke off from dinner to listen to the first transatlantic radio broadcast from London. She leaned toward the walnut cabinet where the radio was enshrined, straining to hear the arrogant and aloof tones of King George V, struggling through several thousand miles of static. It was odd for her to hear that voice, so familiar in a way, so similar in timbre to the dead Czar's, puttering and crackling feebly within this machine of the new age. She snapped off the radio, wound up the Victrola, and the stuffy English king gave way to an American royalty, the stylish Duke Ellington. Her New York friends were musicians, writers, actors, people who did nothing and were just rich, denizens of Broadway and Harlem who drank steadily and sometimes malevolently, their lives a blur of parties and hangovers and car rides too fast between which they found the time to cram in some work. They danced, they laughed, they fell off chairs; they fucked and pretended not to care and said *blah* to the world. To spend time with them was to know that Bolshevism must fail. In New York she never tried to work. She let her friends swarm around her while she watched them and smiled; she'd had enough tragedy in her life, and when she was away from her camera, she wanted jazz.

She wouldn't let herself be angry about what had been done and what was still being done in Russia: to give in to such feelings would be to wreck herself. The news that Lenin was sick and reportedly dying brought her no pleasure. She attended no émigré meetings, read no émigré newspapers. She'd survived in America and married to advantage by dividing her life into compartments and not allowing damage from one to leak through into the other. This was the principle that had made the *Titanic* supposedly unsinkable—but it seemed to be working for her. Her marriage was one thing, not allowed to interfere with her work; her travel was another and came to life for her only when she saw something that made her want to take her camera out; in New

York she gave primacy to MacCormick even when, as now, they weren't actually together. She was very fond of him. He made money, he was amusing,
sometimes brilliant, and he had a sovereign contempt for all sentimental nonsense; this didn't stop him from being jealous, but that was because he valued
her so highly, just as she valued the freedom and ease with which his millions
kept her supplied. She knew quite well that their relationship was more a bargain than an *amour*, but wasn't every mature marriage thus? She'd had quite
enough *amour*, thank you very much; she no longer believed in *amour*, hadn't
for quite a long time. If her realism needed any reinforcement, she had only
to remember the early days in New York when she'd lived in a small room on
Fourteenth Street amply furnished with cockroaches. There'd been little
food, no money. When she knew someone was coming to visit, she ran to one
of the Jewish bakeries on Orchard Street, bought a cake, and sliced it in half.
Guests, out of politeness, rarely touched the cake, knowing that she was starving. She'd eat it later, slowly, with a glass of milk. Once she'd watched in horror while a Greenwich Village poet wolfed it down in one bite, prejudicing
her forever after against writing that didn't go all the way across the page.

Her waking hours were her own now; she controlled them; but at night
her dreams were still sometimes hellishly peopled by the men who'd burst
into the house that night in Petersburg. At night she experienced all over
again the rape, their foul breath on her face, their ramming inside her, the
murder of her mother, her grandmother, and her father. She visited once
more the strange deliriums and fears of those months in Helsinki after her
escape, and it was Esko's association with the memories of that time that
made her recoil when she first saw him in New York. She'd thought him
dead, literally, and then those wires and letters had started arriving, the messages from *Vanity Fair*, and even now, months after she'd last seen him in that
freezing jumble of a space overlooking the harbor, she still remembered the
depression and confusion that meeting him again had evoked. Yes, she cared
for him; but his kindness, his tenderness, his passion for her sped her back
into a tunnel of unhappy memory, at the end of which lay a dragon, a chaos
that she believed could not be defeated, not by love, not by beauty, not by
will. The monsters of her past could only be held at bay; they could not, she
thought, be laid to rest. As for the *pilvenpiirtaja* in the snow—it seemed to her
now that a stranger had done that. She didn't care to confess that Esko was
under her skin; she couldn't afford to admit that; she didn't think it was true.

She heard one morning from MacCormick's people that the penthouse was finished. The news challenged her, made her body tingle with an unease that simultaneously roused her to feelings of resentment. Was she really afraid? Must she really forbid herself to see it? She was a rational, analytical person—it would be absurd, weak, not to go take a look.

She knew that her husband believed Esko to be a remarkable architect, potentially a great one. She herself didn't know what this meant. She would look at certain pictures by Cezanne, by Picasso, by Braque, she would read a lyric by Pushkin, a sonnet by Shakespeare, and the hairs would stand up on the back of her neck. The aesthetic experience was in the end a physical and not an intellectual one—same with Paul Strand's photographs, and Atget's, and even Stieglitz's, though her impression of Stieglitz's work was colored by the fact that she knew him and he always looked at her with weaselly, almost possessive eyes. But she'd never experienced any such bliss with regard to designed space. She'd loved her homes in Russia, but that was to do with comfort, family, memory, not appreciation. Architecture wasn't really her thing, which was a good reason to be unafraid of whatever it was that her Esko Vaananen might have done, she thought.

She came up out of the subway to find Broadway rain-sodden. A savage wind rushed from the sea, and a thousand glistening umbrellas were tilted over a thousand homburgs and cloche hats. Galoshes splashed through puddles, and a passing bus plowed up a wave of spray, briefly obscuring the dripping buildings and the dismal tint of the sky. The continuous patter of the rain made a muted counterpoint to her thoughts, which didn't concern Esko at all; she was remembering, oddly, her first governess at the house in Petersburg, a French woman with dark curls and flashing eyes who had given her a lovely copy of *Madame Bovary*. They'd sat together on a rock in the sunshine—where? somewhere by the sea—reading and rereading the passages in which Emma and Rodolphe meet to make love.

Katerina hurried on beneath her umbrella, came to the threshold of the building, where she paused for a moment, then pushed through the door, walking toward the elevator and pulling the key to the penthouse from where she'd hidden it in the palm of her glove. Going up, she thought of Helsinki and the mirror she'd left behind in the apartment on Fabianinkatu, the little art nouveau mirror that her father had bought for her in Paris one afternoon when they were out walking with that same governess; it occurred to her then that her dead father—of course, how could she have missed it?—must have been having an affair with that sinewy French girl.

She listened with concentration to the whirring, clanking sound of the elevator, pressing the key to her lips. She thought she'd get this over with quickly.

Her first impressions were of warmth and comfort after the rain.

What she'd seen six months ago had been a mess of junk piled high in rooms so cold she'd thought of Petersburg. She'd told MacCormick he was crazy to be throwing his money away. No architect, no matter how gifted, could do anything with this, she'd said. Now, on opening the door, she saw a floor of polished oak and a forest of slender oak columns. Walking through these, touching them with her gloved fingers, she came into the main body of the penthouse and was at once drugged by a voluptuous sense of luxury. The space was high, airy, and luminous; it didn't make her gasp; rather its effect was gentle, reassuring, as if a subconscious chord of harmony had been struck. The walls had been paneled to two-thirds of their height, and the paneling was painted white, as was the space above. The second-story gallery had been extended and now thrust out above the main living area, supported on oak beams that did not meet the upright oak posts until they had gone a foot or more past the balustrade. The air was laced up with wood. Esko had brought the spirit of his forests here, for her.

The oak floor was strewn with fine embroidered rugs. A three-sided brick chimney came down from the roof and stopped five feet above an open brick fireplace. The grate, surrounded by deep sofas, was already piled high with logs, ready for a match. Beyond, in the dining area, a long black table was surrounded by six wide chairs with high, narrow backs and white cushions of shot silk. In the kitchen, plain and elegant knives and forks were laid out like treasures on wooden countertops. She touched the white porcelain dinner plates (sturdy, practical) and then her eye fell with delight on a sleek steel coffeepot; it had an angular wooden handle, so clean and sharp it might have been drawn by Braque; she lifted this lovely thing and was surprised by its lightness.

Everything was quiet. There was only the sound of the rain against the windows and of the building itself, creaking in the wind. Continuing her exploration, on the other side of the kitchen she found a snug den, a room for sitting and reading in, where shelves went from ceiling to floor. A door to one side of the library gave way to a windowless space, perfect for her darkroom, while on the other side there was an open staircase that rose out of the floor like a dizzy corkscrew to the gallery. Ascending, she found that the entire southern side of the gallery had been left open, splendidly facing the harbor.

The chairs here were in the same style as those downstairs, and there were tables so that you could sit with coffee or a drink or a book and gaze at the ever-changing sky and sea. The northern side of the gallery, at the back of the building, had been widened so that there was the balcony rail and a corridor with doors leading off it. The first two doors she came to opened onto the guest bedrooms, with bathrooms en suite. Beyond the third door lay the enormous master bedroom, positioned in the corner of the building, with a right-angled window in the corner; in the center of the room was an oak bed, deep and wide, with curving lines clean as a four-master and a backboard artfully carved with trees.

Katerina understood now the effect that such gorgeous interweaving of light and air and space could have. She felt as though Esko had written her a poem, or painted her portrait, or done both things at the same time. She understood, with her senses as much as her mind, that it was as Esko had promised: every atom of this space had been artfully arranged to evoke in her sensations of comfort, safety, and peace. The vibration in her ears wasn't the wind but her own blood singing. She stood quite still, spellbound, like a little girl handed the key to the great bright unexplored attic of her dreams, like an heiress whose most outrageous whim has been pampered, like a lover kissed on every inch of her body.

14

Kirby came into the Plaza with water streaming off the wide brim of his hat as if he were a fountain. He plucked off the hat, dumped copious further amounts of water onto the marble floor of the lobby, waved away the doorman, took off the wide-shouldered green tweed coat he'd recently bought, shook yet more water off that, and turned, smiling warmly at the woman who'd followed him in and was just now lowering her umbrella. Esko, watching from a chair in the lounge, felt his heart skip. The woman was Katerina. Kirby was with Katerina.

"Look what I found," Kirby said, spotting Esko and coming over, throwing hat and coat down on an empty chair. "The most beautiful woman in New York. Mrs. Kate MacCormick!"

Katerina wore a black cloth coat over a dark woollen skirt and a plain gray sweater, her gray wool stockings were tucked into sensible, low-heeled shoes, and a black beret was pulled down tight over her forehead. She looked snug, not muted, but softened, for a moment younger again, almost girlish, although less sure of herself than when she'd been a little girl, and even more ravishingly beautiful. Just looking at her, smelling the fresh cold air that came off her clothes and skin, made Esko feel as though he'd been deliciously stabbed.

"Let's go to the bar," Kirby said. "I must and shall have a cocktail. There must and *will* be strong liquor," he said, narrowing his eyes so that they were just cracks. "Goddamnit!"

"I won't stay," said Katerina, pulling off one gray leather glove.

"Oh, bullshit," Kirby said good-naturedly. "She was in the penthouse, Esko. What about that? I went around tonight to check on the heating and there she was. Moved in already."

Esko was amused; he gave her a quizzical look. "Is this true?"

"Not exactly. I've only spent the last two nights there," she said in a low voice, twisting the glove in her hands.

This was new to Esko: a hesitant, almost shy Katerina, but then she seemed to catch his thought and jumped straight past her momentary bashfulness. "I was wrong, Esko," she said, looking straight at him now. "It's as if you'd held an enchanted mirror to everything I might want in a home. I don't deserve anything so perfect."

"Yes, you do," cried Esko and Kirby together.

"No," she said, shaking her head, smiling at the two of them. "But thank you. Really—from the bottom of my heart. I adore it. Now I feel embarrassed again," she said.

"My dear young lady," said Kirby, gallantly taking her arm. "Let me tell you right now that any and all such feelings will be surgically removed by prompt attention to a couple of whiskey sours."

"I have to go."

"Don't be absurd," Kirby said.

"No, really. I just wanted to say thank you. Now I really must go."

"Esko—do something," Kirby said, and Esko saw from Katerina's face that the decision was indeed in his hands.

"Stay," he said, proud that he'd moved her.

"All right," she said, her smile a brief searchlight of happiness.

"Even better," Kirby said. "Let's make an evening of it. A night on the town, damnit."

Which is what happened: in the Plaza bar Kirby produced a flask from one of his many pockets and they quickly drank three whiskey sours; then a taxi bore them through driving sleet on Broadway to a small theater in the Village, where they took seats for a Moscow Arts Theater production of Chekhov. Katerina said this was one part of her homeland that she was proud to remember, and Esko and Kirby were sufficiently lit with liquor that it was some minutes into the first act before they realized the performance was to be entirely in a foreign language.

Midnight found them, still laughing, hurrying through the doors of a nearby restaurant, whitewashed walls and red candles throwing shadows in the dimness.

"I guess it was pretty good, considering it was in Russian," Kirby said, sitting down, popping his hat on the back of the chair.

"There was one lovely moment," Esko said.

"When the little boys were watching and the lovers went on kissing anyway," Katerina said.

"They couldn't help themselves," Esko said.

"Of course they couldn't help themselves," Kirby said. "They were in some godawful town on the steppe where everything was gray. The houses were gray. The dresses were gray. The food was gray; probably. Even I understood that." He flipped open the menu, produced another flask from another of his pockets, and gave Katerina a ridiculous wink, as if to say she was very lucky indeed that he wasn't twenty years younger. He twisted in his chair, waving the flask: "Waiter!"

It was jolly in the small, darkened room, packed, filled with laughter, smoke, and raucously rising voices. A waiter duly appeared, mixed their cocktails, and told them proudly that there was wine available, real Italian Chianti.

"We'll take two bottles," Kirby said. He leaned forward toward the candle with one of his cheroots between his lips like a peashooter. Leaning back, he puffed luxuriantly. "I'm not going to let you off the hook, young lady," he said to Katerina. "I want you to tell me about your photographs. You promised you would. Come along now—which is your favorite."

"It's hard to think," Katerina said.

"Don't think—just tell us."

"Well . . ." said Katerina. She'd taken off her coat and her beret; a brooch roosted on her sweater, just below her throat and to the side, a swooping silver swallow with emeralds that picked up the color of her eyes. "It was in Colorado, last winter," she said.

She'd spent three days in a small town, sleeping in a hot, cramped room above the post office while all that time, outside, a blizzard raged. "It snowed for seventy-two hours. Finally it stopped and I could go out again. It was night. The snow was piled deep and white," she said. "The street lamps were on, throwing shadows that made the hummocks of snow look even bigger. I went back for my camera and started shooting. When I printed the pictures later there was one shot with a street lamp in the foreground. The street lamp had a kind of glow around it, as if something wonderful were about to happen. As if visions were about to appear." She accepted Kirby's offer of a cheroot. "And that's my favorite picture," she said, cheroot unlit between her lips. "Now it's your turn, Mr. Kirby."

The waiter returned to the table and, with a humming flourish, uncorked the first of the bottles of Chianti.

"Which is your favorite building—of all the ones you've built?" Katerina asked.

Kirby watched, frowning, while the waiter poured the wine. He rolled his right shoulder a little and rubbed it as though it were sore, nervous gestures that Esko knew by now meant he was upset or worried about something.

"Can't answer that," Kirby said, and emptied his glass.

"Now you're naughty," Katerina said, wagging her finger. "I told you—remember?"

"Oh boy," Kirby said, hand touching the fine hair that stood up on top of his head as if electrified. He blinked, looking tired suddenly, half-filling from his flask a wine glass that was soon emptied again, drinking with a vengeance, holding himself so stiffly in his chair that he seemed to be on the verge of toppling over.

"Was the building knocked down?" Esko asked.

"Fire," Kirby said. He stared into the candle's flame. "Oh boy," he said, "*damnit.*" He shrugged, blew out through his lips. "It's the story of my finest hour—and my ruin. I guess the two are often related, aren't they? Dangerous family members."

"Look—maybe you don't want to tell us the story. It's all right," Esko said.

"No, I do want to," Kirby said, putting a hand to his chest. "My father was a preacher of the gospel. A builder too. He designed and built his own church. And the house where we lived. This was in Kansas. He said that he met Billy the Kid one time and that for a year after that he carried a gun and not only a Bible. But I never knew whether to believe him."

Katerina calmly pushed aside her purse, reached across the table, and took Kirby's hand; Kirby looked at those slender white fingers folded over his gnarly brown mitt and smiled. "When I was a kid I was a whole lot more interested in dime cowboy novels than I was in any of the worthwhile books my mother tried to tell me about. So one day she called me over and said we were going someplace. She took me up on her horse and we rode a few miles outside town and up the hill. It was plenty flat where we lived and there was only this one hill and from on top of it you could see clear fifty miles, maybe a hundred. Read, my mother told me. Educate yourself. That way you'll always be ahead of the game, whatever happens. You'll always be up here. You'll have scope. Vision. I didn't pay much heed to her at the time but later I realized she was right. That was her gift to me. I did read. I did get an education. I did go to college. And so, years later, when I had a family myself, I built a house on top of that hill."

Kirby looked into the guttering candle. He described how men had hauled stone from a quarry over fifteen miles away and wood from a forest that was five miles beyond that. He said, "I was working in Chicago at that time. I'd take the train back to Kansas on a Friday afternoon and keep right on working inside the house while it was rising around us." His eyes glittered with pride at the memory. "Esko, you should have seen that house when it was finished. It didn't sit on the goddamned hill; it was a part of it, like it had always belonged there, like it had grown overnight out of the stones themselves. It was low, wide, and snug. It was a hope, a haven—we were very happy."

He wasn't looking at either of their faces, but at Katerina's hand, folded over his.

"I never kept a picture of that house. It was in 1913 that it burned down. My wife, and Danny, and Billy—our two kids . . . They died, they all died. I wasn't there. I . . . ."

His voice fell away. He pulled his hand away from Katerina's and, with his fingernails, dug into his forehead as if he could peel back the skin from his face like a mask. "I had my own carpenters make the coffins. I dug and filled the graves myself."

Kirby groaned. At last he pulled his hands away from his face. His finger-nails had cut livid half-moons into his forehead.

"You see, Esko. My art became associated with disaster. I lost all my loves in that fire. It's why I'll always be grateful to you. You revived a little of what was fine in me."

In one corner of the restaurant a pianist was playing now, some bouncing new tune that jazzed the air. The waiter, unasked, came and thumped down another bottle of wine. A woman broke out in high-pitched laughter and Esko fingered the scorched skin on his cheek, for a moment no longer in New York, but back in his childhood, running toward a house with flames shooting through the roof and glass exploding from the windows. He thought of Kirby's *Gazette* design, so fierce and pure and refined, and he wondered now if it had called him precisely because he'd sensed that Kirby had walked through fire too. He wished to take the old man in his arms, soothe him, and with some magic spell repair the damage done by the flames of the world. That was impossible Esko knew; the past had broken Kirby's heart—but there was the future and what they still could do.

Esko struck a match and lit again the candle that had died in front of them on the table. "It seems that I owe you both a story," he said. "I want to tell you about my favorite building. I haven't built it yet."

He took a pen from his inside jacket pocket. "I just had an idea," he said calmly. "Wood bends. I think by shaping together wood in long thin strips it will be possible to make a chair like this." The nib of the pen pressed down into the fabric of the tablecloth, making an L and then a reflected L placed on top of the first. Thus: ⌐L

"The seat and back of the chair will be made from pine or plywood. The arms and legs will be strips of the same material, molded together. The whole chair will give. It'll be pliant, like a spring."

Esko slowly screwed the cap back on his pen and laid the pen on the table. He leaned back in his chair, crossed his arms, smiled. "You see, Katerina, now that we've done your penthouse—and I know we've done a good job—we'll get lots of offers from lots of very rich people asking us to do the same thing over and over again. But it's like W. P. told me the other day. It's no good our repeating ourselves. We have to think about the next big thing," he said, gesturing with his chin toward the little ink hieroglyph he'd made on the tablecloth. "This is it."

She tilted her head to one side, examining the two L's first from one angle then the other. "Esko—it's just a chair," she said, puzzled.

"Exactly," said Esko with comic pride.

"I'm sorry. I don't understand." She turned to Kirby, her eyes questioning. "Am I missing something?"

Kirby's cheeks were still wet with tears but his mouth was smiling now. "A detail," he said. "You're missing a detail."

"What?" she said, looking from one of them to the other. "I'm still in the dark."

"Ask who'll sit in the chair," Kirby said.

"Well, Esko?" she said.

"A clerk. Or maybe a secretary." Esko took up the pen again. "Who'll need a desk. And beside the desk, a trash basket. And to the side of the desk, a shelf. And around all these, a room, an office."

The pen raced now.

"An office that is in turn one cell in the floor of a building, a floor that can be endlessly duplicated—like this."

The pen scratched and slashed, bringing forth the bold lines of a skyscraper, something stark and new, derived from the sparse clarity of that original chair.

"And that won't be all," Esko said.

He lifted the plates, the various bottles, the knives and forks, the salt and pepper shakers, and placed them on the floor, leaving only the candle and their glasses on the tabletop, and these he pushed to the side.

"You see, Katerina, when I first came to New York I had this big idea for a utopian city. A city within the city if you like, a city of skyscrapers. I thought— twenty skyscrapers! That way Esko would really prove to Katerina that he loved her. He'd really show the world. But W. P. told me the idea was bull and he was right. It would be too big a shock for the city—like ripping away a limb. So I'll build something smaller, with the original streets still intact, a collection of buildings around a skyscraper and a plaza."

"So the rest of the city can come to it," Kirby said.

"Exactly," Esko said, and then his pen was off again, scoring black lines in the linen. "In the center, the office building, higher than the Woolworth, the highest in the city. At each corner, an office tower. Running away from one corner, a long building for a hospital and a community center flowing into the tower at the other end of the block. Here, a theater. Here, a hotel. In the middle, the plaza, Not like Venice, like New York. People will flock there. To be by the fountain."

"The fountain." Katerina said.

"Of course. The fountain. People will sit, relax, listen to the water. Buy food and things from the stalls in the plaza."

By now the entire tablecloth was taken over by a vision of interlocked cubes and towers, clean walled, majestically sculptural. This project would be simple, convenient, sweet running, and light, and, examining it now by the candle's flickering light, Esko saw that it was the perfect melding of his child-hood ideal with everything he'd learned about life and architecture and New York. He felt, in that moment, as though he'd achieved something at last.

"So you see, Mr. Kirby. You have no call to thank me. It's the other way around. I thank *you*. Now what do you say—will you work on this with me?"

"Esko—it would be an honor."

The next two hours were drawing, talk, drink, more drawing. That first tablecloth was folded away, and a revised rendering was made on a second, and then a third, and by the end of the evening Kirby was so exhilarated, so exhausted, and so drunk, that they had to help him out of the door, into the cab, and back to Harrison Street.

"Where am I?" he said, suddenly starting awake when they were in the loft.

"Home," Esko said.

Kirby sniffed the lanolin in the air. "So I am," he said. "Esko—do you have the drawings?"

"Of course," Esko said, tapping where they were tucked beneath his coat.

"Thank God for that, godamnit. It's a wonderful scheme. Wonderful," he said, allowing Esko and Katerina to maneuver him out of his coat. "Take the drawings to the office right away. Make sure they're safe. Lock them up. You don't want Lazarus or anyone getting wind of this."

"Sure. I'll do it," Esko said. "You should sleep now."

"Should I? Hell, Esko, I feel great about this. We'll really show those bas-tards."

"We will."

"No, we *really* will," he said, and, having thrown himself prone on the camp bed, was snoring within a minute.

Outside, the temperature had fallen, the wind had dropped, and the cut-ting sleet had turned to snow that angled down between the stone flanks of Broadway, drifting on the sidewalk and swimming at their faces as Esko and Katerina walked north toward the office. A taxi went by, engine throbbing, wheels slithering and skidding, and a head raised itself out of the back win-dow, greeting them with some incoherent, ecstatic yell. Then all was silence until they walked beneath a neon coffeepot, endlessly pouring its stream of coffee light into a neon coffee cup. The sign hissed and snapped as the snow hit it, melted.

They arrived at the office and Esko turned on the lights and lit the oil heater. He took down a bottle of whiskey and two glasses from a cupboard. Katerina walked around, glancing briefly through the window toward the prow of the Flatiron, examining the walls where Kirby's old drawings had now been joined by renderings of the penthouse design.

"Is this the way the two of you usually work—by getting drunk?" she asked.

"No," said Esko with a laugh, locking the tablecloths away in the safe. "It's a very sober business, generally speaking. Let me show you something."

He walked to the desk and pulled a sheaf of drawings from the desk. "Did you see your coffeepot yet?"

"Of course—it's lovely."

"Come here. Look. This is how many times we tried before we got it right."

She came and stood next to him and put her hand on his shoulder, leaning toward him so he felt the heat and pressure of her slender body as their heads moved forward and he flipped through the drawings where they lay in a pool of light on the desk.

Katerina smiled. Her white teeth shone faintly. "That's a lot of coffeepots."

"And everything else too. We worked very hard for you, Katerina."

"And for MacCormick?"

"For him too. But mostly for you. And it was a pleasure."

She looked at him, smiling faintly, not a sexual smile, not exactly, but a wondering smile that was followed by a question.

"Esko, do you love me?"

"You know the answer."

"I want you to say it. Is it a very hard thing for a Finnish man to say?"

"Very," he said, his face close to hers. "Katerina—I love you. I love you more than my life."

"Do you think you love me only because we haven't slept together yet? I'm sorry, that sounds blunt. But I know it happens to be true of a lot of men. They want what they can't have and once they get it their interest wanes. Beautiful things shouldn't be attained easily. Received goods are less fascinating than ones that haven't arrived yet. The untaken picture is always the best, because it hasn't been spoiled. And perhaps the unbuilt building is what you really long for. And the untaken Katerina."

From outside came the hiss of snow, melting and dying against hot neon. Her eyes were on him, assessing him, but her voice was soft, almost shy. "Esko," she said, "what if we were to go now and make love all night?"

Esko swallowed hard, swimming in the smell of her hair, the sweet closeness of her perfume, the gloss of her lips, the presence and firmness of her bones. "I'd like that," he said, his voice almost a croak.

"Do you think it would cure you of me?"

"You're not a disease, Katerina. I didn't catch you like the flu. I've always loved you. I always will."

"You don't know anything about me. Not really."

"I know you. When I look into your eyes I know exactly who you are."

"What do you see?"

"That girl with a mirror on her wrist. And by some miracle she's coming toward me, and soon we'll be on the dance floor together." .

She said nothing, letting his words wash over her, soaking them up.

"It gets stronger every time I see you."

She wrapped both her arms around his neck. He closed his eye and she kissed him, her tongue pushing open his mouth and seeking his. He could feel her flesh through the wool of her sweater, a warm passionate heartbeat.

"Katerina," he sighed, and tried to kiss her again, but she pressed her cheek into his shoulder, saying, almost shyly:

"Shall we go somewhere?"

"Any place particular?"

"Home."

15

The streets grew ever quieter once they passed City Hall Park until it seemed that every sound had been shut off, damped down, muffled, and once again—as on that night in Central Park—it seemed that this gaudiest and busiest of cities existed for them alone. Buildings rose all around them, fantastically high, their peaks invisible in the swirling snow. A sheet of newspaper fled across the street, as if migrating. Somewhere in an empty office a telephone rang with frantic impatience. In the harbor a tugboat bawled.

From deep beneath their feet came the rumble of a subway train. These sounds came, and fled, intensifying the silence and the sense of solitude. A policeman came in sight, his slicker gleaming and creaking with ice. He looked at them for a moment, pushed up the peak of his cap with his nightstick, and then he too was gone, like a ghost.

"Esko," Katerina said, stopping when they came to the Kirby Building. "Are you sure you want to do this? You know it will change everything. There's no way of knowing where it will take us. And I'm not making any promises."

"That's all right," he said, taking her in his arms and kissing her again while snow settled in their hair, on their faces.

"This has to happen my way, always," she said, turning to him while the elevator bore them upward to the top of the building.

"Of course."

In the penthouse they took off their coats, kicked off their shoes, and Esko threw more logs into the open grate, where embers were still hot and glowing. Soon the wood caught and crackled, sending up flames and the sweet smell of pine, and they looked at each other for a moment, a small, awkward pulse of feeling, both of them realizing that a border was about to be crossed.

"Will you take a drink?"

"Sure," he said.

"There's some champagne. Someone from Andrew's office sent it over. But it'll be warm. Whiskey, then?"

"Fine."

Esko was surprised by how clean and spare the space still was. The dining room table was spread with some of Katerina's photographs; there were a few books next to her purse on the sofa. In the kitchen there was a can of coffee and a stick of French bread. Esko followed her there and couldn't resist kissing her on the nape of her neck while she poured the whiskey into the heavy tumblers.

"Esko," she said, handing him his glass. "Would you take your clothes off for me?"

"What?" He laughed a little nervously.

"You have to obey me. You said you would. I want to see your body."

"You'll take your clothes off too?"

"Not yet."

His face was a question.

"Do it for me. Please."

He set his whiskey down by the fire. He took off his jacket, his pants, his socks, his underwear, his skin warmed by the flames. "And now?" he said with a wry smile. "How do I look?"

"You look beautiful naked," she said. "Like a picture. Wait a moment."

She disappeared, running through toward the study, and came back a few moments later with her camera and an unwieldy flash attachment.

"Katerina . . ." he protested.

"Don't say anything," she said. "Don't smile. Don't pose. Just be natural."

"Natural!" he said, more or less exploding with laughter this time. How on earth could she expect him to look *natural*?

Then the room was ablaze with the flash and he was blinded, blinking, throwing his hand to his face.

"Esko, my love, are you all right?"

My love!

"I'm naked and I can't see," he said, his arms reaching for her. "Apart from that I've never been better."

"Poor darling," she said, coming close to him, pressing against him now in full embrace, and kissing him on the lips. She kissed his chin and his cheek. She kissed his neck, his chest; she lingeringly kissed his nipples and he fought to suppress a gasp; she kissed his ribs, his belly button; she kissed the scar on his side; she kissed the length of his penis, his balls, murmuring, "Wait, wait." She kissed the insides of his thighs, his buttocks, the backs of his calves. She kissed his feet and each of his toes before her lips began journeying up his body once more, at last reaching his lips, slowing kissing his mouth, her tongue languidly slipping inside; she kissed his ears and both his eyes, the blind and the good. For hours, it seemed, she kissed him, her lips pressing against every inch of his body as if giving him a reward, until it seemed that each pore of his skin had developed a nerve that was screaming with pleasure and for release. At last, when he was sighing deeply, rocking on his feet, moaning "Katerina, Kat-er-ina," she took his bursting penis in her mouth and he came at once, his body jerking and shuddering as if he'd been shot, as she continued to milk from him every last drop of semen.

Katerina fetched rugs and blankets and made a bed in front of the fire before she herself undressed, shyly but without fuss, jumping beneath the covers and beckoning to him to follow. "Well, Mr. Vaananen," she said, her fingers playing on his chest. "Are you cured?"

"Sicker than ever," he said. "Very high fever."

Soon he was erect again and she said, "Now, Esko, come inside me now," and as he did, staring into her eyes, sliding luxuriantly in, he felt that at last, just as he'd tried to make her a home, she'd given him his.

*   *   *

The morning came clear and sharp. It was late when he woke up, and the penthouse was filled with a trumpet blast of light. Standing at the window, Esko stared out at a cloudless sky that seemed soft and powdery blue. A ferry was rolling away from one of the terminals, pitching on the swell. Passengers—specks from this distance—crowded on deck, eager to feel the clean freshness of the air and the soft light of the winter sun now that the storm was over. Smoke plumed into the sky over the Customs House. The Statue of Liberty glanced down on sparkling waves ruffled with white specks of ice. Out in the narrows, spouting fireboats heralded the arrival of one of the great three-funneled liners being dragged into port like a skyscraper knocked flat on the ocean.

Katerina was still sleeping and Esko thought he'd take a walk and bring back breakfast, but then he realized he didn't have any money, having taken his wallet out of his pocket, as he always did, when they'd arrived back at Harrison Street late the previous night.

"Esko, what's the matter?" she said, stirring beneath the blankets, her voice slow and sleepy. "Why aren't you in bed?"

Now he felt like a fool. Why wasn't he? Why wasn't he lying next to her right now, touching and tasting her skin? Why was he wasting a single second of proximity to this gorgeous creature now that he had her? Because he hadn't wanted to disturb her sleeping. Because they'd resume where they'd left off, exhausted, the previous night, when they'd fallen asleep before the dying fire as the gray dawn had begun to light the sky. He'd be inside her and they'd make love tenderly, passionately. Or she'd suck him again. My God, he thought, remembering that, is it possible for a man to die of pleasure?

"I thought I'd bring breakfast. But I don't have any money."

"Ugh," she said not opening her eyes. "I have lots. Just take some from my purse."

"Where'll I find it?"

"Over by the windows somewhere, I think."

Esko kissed her, dressed, and located the bulging oblong of black leather on one of the sofas. He was taken aback by its weight. Snapping open the clasp, he saw the snubby, nickel-plated snout of a revolver poking at him. The revolver was six chambered, and its pearled handle was studded with diamonds; it looked like it belonged in the holster of a Mississippi riverboat gambler.

The curve of Katerina's back was turned to him, rising and falling with the rhythm of her breath; she was already asleep again. Esko shut up the bag, having taken twenty dollars, and returned sometime later with a sack of groceries under each arm. Katerina was in the kitchen fixing coffee. He stood for a moment in awe of that event and made powerfully aware once more of just what had occurred. They were lovers, and there she was, his lover, moving with a quick neatness, spooning grounds from a glass jar, touching the handle of the coffee jug, pouring in boiling water from a kettle, then dipping a streak of jam from a pot with her forefinger and lifting her lips to catch it. Standing there with his brown paper parcels, leaning against one of the oak pillars in the entrance, Esko was reminded once again that although he needed her to make his being whole, to make sense of his life, she seemed complete and self-sufficient. She was wearing a man's shirt and nothing else and she looked shy and alone and invulnerable. Her extraordinary green eyes were as impenetrable, as free from discernible motive as the gun in her bag. There was no way of knowing what she was thinking; but then, sensing his presence, she looked up, her face warmed by a smile whose naturalness and joy flattered him and made his heart bump. "That was fast," she said, licking more jam.

"I hurried," he said.

"What did you get?"

"Everything. Bagels, milk, salmon, eggs, orange juice, bacon. I think I got everything."

"Good."

While they were silently eating breakfast he asked about the revolver.

"Isn't it ridiculous?" she said, gulping coffee, her eyes alive with humor. "It's MacCormick's really," she said, mentioning her husband's name without missing a beat. "He makes me carry it when I'm by myself because last year when we were in the desert we were walking and there was a rattlesnake on the path in front of us. Andrew killed it with a stick. A big stick."

"Do you know how to use it?"

"I'm a good shot. My father taught me. Does it bother you?"

"It just seems a little strange—to be carrying a gun in New York."

"There aren't rattlesnakes here too?"

"I guess," he said. Given everything that had happened to Katerina in her life it seemed perfectly natural that she would wish to walk the streets feeling protected, but in truth he was a little unnerved, both by the gun itself and what it represented—there was still so much about her he didn't yet know and might never know.

"Esko," she said, looking at him over her coffee cup. "We can't stay here, you know. Two days from now we'll look out of that window and there'll be a liner steaming into the harbor and Andrew will be on it."

"Let's leave. Let's get out of New York."

"Where would we go?"

"It doesn't matter. Chicago. Somewhere in the west. Los Angeles," he said, thinking of Gunnar and Cristof. "They're building like crazy there. Lots of work for me."

"They have earthquakes in California, Esko. No *pilvenpiirtaja*. No gorgeous schemes with skyscrapers and plazas and fountains."

"So what? We'd be together."

"MacCormick would follow. He'd destroy you."

"He'd try. He wouldn't succeed," Esko said. All this seemed quite clear; there was nothing to think about. He and Katerina were meant to be together, and they were, they would be, always now. "All these years of working, seeking, searching for something. It doesn't matter, Katerina, so long as I'm with you. I went to war for you. I think I can leave New York. I . . ."

"*Shush*," she said. She came and sat in his lap, stopping further conversation with a kiss. "You'd do that?" she said, unbuttoning her shirt, offering her breast to his mouth.

"Anything."

*　　　*　　　*

That same day, late in the evening, Esko glanced at his watch, overcoat on, hat pushed back on his head, suitcase at his feet in the spacious, murmuring, vaulted dome of Pennsylvania Station. He was waiting for Katerina to arrive with her own suitcase; in his breast pocket he had two first-class tickets for Chicago. They were running away together.

His eye fell on a copy of the *Gazette* left on a bench. The front page was split in two. Alongside a headline screaming "I Did It—Paramour Confesses," there was another story, given equal prominence: "*Gazette* Hails New Midtown Tower." There was a picture of Joe Lazarus, decked out in one of his impressive suits and wearing a flat-topped straw hat, a skimmer. The story noted, as though there were nothing unusual in this, that the *Gazette*'s new skyscraper office would be located on Forty-sixth Street, near Bryant Park, thanks to a trailblazing new design from the eminent modern architect Joseph Lazarus.

Esko didn't get it—the *Gazette* site was over by the East River, nowhere near Bryant Park, and in any event, the competition had been won by that fellow from Chicago, what was his name—Peter Winrob. Flicking to an inside page, Esko reeled. For there, drawn by Hugh Ferriss, the city's most prestigious architectural illustrator, was a charcoal rendering of Lazarus's supposedly new design. It was Esko's old *Gazette* entry, finessed, embellished, but basically the same. There was an interview with Lazarus, where he graciously thanked the *Gazette*, not only for giving him this plum commission, but for arranging the competition that had given him and one of his former employees the opportunity to try out, in very rough form, some of the ideas now crystallized in his superb and, he said, entirely new design. And then, at the bottom of the page, was a boxed footnote: the *Gazette* skyscraper contest had been canceled, it said bluntly; the prizewinners would be allowed to keep their cash awards, despite the fact that the fundamental flaws in Peter Winrob's winning design had been impossible to rectify.

Esko turned his wrist and checked the time. The train was due to leave in five minutes and there was still no sign of Katerina. He looked again at the *Gazette*, trying to make sense of this. Could he call the *Gazette* offices now? Or Winrob in Chicago? No, it was too late—almost midnight now. Somehow Lazarus was at the root of this—but how had he pulled it off?

Esko felt sick, but reminded himself that he and Katerina were leaving New York anyway. It didn't matter, but it rankled. Just then, looking up, he saw Kirby emerge from the arcade beneath the four-sided station clock and come trotting down the steps, heels clicking, spry as usual.

"Where've you been W. P.?" he said, glad. "I've been trying to get in touch with you all day."

"In the steam room, recovering from last night," Kirby said, his face stricken.

"Hangover that bad, huh? I have something to tell you."

"Look, Esko," Kirby said, lowering his pale gray bloodshot eyes for a moment and then raising them to look Esko right in the eye. "I've got some bad news."

Esko held up the paper. "I know. I can't believe it. But it doesn't matter, really. Don't worry. Because the most wonderful thing . . ."

"It's not that," Kirby said. A tweed-sleeved arm stretched out, a bony old hand clutched Esko's shoulder. "You're going to have to bear up, laddie. I just saw Katerina. She said she's sorry."

"What?"

"She's not coming. She's not leaving her husband," Kirby said, wincing for his friend as he saw Esko's eyes fill with a pain he himself remembered, as if his whole world had been destroyed, turned to ashes, as if he'd been shot in the heart.

PART FOUR

Motion Picture

I

It was eighteen months later, midsummer 1925.

Manhattan, blazing noon.

Esko and Kirby, shirtsleeved, were in their office facing the Flatiron, windows flung high, inviting in grit, fumes, noise of traffic, and racket of riveting guns, and even the occasional hint of ocean breeze that somehow vaulted Wall Street and struggled up through the scalding stone canyons. Kirby sat behind the desk, hands clasped behind his neck, a statue. Esko lay flat on his back on the floor, head propped against a cushion. Between the two of them a twenty-four-inch fan played over a coffin-shaped block of melting ice in a tin bathtub. The breeze from the fan fluttered the papers on Kirby's desk, urging them to escape from beneath makeshift paperweights, bottles of bootleg whiskey, gin, and brandy. Neither man appeared to gain much comfort from the fan, though it may just have been what prevented them going crazy in the merciless heat. Both wore dark glasses, as if even here, inside, in the shade, the light was too cruel; or perhaps neither had the energy to take them off. Not a word had been spoken for more than thirty minutes when an agonized creak came from Kirby's chair, indicating that, ill-advisedly, he'd moved, a mistake that caused sweat to roll down the center of his forehead, gather momentum down the slope of his nose, and then pause for a second or two, gathering in a fat drop before falling to the floor, *splat!*

Kirby, jerked out of his trancelike torpor, said: "Esko—are you still there?"

There was a pause of several seconds. Even time crawled, slave to the heat. A few papers lifted on the desk, expired. A police car wailed down on Broadway.

"I'm here," Esko said at last.

"Good," said Kirby. "Very good." There'd been times in these last eighteen months when he'd feared for the Finn's sanity. Esko hadn't screamed or howled when Kirby gave him the news on that night at Pennsylvania Station. Perhaps it would have been better if he had. Instead he'd engaged in a frantic, futile, weeks-long search for Katerina, who was nowhere to be found. And then he'd sunk into a silent gloom. For months. And months. Even the sight of Lazarus's skyscraper, *his* design, growing day by day, rising high over Bryant Park, had done nothing to snap him out of it. Even the fact that various further towers had been announced, all in that modern Gothic style so clearly derived from Esko's *Gazette* entry. He'd merely shrugged, suggesting that such things were inevitable. That was how things worked in this world, he'd said. True, Kirby had said, sure that's the way things are, but *phooey*. And then one day, at last, showing a resilience that Kirby could only admire and wonder at, Esko had taken himself by the scruff of the neck and begun to shake himself out of it, even though he'd still steadfastly refused to let them accept any of the work that Andrew MacCormick tried to throw their way. And there'd been a lot. The whole of Manhattan vibrated to the dissonant song of construction. Hotels, apartment houses, office buildings were soaring up everywhere. The daylight hours were deafened by riveting guns. Like human spiders, the sky boys spun their webs of steel. Towers struck skywards with smart setbacks and ever higher swagger. It wasn't German Expressionism. It wasn't Soviet constructivism. It wasn't Le Corbusier's boxy modernism. It somehow partook of all this with an added something special. It was Manhattanism, an era of light and dark, a carnival of flappers and sophisticates, of silk stockings that led high, like the stock market, to a realm of infinite promise, of bathtub gin, of doe-skin spats and fads for mah-jongg and flagpole sitting, of contests where people danced and danced until they died, of ceaseless blunt rude truffling for cash that was syncopated to the rhythms of jazz, jazz, jazz. Everyone said it couldn't last, but it was lasting. And yet even in this situation so welcoming to architects, where high art and low life were meeting with a vengeance, not only embracing but getting down on the floor and inventing the positions, Esko and Kirby were having a tough time getting work. Their ideas were too advanced and their contacts nowhere near good enough. They couldn't hustle, or they didn't hustle in the right way. Their ideas were a problem.

Kirby turned his head but wished he hadn't, for he glimpsed the thermometer on the wall: 105 degrees, it said, and somehow it was much worse knowing.

"Let's review the situation," Kirby said, rivulets of sweat coursing through the lines on his cheeks. "In the last three months we've earned—what?"

Esko didn't open his eye. He concentrated on the sound of traffic, trying to imagine that it was really the swish of skis, and he was in Finland—cool, cool. "Two hundred fifty-two dollars—and sixty-five cents."

"What's on the horizon?"

"The buyer from Saks still has the design for the chairs and the glasses and the knives and forks. I'm optimistic, believe it or not. And I've sent some stuff to that new magazine. *The New Yorker.*"

"Stuff?" Kirby said. "What stuff?"

"Artwork. Cartoons."

"Jokes, you mean?" Kirby's voice rose. "You never tell me any, goddamnit."

"You don't pay me anything."

"Hah!"

The fan kept up its rhythm over the dwindling block of ice. "I think I'll go out," Esko said.

"In this filthy heat—are you nuts?"

"To the movies. Chaplin."

"I'll come with you."

"And Keaton."

"I like Keaton too."

"Still afraid to let me go out by myself?"

"No, I know you're all right now. You're over all that nonsense. Aren't you?"

"I'm over it."

"Completely over it?" said Kirby, brushing his palm softly across his stiff white hair.

A man came in without knocking. He was dark suited, with a blotched complexion the color of porridge, and he had on a dark hat that sat precisely on his head as if he'd spent a month in front of a mirror getting it straight. His eyes were so far back in his head, you'd have to fish them out with hooks; they had dark rings under them. He didn't say anything. He didn't move. He simply stood in the doorway with his huge hands hanging ready by his sides and sweat streaming down his face while those hard, glittery little eyes traveled the room like searchlights.

Esko, sensing danger, quickly got himself up off the floor. Kirby stood too, his chair scraping back across the floor, flakes of hours-old cigar ash tumbling from his shirt.

"Can we help you?" Kirby said.

The big man said nothing, his expression impassive beneath the hat, his eyes tracking the floating ash as though it were an offense to his secret sense of dignity and decorum. A faint smile pulled at his lips, then he took a step to one side and Paul Mantilini was in the room.

That was how Esko would think of it later. It was like a conjuror's trick, a magical appearance. The big man stepped away and Paul Mantilini was in the room, had crossed the room, and was standing by the window, loafing with his back to them, gazing down onto Broadway, one hand in his pants pocket, jingling the coins there.

"Hello, Esko. It's been a while," he said, turning his head just a fraction, speaking in that low voice, as if it were only to be expected that the world should have to strain forward to listen to him. And yet there was a likable courtliness to him as well as the restlessness and the arrogance, Esko thought, realizing that he'd pretty much forgotten about Paul Mantilini until this moment. It was months since he'd given the scar on his hand more than a passing glance; now it started to itch like hell.

Mantilini had evidently come up in the world. He wore a shirt of mauve silk beneath a three-piece banana-yellow suit that was one of the most extraordinary things Esko had ever seen. The buttons were of ivory, the lapels were sumptuously wide, and the fabric must have passed through the dye a thousand times to get that golden, buttery hue; it was a solid wall of color, and yet it looked miraculously soft and light. Its folds kept Mantilini cool on that ferocious day. He wasn't sweating at all. His skin was smooth and pampered and gave off a sharp smell of lime. His shoes, two-tone, chocolate and white, were of highly polished leather, delicate shoes that fit his nimble feet like gloves. Whatever Mantilini didn't have, he had grace. It was as natural to him as his flashing smile and his mean streak. A mauve silk handkerchief rose from his outside suit pocket like an orchid. He'd acquired a small, deep scar on his left eyelid since Esko had seen him last, a nick from a knife, perhaps.

"Paul Mantilini," he said, in his low, commanding voice, offering his hand to Kirby.

"I didn't quite catch that," said Kirby, taking the hand. "What did you say your name was?"

Mantilini's smile was far away; he'd moved on and, anyway, wasn't in the business of repeating himself.

"W. P. Kirby," Kirby said, looking at Esko with a puzzled shrug.

Mantilini nodded, as if he knew that already, pushing his hands into his pockets, strolling about, behind the desk, in front of the desk, taking in the framed designs, the absence of a secretary, the tin bathtub with the ice in it, the whirring fan, the worn but well-ordered state of things. He examined the label of the bootleg booze on the table with a smile.

"Nice view," he said, and he wasn't talking about what he could see from the window. "A speakeasy," he said, touching the scar over his eye gently with a fingertip. "I want you guys to build me a speakeasy."

The fan hummed over the bathtub while Esko and Kirby traded glances of amazement. Mantilini didn't miss a beat.

"You are architects, right?"

Esko and Kirby were still looking at one another, Kirby's eyebrows a questioning brace.

"We are," Esko said.

Mantilini relaxed, a smile playing around his lips. In all this he seemed to know ahead of time exactly what Esko and Kirby were going to do. "Yeah, you told me. An architect. And Bo, the Swede, said something about it. A while back," he said. "Just make me a speako deluxe. The best in the city. With a bar, a big round one. And a dance floor, and places where people can eat. And a piano—I know someone who likes to sing."

"By any chance is his name Caruso?" Kirby said.

"Very funny," Mantilini said, gazing down at his shoes, then glancing at Kirby with one of his quick sharp looks. "The singer's a she; I doubt you'd know her," he said. "So—how long it take you to do something like this?"

"That depends," Esko said.

"On what?" His voice sharp and engaged. "Money?"

"That comes into it."

"Damn right it does," Kirby said.

"There's also the question of the site," Esko said.

"The *what*?" said Mantilini.

"The place where you want us to build it. Do you have anywhere in mind?"

"Oh sure," said Mantilini lazily. "I've got a building. Several. One in particular that I have—*in mind*." He smiled again, once more ahead of the game, leaning against the desk, picking up a pencil, putting it down again. "What do you say?"

Esko cleared his throat, looking at Kirby, but Kirby was no help here. He just seemed very amused by the situation and went on making more music with his eyebrows.

"How big is this place?" Esko said.

"It's big. About one-third the size of the ballpark they built for Babe Ruth. I mean, it's *big*. The basement of an entire city block, basically. That big. About twenty-five feet high. Do you think you guys could do something with that?"

"It's empty?"

"Yeah, completely."

Esko whistled, beginning to appreciate the possibilities.

"You guys could probably knock something together in a couple of weeks, right?"

"Hah!" said Kirby, and Esko laughed. Mantilini looked from one to the other of them, wondering if they were making fun; he realized they weren't— probably as well for both of them, Esko thought.

"It'll take longer?"

"Much," Esko said.

"I need this place fast. Money's not a problem."

"I can't tell you how glad we are to hear that," Kirby said.

Esko said, "Why don't you come back tomorrow? In the afternoon. We'll rough a few things out for you to look at."

"Is that how this works?"

"That's how it works."

"So we're set?" said Mantilini. "That's it?"

"That's it."

Mantilini was gone, his absence conjured as swiftly as his arrival; he paused only at the door, raising his hand for a second to show the scar.

"What's with the scar?" said Kirby, while he and Esko crowded together at the window, looking down onto Broadway. "It's like yours."

"I saved his life once. We were working together on the steel."

"Is that a fact?" Kirby said. "Jeez—just look at that!"

Beneath them, on the other side of the street, crouching and gleaming in the shadow, was a wondrous automobile, a Rolls-Royce, golden, long, and sleek, bright with chrome and bulging with boxes. A silver lady rode the dazzling radiator between two wide-eyed headlamps. A figure, a woman, sat in the back of this gorgeous wagon leaning against the red leather upholstery, her face hidden in shadow. A suited fellow was smoking a cigarette with his foot on the running board when Mantilini and his bodyguard came out of the building and crossed the street. Yet another man, another beefy bodyguard, was with them; he must have been waiting all that while outside the door to the office, or perhaps down in the lobby.

Mantilini got in the back, leaning toward the woman, kissing her briefly on the lips, while the two bodyguards positioned themselves in the front with the driver and the car pulled into traffic and drifted down Broadway, a wanton shimmer of silver and chrome.

"Life just got exciting," Kirby said with a smile.

2

They went to work for a bootlegger, a racketeer, a gangster; they went to work for Paul Mantilini. They roughed out some designs for the speakeasy, Mantilini spent a few minutes silently flicking through them, nodding his approval, and the next day the bodyguard with the precise hat—his name was Gardella—came alone to the office bearing a suitcase of pale creamy leather that had solid gold fittings. The suitcase in itself was worth a fortune and for a moment Esko wondered if this was their fee, a bizarre joke; but Gardella flipped open the suitcase and Esko noted simultaneously the smell of rich leather and Kirby's gasp. It was full of money.

Kirby fingered the stubble on his chin. "There must be fifty thousand dollars in there," he said.

"Seventy-five thousand," Gardella said.

"God-*damnit*," Kirby said, riffling the bills. "I'm going to like working for this guy."

From then on Mantilini put a car and a chauffeur at their disposal to ferry them from their office to the site, nearly thirty blocks north, in the indeed cavernous basement of a building at the corner of Broadway and Fifty-fifth. Kirby invested in a rack of new summer suits and several white panama hats, playing the part of successful architect with flamboyant delight. The worries they had about Mantilini interfering or standing at their shoulders dictating this and that soon proved groundless. He came to the site infrequently and without fanfare. It was as if he'd practiced his entrances and exits so often that they were invisible. Suddenly he would be there, dressed in the banana-yellow suit, or one that was grass green, or electric blue, announcing himself with a little cough, or by the jingling of keys or coins, or by the scratching of a small gold pencil in a black leather notebook that he had extracted from his pocket. Once Esko happened to glimpse a page of the notebook; it was filled with columns of figures; no dates, no names, no letters of the alphabet, just numbers, astronomically high numbers, lots of zeros, which Mantilini juggled with the agility he'd formerly displayed on the steel.

The heat belted on through July and August. One morning Esko looked up from his workbench at the site and saw a shadowy figure coming toward him from the roaring light of the doorway. It was Mantilini, dressed in a pink suit, cool as ever. Esko didn't know how he did it. His tanned skin was smooth and fresh. His shiny, slicked-down hair looked as though it had just been barbered. His teeth flashed sharply but even so Esko could see nothing sinister about him. Of course he'd read the stories: that when bootleggers weren't shooting their rivals they were beating them into a daze, drowning them, hoisting them by a rope; they hobnobbed with mayors and movie stars; they hauled trucks of whiskey down from Canada and ran rum up the coast from Miami, defying a law that nobody wanted in order to provide a product that everybody did. But he saw none of that; as far as he and Kirby were concerned Mantilini was a model client; he didn't interfere, and he never argued about money. His only concern was speed, getting the job done quick and smooth, and Esko was happy to accommodate him. He knew of other architects who were designing speakeasies; indeed it was quite the fashionable thing, and if this was Mantilini's way of rewarding him for what had happened on the high steel three years previously, well, Esko thought: so be it. He was curious, naturally, to learn just how Mantilini had come so far so fast, but he didn't ask, guessing that the less he knew about Mantilini's business the better.

Mantilini glanced at the plans on Esko's bench, restlessly turning a coin between his fingers. "Let's go for a drive," he said, and so Esko found himself sequestered amid chrome and gleaming walnut and firm cushions of red leather while the Rolls-Royce whispered downtown and across the bridge toward Brooklyn with the waters of the East River shining beneath them like crinkled tin. On the other side of the bridge they approached a warehouse and got out of the car while gulls cawed over their heads. The warehouse looked dingy and deserted. At one basement entrance, however, approached down a ramp, there was a white door.

"Come on," Mantilini said, knocking three times on the door and leading the way into a space filled with steam and the whiff of alcohol. The echo of their footsteps gave Esko a sense of the vastness of the space, and through the steam he now made out row after row of bright copper vats. The plump vats seemed to stretch on endlessly. There were perhaps fifty of them, and each seemed to be attended by five or six men under the direction of a manager in a smart white coat. A constant chime of glass came from a conveyor belt that bore tinkling bottles toward the far side of the warehouse to be filled.

"This is where those bottles in your office came from," Mantilini said, raising his voice to contend with the glass. "In fact a lot of the whiskey drunk in New York tonight will have come from here." He raised an arm. "See those stills—they come from England at fifteen thousand dollars apiece."

It was here, he said, that government alcohol was redistilled, removing the impurities; then it was cut with real whiskey brought in from Canada or Europe. "We import all our bottles from England. The labels come from the same classy printers that do the best Scottish brands. This whole establishment is worth a little over one million dollars. This particular operation will net maybe ten million dollars profit this year. Our syndicate has eight of these around the city. We're not trying to hide anything. How could we? Tammany Hall knows where we are. They like us, because we make decent liquor, not like the poison some other guys peddle. Of course they also like us because they get graft. The bills are big, I don't mind telling you."

His hands were in his pockets and his manner was a mixture of pride and tough control. His eyes roved around the still, checking details, making sure all was well. Gardella whispered something in his ear and he sauntered off for a moment, chatting amiably with one of the men who wore a white coat, leaving Esko to wonder at the scope of his operation and the sums of money involved. He'd understood that bootlegging was big business but this was staggering, astonishing. Mantilini had created a world.

"Yeah," Mantilini said, back now, showing his teeth. "I've done good and I ain't done yet." He touched Esko on the shoulder. "I want you to know that I appreciate what you did. Not just saving my life, but coming to the funeral, showing your respects. My mother—she still talks about you."

"How's Steffano these days?"

Mantilini nodded, brightening. "Good. Much better. He's walking now. He's got his own restaurant now. You should go eat there. He'd like that."

"And Teresa—is she still with Bo?"

Mantilini was still smiling but his whole expression changed: what was generous the previous moment became hard and cold. "He cheated on her. Can you believe that? He cheated on her and I slapped him and he went right on doing it," he said. "What's funny?"

"Bo."

"Yeah, Bo," Mantilini said, shaking his head. "That fucking operator. I'm serious. I ever see that guy again—he'd better watch out." He frowned, glancing down at his neat white shoes. "Kirby was telling me you had some trouble with a woman yourself. Got you down for quite a while, he said."

"He told you that?"

"Actually he said she broke your heart. Yeah, well, that I *can't* fix. But you're still standing, you're still a man with two legs. D'you know where she is, this woman? D'you ever see her? You love her, you should go get her."

"She doesn't want me," Esko said.

"So—forget her. Me, I got a wife. Nice Italian girl. She's pregnant now."

"Congratulations."

"Yeah, you can't beat a family." Mantilini bounced up and down on his feet. He turned the lapel of his gorgeous pink suit, examining a diamond pin that was stuck there, sniffing at it like a rose. He glanced at his watch. "See this?" he said, evidently having decided this was quite enough sentiment for the day. "Cost me ten thousand dollars. C'mon, there's some other stuff I want you to look at."

They drove back toward Manhattan and Mantilini told Esko how protection worked, how important men in certain federal offices were in the pay of the syndicate and gave information about coming raids. He recounted the long story of a trick he'd come up with the previous year, involving a pretty woman and a roadster, diverting police attention from a convoy of liquor his people had been bringing up from Miami. He'd put on dark glasses now, and was leaning back against the red leather. From time to time he glanced up, his attention caught by the shadows flashing through the cables of the bridge. Then he went back to his little black book, listing numbers with his gold pencil. He had small, surprisingly neat handwriting. "See, it's like this," he said. "At any one time, in any one situation, there's one person who can help you, who can make things go. You have to know who that person is. And you have to know how to make them do what you want. Maybe they want money. Maybe they want a little fire truck for their kid. Or a tip on the next race at Saratoga. Could be anything. Sometimes you'd better put a gun to their heads. Or maybe you just have to ask them. It doesn't matter. Keep it simple. The less there is to it, the better."

When they reached midtown he instructed Gardella to go on with the car. "Go to Saks, get me some socks," he said. "The silk ones with the little arrows."

Gardella frowned beneath the straight brim of his hat.

"I'll be fine," Mantilini said. "Now beat it."

They stood on the sun-drenched sidewalk until the Rolls had disappeared in the traffic; then Mantilini took Esko by the arm, leading him across Broadway and into the shadows of Fifty-seventh Street that fell across their faces like cool water. They paused beneath the awning of an apartment building while a woman walked by, her white cloche hat glowing like a halo as her heels clicked on the sidewalk. A taxi threw out clouds of fumes, clattering down toward Fifth Avenue. A newsboy sandwiched between boards for the *Evening Graphic* shouted about the latest murder. From less than a block away came the spurt of a riveting gun. An ice man stood with his cart on the corner. Another guy was selling 100 percent pure whiskey candies—three for ten cents. Hands in pockets, head tilted back, Mantilini looked across the street.

"See that building? Up on the fifth floor I have my other business. A real estate business. None of my Broadway friends know about it. Not even Gardella. It's a corporation, a completely legitimate corporation. In my mother's name. Got five guys working there. Secretaries. Everything," he said. "You see, Esko—I won't always be a racketeer."

Now he led Esko beneath the awning and through heavy doors of glass and bronze into the lobby of an apartment house where tall potted palms grew from urns set on black marble. An elevator bore them to the sixth floor. Mantilini approached a door, tossing a brass key in his hand and, without knocking, turned the key in the lock of a door that had the number 510 on it in silver letters.

"Hey, Ruthie, it's me," Mantilini called, sauntering through, beckoning Esko to follow.

The room was stuffy and full of cigarette smoke. The windows were closed and the sunshine coming through the white blinds showed layers in the clouds of smoke. *Vanity Fair* and *Vogue* and the latest Broadway magazines were littered on a low white table. The furnishings were spare and new, all black leather and shining tubular steel.

"Ruthie!"

A door opened and a black girl appeared, straightening her dress, followed by a tall, skinny, loose-limbed, white-suited black man, about six feet tall, who leaned over a chair to pick up a white hat with a band and, without either putting on the hat or uttering a word, walked slowly to the apartment's front door, which closed behind him with a tremendous bang.

"Who the hell was he?" said Mantilini, puzzled but calm.

"Paul, would you light me a cigarette, please?" said Ruthie. She wore a short white dress that hugged her body and gleamed with beads; her bobbed hair was slick with oil. "He's my dance teacher."

A light flared between them while Mantilini watched her.

"Are you making fun of me?"

"No . . ."

"I wouldn't do that if I was you. Now look me in the eye, Ruthie. You know I'll know if you're lying. And you know that if he's been fooling around with you I'll find that nigger. I'll kill him."

Mantilini's tone was as calm as it was chilling, although Ruthie gave him a defiant look.

"Like I said, he's my dance teacher." She sighed smoke. "He sells me stuff too."

She was lovely, a handful, and very much not Mantilini's wife, Esko saw.

"Dope? Morphine?" Mantilini said. "You'll kill yourself with that."

"Oh big deal," she said in a flat voice.

"Give."

"So who's the new thug?" Ruthie said, looking at Esko, at his scars and the patch over his eye. "He certainly looks ugly enough to be a gangster."

"Give," Mantilini repeated.

Ruthie raised the hem of her skirt and handed over a white packet she had concealed in the top of her stocking. "Don't hurt him—promise me, Paul."

"Thank you," said Mantilini with a polite nod, pocketing the little white slip of paper. "Now say hello to Esko. He's an architect. He and his partner are designing our club."

"Are you really an architect?" she said, her sleepy brown eyes showing mild interest.

"That's right."

"Does the club have a name yet?"

"Yeah, Esko—how about that?" Mantilini said.

"Don't you want to call the place Mantilini's?"

"God, no," he said, raising his hand.

"How about—The Sky Club?"

Mantilini considered this for a moment. "Ruthie—what do you think?"

"One name's as good as another," she said.

"I like that. The Sky Club. I think that's good," Mantilini said. "Ruthie's gonna sing there."

"You're a singer?" Esko asked, and she gave him a look, tilting her head to one side, as if to say what was it to him anyway? She went to the corner of the room, wound up a Victrola, and put on a record. Next thing she had her long bejewelled hand around Mantilini's neck, he had his around her waist, and they were dancing, spinning around the room to some tooting jazz. She was laughing, and Mantilini had a serious, almost studious expression, holding her lightly, moving nimbly in a graceful foxtrot.

At which point Esko tried to leave, but they wouldn't let him, insisting that he stay for a cocktail, then a second, then several. Only when they disappeared into the bedroom did he and his spinning head make their escape. He gathered himself in the corridor for a moment, straightening his tie and jacket beneath a humming, flickering ceiling lamp; then he stepped across the zigzagged carpet and pushed the button for the elevator.

In the street it was twilight, still hot, a little after seven o'clock. On Broadway the taxis stood five deep outside the theaters, and the crowds flowed up from the subways into an electric world of dancing neon signs and awnings ablaze with lights that grew ever more brilliant as the sky darkened moment by moment. Esko felt tired and dizzy from the liquor. There was no point in

going back to the site, he thought, and so he walked, heading east, against the
flow, crossing Fifth Avenue before turning south.

Soon he found himself beside the New York Public Library, looking into
Bryant Park. The skyscraper had been completed just a few months before. It
was built, finished, and it was Esko's design basically, a stripped-down Gothic
tower in dark brick, beaconed at its crown, floodlit at its flanks, and with
another searchlight on the roof shooting a circling beam into the sky that
pilots reported they could see all the way from Boston. This was the first time
he'd been able to bring himself to look at the structure; it was dynamic and
pure; it was, in fact, lovely, even though a plaque outside said: THE GAZETTE
BUILDING, Architect Joseph Lazarus.

Esko approached the building and kicked it, rousing startled stares from a
couple of drunks sitting on a bench in the park. Lazarus had built a skyscraper, while he was now laboring in a cavernous basement building a
speakeasy for a gangster. Well, this was America: you trod on the other fellow's head if he happened to block your way up the ladder; you took what you
could and didn't ask questions and moved on; you didn't look around corners—you *cut* them. Oh yes, there were lessons here, he said to himself, and
he thought back over the day. Mantilini had shown him the various secret
strands of his life, had taken him to the top of the mountain and shown him
his world, demonstrating that in America—if only you were bold enough—it
was possible to step through the looking glass of legality and build on the
other side a precise vision of order and productivity. Mantilini had power,
wealth, glamour, a growing fame. He had the whole American package, he
was the architect of his own empire. Perhaps he even wants a *pilvenpiirtaja*,
Esko thought.

3

It was the night of the opening of The Sky Club. Esko and Kirby were seated
on round leather-and-steel stools at one of the semicircular bars. Behind the
bar there was a mirror—ten feet high, twenty feet long, etched with skyscraper motifs, all edges and flowing curves, with zigzag borders and sun-
bursts—whose symmetry had the precision of an engraving. In front of the

mirror stood a hundred shining bottles of liquor, which the white-jacketed barmen tossed and sloshed, mixing their cocktails. The bottles stood on a flat platform that would, at the touch of a button, disappear down into a cellar should there be a raid, though no one expected one, since the New York city police commissioner was one of the guests of honor. Mantilini had thought of everything.

Dressed in red, Ruthie had just sung the blues, her voice as melting as her liquid eyes, and Mantilini was still applauding, calling "Bravo! Encore! Bravo!" raising his fingers to his lips and whistling now, waving his white tie in the air above his head. Kirby told Esko he'd seen three senators along with several movie stars, too many millionaires to count, numerous gangsters, and entire squadrons of chorus girls. The place was packed, the evening an indisputable success.

Ruthie made her way off stage, running and jumping at Mantilini, who caught her in his arms and bore her away up one of the corner stairways that led to the balcony and the private booths, while, across the room, another dramatic couple appeared on the majestic mirrored stairway that swept down from the street-level entrance. It was MacCormick and Katerina.

"*Uh-oh*," Kirby said, his eyes tracking Esko's gaze. "Here comes trouble."

MacCormick had his hands in his pockets and loitered for a moment, aiming thumb and forefinger as if a gun at someone he knew. Katerina's arm looped through his and her cool green eyes darted around a little anxiously.

On the glittering steps she swayed in a tight black dress that hugged her thighs and reflected no light. Her hair was swept back from her forehead in smooth waves, and triangles of black ebony dangled from her ears. Her fingernails were painted silver, and while she was waiting for MacCormick, she lit a cigarette and blew a ring of soft, gray smoke. How old was she now? Esko wondered. Thirty-two, thirty-three? Age had put a few new lines around the corners of her eyes, had hollowed her cheeks, but had done nothing to wither her; she was lovelier, more beautiful than ever.

"Steady, laddie," Kirby said, gripping Esko's arm. "Ignore them."

"Just what I intend to do," Esko said, perhaps even thinking he meant it; but then he spotted Gardella and summoned him over. "See the couple on the stairs? They've just come in."

"Sure," said Gardella, whose face looked pale and unnaturally long tonight; he wasn't wearing his hat. "The rich guy with the classy, skinny broad. Who are they?"

"Never mind. Make sure they get the best table. And a bottle of champagne on the house. The real stuff, all right?"

"Sure thing," Gardella said, ambling away, huge hands hanging at his sides like clubs.

"Esko . . ." Kirby began.

Esko waved Kirby off impatiently, finishing his whiskey and calling for another, a large one. "Leave me be, W. P."

He watched while Gardella guided the couple toward a table next to the dance floor. A waiter popped the cork on the champagne, and MacCormick's eyes followed Gardella's gesture toward the bar where Esko and Kirby were sitting. Kirby raised his glass, and MacCormick's surprised expression turned to pleasure. He said something to Katerina and made his way toward them, not hurrying, but with all his usual languid self-confidence.

"How the hell have you guys been? *Where* the hell have you been?" he said, running his hands through his long blondish hair, that youthful face of his lit by a smile that seemed genuine. Then his eyes quickly absorbed a few of the speakeasy's details, and a look of recognition spread across his face. "This is your work, isn't it? You built this place!" He shook his head, mingling admiration and surprised displeasure. "You work for a bootlegger now?"

"He pays well," Kirby said. "Better than you did."

"You should still be working for me."

"Never," said Esko, knowing this was stupid, but unable to stop himself, the jolt of love and remembered lust and unfinished longing that he'd felt on seeing Katerina turning to anger now.

"Why's that?"

"Ask your wife," Esko said, rattling the ice in his glass.

"What?" said MacCormick not angry, startled.

"Just ignore him," Kirby said. "He's drunk and Finns make damned poor drunks. At least this one does. How are you enjoying the penthouse?"

"We love it. The two of you must come and have dinner with us. There are some things I'd like to talk to you about."

Esko's guts milled with stupid rage. "Go to hell," he said.

"Excuse us, MacCormick," Kirby said in his lively but kind voice, brushing his cropped hair with the palm of his hand the way he did when he was nervous or afraid things were slipping out of control. "I'll take Esko to the bathroom and cool him off. Please say hello to Katerina for me."

"Sure," said MacCormick, confused. "Good night to you both. And congratulations on the club. It's quite something."

Esko fumed, watching MacCormick stride from the bar back across the dance floor toward Katerina, who turned her head when he sat down so that his kiss just grazed her cheek.

"That was clever," Kirby said.

"Wasn't it?" said Esko, reaching for his whiskey, anger dwindling again as he emptied the glass. Now despair washed over him. "Jesus, what a fool I am. Perhaps I should apologize," he said, thinking this would at least give him the excuse to sit next to Katerina, smell her, inhale the cigarette smoke that had passed through her mouth and nostrils, feel the heat of her body a chair's width away.

"Too late. They're leaving already," Kirby said.

Esko turned to watch them in the mirror at the back of the bar, then swung himself off his stool, preparing to follow. Kirby grabbed him hard, ensuring that the MacComicks made their getaway.

"You're a diplomatic, interfering old fuck, you know that?"

"I love you too," Kirby said, releasing him at last, and Esko was forced to smile, realizing that Kirby did indeed love him.

Kirby signaled to the barman, calling for two more whiskeys. "I think I'd better get you drunk, laddie," he said.

"Fine by me," Esko said, touching the glass but then pushing it away as the band kicked into a new number. He felt miserable, but he wasn't going to give in and drown his sorrows. A sigh shook his body as he remembered the last time he'd seen Katerina. His skin tingled, on fire with the memory of her touch.

He turned the shot glass on the counter, tracing a perfect circle.

"W. P.," he said. "I'm thinking of the idea for a skyscraper I had. That night, in the restaurant with her. The skyscraper that would have the fountain in front of it. The water that would play so gently in the summer and freeze like crystal in the winter. Is that really such a crazy idea?"

"I always liked that idea," Kirby said. "I thought you didn't want to talk about it anymore."

"I want to start working on it. Tomorrow. Let's draw up some plans. Start looking for a backer. The *Gazette* didn't build over there — so the land's available."

Kirby sipped at his drink. "Who'll pay for it? You just did a pretty good job of pissing off our best friend in the big money business."

"What about Mantilini?"

"What about him?"

"He knows people."

"And lots of them have bullets in their guns. Don't get me wrong—Paul's a good guy. I like him." Kirby raised an eyebrow, attending to his whiskey, placing his glass down carefully on the bar. "But he may not live that long."

*   *   *

Esko and Kirby did a second speakeasy for Mantilini, up in Harlem, this one in the style of the shaman artisans of Africa and Oceania, its walls encrusted with fetishes and ceremonial carvings. They did another in midtown, only two blocks east of The Sky Club, in the sleek and shining industrial manner of the Bauhaus. They were creating stage sets in which the audience became the players, drinking and dancing and fucking and fighting and spending and stealing, losing themselves in a spree that was as desperate as it was cocky and headlong. But after that night Kirby never let Esko forget about the skyscraper, about the project they called East River Plaza. Several times each week they took their fingers out of the bootlegging barrel and walked across town, studying those ramshackle city blocks that spilled down toward the river, planning what they could do, constantly honing and improving Esko's drawings, incorporating whatever new trick and refinement they'd learned or discovered. Kirby's enthusiasm was so far from being undone by age that he seemed like a young man again, and Esko realized again how refreshing and inspiring work for its own sake could be.

One day Mantilini took Esko for lunch. The restaurant was a small place with red-and-white-checkered tablecloths and a stricken, slow-moving fan that didn't cool the air but stirred it like hot soup. Mantilini loosened his tie, stretched his neck, and called for highballs, while Esko blinked, his eye adjusting to the dimness after the dazzling light outside.

It was the summer of 1926.

"Did you hear about Valentino?" Mantilini asked, almost grudgingly, reluctant to mention the name of someone who was even better known in New York than he was. "He died. Complications with his appendix, or something." He restlessly broke bread between his fingers and rolled the pieces into pellets before shooting them into his youth. "My wife," he said, chewing. "She's real upset."

Mantilini had a baby now, a boy, Antony, named after the oldest of his dead brothers, but he was still seeing Ruthie. Or at least Esko was pretty sure he was; it was no easy thing to keep track of Mantilini's movements these days. He traveled out west, to Chicago and the coast, and the other way, to Europe. His business seemed to be expanding as always.

"You come, you go—I guess," Mantilini said philosophically. "I almost got mine when I got this," he said, touching the scar on his eyelid. "I'd met this older guy. A bootlegger, a gambler, a fellow in the line of business that I wanted to get into. I went to him with a proposition. I told him I had some booze. A lot of booze. He asked me where I got it and I told him I didn't have it yet but I soon would. He smiled and said I was an enterprising young guy and I should come back and see him when I was ready."

Mantilini leaned back, rocking his chair on its two back legs. He was in his shirtsleeves, his belly taut against a vest that was like a corset of sky with pearly buttons. "Me and Bo, the Swede, met a couple of trucks coming down from Canada with sawn-offs." He popped another rolled pellet of bread into his mouth, nodding in an offhand way at the waiter who put the highballs on the table, ice clinking against frosted glass. "The driver of one of the trucks took a shot at me with a pistol. I didn't even know I'd turned my head. The bullet just grazed me." He gently fingered the scar again. "There was a lot of blood. Sheets of it. Bo blew the guy's head off with the shotgun. All the other guys ran away. We got the trucks and I was in business. An inch the other way and the bullet would have gone through my eye and I'd be dead. Just blind luck. Think about it too long you go crazy."

The chair clattered forward. Leaning across the table, he took one of the highball glasses and rocked back again. "I got a tip today. There's something big happening on the market. This guy's very reliable—he wouldn't cross me. Now if you want . . ."

Esko held up his hand. "Thanks, but no," he said.

Mantilini shrugged and showed his white teeth, not prepared to worry about Esko's problem, whatever it was. "Do you think Valentino was good in the sack, really? Or was he just a pink powder puff? What should I tell my wife? What do you say, Esko?"

Esko shrugged noncommittally as he pulled a pair of dark glasses from his pocket and masked himself with them, watching carefully while Mantilini sipped at his highball.

"Will you guys be ready to start on another club soon?"

"Next week," Esko said, still eyeing Mantilini, who had opened his menu now.

"Good," he said, bouncing his knee furiously up and down, even more restless than usual. "I wanna get moving on it."

"Paul, there's something I'd like to talk to you about. Something I might need your help with."

"Trouble," Mantilini said, looking up from the menu, almost pleased.

"No—nothing like that. I just need to know if I can come to you when the time's right."

"Any time, for any reason." Mantilini said with a strange, perhaps predatory smile. "I'm sorry you think it's even a question, my friend."

Back on site the workmen were standing around, but not with their accustomed air of temporary ownership; rather they all looked a little lost and sheepish. There was no drilling, no music from the record player that the painter who was doing the murals had brought with him, and Esko knew instantly that something was wrong.

Kirby had fallen; he'd gashed his scalp and been rushed to Bellevue.

At the hospital Esko spoke to the doctor, a young, small, balding man who told him they stitched Kirby's scalp and operated on him for a blocked intestine that had been caused by a hemorrhage—hence the dizziness and the fall. "I'm sorry," the doctor said, in a nasal, high-pitched voice, sounding almost sprightly. "He's unlikely to last the night."

The words buzzed around Esko's head like wasps. He was in a daze, trying to take back control. What if he hadn't gone to lunch with Mantilini? What then? Would Kirby be all right now? What if he'd come back thirty minutes earlier, taken a cab rather than walked?

Kirby lay sleeping with the sheets up to his neck and his arms stretched out on top of the covers. A bandage was wrapped around his head, almost obscuring his eyes, and his breath came faintly and in flutters. Esko drew up a chair and took a cold hand that grew no warmer even as he rubbed it. "You're going to be all right," he whispered, brushing his fingers against the rough white stubble on Kirby's cheek. "You'll be back at work in no time."

Kirby didn't speak or open his eyes or even move. In the early hours of the morning he died.

Esko watched the nurse take Kirby's nonexistent pulse. He listened while the light from the bedside lamp glowed through the fuzzy nimbus of Kirby's cropped hair and the small, balding doctor confirmed that the old man was indeed gone now. He agreed that he would make the funeral arrangements and followed the two whistling porters while they wheeled the corpse down into the icy vaults of the morgue.

As he walked away, stumbling through the hushed, darkened Bellevue corridors, nausea and a panicky breathlessness set in. More than anything he wanted to call Katerina, to go to her, to hold her and to talk to her about this, because she'd understand about Kirby, had known him, had loved him too. But that was impossible, he realized. This grief would have to be endured alone. Tears came, and Esko pressed his head against a wall, letting them flow.

4

None of the New York papers ran an obituary, so Esko called Marion Bennett. "Everything's crazy with Rudolph Valentino right now," she said. "Tell me about the guy and I'll see what I can do."

She managed to get something in the *New York Times* the following day, under her own byline, and Esko called again to thank her.

"Don't mention it," she said. "No, *do* mention it. I like to hear praise."

"Thank you," he said. "It means a lot."

"Don't go gooey on me, Esko. You're my tough Finn. What you should thank me for is not writing anything about the fact that you and Kirby have built all those speakeasies for Paul Mantilini."

"You know about that?"

"Don't get me wrong. I've got nothing against speaks. I love 'em. Nor against Paul Mantilini, even though he's a gangster. God knows, there are enough of them around. At least he's attractive. But maybe it's not a connection you want made in your *Times* obituary."

"Point taken."

"How do you know that guy anyway."

"Is this the reporter asking?"

"Just curiosity."

"I met him years ago when I first came to New York. I saved his life."

On the other end of the line Esko heard a sharp inhalation of breath, as though she were sucking greedily at a cigarette. "How did that happen?"

"It's a long story."

"Oh yeah? Here's another one," she said. "About a month ago, on Park Avenue, one car pulls up alongside another. Two guys get out. The first guy shoots the driver of the other car. The second tommy-guns some schmuck as he's making a call in a phone booth."

Esko remembered the story from the papers. There'd been outrage about these violent men bristling to take over the city much as Capone was doing in Chicago; but the mayor had smoothed his oil on the situation, saying that New York was the grandest and safest town in the world. Esko had wondered at the time how much graft *he* was taking.

"Mantilini was involved?"

"He didn't pull the trigger himself. He's too smart for that. But by some strange coincidence he did happen to be on the other side of the street. Watching. He even gave a statement to the cops, saying how shocked he was, how truly shocked. And then he kept his name out of the papers. He's got nerve, and pull." She drew on her cigarette. "A life you saved."

And Marion Bennett wasn't finished yet.

"He's a dangerous killer, Esko, a hoodlum who does anything and gets away with it. And you're an architect with ideas about beauty and justice in society. Does that sound like a clever combination? Forget that, it sounds like I'm making a judgment here. But watch yourself, my tough Finn."

*   *   *

Esko arrived early for Kirby's funeral, pacing to and fro while gray and purple storm clouds loomed dark in the sky, making the rows of white headstones stand out like teeth. From beneath a tree he watched while the cars pulled up one by one. Ruthie arrived first, her two-seater slithering to a halt in a spray of gravel; next came Mantilini's Rolls, one back door opening to let out Gardella while Mantilini waited a few moments before stepping out of the other, dressed in a suit of the same somber gray that Esko had seen him wearing once before, at this very same Queens crematorium, when his brothers died. Next came MacCormick, chauffeured in a black Hispano-Suiza, and Esko was surprised, and grateful, to see that Katerina was with him, wearing a black hat with a black feather trailing from it, her face hidden by a veil. Only when a taxi came and a lean, gray-haired woman stepped out, looking around her, wondering if she was at the right place, did Esko leave the shadows of his tree, guessing that this was Kirby's sister.

"Hello, I'm Esko Vaananen," he said. "I sent you the wire."

"Grace Kirby," she said, voice to the point as her brother's had been, face sharp and hawklike. "Thank you."

"How was the trip?" She'd traveled by train from Kansas.

"Long. A long way to come. Poor Billy."

The service was brief. Esko read a short piece from Whitman. Grace Kirby spoke of her brother as a little boy, her emotion sincere and understated, the way Kirby would have preferred. And MacCormick, surprisingly nervous for once, coughing to clear his throat, paid tribute to Kirby the architect. The pink-faced minister hurried through the rest of it, slackening his pace only when the organ struck up and Kirby's coffin began trundling down the runway. The minister made unctuous ushering motions, sending it on its way, and Esko thought for a moment about the funerals he hadn't been able to attend in his life—Klaus's, and his mother's. He didn't see much dignity or comfort in the event. The attitude here seemed to be to shuffle Kirby out as quickly as possible, but then these moments were perhaps inevitably like that—liminal, unsatisfactory, and oddly incomplete however you looked at them—despite their apparent finality, a mixture of the sad and the absurd and the chilling. What did it mean to die anyway?

The hand that Grace Kirby laid on his sleeve as they left the chapel was mottled with age, pale as parchment, and surprisingly strong. "I hate fuss and so did Billy," she said. "We hadn't spoken in fifteen years. Lately he'd been sending me letters. He wrote a lot about you. He said you were his good friend."

"I'd like to think so."

"Tell me something straight, Mr. Vaananen," she said, while Esko stood aside to let her pass first through the open door.

"If I can," Esko said, following her out onto the gravel.

"Was he a good architect?"

Esko glanced up. Smoke puffed out the crematorium chimney, a twisting rope of white that climbed against the darkness of the clouds—Kirby, presumably, and Esko hoped that some of him blew over to Manhattan, mingling with the porous brick and stone.

"The best," he said. "Your brother was a genius plain and simple."

"Thank you," she said, smiling with her eyes, reassured. "I always thought that Billy did fine things."

"Better than that. Inspiring things. I promise you this—years from now some young man or young woman will walk into one of your brother's buildings and his or her life will change."

She raised her lips to his cheek, planting a kiss.

"Thank you, Mr. Vaananen."

Esko walked her to the taxi where the driver, a short roly-poly Italian with sad, doglike eyes threw down his newspaper, stamped out his cigarette, and fussily opened the back door. Soon the car was trundling away, bumping toward the black iron gates, and Grace Kirby turned only once, offering a brief wave through a distorting oval of glass.

"She looks a lot like him," MacCormick said, at Esko's side now.

"His sister."

"I gathered," MacCormick said, his handsome face heavy and reflective. "He was an extraordinary man—but you know that better than anybody. I liked him. I liked him a lot. So did Katerina."

Esko nodded, guarding his eyes again with the dark glasses. Katerina stood by the arched, redbrick entrance to the crematorium talking to Ruthie.

"I wanted to clear something up," MacCormick said. "I know why you were angry with the two of us that time when we came to the club. Katerina told me."

Esk felt the blood drain from his face, leaving him dizzy with sudden alarm. "She did?"

"She said she'd been out with you and Kirby one night in a restaurant and you and Kirby had been talking about some big scheme you had and she poured scorn on it. Is that true?"

Esko was silent, poised between puzzlement at the lie and excitement at the suggestion of complicity, even hope, it held out.

"What can I tell you?" MacCormick went on with his easy smile. "Katerina knows photography and art better than anyone I know. She knows music, and she knows books—but architecture is one book that's closed to her. She's even a little frosty about the penthouse, to be honest. Tells me it's so perfect it makes her uneasy."

"That's a pity," Esko said.

"So I'm sorry about that," MacCormick said, his sharply observant eyes watching Esko carefully from beneath the brim of his homburg. "I'd like to hear about that big scheme. That is, if you ever went any further with it."

"We did."

"Well," said MacCormick, moving forward on his toes, and then stepping back, assuming his usual languid pose, trying to disguise his enthusiasm. "I guess I'd be quite interested, very interested. Maybe you'll show it to me?"

"Maybe," said Esko noncommittally, seeing Mantilini coming toward them, his quick feet on the gravel like gunshots.

"Say, Esko, you coming? I'll give you a ride back to the city," Mantilini said, appraising MacCormick with a dismissive nod.

"I was just about to make the same offer," said MacCormick, grinning widely, speaking in his most honeyed tone. "Katerina and I would love your company."

Something about MacCormick put Mantilini's back up straightaway. "I don't think we've been introduced."

"Paul—this is Andrew MacCormick. Andrew—Paul Mantilini."

The two men watched each other, the one bored and haughty, the other tough and ungiving, jingling coins energetically in his pockets.

"So, Mr. MacCormick," Mantilini said. "What do you do?"

"I'm a man of leisure, Mr. Mantilini," MacCormick said, quite happy to play this sort of game all afternoon. "What about yourself?"

Mantilini laughed, determined not to be daunted by the other man's old-money assurance. "I'm a businessman," he said.

"Really," MacCormick said, stretching out the word as though it had about eight syllables.

"Yeah, really," Mantilini said, tanned skin drawn tight on his face. "Esko, are you coming?"

"Yes, Esko. What *do* you want to do?" MacCormick said. His eyes held the question he didn't ask. So, Esko, are you your own man or do you belong to this gangster now?

"I think I want to ride with Ruthie," Esko said calmly. "I'll see you gentlemen later."

He let his feet lead him across the gravel to where Ruthie stood talking with Katerina; he'd covered about half the distance when the two of them turned, watching him the rest of the way. By the time he got there those same feet felt as though they no longer quite belonged to him, as though in the presence of Katerina he was sure to fall apart all over again like a broken puppet; but he controlled himself, holding himself together even when Katerina lifted her hands and raised her veil, revealing her green eyes and the smile that was playing across her lips.

"I'm so sorry, Esko," she said, and into that short sentence she seemed to cram a multitude of apologies and all her vulnerable emotional vitality. She took his hand for a moment; then, just as quickly, she was walking back to MacCormick.

"Ruthie," Esko said. "Can I ride with you?"

"Sure, honey," she said.

Rain started to fall as they were crossing the bridge, pimpling the windshield and pinging on the two seater's taut canvas roof. Ruthie squinted her eyes, peering shortsightedly through the sweeping wipers at the wet asphalt and the rain-speckled steel girders of the bridge rushing by. Esko glanced at her face, a profile whose innocence belied the experience she'd gained; Ruthie, so young, seemed to have several lifetimes worth of pain stored in her frail and beautiful body; it was why she sang so well; it was why she didn't give a damn, and he wondered if this not caring was the source of her power. Even if so, he thought, the insight was of no use; it might work for her, but not for him; he would never not care; that was his burden, his saving grace, perhaps.

Ruthie, aware of his attention, dropped her bombshell: "Your friend, the Russian lady. She says she's heard me sing and she wants to take my photograph. Is she any good?"

"Very. You should let her do it."

"That's what I thought. She's an interesting lady."

The car roof was drumming now. On the other side of the divide a truck lumbered by in a mist.

"You know her pretty well, don't you?"

"What makes you say that?"

"I see the way she looks at you. A woman knows when another woman has fucked a guy. Something in her eyes, the way she looks at him. Asking: could I have him again? Do I *want* him again? The way she was looking at you, I'd say she wants you, but bad." Ruthie kept her own eyes on the road, her smile a wistful note to herself concerning her sharp perceptions and dreamy addiction to excitement. "Course, she may love you. But I don't believe any of that Romeo and Juliet bullshit."

Esko shifted in his seat with a quivering sense of his core having been observed.

"I got cat's eyes, other people don't," she said, reading his thought, and Esko relaxed, leaning back and watching the energy of the rain dying in its rush to obliterate the windshield of the car.

5

Katerina was his passion and his flaw; his inspiration, his blindness; his history, his future; she was the million stars that pricked and made brilliant his soul; she was the one reason why he shouldn't have gone to MacCormick with the East River scheme and the real reason he did. Of course there were other reasons: MacCormick had class, connections to the decision-making process at city, state, and federal levels; he was so rich that he could pick up a phone and raise $50 million, every cent of it legit. He knew building, he understood architecture and applauded the architectural revolution that was hitting its stride. He knew and respected Esko's work, revered it even. MacCormick made sense for any number of reasons, but none of those, finally, mattered a damn. Esko went with MacCormick because of Katerina, knowing all the while that she might be infuriated by what he was doing; she might spit in his face and flee to the other side of the continent, or back to Europe; but even there she would not escape the knowledge that Manhattan's most ambitious architecture ever was a monument to his love for her.

Esko's designs were ready, the moment had arrived. In his mind a hundred riveting guns drove him forward to the thumping rhythm of the Kirby edict: *get the job, get the job.* He believed completely in what he was offering. He'd imagined this moment and had prepared for it for years, for all his life in a way. He'd made studies of every old skyscraper in New York and knew how the procedure could be made faster, quicker, cheaper. From his time on the steel he knew this process inside out. So he was ready to tell MacCormick a story about money and art and social use; and it was a true story.

In MacCormick's office the stock ticker tapped away, spewing paper. Phones rang. Assistants, suited acolytes, moved soundlessly to and fro, a part of the boom, fanning it higher.

"Have a seat, Esko," MacCormick said, not getting to his feet, rocking slowly in his chair behind his desk in front of two high windows set at an angle, one with the startling view over the harbor, the other staring west toward the Hudson and the jumble of the Jersey shore.

"Thanks, I'll stand, Andrew, and I'll get right to it. I don't want to waste your time."

Unlooping his portfolio, he took out a stack of drawings. The first he showed was the most striking, five feet by three, a rendering in charcoal, dramatic precisely because the medium itself was incapable of showing decoration or surface trivia.

"I propose a metropolis within the metropolis," Esko said. "Covering three full city blocks. The central tower will be more than a thousand feet high. It will be modern, not Gothic—slablike, with the setbacks emphasizing a simple sculptural mass. An office building."

"And the other buildings?" MacCormick said, giving the rendering all his concentration.

"Four more office towers." Esko laid down the renderings, one by one. "A theater, a hotel, a hospital, a community center."

"A *community center,*" said MacCormick, rising out of his chair like a startled bird. He ran his hands through his hair. He touched the knot of his tie, checking that it hadn't run away in panic.

Esko smiled, never having seen him so disconcerted.

"Come along now, be serious. I have to make some money here," Mac-Cormick said, throwing up his hands in mock surrender.

Esko was patient, prepared; he told MacCormick that he would make money, lots of it, precisely because of the hospital and the community center. "The land is cheap here, and once we persuade people there's a good reason to come to this neighborhood, its value will soar. Everything about this project is designed to make money. And to be beautiful. And to be of use to the city and become a living part of it. People will come here to work. And it will beckon others in because it will be a good space to be."

Esko touched one of the drawings, not letting himself waver. "The central skyscraper will be clad in limestone. I suggest from Indiana."

"Because it's the most expensive material you could think of?"

"You're right. I could use brick. It would save maybe a million. Or why not corrugated iron? That would be even cheaper. Another million in your pocket, and we could paint it any color you like. What color would you like MacCormick Tower to be, Mr. MacCormick?"

"MacCormick Tower?" MacCormick squinted—eyes like slivers of gray granite. It was impossible to say whether he was surprised or flattered or both.

"You're putting up a skyscraper for all to see. Why not call it after yourself?"

MacCormick pondered the possibility, obviously intrigued.

"And perhaps it would be a *good* idea if the people of New York thought that Mr. MacCormick was so proud of what he'd done that he'd insisted on Indiana limestone rather than corrugated iron." Esko didn't smile. His voice was even. He looked MacCormick right in the eye with a direct challenge.

"I rather like the idea of the limestone," said MacCormick in his languid way.

Esko let go with all his enthusiasm now: "The world has never seen anything like this, Andrew. Be a part of it. Take the chance, come on. You'll be rich, but you're already rich. Do this and your name will be a glory in New York, damnit." He smiled, realizing he was sounding like Kirby.

MacCormick had a small gold pencil in his hand, just like the one Mantilini used to mark up figures in his black book; leaning over his desk, he made swift calculations on a blotter. "Property might be cheap in that neighborhood," he said. "But do you have any idea how many tenants and owners there are in any three city blocks in New York? Hundreds usually. Do you have any idea at all of how difficult it will be to assemble this parcel of land?"

"Not really," Esko admitted with a smile.

"Me neither," MacCormick said in his laziest drawl, rocking back in his chair again, watching Esko with an expression that was poised between humor and excitement. "It'll sure as hell be fun to try."

And so they went to work. In the forty months or so since the *Gazette* contest, yet another of Esko's ideas had been adopted: it had become usual to make a model of any proposed project in plasticine or clay, to impress potential investors. MacCormick hired the city's most prestigious commercial sculptor, putting him at Esko's service. MacCormick didn't tell either of them that it was essential for the scope of the plan to be kept secret, to protect against holdouts. There was no need for threats. The sculptor simply understood that he'd never raise his hand in Manhattan again if he whispered a word.

As an architect in midcareer Esko had naively assumed that he knew

something about the hullabaloo behind any big building project. Now, wit-
nessing MacCormick's wheeling and dealing, he realized how wrong he'd
been. MacCormick had a hundred tricks and dodges. He sent men incognito
to the City Hall to discover who owned what and who had leased to which
tenants within those three East River city blocks. He lunched one important
owner, hinting at market tips that would be forthcoming should he do the
smart thing and rid himself of that stinking factory by the river. He sent out
twenty different agents, each buying up smaller properties in secret. One
entire block, the northernmost of the three, was owned by a colleague who
had been on the swim team at Harvard. Such was MacCormick's universe,
and, thus, he quickly secured an option. Two-thirds of the southernmost
block belonged to the Roman Catholic Diocese of New York; he gained the
cooperation of that august organization by guaranteeing that the complex
would include a Sunday school, a promise that Esko heard with amused
astonishment.

"You don't mind?" said MacCormick afterward, leaning back in his chair
with a self-satisfied smile, immensely pleased with himself. "It won't affect the
integrity of your scheme."

"Not at all," Esko said. "In fact—let's throw in a soup kitchen for good
measure."

MacCormick handled the telephone with a familiarity Esko had never
seen before, not barking at it the way Joe Lazarus did, but caressing it, wooing
it. MacCormick smiled more than ever, spinning his monologues of money,
and the brightness of that smile usually meant bad news for somebody.

Once Esko heard him talking to Katerina, his voice hushed as he breathed
intimacies into the receiver, while Esko stared toward the corner of the office
where a series of her photographs were framed on the wall. They'd been taken
in desert country, silvery prints of sagebrush and twisted palm, fallen trees and
dried-up riverbeds, lonely mesas with not a human soul in sight, a terrain that
couldn't be humbled or even much modified by use, was just too strange and
immense. They were haunting pictures—desolate, timeless.

"Wonderful, aren't they?" said MacCormick, swiveling in his chair when
he'd put down the receiver. "She took those in Arizona. We spent our honey-
moon there and bought a house. That's where she is now."

On this late night Esko and MacCormick were alone in the office, all the
other aides and lawyers and secretaries long gone. Red light from the
torchettes rained down, and to mask his confusion, Esko turned his head

toward the undrawn drapes of the corner window, concentrating for a moment on the bobbing firefly specks of ships and boats on the river and, much nearer, an oblong light in an office building hanging in midair like a lit-up coffin.

"Does she know about the project?" Esko suddenly had to know.

MacCormick was making notes on his blotter beneath the light of a heavy brass lamp that was green above and golden inside. Esko stood over the plasticine project model, *puukko* in hand, shaping one of the cascading setbacks.

"Of course, how could she not? Despite the remarks she made that time at dinner, she hopes you'll give her a second chance. Let her look at it again when she gets back to town," he said, giving Esko a hopeful smile. "Maybe she'll change her mind."

For a moment he wanted to tell MacCormick everything and be done with the confusion and the deceit.

"What?" MacCormick said.

Esko pointed with his *puukko* at the model. "I was thinking that office space looking out onto gardens would be worth more than any other space. How much more per square foot do you think space like that would be worth?" he said.

MacCormick was sitting back in his chair, his arm stretched forward toward the desk, idly doodling on the blotter. "I'm not sure," he said.

"Don't give me that—your mind is like an abacus."

"All right then," MacCormick said, abandoning his nonchalant pose for once, his face reflecting a passion and knowledge he generally made it his business to disguise, studying his hand where it lay within the rectangle of light from the banker's lamp; then he quickly wrote a figure.

"I'd say seventy-five cents per square foot extra. Maybe even a dollar."

"With all that money we could make gardens like Versailles. We could even sell tickets," Esko said. "We put them on sunken roofs so they'll be invisible from the street and won't interfere with the lines of the building. I've also been thinking for a long time about a fountain," he said, aiming the *puukko* at the plaza in front of the central skyscraper slab. "People will leave their offices and hear the sound of running water. You know how much that will cost?"

"No. But I bet you're going to tell me."

"I can recirculate thirty thousand gallons a day for three dollars."

"You never quit, do you?" MacCormick said admiringly.

"In Italy in the seventeenth century rich patrons put painters under contract like ballplayers. They used them. They didn't just buy authenticated pictures by past masters and throw them into a bank vault and let them gather dust while they became more valuable. This country is so rich, something must be done with the money—I salute you for trying."

MacCormick blinked, wondering to what extent his prodigious vanity was being played upon, massaged. The answer was not at all: Esko had surprised himself, realizing for a moment how much he truly did appreciate his business partner.

"You're paying for my best, Andrew. I'm going to give it to you even when at first you say you don't want it," Esko said. "And, no, I don't quit."

And then, with a flutter of shame, he remembered saying much the same thing to Marion Bennett, with regard to his pursuit of Katerina.

MacCormick pushed himself back from the desk and stood. With a smile, straightening his suspenders over his precise white shirt, he came toward Esko, asking, "What's that knife you always use?"

"A *puukko*. Every Finnish boy is given one by his father. To learn how to be a Finnish man."

"Oh, and how do you do that?" said MacCormick with merry cynicism.

"Gutting fish. Handling wood. Carving ice."

"I was always more of a city boy," he said. "May I see?"

Red light flashed down the length of the blade; Esko gave it to MacCormick, handle first.

"My dad preferred jade," MacCormick said, testing the sharpness of the point. "I was fourteen when he died and I found myself heir to a whole lot less than I thought. A crumbling old place in Baltimore and a fistful of bills. And jade. A warehouse full of jade. He traveled the world for it after he left my mother and me. The collectors used to see him coming, and when he was dead one of them saw *me* coming. Bought the whole lot off me for fifty thousand dollars. Turned out to be worth more than two million. That was twenty years ago now. It was the last bad deal in my life." His tone was almost rueful, apologetic. "I make money. Even when I'm not trying to, I make money. Sometimes I wish I could stop making money. I can't. It's who I am."

"Not only that," Esko said, filled with fondness for the other man, despite himself won over by MacCormick's charm and sudden honesty.

"Maybe," MacCormick said, pushing his hands through his hair, shrugging something off. "You knew Kate when she was a little girl, isn't that right?"

"Only very briefly," Esko said carefully.

"Tell me. What was she like back then."

"Very sure of herself."

MacCormick nodded, comparing this with the Katerina he knew. Satisfied, he said: "You were in the war over there, weren't you?"

"Did she tell you that?"

"There was some other guy."

"Klaus . . ."

"He was killed?"

"He saved my life. And then he was shot."

"I only worry about what happens now. I protect my assets. And to do that I concern myself with the present tense. Strictly. Whatever's happened in the past doesn't bother me. Whatever," he said, smiling at Esko from the generous height of his mood, happy to be rich, happy not to be dead, happy to be married to Katerina. And then he handed back the *puukko*.

*   *   *

An Italian shoemaker was the last stubborn holdout, the only remaining tenant who refused to be bought out of his lease, turning down every offer and blandishment. "He's an old fool," MacCormick said, slamming down the phone and swinging his feet off his desk in a rare display of temper. "This whole thing's going to fall apart."

Early one morning Esko went around there himself, feeling at his back the nipping chill of November. In the untidy streets by the East River the first exhalations were wafting from the breweries, impregnating the air with the heavy, heady smell of malt. In the window of a delicatessen a sign said, ITALIAN HEROES SOLD HERE. Another small store had a sign in Hungarian. All these operations looked bright and brave starting the new day. He opened the door to the dim cavern of the cobbler's shop and was greeted by the smells of leather and boot polish, and a bell that went off like the gong at the beginning of a prize fight. An old man sat beneath the rough counter in the yellowish, waxy light that fell from a solitary bulb hanging on a cord. His name was Dino Bitale, Esko knew, and he looked up only for a moment before returning to the task at hand, spitting a nail into his hand and then tap-tap-tapping it into the upturned heel of a shoe. Behind him, a burlap curtain cut the shop in half.

MacCormick's people had apparently threatened Dino Bitale—stupid and unpleasant and unnecessary, Esko thought, knowing Mantilini wouldn't have stooped to such a tactic with an old man. Esko arrived with apologies, his renderings, and a bottle of Chianti. He showed Dino Bitale what he intended to do, and why, and promised that the old man would soon be opening a new shop in one of the arcades off the central skyscraper lobby. He showed Dino Bitale photographs of the Church of the Shadow Cross, saying that although MacCormick Plaza would be grander he hoped it would be no less beautiful. He wooed him with his enthusiasm, just as he had Mac-Cormick, and within an hour he left with a signature on the contract. For once, good faith and passion were more powerful than the gun.

6

MacCormick called a press conference, high in that office with the windows, the red mosaic ceiling, the heavy velvet drapes that were always open, framing the action like the curtains in a theater. Close to noon, he and Esko stood in the center of the room next to the model, waiting for the reporters to arrive. "Nervous?" MacCormick said, snapping a flame from his gold Dunhill lighter.

"A little," Esko said.

"How do you say that in Finnish?"

"*Pikkusen.*"

"*Pikkusen* nervous. I like that," MacCormick said, drawing on his cigarette, slowly exhaling, pointing his chin in the air. "Don't be. This'll go fine. We'll get lots of publicity and that will lead to lots of tenants and lots of money. That's the way it works. It's simple. We've told them your design is a work of genius and they'll believe it. Because they don't know any better. And because maybe it is."

One of MacCormick's aides stood at the elevator door, greeting the arrivals with a prospectus printed on thick, glossy paper and embossed in a colorful, cubistic style with the words MACCORMICK CENTER. Various of Esko's plans were included, along with a text whose prose tended toward the purplish:

> In deepest India, the Taj Mahal lies in solitary grandeur on the shimmering banks of the Jumna. MacCormick Center will stand proud on the teeming river that is New York. The Taj is truly an oasis in the jungle, its whiteness tense against the verdurous gloom of the forest. MacCormick Center will be a jewel, a still point in the swirl of our great metropolis: its cool, sharply edged heights will stand out against Manhattan's agitated man-made skyline. As the Taj speaks to India of spiritual serenity, so MacCormick Center will bring New York's business and social and artistic worlds into a companionship previously undreamed of. MacCormick Center is an urban ode, a prayer to a place, to our fantastic city of hurried and sparkling waters. It is the future. It is our future, bold and pure.

"My God, I'm getting a temperature," said Marion Bennett, fanning her face with the prospectus. She wore no hat and a straight black hipless flapper dress that stopped above the knee with a wide red belt dragged down over one hip. She looked like a gunslinger, and indeed she was now for hire, having left *Vanity Fair* and gone freelance. Her lips were rouged into a taut, businesslike bow. "I've got twenty dollars says MacCormick hired some Vassar jazz-baby poet who wears a green hat to write this overheated bilge."

"She arrived in a cloud of perfume and cigarette smoke," Esko said. "She wrote in pen and violet ink before the secretary was allowed to put her magic words through the typewriter."

"Well, well," said Marion Bennett, amused and a little impressed. "I didn't know you went to Vassar."

"And I never wore a green hat. Not yet, anyway," Esko said. "MacCormick gave me the idea. He told me that nothing can be itself anymore. Everything has to be like something else, otherwise people won't understand it. So I thought: Why not the Taj Mahal?"

"You're beginning to understand this, aren't you?"

"*Pikkusen*," he said. He gestured around the room: at the reporters, the prospectus. "All this is just the froth. The project is the thing. Nothing else matters."

"And the project's pure? Even though it's called MacCormick Center?"

"It doesn't matter what it's called. Or how it's described. Or who thinks he's being remembered. It is what it is. It will be what it will be—a part of the city, for everybody."

"I'll see you later, Esko," she said, and her gaze had both a casual friendliness and a hint of something else, a watchful, intimate awareness. "You're about to be someone. Do you know that? Maybe I'll have to corrupt you after all."

Katerina appeared some thirty minutes later, having returned to the city only that morning. She stepped out of the elevator and Esko saw her hesitate, startled by the busy scene. MacCormick raised his hand and smiled and nodded at her, a code that meant he was talking to someone important, so she walked through the crowd, combing one hand through her hair—a gesture she seemed to have acquired from her husband—pausing in front of the project model, examining it for a long time, her expression intent, lips parted, hips swaying in elegant long pants. Her skin was tanned and freckled from the sun, and her eyes shone out of her face like jewels. Esko gazed at her, suddenly unaware of everything else around him; he was astounded that Katerina, such a ravishing lifelong idea of his, could be new to him again, as if every detail he remembered about her had to be viewed once more from a different angle. He looked away, startled by the hallucinatory intensity of the moment.

A few moments later, she came over, said: "Hello, Esko, I'm in New York for a little while. Perhaps we can get together."

"I don't think that's a good idea—Mrs. MacCormick."

"Maybe I just want to go for a walk," she said, putting her hand on his sleeve.

"It can never be just a walk. You know that."

"I suppose I do," she said, glancing away, a little saddened. "What if I were to ask you to come away with me right now? What if I were to say, 'Let's get on a train together'? What would you do, Esko?"

"We went through that once already."

"You sound very rational about everything."

"Do I? I don't feel that way."

"I've caused you a lot of trouble, haven't I?"

"Not enough," he said.

She smiled, saying, "Kirby would be very proud of you today," and turned quickly, going to join her husband, an action with more mercy in it than coquetry. Esko sighed, wishing he'd taken her in his arms, glad that he hadn't.

The *World* fell in squarely behind the plan for MacCormick Center, thus guaranteeing that the *Times* would attack, which was fine, because the *Tribune* at once rushed to the scheme's defense. The *Graphic* printed a Composograph, a mock photograph of the scheme, next to a clock indicating the number of hours a death-row killer had left to live. *Vanity Fair* reproduced the renderings across a double-page spread with the headline: "The City of the Future." *The New Yorker* ran a cartoon picturing two puzzled construction guys holding a pane of glass and looking down from the peak of Mac-Cormick Tower, asking: "Which window did we miss?" The *Gazette* featured a cartoon of Esko alongside a plan of the project asking, "Which Is Beauty, Which the Beast?" Esko was asked whether he was a Communist, what he thought of Babe Ruth, if he could run like Paavo Nurmi, the name of his favorite motion picture star. Clubs he'd never heard of sent membership cards and Park Avenue hostesses whose Rembrandts were more authentic than their scotch invited him to parties where uniformed barmen twirled cocktail shakers that played "O Lady Be Good." Esko was feted, celebrated, and for the first time in his life, he saw the shock that customarily greeted his disfigurement turn to eager indulgence. He was, after all, a man of talent and burgeoning fame, the architect of the hour—hadn't Walter Lippmann said as much in the *New York World*? Publicity was more than a mask that made a deformed face seem appealing; it was a veritable social X ray, revealing the true structure, perhaps the very soul itself. Publicity was magic, making people believe he could produce beauty because he was a freak. "Lon Chaney, Architect," said the *Gazette* in another story. Invitations stacked up on his desk and if he was bold and foolish enough to go to these parties, and sometimes he was, he found himself pursued by flappers who'd read that he'd once painted and who were now eager to pose nude for their portraits; by their mothers, who clamored for their apartments overlooking the serrated skyline of Williamsburg to be redone in the *moderne* style; and by their fathers, who wondered if he couldn't knock up a quick house or even an office building or two while he was waiting to get going on the big thing. Within a matter of days he could have accepted enough commissions for a lifetime. He was fascinated, appalled, a little turned around by the city's self-conscious regard of his talent and disfigurement. Fame had hit him on the head like a flowerpot tumbling from a smart Manhattan setback; he was duly dazed.

Esko's celebrity reached its climax with two events.

First, there was Marion Bennett's profile in *The New Yorker*.

> *Vaananen is thirty-seven, a big solid man with a scarred face and a mystery about him that defies analysis. The patch over his eye gives him a dashing, secretive air. Perhaps, sometime long ago, he met an angry bear on a hunt in the forests of northern Finland. Or maybe he was the victim of a fire. We couldn't find out. He wouldn't talk about it. In any event he has absorbed the lessons of both America and his native Europe and has burned out of himself any idea of service to traditional design. Vaananen is building what Vaananen himself feels. Old-school architects hem and haw and clear their throats and decline to comment on MacCormick Center's unashamed modernity. Others are thrilled by its passionate fusion of ideas, some of them from Europe, even though the buildings will be as American as a sawn-off shotgun. He builds for today, not posterity. His chief architectural theory is to build buildings whose exteriors gleam with the granite purity of his vision. Inside, his concerns lie with the comforts, needs, and practicalities of those who will have to work and live there. He is quite pragmatic, belonging to no school. He's unashamed about wanting to make money for his backers. He says that's just good architectural sense. He's equally unashamed about wanting to make our city a better place for all its inhabitants. He says that's just good architectural morality. One morning in drizzly November, when it seemed that winter was about to descend in earnest, he gave us a tour of the site, quoting Finnish classics and telling us how he almost died in the war that took place there in 1918. His mind is quick and his tongue flipped off grand phrases, and we were quite unable to discern when he was being humorous and when he was not. He gets on well with most men and behaves*

with the courtesy of an anxious cavalier toward women, as if he
likes them really but needs to be reassured regarding their
intentions.

The piece went on for two more pages. Marion noted with amusement (it
was not an obituary after all, nor would it run in the *Times*) that Esko had
designed several speakeasies for a certain eminent bootlegger and that an earlier skyscraper effort of his, submitted for the *Gazette* contest in 1922, had
been copied all over America, most notably on *The New Yorker*'s very own
doorstep, in Bryant Park, by the German architect now based in New York
and Miami, Joseph Lazarus. She got that story from MacCormick, although
Esko was not displeased to see it in print.

Then, on New Year's Eve, he was invited to give the keynote speech at the
annual costume ball of the Architectural Association. The theme was "New
York, the Modern, a Building Boom." The event took place on the third floor
of the Astor Hotel in a chandeliered ballroom with forty-foot ceilings that ran
almost the entire breadth of the hotel. In the center of the room was an imposing reproduction of the Statue of Liberty, spotlights beaming from both eyes.
Painted on a frieze hanging from the balcony was an epic depicting man's
progress through the ages. Hanging opposite was a second frieze, scenes from
the history of New York itself: an Indian handing over the title deeds to Manhattan, the assassination of Jim Fisk, society taking its pleasure in Central
Park, the Bowery at night, the construction of the Woolworth. There were
more than one hundred white-clothed tables, each with a shining red lamp
rising like a muted beacon on a stalk at the center. Two rival jazz orchestras
played in rivalrous alternation, their din nonetheless failing to drown out the
hubbub of the crowd surging to and fro. The place was alive with the brazen
hooting of the orchestras and the clash and strain of a thousand different personalities in fancy dress. Esko himself hadn't bothered with a costume, rea-
soning that as the main attraction he'd be forgiven. And there'd always be
those who would look at his face and assume he was wearing a mask anyway.

The jazz orchestras fell silent, dinner was announced, and everyone took
their seats. At the head table Esko found himself between an eminent member of the Choate family and a woman whose shining black hair was streaked
modishly with green and who was something big to do with the Metropolitan
Museum. A waiter kept him primed with cocktails from one of those musical

shakers that were all the rage at the end of 1926, this one tootling a prelude by Rachmaninoff.

Esko wrangled with spinach soup, a large steak, and a mountain of potatoes slopped in gravy, and, for dessert, an enormous sparkler-adorned scoop of ice cream that looked like an anarchist's bomb. Brandy was served, cigars offered from cavernous humidors. The master of ceremonies heaved himself to his feet, belched, and introduced the speaker, a fellow described in terms of such outlandish achievement that Esko looked around for a moment before realizing that he himself was the subject under discussion.

The main ceiling lights went dim. Rising to his feet, Esko saw the hundred or more red table lamps glowing in front of him, heard the dying murmur of conversation. A spiky round microphone was placed in front of his face.

Giving a speech: this was every Finn's idea of a nightmare. Not his father's, of course. Timo had made a thousand speeches in his time, rousing men and women in lecture halls and in dingy basements and perhaps even on battlefield. Now Esko surprised himself by warming to the task, calling for a toast to the memory of a great American architect—W. P. Kirby.

A chair banged, falling, and glass shattered. Someone was coming in late, a looming figure dressed in white, muttering apologies in harsh guttural tones so that his progress was like a series of firecrackers going off. The man stood up straight for a moment and Esko saw that it was Joe Lazarus.

His pulse quickened.

He went on, recapturing his confidence: "Kirby taught me that a city is not just a human operation directed against nature. It is a creation and also a living thing. It makes demands on us, just as we expect much from it. New York is a mighty image that stirs our minds."

Lazarus called out, "Hear, hear!"

"The architectural problem of old Europe lies in the great city of today—here in New York, in other words. The architect must solve it with action—"

Lazarus: "Hear, hear! Bravo!"

"—not bothering whether he creates the city of the future but caring deeply about the life of the present," Esko hurried on. "And in doing so, of course, he will create the future. Organic and lasting. Ladies and gentlemen, thank you. I'll see you down at MacCormick Center."

Esko was sweating a little when he sat down, surprised by the thunderous applause that greeted him, and was soon on his feet again for questions, unable now to make out the figure of Lazarus beneath him in the crowd. But at the end of the evening, as he collected his coat, he sensed a presence behind him, and knew it would be Lazarus, and indeed it was. Lazarus was dressed remarkably, extravagantly, comically, in a costume representing the *Gazette* skyscraper. His face was bearded, ruddy, and sweating, his already heavy body struggling beneath the weight of his extraordinary getup.

"Good speech, Esko, *sehr gut,*" he said, headpiece nodding, self-possessed, but making no attempt to disguise his energized malevolence. "You can spout intellectual nonsense to match the best of us these days. Now you really know how to be an architect. A pity it will be your swan song in New York."

"I can't talk now, Joe," Esko said breezily, his brief moment of anger and unease having passed. What Lazarus did or didn't do didn't matter anymore. So what if he went on claiming the *Gazette* design, so what if he continued to build that same skyscraper over and over again? Esko would only be losing what he'd dismissed as unimportant long ago—credit for something that was merely a stop-gap, an inspired judge-pleaser, a contest compromise. "I'm on my way out."

On seeing Lazarus hug himself with fiendish glee Esko started to turn his back, but a costumed arm shot forth, creaking with metal and wood, and restrained him.

"Quite correct, Vaananen," he said. "You are out."

Esko tried to shrug off the hand.

"You are out and I am in. Andrew MacCormick, you see," he said in his rattling staccato. "Such a nose for business! He has settled the matter. He has quite cooked your hash."

"I'm leaving now," Esko said, determined to keep calm.

"No, you stay," Lazarus said. "You go nowhere. Ever."

Esko smelled the liquor on Lazarus's breath; the man was drunk, perhaps dangerous—he looked mad, on fire with hatred and gloating triumph. "You have MacCormick," he said. 'You *think* you have Andrew MacCormick in that pocket of yours. But I have my own man. He's buying out MacCormick's interests in the East River lots."

"Andrew won't sell."

"You are quite wrong—it's all agreed."

Esko slapped down Lazarus's hand. "Don't be ridiculous!"

"Your scheme—quite excellent in its way," Lazarus said, blinking, stroking his beard. "Perhaps even one or two details from it will feature in my own grand plan."

Esko didn't want to think about it but the fact was there: the East River lots, now legally assembled in one big parcel, were worth many times the sum of the individual parts. MacCormick would make a fortune if he sold, if there was a buyer.

"Andrew would never agree," he said again in a low voice.

"It is a pity, *ja*. A great pity," he said, moving so close that Esko could smell his rank body odor and not only the booze and garlic on his breath, and so that Lazarus could sniff the vapor of Esko's doubt. "Lazarus wins, you lose."

7

Esko hurried through the revolving doors of the Astor. His arm shot out for a taxi. Settled in the back, he was buoyed by the crowds and the festive lights in Times Square, but then, appearing in his mind like a picture, came the face of Lazarus gloating in that ridiculous costume, and his throat constricted with unbidden anxiety, the pathways and currents of his body already anticipating the full calamity of what Lazarus had said before his mind would accept it. He tried to tell himself there was no reason at all why MacCormick would seek to destroy him; then he instantly stopped short. In fact there was a reason, a very good one: Katerina. What if MacCormick had discovered the truth?

The cab dropped Esko at the Kirby building. He rode the elevator to the top floor and found the doors to the penthouse open, the lights on.

"Hello? hello?"

There was no answer. His voice sounded hollow and empty. He went in, and gasped.

The space had been gutted. Sledgehammered. Destroyed.

The walls had been smashed. The furniture—what was left of it—lay in broken heaps on the floor. The drapes had been wrenched from the windows and torn into strips with fanatical deliberation. Glass crunched and splintered beneath his feet, and the air was filled with the smell of plaster. As he moved around Esko caught an acid whiff of something else: urine. The kitchen was a chaos of smashed crockery and food. All the taps were eerily running in the bathroom. In the bedroom the oak bed had been smashed. It lay in pieces and splinters on the floor like a ship on a shoal.

Was Katerina safe? Had she been hurt?

He ran back to the elevator, but the elevator clanked and groaned, its slow descent endless. In the street he again broke into a run; coat lifting behind him, he felt the whisk of his feet on the sidewalk, the rush of his breath.

"Hey, what's the rush, pal! Come back here a minute!"

It was the night cop, patrolling the other side of the street. Esko ran harder, easily outdistancing the cop and his whistle, darting down streets this way and that, racing toward the banks of the Hudson, toward MacCormick's office.

The building rose before him, high and stark against the moon. The moonlight was blue, almost powdery, and it soothed Esko, making him pause for a moment to catch his breath before entering the interior street of the lobby, designed as a long shot, a corridor that ran clear through to another entrance at the other end and made getting in and out of the building easy. Esko picked up his pace again, heels clicking on marble, racing past the bronze light fixtures and murals that depicted the long-ago roots and future dreams of America: Vikings in their long ships, Columbus in midocean, Lincoln at Gettysburg. Esko thought of Kirby—get the job, get the job. It wasn't supposed to be like this.

Esko rode upward alone in the swaying express elevator, there being no man on duty.

MacCormick stood in the red dimness of that huge and theatrical room, the gold light of the lamp with its green shade glowing on the desk in front of him. He looked up, dressed in tuxedo and bow tie, and he smiled.

"Good evening, Esko," he said in a calm and unsurprised voice.

And then Esko saw Katerina. She stood in the far corner of the room, in front of one of the tall windows, sheathed in a black, diamond-patterned dress that both covered and suggested her body. Baubles of black glass glittered beneath her ears. Her feet were tucked into black satin pumps and she was holding a champagne glass, as if posing for an advertisement in *Vanity Fair*. There was something shocking and incongruous in the scene. It might have been entitled "The Rich at Leisure." It was the sort of thing, Esko thought, that Katerina wouldn't have the least interest in photographing. And yet here she and MacCormick were. The torchettes gave off their strange, rubylike light. The ticker tape machine was silent, a mound of paper spewed on the floor in front of it.

"We've been talking and thinking about you, Esko." He took a cigarette from an ebony box on his desk and snapped a lighter. The air filled with the smell of Turkish smoke. "Kate?"

Katerina turned away swiftly, showing them her bare back. Light glanced from a diamond clasp on the pearl necklace at the back of her long neck. For a moment there was something else crackling in the air.

"Champagne?" said MacCormick. "As you can see I have a couple of bottles on ice." He gestured to where they were, in a bucket carefully positioned in the model of Esko's project that had been sculpted by the most prestigious commercial artist in the city. "We've been hitting it, Kate and I—shamelessly. There's some cold chicken around here someplace, if you can find it." He shook his head, as if at the hopelessness of the task—trying to find anything in this vast, red-lit space. "This room is simply so improbably big. Did you ever notice? Esko, whatever's the matter? Are you feeling ill tonight?" His darting eyes were filled with malicious humor. He touched the front of his immaculate white silk shirt. "Should we call a doctor? I'd hate for you to get sick."

"I saw Joe Lazarus," Esko said. "He tells me I'm out, that you're selling the East River lot to someone else."

MacCormick hummed a tune, something by Gershwin. He hurried through a few bars, stopped, grinned drunkenly. He'd found a bone of chicken on his desk with some meat left on it. "*Did* he say that? *Why* would he say that? That's such a *terrible* thing to say."

"Is it true?"

MacCormick wasn't through. "This chicken's really not too bad, you know." He tossed the bone onto the desk. "Could use a little salt."

Esko repeated: "Is it true?"

"Ah, but what is truth?" said MacCormick, mouth widening in that boyish grin. "It's true that my hands are greasy now from the chicken," he said, moving out from behind the desk and ambling slowly over until he and Esko were standing face-to-face, so close that Esko could smell the champagne and the meat on his breath. Then Esko felt a pressure on his coat lapels as MacCormick placed his hands there, wiping them to and fro.

So, Esko thought: he knows, he definitely knows. Esko thought he understood something else—restraint was the only way he could win this. "Andrew, I asked a question," he said in a level voice.

"But I didn't say I'd give you an answer, did I?" he said, his eyes flashing.

He wagged his finger. "Maybe I'd rather talk about theater. Or art. That's always a splendid topic. Art. Perhaps we can persuade Kate to join in. Kate, darling?"

Katerina said nothing, facing the night high above New York. A flame from her lighter flashed in the blackness of the pane.

"No? Frankly, that's a pity. But then Kate's not been in a talkative mood this evening, has she? Except with regard to a certain architect."

Whistling, MacCormick moved back behind his desk and sat down heavily. He reached for the little brass chain on the banker's lamp and the desktop went dark. "If you're forcing me to deal with dull old business, so be it," he said, his face strange in the reddish light. "Here's the deal, Esko. Lazarus is right. You're out. The contracts are here in front of me, waiting to be signed. Lazarus has his own scheme, another speculator, I'm cashing in my chips, and you are *out*. The comedy is over."

Esko had been steeling himself for this; all the same he felt as though he'd been struck in the face.

Behind the desk MacCormick turned the lamp back on, its golden light disclosing fountain pens, the cigarette box, an onyx clock in the shape of a pyramind, piles of papers, stacked and orderly. Esko gathered himself.

"You're making a mistake."

MacCormick looked at him sharply, throwing himself back in his chair and locking his hands behind his head. "Really? And why might that be?" he said, as if he was looking forward to hearing this.

MacCormick simply never made a bad deal, and Esko knew that he was about to make one now. The world within the world that Esko was going to build down on the East River was not only better than whatever Joe Lazarus had it within him to design, it would ultimately make more money. Esko hadn't lied about that. He was sure of it. In this instance the purity of his inspiration had been allied to a sound grasp of commercial reality and the requirements of New York. "Lazarus is a hack. In the end you'll make more money with me," he said.

MacCormick's chair scraped across the floor. He got to his feet suddenly. "Here," he said, moving with restless energy. "Take this book."

It was a wide but slender volume, tooled in gold, bound in leather, inlaid with jade. The leather was so soft and grainy to the touch that it almost crumbled in Esko's fingers, and his nostrils were filled with the sweet, slightly musty smell of it.

"It's the one thing belonging to my father that I still possess. Eleventh century. Japanese. Just to handle it is to decrease its value. Laugh at me if you want—but this really *should* be in a bank vault someplace."

"It's beautiful," Esko said. His fingers were covered with brown dust.

"You know what's more beautiful?" He moved out from behind the desk again and stood in front of the plasticine model of the project. Gently he lifted the champagne bucket from the middle of it. He laid the bucket on the floor, ice chiming. "This. MacCormick Center. Your buildings, your design. It's maybe the most remarkable thing I've ever seen and I've seen some remarkable things. *This* is beautiful. How much do you want to build it?"

MacCormick's expression was different now. He seemed studious, almost serious, fingering the dimple in the center of his chin. The stakes of the game seemed to have changed.

"You know how much," said Esko quietly.

"But I don't—not precisely, not down to the last dollar of your desire." MacCormick sauntered across the room. The perennial youthfulness of his expression seemed worn; his face sagged. "Are those burns that you have, Esko? Or saber wounds? Were you in a duel? We never did discuss the issue of why you came to America. Was it terribly romantic? Will you tell me now?"

A footstool came skittering across the floor from beneath MacCormick's exquisitely shined shoe.

"There, stand on that. It'll hold your weight."

Esko glanced toward Katerina. The reflection of her cigarette no longer burned in the window. She had her black-gloved hands over her ears.

"Kate won't help you. Now come on," he said, beckoning Esko toward the stool. "Up you go. Or isn't your dream worth quite so much as that?"

Esko looked at him for a moment, shrugged, and got up on the stool. Almost slipping, the stool wobbling beneath his weight, he threw out his arms for balance.

"There we go. Now, what do we think?" MacCormick said, his eyes filled with a terrible gleam. "Is this the man who will invent a new New York? Our great materialist of the abstract? Purveyor of the ultimate twentieth-century environment?" MacCormick's voice rose with ferocious command. "Or a dull old Finnish bear who should be led back into the woods. Can we transform him into the ultimate human? C'mon, Esko. Let's get into the spirit of this. Improvement is in the air."

MacCormick got down on the floor. On his hands and knees he fussed at Esko's shoes. He tugged at the bottoms of Esko's pants and prodded his foot. He made a great display, as though he were a tailor, measuring a new design. This little theater seemed to amuse him very much. "Mmm. Maybe the toes could be eliminated. They were given us to climb trees with and we don't really climb trees anymore. Not here in New York."

Back on his feet now, he stared into Esko's face with a grave expression. He reached out and yanked Esko's left ear with a sudden tweak. "The ears could be turned around, slotted to the head. The hair, of course, would be used only for accent and decoration. Streamline the nose."

He stood back, picturing this notional handiwork and, with another of those quick, unexpected motions, jabbed a finger at the patch over Esko's blind eye. "This will be of polished steel. It will gleam. We could create the perfect being, couldn't we Kate? Kate?" He raised his voice a little, turning his head, and then shrugged. "She's still not listening. Oh well, we'll have to go on alone you and I, pursuing this little idea of ours, this fantasy about improving life, calling forth the ultimate human, the inscrutable machine. Of course that was Baron Frankenstein's idea. And we've already got our terrible creation—*Esko Vaananen.*"

MacCormick shuddered, overcome with a frisson of mock horror. "Spiritually, of course, it's another matter. We know we have flaws that cannot be corrected. At heart maybe we're all unhappy freaks. Only money helps. And love, I guess. The delusion of love."

Everyone's acting tonight, Esko thought, everyone's playing a game, showing their cards, hiding their cards, bashing their cards down on the table; this was a game with something real and final hovering behind it, an ax waiting to drop. The strain of standing on the stool made his legs quiver. His eye stung from where MacCormick had jabbed it. His ear smarted, hot, pulsing as though it were leaking blood. And yet still Esko stayed calm, believing that in this game he possessed a good card, a winning card.

"Money does help, doesn't it Andrew?" Esko said calmly. "Money overcomes everything. My project is more work, more risk, more fame, and much, much more money. So what if you get a quick return on your investment? Where's the glamour in that? You do that every day. But this." He nodded toward the plasticine model. "It's what a Medici prince would have done. It's special. You know that."

MacCormick sniffed. He circled the desk, gulping champagne and setting the glass down within the light of the lamp. "Maybe I do at that," he said, his pale eyes narrowing to cracks. "Maybe I do know. A Medici prince. Mmm." He stuffed his hands into his pockets. "Are you still holding that book?"

"You can see that I am."

"Are you sure? It's very valuable, you know."

"So you said. I'm taking good care of it."

"That's excellent," said MacCormick, shrugging his shoulders a little, like a boxer. "I want to tell you something about it." With sudden violence he yanked up the heavy brass bankers lamp. Its bulb popped, showering glass, and a blotter flew off the desk together with a Harvard beer mug, scattering pencils; the pyramid clock bounced, spinning toward the foot of the stool where Esko stood. "I had that book translated. It was written by a woman at the Japanese Imperial Court. Turns out to be pretty fascinating, because you get a good picture of what life was like for her. Of course, there's a lot of personal stuff. Lists of things she likes and things she doesn't. Gloomy things. Happy things. Shameful things. Things that make her hot." He pulled a face, guying each of these emotions. His glance fell on the lamp in his hand, as if in surprise, wondering what it was doing there. He hefted the thing, trying its weight. "The interesting thing is that they screwed around a lot back then. They had a sense of sin, but it didn't extend to sex. Think of it, Esko. I implore you to think of it. All those Japanese people in the eleventh century fucking each other like rabbits and feeling no guilt. Isn't that tremendous?" he said.

MacCormick looked calmly into Esko's face. "Do you feel guilt, Esko? About sleeping with Kate? About fucking my wife?"

Esko said nothing. At the window Katerina had turned to face them both. Her expression was blank, her lips slightly parted, her eyes gleaming a little in the red light that flashed from the beads swinging on her ears.

"Yes, Andrew, I do," Esko said.

"You do what?"

"I do feel guilty about sleeping with Katerina."

"Oh, Esko, you fool," said Katerina, and her hand flew to her mouth.

"I feel guilty but not ashamed. Guilty because you're my friend. Unashamed because I love her. I always have," Esko said.

In his head, MacCormick knew this, had known it for a long time; but never, until now, did his bones have the information; never, until now, had his nerves been dulled by the absolute certainty of this truth. His face flushed.

He started to speak and then stammered to a halt, as if something in his throat had run down or was broken. He took a step, paused. And then strode quickly across the room smashing at the plasticene model of the project with the heavy base of the brass lamp, striking one blow, grunting, raising the lamp and striking again, scattering glass and plaster, not quitting until Katerina— who stood close by the model, and moved not an inch throughout this—was speckled white with broken fragments and all that remained of the model were the shattered bases of the buildings, sticking up like stumps of teeth.

"There. It's done. It's finished," MacCormick said, allowing the heavy brass base of the lamp to drop from his fingers. Sweeping back his hair, he left a streak of blood on his forehead from where he'd gashed his hand. All around him Esko felt the waves of MacCormick's rage and hate, but he stood quite still.

MacCormick passed his hands across his eyes. From faraway, out in the night, came the wail of a boat on the river. Katerina was trying to light a cigarette.

"Katerina, are you all right?" said Esko.

"Here," said MacCormick, stepping forward with his lighter, not giving her the chance to answer. Quickly pocketing the lighter, he leaned toward the floor, picking up a piece of the broken skyscraper, tossing it away. "I'm bored by this. I'm bored by you, Esko. I'm bored by your hideous face." Behind the desk, he unscrewed the cap of one of his fountain pens, squinting in the dim light, before his hand began moving with a scratching, almost furtive sound across the contracts. "Tell me something," he said, looking up at Esko as though an idea had just occurred to him. "What if I were to say that even now there's a chance for you? What if I were to say that all you have to do for me to tear up these contracts is to tell me that you've never loved Kate? Not at all? Never for a moment. And that all you'd thought about, ever, was building your precious skyscraper. What would you say, Esko? What would you do then? Would you renounce her?"

"No," said Esko, without hesitation. He could design another skyscraper, a dozen more. Nowhere in the world would he ever find another Katerina.

"Katerina's right. You *are* a fool," MacCormick said. Rage spent, he spoke with bitter calm. "There won't be any big projects for you. You've been had, Esko. It was a scam right from the start. From the moment you came to me after Kirby's funeral I've known I was going to do this. And you know the most glorious thing? Kate's been in on it too. Haven't you, darling?"

Esko was swept by nausea. He felt as though he'd lost his grasp on every-thing. Now he was sinking. "Katerina," he said, his voice cracked, precarious. "No—please." He dropped off the stool, sinking to his knees on the floor. He'd been tricked, gulled.

"Esko!" she said, but nothing more.

He slapped his own face, first the scarred side, then the other, deliberate, heavy thumps that made his head ring as if he were in a bell tower. At his hand on the floor he espied the chunk of plaster that MacCormick had thrown, and so, with the topmost pinnacle of the model of the skyscraper he had dreamed of building, he smote his forehead, driving in the plaster until sharp splinters cut his flesh and the blood ran down in front of his eyes. The full weight of the deception and the betrayal was borne in on him now. Kate-rina had been in on the plot all along. He was crushed, he was at rock bottom.

Now he heard MacCormick, whose lies had breathed such sincerity. "Well done," MacCormick was saying. "Oh, most *excellently* done. The wounded Finnish bear performs. The piece is called The Descent into the Abyss of Self-Pity."

MacCormick's moneyed hands went: *clap, clap, clap.*

"It's better than the Metropolitan!"

Something inside Esko made him smile. He who is blind in one eye can still see out the other. He who limps is still walking. There was the taste of blood in his mouth and suddenly he saw himself back in Finland, in the vil-lage, running toward a house where flames were shooting out the windows. A beam crashed. Another pane of glass exploded. Smoke clawed at his eyes, making them smart. His flesh turned hot. A carpet rose and rippled beneath him, surging with heat. He heard his mother's voice, screaming, and a great howl of fury rose up inside him. He threw himself across the desk, scattering pens and contracts, lunging at MacCormick with the unsheathed *puukko.* Hot blood jetted from MacCormick's cheek while Esko slashed again, cut-ting at the silk-enshrined arms that MacCormick threw up to protect himself. It was violence, it was chaos; Katerina was yelling, begging them to stop.

MacCormick scrambled away from the chair and was on his knees now, in front of the desk in a position of lopsided prayer. More blood dripped from his face, splashing the floor as Esko pounced. An image from Tampere appeared before him, and he stepped forward, *puukko* ready, as he'd seen Holm—killer Holm—do many a time before slitting a man's throat. Mac-

Cormick's eyes were filled with shock and fear; he was too stunned even to beg; he didn't know what was happening to him, what was about to happen.

"Don't," said Katerina. "Please."

Esko hesitated, glancing at her. Light flashed on the diamond patterns of her dress.

"Let's leave," she said. "Let's go Esko. Let's go together, you and I."

As Esko moved toward her his right foot slid from under him, skidding on marble made treacherous with blood. He fell as if in slow motion, *puukko* carving thin air, his ass banging the floor a split second before the back of his head. He blacked out for a moment, awakened to stars. The scarlet mosaic was looking down at him, twinkling like a sky soaked in blood. The lights in the melting torchettes seemed to flicker. He was conscious of a throbbing, pounding pain in the back of his head and the faint, almost surprised tone of MacCormick's voice:

"I'll be scarred for life, you son of a bitch."

MacCormick was behind the desk, mopping at his face with a handkerchief that was turning slowly red. In a drawer he found what he was scrambling for, a pearl-handled revolver with six chambers and a bullet in each. "I won this from some dumb bootlegger at poker," MacCormick said. He was unsteady on his feet. Seeing a half-filled bottle of champagne on the desk he took a pull from it, dropped the bottle. "You're going to die now, Esko. I'm going to shoot you with this bootlegger's gun. In self-defense, obviously. Don't they say the best story is the one that sticks as close to the truth as possible? And Kate will back me up. Because Kate's a good little girl who knows where her bread is buttered."

Spittle had gathered around MacCormick's mouth. He wiped it away with one hand while coming toward Esko with the revolver outstretched in the other. In his mind Esko found himself once again back at Tampere, on the dam with Klaus moments before they were shot. His eye flicked about, searching for the *puukko*—nowhere to be seen. Kicking upward, he flailed at MacCormick with his feet, knocking at the gun.

Afterward when he tried to picture what happened in this instant, he would never remember the noise, only the searing flash, as if everything else had been transformed into visual sensation, pure and explosive. His head whirled with blobs and sparks and smears and squirming snakes of fire. He and MacCormick were rolling on the floor, beating at each other, pummeling each other. Then Esko realized he had a hold on nothing. His arms grasped empty air. MacCormick had escaped his bear hug and Esko was squeezing only himself.

MacCormick's voice rasped, "Shoot him, Kate. For God's sake, finish this. Shoot him like a dog."

Esko raised himself to his feet, groggy, staggering, spattered with Mac-Cormick's gore and with fireworks still exploding in his skull. His flopping tongue discovered that he'd lost a tooth; he bled from his gums without relief. The black and gold pattern of the marble floor slowly reordered itself in his vision.

The revolver—diamond studded, he now saw—was in Katerina's left hand. She was aiming it right at his heart.

"Shoot him! For Chrissakes, shoot him now!"

Run him down. Katerina regarded him in an impersonal way. Perhaps it's finished after all, he thought. Perhaps this is where it ends.

He followed her every motion as she crossed across the floor toward him: the shimmer of her dress, the leonine movement of her legs, the flake of white plaster falling from her hair. He remembered a young girl stepping toward him with a mirror in her hand. He smiled.

MacCormick: "Shoot. For God's sake, Kate—"

She raised the gun to her own head and Esko had already started to cry out lest she shoot herself. But she was only stroking her skin with the cool metal of the barrel, brushing something away, or trying to think. "I can't do that."

"Give me the gun," MacCormick said, his voice striving for calm, his pale eyes half closed as a rivulet of blood ran down his cheek into the already bedrenched collar of his shirt. "Be careful, Kate, I don't want you to hurt yourself. Give me the gun. I'm going to end this."

The first bullet took MacCormick in the shoulder, cleaving away a chunk of tuxedo as if with an ax. "What—why?" he said, shocked eyes scrutinizing the wreck of the garment, advancing toward Katerina with his hand stretched out. "What the hell—"

She shot him twice in the chest; as he staggered back, already falling, hand clutching feebly at the edge of the desk, she shot him once in the belly. On the floor he raised his head and tried to sit up but he didn't have the strength. He slumped back down, his body wheezing and sucking as blood spilled from his wounds and air tried to get in. "Jesus, Kate," he said, and tried again to pull himself up. His hand pawed feebly at the blood spreading over his shirt front. He gasped, spurting more blood from his nose, and the heels of his shiny shoes scratched at the floor as if he were still trying to raise himself.

In the war, Esko had seen men die and there was always a moment when the look in their eye seemed quite distinct from the agony that the body was feeling; a merciful numbing, perhaps, or a flooding of memory. He saw that look now in the eyes of MacCormick.

"Kate," said MacCormick, the word a sigh, a dying breath; his feet stopped twitching; in his eyes that last fading light was gone.

Katerina held the gun outstretched. "It hurts, doesn't it?" she said, her own eyes huge, dazzling through tears, her voice neither scared nor surprised nor exultant.

"Katerina," said Esko, crawling toward her, just needing the affirmation of human contact and assuming that she did too.

"Don't," she said, swinging quickly around so that the revolver pointed at him again. "Just don't."

Esko fell back, holding up his hands. From outside came no sound, not the hooting of a boat, or the ringing of a phone, or the clamor of a siren. It was as if they were alone in the universe.

The gun fell to Katerina's side and then slipped from her hand, clattering on the floor. Esko picked it up quickly, slipping it into his coat pocket.

She turned. "Did you say something?"

"No," he said in a soft voice.

"I thought I heard you say something."

"It was the wind."

She raised a glove to her forehead and shivered, at MacCormick's face. Esko stepped over, leaning across the corpse, shutting the eyelids with gentle pressure of thumb and forefinger.

"It's a—spectacle. Isn't it?" Katerina said in a low, halting, wondering voice, as if speaking of some distant event, some earthquake or volcano or iceberg-sinking on the other side of the world, some happening she was now hearing about at second hand. "If only I had my—my camera," she said. She paused. "Shouldn't we call the police?"

And then what? thought Esko. Was there really nothing for it but to tell the cops the whole messy story, to feed themselves to a machine that would grind them into the sensation of the next tabloid murder before it packed them off to jail and the chair? Outside, everything was still, quiet, and the lights of the boats twinkled beckoningly on the harbor's wintry depths.

Esko saw that his own hands were wet and smeared with blood. Katerina's were clean. "Who knew you were going to be here tonight?"

"I've no idea," her voice rising a little with exasperation. "No one. I returned this afternoon."

A million questions demanded an answer. How long had MacCormick known? How had he found out? When and why had the penthouse been destroyed? What had been Joe Lazarus's part in all this? And Katerina's? Had MacCormick really been setting him up from that moment when they met again after Kirby's funeral? Had she truly encouraged the betrayal?

None of this mattered right now. Many thoughts raced in Esko's mind, but he knew that if anything were to be saved, action was required. At this moment he wasn't going to wear a hair shirt over MacCormick.

"I want you to leave. Right now. Clear out. Get out of New York. You were never here tonight. This never happened."

"I'm not sure what you mean."

"Just do as I say. Please."

"Esko . . ." She looked at him closely. "You don't imagine you can get away with this?"

"Just go," he said, spotting her lustrous fur coat lying on a sofa beneath one of the tall windows. He crossed the room and was on the point of picking it up when he remembered his hands and told her to wait a moment.

The bathroom, tiled in black and yellow and salmon pink, softly lit from above, with a shower and a bath stall behind doors of steel and frosted glass at the far end, was a haven. Esko shut his eye and tried to expunge from his mind the terror of what had happened. He shrugged off his coat and wiped his hands on it. He nudged on the cold-water tap with his elbow, splashed clean his hands, rolled up his sleeves, and lathered himself with soap. The ritual calmed him. He washed; he massaged his face with warm water; and, on catching sight of his face in the mirror, was surprised to see an expression of such calm determination reflected back at him. This Esko Vaananen looked to him like a fellow who could still build a skyscraper. He looked like the architect of *something*. Esko didn't know yet quite what he was going to do. He only knew that he'd come too far from the village and the ice for it to end here like this.

He helped Katerina on with her coat, smoothing the fur around her shoulders. "Walk a few blocks before you try to find a cab. Better yet, take the subway to Times Square and get one from there. Katerina, are you listening to me? This is important."

"I'm listening," she said, her tone questioning. She hugged herself tight, confused.

"Leave this to me." He had to get Katerina out of there so he could think.

"Are we conspiring together?" Her husky voice was cracked and pained. "Oh Esko—what have I done to you?"

"You saved my life, remember? He was going to kill me. Don't forget that."

Her forehead puckered, as if that wasn't what had happened, or as if she didn't accept the burden of his gratitude. "I didn't know about any of this tonight. I didn't know what he was planning." She glanced down at her hands. "He never spoke to me about business. It was part of the arrangement."

"None of that matters," Esko said. "What matters is what happens now. What we do next. What we make of this. Come. I'll take you down."

In the elevator they stood silent, holding hands, watching as the sweeping arrow above the door marked the velocity of their descent. Only when they'd walked to the far end of the lobby corridor did she speak, approaching him and laying a hand softly on his chest.

"What *is* going to happen now?"

"I'm not quite sure yet."

"Will we meet?"

"Best if we don't."

She said nothing, putting up the collar of her coat and pulling the fur tight to her cheeks. He'd brought her to the quieter side of the building, away from the piers, which were busy even at night. Opening the door, he found that the narrow downtown street was deserted. The night was clear and chill. The moon bore into the flat stones of the sidewalk like a hole driven deep into the ice on a lake in midwinter. "Good-bye, then," he said, his fingers crackling with static as he gently brushed them across the fur on her shoulder and watched her depart.

8

A hand was in Esko's coat. He spun around, facing a pickpocket, a rubber-faced man who winked, grinned, made no apology, and, with a bold backward stare, sidled on. Another man at once lurched toward him, belching and offering a hip flask: "C'mon sport, join the party!" There were men in top hats and women in fur coats and scores of taxicabs panting and honking, throbbing, waiting, trapped by crowds on the Great White Way. A frantic Charleston jumped and jittered on top of one of the taxis and beneath the rolling, writhing neon, the electric signs that made moons and planets and coffee cups and cigars and grinning faces.

"Happy New Year!"

Every time Esko managed a few steps forward through Times Square the crowd picked him up and good-naturedly threw him back, buffeting him, shouting their boozy celebrations into his face and insisting that he join in.

"Happy New Year!"

Esko had quite forgotten: it was New Year's Eve, and this endless night wasn't over yet. People thronged, whooped, yelled:

"Get your hands off, mister! You ought to be ashamed!"

"I've drunk a bottle and a half and I'm not responsible for my actions."

"Happy New Year! Happy New Year!"

When at last he had made it to the well-lit awning of The Sky Club, he found that this density of human matter had only increased. It seemed that half of Manhattan was determined, like him, to get in.

"Hey, come on!"

"I need a drink! Just a little drinkie!"

"Liquor! Lovely liquor!"

"Let us in! I demand to be entertained!"

"The hell with it! Away to Harlem!"

Esko's thick hair was soaked, despite the cold. The crowd had possessed him with its chaos and heat. He closed his eye and willed himself to make one more effort, pushing down his head and shouldering through, twisting, turning, until he saw the wide black door and a bulky figure positioned in front of it, hands crossed, hat brim making an uncannily precise line across the middle of his head: Gardella. The sight of him felt like Esko's first lucky break all night.

"Gardella! It's me, Esko Vaananen."

That was all it took—the crowd parted as if in a biblical miracle, and Esko was walked through amid a ripple of envious nods and calls.

"Hey, who's he?"

"What the hell!"

Inside, Esko found himself descending the sweeping staircase into jazz. On the dance floor countless bodies twirled in the cascades and arrowings of mirrored light. The air was thick with smoke and musk and an eight-piece orchestra was going full tilt on the bandstands. A balloon floated in the air, evading a score of clutching hands.

Mantilini was alone, in one of the semicircular booths on the balcony. His hands rested on the white tablecloth along with a cigar case, a platinum lighter, his gold pencil, and one of his narrow black notebooks. His suit was white, spotless, his shirt and tie of sumptuous gray. He kept a casual but alert eye on the bar with the skyscraper mirror behind it, where a party of swells were clustered around a boxer and a motion-picture actor. He didn't look as though he was expecting trouble, but as though he expected to deal with any trouble that happened to come along. On seeing Esko his expression didn't change. He looked at the cigar case, turning it between his fingers, raising an eyebrow.

"I need to talk to you," Esko said.

"Talk," said Mantilini, gesturing to the other side of the booth.

"In private," Esko said, not sitting.

Mantilini tapped the white cloth. With a faraway look, he inspected his fingernail. "How come you're not with your friends on Park Avenue?" he said in his soft voice, looking at Esko for the first time. "Or wherever it is they live. Didn't they invite you to their New Year's Eve party? Or aren't they having one?"

"You once said if ever I needed help I should come to you."

"You're touchy." Mantilini eyed him with greater care. "It's been a long night, has it?"

His voice was colored with kindness now, and Esko nodded, unable to speak for fear of breaking down.

"Well, friend, your trouble's are over." Mantilini gestured once more. "Sit down a minute. Ruthie's going to sing."

Esko eased himself down on the leather bench. A glass of whiskey appeared in front of him on the table and he knocked it back, feeling the liquor warm his belly.

"You needed that," Mantlini said.

"A little."

"Have another."

"No. I'd better keep my head straight."

Mantlini nodded. "Here's Ruthie. She looks lovely tonight," he said, warmth and pride creeping into his voice as he leaned over the table, shifting his weight forward, eager not to miss a word as the club went quiet and Ruthie's melting voice pierced the silence, a lonely floodlit figure, sparkling in gold, singing about the man she loved.

Mantlini waited until she'd finished and the applause died away. He said to Esko: "You're in a jam?"

Esko nodded.

"How bad?"

"Very bad."

Mantlini absorbed this without change of expression. He turned the lighter a little more slowly, concentrating on it. Suddenly he threw the lighter in the air and caught it with a deft flick of the wrist.

"Come on then."

In the small back office Mantlini snapped on a light over the desk. "Seat?" he said.

"I'll stand."

"Suit yourself," he said, working his way behind the metal desk and throwing himself into the chair. "Shoot."

Esko pulled the gun out from his pocket.

"Hey, I didn't mean—" Mantlini flashed his sharkish smile.

The diamond-studded revolver clattered down on the desk. Mantlini observed it for a moment, his mind beginning its calculations.

"Your gun?"

"No."

"Fancy," said Mantlini, pushing out his lips, rocking in the chair.

"I killed a man."

Mantlini nodded, no more perturbed than if Esko had told him he'd just cut himself shaving.

"Do I know the guy?"

"You met him once. At Kirby's funeral. His name was Andrew Mac-Cormick."

"The rich guy?"

"A financier. He was backing me on a big project I've been working on. For years. Before I did the speaks with you. This project—it's the reason I came to New York. To build a skyscraper. Tonight he pulled the rug from under me."

Mantilini's chair creaked a little. "You killed him with this?"

"We argued and there was a fight. He tried to kill me but I was lucky and . . ."

Mantilini waved this away, not impatiently, but as if the reasons didn't matter, only the situation. "You shot him?"

Esko nodded.

Mantilini reached for a cigar. Didn't light it. Just sniffed it. "He's dead and he's lying there. A big mess, am I right?"

Another nod.

Mantilini passed the cigar under his nostrils. "Yeah, it can happen like that." He slipped the cigar back in its case and took up his gold pencil. "Address?"

Esko gave it, and Mantilini made a note of it, not in his notebook, but on a scrap of paper.

"Any witnesses?"

"No."

"You're sure," Mantilini said, eyeing Esko sharply.

"I'm sure," Esko said, holding his gaze.

The chair squeaked as Mantilini rocked to and fro, tapping the edge of the pencil against his perfect white teeth. "Good, that's very good, that's the important thing, the only important thing." He made a doodle on the scrap of paper and then gave Esko a reassuring smile. "You want that other drink now."

"I'm dying for one," Esko said.

"Yeah, well, you don't have to. You've come to the right guy, remember?" He brought down a bottle and two glasses from a shelf. "This is some of the good stuff. Brought it last month from Scotland."

"There are contracts. On the desk. With his signature. I'll need to have those," Esko said. "They must be destroyed."

Mantilini screwed up his eyes, squinting, smiling, unworried by the complication. "Sure," he said, touching the gouged scar above his eye, splashing out the whiskey, which filled the stuffy room with a rich aroma. "This big project—it's the one I been reading about in all the newspapers? It looks like a fine project."

"Thanks," Esko said, sighing, suddenly exhausted.

"Esko, don't worry," Mantilini said, very quietly, very calmly. "Your problems are over. You ain't got a thing to worry about." He held up his head, showing the scar on the inside of his hand. "You're my brother, remember? And for my brother, problems go away, always."

Esko stared at the diagonal gash on Mantilini's palm, his eye laced to it, remembering: "My *puukko*. My knife—it's there, on the floor, with blood all over it."

Mantilini was unruffled. "You cut him too?"

"Like I said—we fought."

"You really made a job of it, didn't you?" he said with one of his ravishing smiles, and he held Esko's gaze for a moment, almost in an admiring way, as if to say that he really wouldn't have guessed that Esko had it in him; and Esko shivered a little, because he hadn't known either, and because while he had no exact idea of what would happen now, he was well aware of the nature of the bargain he'd just made.

"Happy New Year," said Mantilini, raising his glass.

"Happy New Year," Esko echoed, and the whiskey cut against the back of his throat.

PART FIVE

Architecture

I

The pilot was a sleepy-looking man with a blond mustache and a sloppy hat of gray felt. His name was Charlie. He charged fifty cents a mile and called his burnished silver monoplane a ship.

"Shut the door," Charlie said in a drawl, seemingly with a clear idea of how flying should be brought off. His wrist was draped lightly over the stick, as a flaneur might rest his hand on a cane. His other arm was thrown with equal casualness over the back of his seat.

"Are you ready?" he asked. "Let's get this ship aloft."

Esko and Mantilini glanced at one another, shrugging, not without a trace of anxiety, while the motor started with a cough and a growling hum.

Through the little window on his side of the cabin Esko saw the grass for twenty yards around them flowing in one direction like a stream, flayed by the wind from the propeller. The plane's wheels strained against the chocks and then lurched forward, swaying, taxiing slowly. Charlie smiled with the same careless ease that Esko remembered so well in Klaus. He pulled back on the stick and they made a startling leap, bumping across the field with the sound of the motor swelling, heightening in pitch. There were more bumps and it was only when Esko looked out the window again that he realized they were already off the ground. The air became smoother once they cleared the trees bordering the field. He saw the concrete hangar dwindling in size, trailing a red and white wind sock like a caterpillar and then, as the airplane climbed higher still, was treated to a view of the lake and downtown Chicago, where the skyscrapers stood up so differently from their Manhattan counterparts, arrayed in spacious and well-modulated harmony, singing together in mannish barbershop rather than yelling and bragging at each other the way tall buildings did in Manhattan. Low clouds wafted at the window, smudging a view that was sadly beautiful and soon gone entirely.

Charlie had warned that it would be cold, and both Esko and Mantilini were bundled up like bears in fur-lined coats. It was May 1928, the first time in the air for both of them, and the first time they'd met since the night of MacCormick's murder. Esko had come to Chicago by train, on the Twentieth Century—for a meeting with the sculptor designing the skyscraper fountain. Mantilini had contacted him at his hotel, suggesting they fly back together. Mantilini had been excited. "We'll be taking a big step into something," he'd said. Since Lindbergh's transatlantic flight, aviation seemed an important and even necessary exercise, where previously it had been almost unreal and entirely blurred with romance. It was now easy to believe that flying through the air would one day be a commonplace and that the airplane would replace the ship and the automobile as the symbol of the time. Esko had been filled with curiosity, and was still, and not only about this new experience; he was wondering what Mantilini might want; Mantilini—his savior; Mantilini—who'd said he'd take care of everything and had made good on his promise; Mantilini—who'd been the force behind the scenes, ensuring that East River Plaza (MacCormick Center having been dropped as a name) should proceed as planned; Mantilini—who'd warned that it might be best if they didn't see each other, who'd insisted on the fact, until now.

Esko eyed his traveling companion. Mantilini had put on some weight, had acquired a few premature gray hairs even as the last year or so had invested him with the halo of celebrity in a very special way. The New York papers wrote about him only a little less often than about Chaplin. When Tunney beat Dempsey for the second time, Mantilini was pictured ringside. When Tammany Hall tried to do something about those machine guns that fired six hundred bullets a minute, Mantilini was quoted in all seriousness and with great respect, as if he were a professor with unique and special knowledge of the subject, owing to his connections with the University of Chicago. His opinion was sought on the latest murder and the upcoming execution. Sometimes he gave that opinion, sometimes not; he understood the danger of spreading himself too thin. The papers would cook up some story about him, anyway, not front-page stuff, but funny fillers on the inside: "Mantilini Gains Ten Pounds," "Mantilini Goes to Church on Sunday in Jersey City," "Mantilini Picks Yankees for 1928 Flag," "Mantilini Reads Life of Napoleon."

Mantilini was as famous as the president; his notoriety was an asset that gave him almost complete respectability. People were upset, of course, and not *only* thrilled, when racketeers were slaughtered in nightclubs, when the refrain of machine guns shattered the tranquillity of Broadway on a Sunday afternoon. So for a while Mantilini would denounce these events as vehemently as he distanced himself from them, amid a scurry of ineffectual activity at police headquarters. In truth the threat of violence was more useful to him than violence itself, for his chief mission was protective, the guarding of his syndicate's traffic in alcohol and dope. He believed that killing was inefficient and was proud to point out that Ford salesmen didn't try to shoot their rivals from Chrysler. He called himself The Good American. He was still confident and cocky and unself-conscious, as those who pass through mirrors must be. He seemed charmed.

Charlie, the pilot, had his felt hat pushed back and now scarcely seemed to be holding the stick at all. He crooned and sang, bringing his ship down out of the clouds to follow the line of a river Esko identified as the Hudson, a vein of silver pulsing through a landscape that robed itself in color once more. Everything seemed glittery and sharp. The woods spread out on either side and the hills rose and fell, giving the impression that the earth was breathing. Charlie gave a kick to the rudder and the whole landscape went topsy-turvy.

"So," Mantilini said, even he looking a little green when the airplane completed this maneuver and returned to the horizontal. "How are things in the architectural business?"

"Fine," Esko said. Everything at East River was proceeding smoothly, according to plan, slightly ahead of the schedule he'd spent months working out with O'Geehan, his chief contractor, a foul-mouthed Irishman, a thin wiry man with a head of tight curls and formidable skill for organization and not-always-good-natured bullying. During demolition twelve hundred men removed twenty thousand tons of steel and dumped twenty-five thousand truckloads of debris into the harbor. Then men swarmed into the excavation, burrowing, digging, gouging, drilling out the clay until they hit bedrock and then went to work with dynamite. A month later the foundations had been laid and Esko had begun to set steel, starting with the central tower, his sky-scraper. Three and a half stories a week was considered a good mark to aim at. East River Tower was currently rising at the rate of one story a day, with thirty-five hundred men in fifty different trades on the job, and a payroll of $250,000. "So far no one tried to hold up the truck that brings the money every week. I guess it's something else I have you to thank for, Paul."

Mantilini clapped his hands, delighted. "I heard you're planning a trip to Europe," he said.

"How do you know that?"

Mantilini's lips moved just a fraction, as if to say that the question really wasn't worth answering; what he needed to know, he knew, and what he didn't, wasn't worth knowing. It was one of those imperturbable looks that said: I'm Paul Mantilini.

And it was true; Esko was planning a trip to Europe. As the East River project proceeded, other offers were coming his way, including one from Helsinki. Alexander Diktonius, returned from Sweden now that Finland was once again safe for Finland's richest man, intended to build Finland's first skyscraper on the site of the old Diktonius department store and he wanted the famous Finnish architect Esko Vaananen for the job; Esko was interested in the proposal and had another reason for wanting to return to the country of his birth. He'd conceived the idea that each of the twenty-four elevators in the East River skyscraper would be, unto itself, a work of craft decorated with fres-coes painted by commissioned American artists and furbished and inlaid with wood from the forests in the village where he'd grown up, bringing the old world where he was born to the new world that had transformed him, con-necting two different parts of Esko Vaananen in a device—the elevator—that was integral to his sense of who he was and why.

"There's a reason why I hired this airplane for us today. A couple, in fact," Mantilini said. "I want something from you, Esko. I'm hoping you'll do some-thing for me."

There was a kick in Esko's stomach. Now I'm in for it, he thought, groan-ing inside, now it's judgment day. He awaited the presentation of the bill.

"First off, you can say no to this. All right? No obligation here. But I'm asking you as a professional guy—not as a friend. You gonna laugh now, Esko. But I found out something about you."

"What's that?" Esko said, easing a smile onto his face.

"You're a really good architect, aren't you? I mean, a *really* good architect. When I hired you to do the speaks I thought I was doing you a favor. I didn't get it. Now I know better," he said. "Here's the deal. I just bought three hundred acres in Connecticut. My wife, she's got another baby on the way. That'll be our third. I wanna build her a new house. Something beautiful. Also—she'll be in Connecticut. Not too far away, but far enough. Hear what I'm saying?"

Esko's smile was genuine now. "Ruthie causing you problems?"

"I don't know what it is with that little nigger girl. She's got me twisted around her little finger. I must be getting soft in my old age."

Esko looked at him—Mantilini was all of twenty-seven years old now.

"What do you say?"

"I'd be happy to build you a house."

"You would?"

"Sure."

"Gee, that's great." Mantilini said, the curve of his mouth soft, almost shy for once. "I've got some business in Europe. I thought we could maybe go over on the same boat. Talk about it then—you'll meet my wife."

Esko nodded; it sounded fine; he saw no reason why not.

The plane throbbed on like a great bumbling bee, following the line of the Hudson until Manhattan rose to greet them. Over Harlem Esko was thinking how solid and logical and actually understandable the city seemed from the sky, like a plan, with the grid so clear, and they swung toward the East River, where a coal barge plowed the calm waters, a tugboat proudly plumed white smoke, and cargo ships sat tight to the piers. Esko saw his skyscraper rising to greet him.

Charlie touched his hat, turning to face them with a casual smile that was like an unexpected gift of grace. "This it?"

Mantilini nodded. "This is what we want to see."

"I'll cut the motor."

The plane glided on, suddenly soundless, buffeted by the wind. Charlie swung his ship closer and closer to the flanks of the skyscraper until, looking out the window, Esko saw a man sailing by, a little beneath them to the right, and only about fifty yards away. The man rose astride a beam that a derrick crane was bringing in toward the top of the building, where four other men, striding through an upright forest of steel, waited for the beam so they could get it set up for the riveters. The beam tipped forward as the man atop it moved forward, guiding it toward the other guys, who quickly attached a chain so that it could be hoisted to the vertical; then the rider slid off, jumping onto the top of the building.

"Remember?" Mantilini said, shaking his head. "I tell you, Esko—I wouldn't do that again for heaven or hell. Did anyone die on this building yet."

Esko held up his crossed fingers.

"Good for you."

The motor burst back into life and Charlie climbed for height, banking the plane so Esko could look down from another perspective. On either side of the tower, the excavations for the hospital, the big hotel, the theater, and the smaller office buildings were already complete. The skyscraper itself was almost at its full height; forty-five stories already wore their cladding of that fine, and expensive, Indiana limestone; the top part of the frame was still naked, an interwoven tracery of steel. Some of the windows were in place, sunlight glittering off them. As the plane circled Esko saw four flatbed trucks pull up, beetles jerking in a line, bringing supplies. His skyscraper was real. The world of dignity and possibility and clear light that it proposed was rising higher every day. Esko was circling around it in an airplane. It soared from the ground and touched his soul with something approaching ecstasy.

Mantilini saw on Esko's face an expression of pride and intense joy. "I was just the means, Esko. Or not even that—a part of the means, and proud to be. This is the end. It's like Lindy," the gangster said. "It reminds you of what's best about America."

2

Thanks for agreeing to another interview—at last," said Marion Bennett, a cigarette in her hand, pale smoke drifting from her red lips, as she leaned back against the desk in O'Geehan's office, a steel cabin at the base of the skyscraper. She wore flowing gray pants, mannish gray shoes, and a white blouse with lots of flaps on it; her fingernails were painted jungle red. "You look well, Esko. And the skyscraper—I'm amazed, darling. I didn't expect it to shoot up so quickly."

"We don't hang around," Esko said, pointing to a wall of the cabin that was entirely dominated by a chart that he and O'Geehan had drawn up, with different-colored lines racing and overlapping across it, each line representing a different phase of the construction process. "In this game, everyone loves speed and efficiency. You want to know the most important things in building a skyscraper?"

"Tell me," she said.

"Plumbing and elevators. Get those right, and everything follows," he said. "We break one huge job into lots of little ones. After that, it's automation, building the same thing over and over until the top. Just like Mr. Ford in his factory."

She exhaled smoke. "It's really happened, hasn't it? You're building your skyscraper. The tallest in the city."

"In the *world*—for now."

"How high is this thing?"

"One thousand twelve feet."

She sprang away from the desk, standing up straight. "Can I go to the top?"

"Of course—isn't that why you came?"

Her shrewd, dark eyes assessed him, harder now, something snapping shut in her mind like a trap. "Esko—have you been avoiding me?"

"I'll show you around," he said, throwing open the cabin door and inviting in the din of the site, aiming himself into the mess of trucks, drills, cement mixers, riveting guns from which his vision of civic order was emerging, leading Marion Bennett down the wooden steps from the cabin into the potholed battlefield. He raised his arm, pointing. "On each floor that we're working there's a miniature railroad, like a little kiddy train. It brings all the materials. A timetable's printed every morning so that at every minute of every day each man knows what to expect. He won't have to look around for what he needs. It'll be right there at his elbow. We keep the trains fed with the trucks. For each truck that comes in, everything's been thought out, planned to the last detail—the moment of departure, the length of time for the journey, the moment of arrival, some allowance for delays. And so on."

"It's like a military campaign," Marion Bennett said, holding his arm while they picked their way across the site.

"I've been in a military campaign," Esko said. "Believe me. It wasn't as well organized as this."

He went on quickly, "A big problem with the tall buildings of thirty years ago was the number of elevators and their speed. Too much wait time. People couldn't stand it. So you lost tenants. No one should have to wait more than thirty seconds. My friends at Otis promise me that my elevators will have a speed of twelve hundred feet a minute. But the city code was written in 1910. It still says seven hundred feet is the maximum. That's back from the time when you had to wait all day to get to the top of the Flatiron. We're trying to eliminate all that nonsense."

"You want me to write propaganda?" Marion Bennett said, with a wry, almost fretful look.

"A little." Esko made a narrow space with his thumb and forefinger. "*Pikkusen.* Would be useful, you know."

They rode the outside hoist, a plank cradle like the one the riveters used that went up the south side of the building. They rose above the fence that surrounded the street, above the channels of the surrounding streets, above the slowly moving boats on the river. They rose above the spaghetti of railroad tracks that disappeared into Grand Central as if into a throat and above the movie marquees that looked like upturned prayer mats. Soon the hundreds of automobiles in the avenues below were no more than streaming lines of insects. Fifteen-story office buildings looked like dirty sugar cubes. Even the Brooklyn Bridge seemed a toy. Sunlight glinted from a distant bauble atop one of the midtown towers and still they rose. The wind slapped at their faces and plastered the thin wool of Marion Bennett's pants tight to her flesh. A nerveless woman, she stood close to Esko, holding his arm, just in case. They rose and rose, the ropes creaking and screaming in their pulleys. They rose against the building, rattling ever upward, passing the line where the masonry ended and the structure was thin air sandwiched by steel. They looked down on another skyscraper that was under construction on Madison Avenue. They went to the top of the world's tallest building, and it was being built by Esko.

One of the foremen stood waiting when they arrived at the seventieth story. He took Marion Bennett's hand while she stepped off the hoist and onto the temporary wood floor. Esko, waving aside the offer of help, jumped down himself.

Marion Bennett was turning slowly around, her eyes looking east, then south then west, swallowing the views. "This is better than Coney Island," she said.

"I come up here almost every day and I'm still not used to it," Esko said.

"You must be thrilled. Esko, you've *done* this."

"Yes, I'm thrilled," he said, feeling that even if he was sullied, this, his building, was pure. The skyscraper represented opportunity, the possibilities of one man's vision, his own, and he'd spilled blood to achieve it. The skyscraper appeared sinister to him sometimes, but that was because of his unique and flawed relationship to it; everyone else saw only the clean lines, the soaring height, the crystalline perfection.

Marion Bennett had lit another cigarette. She fiddled with the clasp on her purse, returning the lighter there. "What about Andrew MacCormick? His disappearance—what do you know about it?"

"The same as you," Esko said, uncomfortable, hating to lie to this tough and ambitious woman he liked. "What I read in the newspapers," he said.

"Which have been full of crazy rumors. Do you know where he is?"

"No I don't," he said, which was the truth, strictly speaking. Mantilini had never told him how the body had been disposed of, had said it would be best if he didn't know.

"Look at it this way. One of the wealthiest men in America is seen getting on a boat to Buenos Aires. The steamship company records that a ticket was issued in his name. But he keeps to his cabin the entire voyage—and then vanishes. Eighteen months go by and still he hasn't come back. That's a long time. I never even had a hangover that lasted that long. What's in Argentina? Cows and cowboys and too many English people. Why would he want to go there?"

"You tell me."

"I'll tell you this, Esko. Joe Lazarus came to see me a couple of months ago. He had a wild story. An interesting story. He said that he'd been about to take over this project, that MacCormick was about to sell out to him and his backer." She'd taken out her notebook and had her pen posed, her smile not disguising her steel. "Do you have any comment about that?"

"Joe Lazarus is crazy. He's an old man who's lost his grip. What he thinks or does or says is irrelevant."

"Are you prepared to go on the record about that?"

"Why do you think I said it?"

Marion Bennett smiled, making a note. "Still see much of Paul Mantilini?"

"Not much."

"When did you last see him?"

"A few weeks ago. We just happened to travel back together from Chicago."

"What were you doing there?"

"Skyscraper business. Nothing to do with him."

"And what about Mantilini—what was he up to?"

"I've no idea. We didn't discuss it. Whatever it is that Paul Mantilini does."

"That could mean a rack of new suits. Or murder."

Esko took a deep breath. "I don't really know about any of that," he said. "I like Paul Mantilini. Kirby and I built him three speakeasies and found him very businesslike to deal with. I've seen very little of him since then."

"Not since coming back from Chicago?"

"No," Esko said, again truthfully. He'd been out alone to look at the land Mantilini had bought in Connecticut; he'd stood on top of a hill, looking down over a spread of lovely acres that descended to the shore of a lake. "This is starting to sound like an interrogation."

"Isn't that what an interview is?" she said, archly sweet. "So you really have no idea where Andrew MacCormick is?"

"No."

"Do you think his wife does?"

"I've no idea. You'd have to ask her."

"I did."

Esko was surprised for the first time. He paused, letting one of the riveters go by with his gun. The lunch break was almost over now, and soon everything would be deafening activity up here. "You've spoken with Katerina?"

"She's back in New York," Marion Bennett said. "She said she was sure that if the papers said her husband was down in Argentina then that was where he was. She said she'd had several wires from him down there."

Really? thought Esko; he supposed Mantilini must have arranged for someone to send them; it was the kind of detail that Mantilini was good at.

"It's a very modern marriage, I guess," Marion Bennett said without malice. "Maybe I'll write a play about it. Meanwhile I hear she has access to all that money of his. And gets to make the important decisions about his building projects. I'd say she was a very lucky lady."

3

On that warm clear evening Esko didn't bother with his coat. He left the office, heading crosstown at a brisk clip while office workers streamed from the tall buildings, heading down the subway steps or for the nearest speak. Cars were jammed in the streets, honking and puttering, and in the theater district, the neon was already beginning its protest against the outmoded restrictions of night. Summer was in the air, a fresh tang of expectancy and hope.

He was climbing the stairs toward the gallery on the first floor when a man backed onto the landing, a balding man, big eared, beetroot red with indignation, cartwheeling his arms.

"Fucking outrage!" the man said. "Whoever perpetrated this horror should be put in jail."

A younger man faced him now, saying, "Ah, shut up you old bum," and the two raised their fists, the one truculent as a fighting cock, the other insolently drunk.

"Excuse me," Esko said, dodging past the pair, going into the gallery, where a woman was on the floor being fanned, while several others were on their hands and knees, chasing the gems that had popped loose when her necklace broke.

"Let her breathe," someone said, mopping at her brow with a silk handkerchief dipped in fragrant cologne. A nervous laugh pricked at Esko's ears. Someone shrieked, and he turned to see a woman in a long white gown, wearing a stunned gaze, like she too was about to faint.

Esko picked up a catalog from a table by the door, reading: "Eye on America—A Show of New Photographs by Kate Malysheva."

He looked at the first image, a black-and-white of a body sprawled in an empty poolroom, positioned in a way that no living person could ever fall, eyes open, his face wearing an expression of startled surprise. The man's pants were stained where he'd wet himself, while above his head the inert billiard balls were racked, undisturbed, reflecting light, waiting for a game that would never begin.

Esko moved to his left. Here a corpse lay on the sidewalk, the shadow of

black blood puddled by its forehead glistening a little from the camera flash.
A shoe lay beside the dead man's face while excited onlookers, trying to press
closer, were held at bay by a pair of cops with their nightsticks.

He viewed the next, of a man sitting at a table, head snapped back, neck
broken by the force of a gunshot that had pierced and shattered the window at
his side; on the wall beside him was a picture frame tilted at a crazy angle
with the picture gone from inside it. In the fourth a corpse lay with its head
poised over a gutter, blood gushting from the eyes as if from uncorked bottles.
In the fifth a corpse lay twisted in filthy melting snow. In the sixth . . .

There were forty-eight such images, wild and fever bright, shocking in
their detachment, the camera always placed in the middle distance so that its
lens could pick out the heightened surrounding detail as much as the victim,
as if to comment on the world's indifference to the removal of yet another citizen. In each photograph the victim was male, and each was a calm glance
into the cabinet of some icy hell.

Taking a glass of red wine, Esko moved into the second room. Here the
first subject was a woman, photographed up close so that the pores of her skin
stood out like craters, her expression of troubled dismay both beseeching and
reproaching the observer. The next picture was also of a woman, her wet yellowish face set hard and deeply lined. Her eyes burned madly. In the third the
woman's face was smooth and seemingly untroubled, save for the mouse's tail
that hung from between her lips. The fourth woman was straight and proud,
beautiful, but blinking away tears. The fifth . . .

There were thirty-six images of women, each one desperately sad. All of
them seemed to be sliding toward a tragic abyss. The colors, the very texture
of the prints, were more expressive here. In the band between black and
white Katerina had found whole Himalayas of modulation and emotion.
Some were dark, almost smoky; others flared harsh with silver. Esko felt as
through he'd been given a new eye through which to view pain and sadness.

A tingle in his spine told him to turn and he did, expecting to see her, but
instead it was Paul Mantilini, ambling across the room in a suit of sky blue
with Ruthie on his arm.

"Is this what art shows are like?" he said, teeth flashing sharkishly.
"Maybe I could get my own show . . ."

"In a pig's eye. You don't know nothing about art," said Ruthie, her liquid
eyes huge beneath a cloche hat of delicate gold mesh.

Mantilini had his hands in his pockets, a relaxed chairman-of-the-board attitude. "Is that so? I thought that was why you brought me to these events—to get an education."

"Fat chance," Ruthie said.

"Who's the guy who took these pictures, anyway?" Mantilini said.

"For your information—it's a woman," Ruthie said.

"You're kidding?" Mantilini said. "How do you know that?"

"Because it says so on the catalog. Because she took my picture once."

Mantilini frowned. "She did? You didn't tell me that."

"My secret," she said, putting her hands to his cheeks, raising her open mouth to his mouth, pressing her body flat against his.

"I don't like secrets," Mantilini said, with a strained smile. "Only my own."

"I thought all your secrets went to the bottom of the river," she said, the metallic mesh of her hat glittering under the light.

"Yeah—and what do you know about it?" Mantilini said, his temper rising a little now.

Esko was about to go away and leave them to it, but then Katerina came up, and stood between them, her short hair crowned with a beret, her long neck rising, swanlike, from a collarless jacket cut like a man's, her green eyes smarting from all the smoke in the room. Esko held his breath and then emptied his lungs in a long, silent exhalation, his mind a storm. He knew he shouldn't have come, but he'd been unable to keep himself away. It would be madness for them to be together with the memory of MacCormick hanging over them, the reality of MacCormick too, an invitation to the electric chair. Yet at that moment he wished nothing more than to take his chances.

"It's nice to see you, Ruthie," she said, and turned to him. "Esko . . ." she said, her voice definite, as if she'd expected to see him here, had even hoped for it. She looked well, despite the pictures, or perhaps because of them.

"I'm Paul Mantilini," Mantilini said to her, his eyes narrowed, and Esko guessed that he didn't remember having seen Katerina at Kirby's funeral, if indeed he had.

"Kate Malysheva," Katerina said, her curious gaze absorbing Mantilini's suit, his quick, arrogant eyes.

"Maly . . . ? What kind of a name is that?"

"A Russian one," Ruthie said. "She was in the Revolution."

"Is that a fact?" Mantilini said, hands in pockets, coins rattling. "On which side?"

"The losing one."

"I guess that explains the murder shots," Mantilini said ceremoniously, thoughtful—Paul Mantilini, art critic.

"In a way," Katerina said, her brow puckering. "I hadn't quite looked at it like that, I must confess. Is it a subject that interests you very much, Mr. Mantilini?"

Mantilini's white teeth glittered in a crescent. His smile was amused, and he wasn't even considering answering the question. His hard eyes watched Katerina, wondering who she was, what she was like, whether she could ever be of use or perhaps even a danger to him. Something about her intrigued him, Esko sensed, but then maybe it was because he'd never met anyone like her before.

"You must have been through quite a bit to take those pictures," Mantilini said.

"The camera protects me. I've been through worse things."

"Such as?"

She shook her head slowly, no, now it was her turn not to answer, and Esko found he was holding his breath again.

"And you, Esko, what did you think of my photographs."

"They terrify me. It's beautiful work," he said.

Katerina smiled mysteriously, and whispered so that only Esko could hear. "And if I were to ask you again, if I were to ask you for the third time—will you leave New York with me—what would you say?"

"Which train do you want to catch?"

"The last time we discussed it you thought it was a bad idea."

"And now it's an even worse one."

Katerina laughed, while from the corner of his eye Esko saw Mantilini take something from his pocket, a knife, a blade, and not just any knife—the *puukko*.

"What the . . ." he began, then saw Marion Bennett, and with her was Bo, Esko's old colleague from the riveting gang, the Swede who'd once been engaged to Mantilini's sister and had run liquor with him.

Bo at once stepped over, his cropped red hair damp with sweat, and shoved Mantilini in the chest. "Come on," he said, pushing Mantilini again with the flats of his palms. "Fight, fight me if you dare, you guinea pussy. You think you're a big man. You ain't so tough. Where are your goons now, Paul Mantilini? They ain't here to help you now," he said, bearing down. "It's just you and me, pal."

Bo hadn't seen the *puukko*, hanging down at Mantilini's side.

Mantilini just kept stepping back. With each of Bo's shoves he retreated, and then paused, shrugging again, looking Bo right in the eye and wearing his cruelest smile, biding his time, luring him on. His eyes had a look of icy murder.

Mantilini darted forward, slashing at Bo's throat with the *puukko*, only to find Esko's strong hand closing over his wrist.

"Don't," he said. "I mean it, Paul. *Don't*."

The blood drained from Mantilini's face and his dark, dotlike eyes stood out bright from the pallor of his skin. His expression was still murderous, but all that venom was directed at Esko now. Esko was by far the bigger man, and no weakling, but still he couldn't prevent Mantilini inching up the blade and aiming its point straight at his good eye.

"You know this, Esko? You recognize this piece of steel?"

The room was filled with silence and Mantilini's grin and the smell of automobile exhausts rising from Fifth Avenue.

"Sure, Paul. I recognize it. I'm going to let go your hand now and you can do what you want."

The *puukko* hovered with an inch of the jelly of Esko's eye, then flashed away, carving air.

"You got that right," Mantilini said, rolling the taut muscles of his shoulders beneath his suit. "I can do anything. I can do whatever the hell I like. I'm Paul Mantilini. And don't you ever forget it."

Mantilini relaxed, smiling now, pushing the *puukko* back into its sheath in his pocket. "Show's over, folks. Enjoy the rest of your evening. Stop by one of my clubs when you're done. Say Paul Mantilini said to say it's on the house. C'mon, Ruthie, let's go," he said, taking her arm. "Interesting stuff, this art."

A babble of relief filled the room while waiters circulated with liquor and Paul Mantilini's name was on everyone's lips like a chant. Esko felt Katerina's eyes upon him. She was pinching her lower lip between her teeth, and he grimaced, and then he saw that Marion Bennett was watching, sensing the flashing of some secret, something, between them, and Esko felt a contraction in his gut, a feeling that everything was about to explode, that forces beyond his control were starting to turn, had always been turning, waiting.

Only Bo, the Swede, was oblivious to these undercurrents. He scratched his groin, knocking back his fear with a glass of wine he grabbed from a passing waiter's tray. "I guess I showed him," he said, smiling at no one in particular.

4

Mantilini was in great spirits on board the *Ile de France*. He and his family were in the presidential suite, while Esko had been given a prestigious *apartement de grande luxe*. "I told them you're the most famous architect in New York. Certainly the greatest," he said, showing Esko the opulent fruit baskets, the flagons of champagne. "These French, they love that kind of stuff," he said, whistling as he shut the door, shouting for Gardella.

Esko sat down on one of the sofas and looked at his watch. There was a knock, the door flew open, and it was Mantilini again with a list of the first-class passengers in his hand. "We're at the captain's table tonight, right where we should be," he said. "Along with two governors, a bishop, the foreign minister of Brazil, and guess who?"

"Who?"

"Esko, you're going to love this," Mantilini said. "*Chaplin.*"

"*Charlie* Chaplin?"

"It says here *Mr.* Chaplin," Mantilini said with a frown, touching the top of his ear with thumb and forefinger, smoothing his slick, shining hair with his palm, forced to contemplate the unpleasant idea that this particular Chaplin might not be the right one. Mantilini lounged against the door, one foot crossed over the other. "Esko, about the other night . . ."

Esko held up his palm. "Forget about it," he said.

A muscle twitched in Mantilini's jaw, and Esko realized that Mantilini wasn't used to being interrupted, that Mantilini might not, after all, have been about to issue the apology that he, Esko, deemed unnecessary. There was an issue, here, of who was calling the shots.

"I could've done something in front of that bunch of people and that would have been a mistake," Mantilini said. "So thank you. But that Bo . . ." Mantilini shook his head. "People can cross me one time too many," he said. "I'll see you at dinner."

A half hour later there was another knock on the door and it was Katerina, a steward standing behind her with her bags. "May I come in?"

"Of course," he said, blinking, taking in the smell of her, standing aside while she came in, smiling as she fell into his arms and pressed her cheek to his pumping heart. "I was afraid you wouldn't come."

"I know," she said. "But here I am."

Esko tipped the steward while Katerina looked around, trailing her fingers along the glass and polished walnut decor, inspecting the bedroom, coming back again.

"Did you tell Mantilini yet?" she said, when the steward was gone and the door was closed.

"Not yet," Esko said.

"Esko—I'm not going to spend five days hiding in a closet even if that gangster did clear up our mess."

He'd told her everything about Mantilini.

"I know," he said. Her eyes, shining beneath a green hat, glanced down; she fitted a cigarette into an ebony holder.

"What then?" she said as he sprang forward with a lighter. "What do you propose?"

"Maybe he'll get seasick."

She laughed, an unexpectedly carefree sound, and swayed against his body, kissing him; then she broke away, her eye falling on the drawings that Esko had spread out on the table; they were some modifications to the East River theater, for the proposed Helsinki skyscraper, for Mantilini's Connecticut house. The sight of them made her shiver. "Such wonderful, such marvelous things," she said. "Esko, have I destroyed you?"

"You've *made* me," he said.

She wouldn't meet his eye. "It's my fault," she said, her body trembling. "I shouldn't have married him. It was for all the wrong reasons. But I liked him—he wasn't a bad man."

"I know," Esko said softly.

"And I *killed* him."

"We both did," Esko said, in the same low voice, leaning close to her over the table. "Because he was trying to kill me. And in the end I'm very glad it was him lying there. Because otherwise it would have been Esko Vaananen."

She looked at him now, touching her finger to his lips. "Can we really be happy together, you and I? Is there any chance of that? What are we going to do?"

"Forget," he said, kissing her fingers, her mouth. "Bad things have happened, but we're not bad people. We'll put those things out of our minds and get on with our lives. We will be happy."

Esko felt the ship begin to vibrate and pulse beneath his feet. The engines had started, the propellers of *Ile de France* were churning through the deep waters of the harbor, and soon from the window of their suite, they saw the serrated Manhattan skyline slip behind them. There were things that had to be faced, Esko knew, but not tonight; this night was for them alone; he took Katerina in his arms, and to bed.

The next day, before lunch, Esko found Mantilini alone in the first-class bar, smoking a cigarette, sipping a whiskey, eye moving from his black notebook to the frosted mirror behind the bar in which he observed Esko's arrival. "Not sick then?" he said, not looking at Esko, his gaze sliding above the mirror, squinting at a mural painted there. The mural depicted figures cavorting to jazz, some falling, some recovering themselves, others whirling on and on. "I missed you at dinner."

"I don't get seasick," Esko said, taking a seat beside him. "You?"

"No. The ocean doesn't bother me. Ain't we the lucky ones?" Mantilini said, his manicured, long-fingered hands resting on the shiny bar top beside the ashtray that had his cigarette burning in it. "Guess who I just saw on deck?"

"You saw Kate Malysheva," Esko said calmly, signaling the barman. "And by now you know she's also Kate MacCormick, the wife of the man I killed. Yes, we're having an affair. Yes, we were when I killed him. Yes, she's with me."

Mantilini rocked back on his stool, blowing air out through his lips, snorting and throwing his hands to his face. He sighed. He squeezed his fingers to his temples and screwed up his eyes, the veins in his neck throbbing. "You idiot," he said. "You fucking *idiot*. Jesus, Esko—" He wiped a hand across his mouth, shaking his head. "What else do I need to know?"

"Nothing. That's all."

"That's *all*. Je-sus." He jumped to his feet and seemed to be about to kick a chair but the chairs were bolted to the deck, and he thought better of it. He straightened his tie, fastidious, glancing once again in the mirror, smiling at the barman, gathering his control.

"Am I still building you a house?"

Mantilini wagged his finger. "Don't tempt me, Esko, don't push me, otherwise the only thing you'll be building is a mausoleum and I'll put you right in it. Have you told me everything now?"

"Everything."

"You'd better be telling me the truth."

"I am."

With an effort Mantilini sat himself back down on a stool at the bar; he placed his notebook in front of him and took up his gold pencil. He made an epic calculation, swiftly writing and toting figures, and then snapped shut the book. "Come on," he said, his smile a little warier than usual, as if Esko had damaged it in some way. "I want you to meet my wife. My children."

Later Esko told Katerina what had happened. "He didn't like it, but it doesn't really change anything from his point of view. He won't trust me so well from now on."

"Does that matter?" Katerina said, taking his arm while they struggled against a gusting wind on the promenade deck. Inky clouds loomed low over the ship, the sky having lowered itself to join the ocean.

"No," Esko said; it was odd, but he realized he wanted Paul Mantilini to think well of him. "It doesn't matter."

Esko held the rail and Katerina held onto him while they fought a path aft; but there they met a young man with black hair, his boyish face sandwiched between a check cap tilted at an angle and a check jacket buttoned to the neck with the collars turned in. "I am the mail pilot," he said in anxious English, drawing their attention to a seaplane that was being affixed to a steam catapult on the deck below. "That's my ship down there." A few days from now, when the *Ile de France* was six hundred miles out of Le Havre, the plane would be hurled off the deck with him in the cockpit. The aim was to clip more than twenty-four hours off the time taken for a letter to travel from New York to Paris. This was the first time the French line had tried the experiment; no one was quite sure whether the catapult would work or not.

"And if it doesn't?" Katerina said, gripping Esko's arm tight, her eyes moving from the tiny seaplane to the huge Atlantic seas rearing up like a sawtoothed mountain range.

"Then, mademoiselle, I will sink," the young man said, and Esko was struck with pride and sadness and the blind, reckless courage it required sometimes just to venture one more step.

"It will be all right," Esko said. "Everything will be all right."

The weather cleared, beckoning the *Ile de France* through calmer seas. It turned out that Chaplin was indeed on board, and Esko saw him one morning outside the first class stateroom, a small, debonair, exquisitely handsome and now slightly plump man in a pinstripe suit and spats. His soft eyes grazed Esko's face with a tender inquisitiveness; Chaplin was standing beside Mantilini when the mail pilot completed his checks, doffed his rakish check cap, handed the cap to the catapult operator, pulled on his flying helmet and his fur-lined goggles, and then, in the movie star's honor, walked splayfooted in the direction of the seaplane, twirling an imaginary cane. Everybody, including Chaplin and Mantilini, laughed and cheered, clapping their hands.

Katerina gripped Esko tightly while the pilot shut his cockpit window with a clunk, a sound like both the beginning and the ending of something, like the closing of an elevator door. The motor started with an unseemly racket and the pilot adjusted his goggles and jerked up his thumbs. Hurled forward by the flaming catapult, the plane dipped from view for a moment, as if it had indeed dropped off the end of the ship and plunged into the ocean; Katerina groaned, but then her eyes brightened as she saw the plane again, skimming the wave tops with its belly before rising and soaring, aiming itself like a dart at the sun.

5

The train rolled through a landscape that was soon more water than land. It was the time of thick and enchanted northern light. The sun had just gone down but there was no darkness. Mist hovered over the lofty trees, as if the forest floors themselves were exhaling, wearied by the endless day. The lakes, like enormous eyes, seemed to have stolen the light from those millions of stars that summer had banished from the sky. Katerina lay asleep while Esko stood at the window to the compartment. They were heading north after spending three days in Helsinki, where Esko had met with Diktonius and the other businessmen planning the Aleksanterinkatu skyscraper and had endured interviews with reporters from *Hufvudstadsbladet* and *Helsingin Sanomat*. Part of the strangeness of being back in Finland was that he found himself far more famous here than in America. For his countrymen, he was now money in the bank, a successful export who might usefully be employed at home. "Architecture or revolution," Le Corbusier had written in his book. Finland's revolution had failed—it was going to have architecture. Esko Vaananen was going to give them a skyscraper of glass in the center of the capital.

During their time in Helsinki Esko and Katerina had also visited the Diktonius Building, soon to be destroyed, and Esko had arranged for his elevator, their elevator as he now thought of it, to be salvaged and shipped back to O'Geehan in New York; he planned to strip out his murals and install them in the interior of the express elevator in East River Tower.

A dappled white horse behind a little black buggy on springs was waiting when they stepped off the train. No driver was in sight, but the horse waited with patient indifference, a true Finn. The sturdy new buildings of the station, freshly painted, were already surrounded by the rough beginnings of a town now that the railway had reached the area at last. Esko glanced at a new building that was under construction, using logs cut by mechanical saw rather than ax hewn—a real sign of modern times. There was a post office and a small *hotelli*.

"Where is everybody? The place is deserted," Katerina said.

"Believe me, it looks a lot busier than it used to," Esko said, and she smiled, taking his hand and swinging it.

The doors of the *hotelli* swung open and out stumbled an old man, who glanced around briefly, drunkenly, and fell down, smitten by the sunlight. He lay on the ground for several minutes, picked himself up, dusted himself off, and turned around and launched himself back toward the *hotelli* with offended dignity, having earned himself another drink. It's Finland, it's nine o'clock in the morning, Esko thought to himself, and even though the outside world is pouring in, some things will never change.

Another man came out, the buggy's driver, sober (or at least it so appeared), and soon they were rolling off the smooth concrete of the station approach, bouncing along the rough track that ran beside a forest of slender silver birch next to the lake. It was a windless summer day, although every now and then Esko saw a shadow ruffle the lake, a breeze like a brush stroke, deepening the blueness of the water. A few fleecy white clouds stood high in the sky. The smells of hot birch and dried straw wafted into his nostrils like innocence itself. A farmer walking through his meadow paused for a moment, pushing up the brim of his hat and regarding the buggy with curiosity as it went by, and Esko remembered that they didn't much care for strangers around here. Well, he wasn't a stranger—not quite; but he didn't quite know what to expect, nor what emotions would be stirred as the buggy turned a corner on the track, sweeping away from the lake, with the sunlight dappling through the treetops and Katerina's hand resting lightly in his.

"There they are," he said, springing up in the back of the buggy, pointing to the twin towers of the church. He was still on his feet when the buggy rattled past the first of the village's four cemeteries, where late summer flowers adorned the neat headstones of black marble, where his mother was buried. They went by the overgrown ruin of the house where he'd almost died in the fire, and then the other, still standing, from which one night he'd fled his father's fists. Somehow these memories no longer struck him as unhappy or painful. They were the shadows of the events and tensions that had made him; there was something reassuring and right about them now that he was back. The village was the history of all that he'd tried to become, and he knew now that coming here was a good idea.

In the corner of a meadow he saw a barn, red painted, built in the old style with chinks showing between the logs; it was in that meadow that he and Katerina had met.

At the vicarage they found the surveyor waiting for them as arranged, a spry old gentleman with a *puukko* at his belt and a map in his hand, armed with all the information Esko needed—about which small areas of land still belonged to the Vaananens, and which other areas were owned by farmers willing to sell—and for the rest of the day they roamed these dense forests, picking out trees to be felled and shipped back to New York. In Helsinki Katerina had bought a little hand-held movie camera, a Pathe 9, and from time to time she would raise it like a gun and the film would whir, while Esko chatted with the surveyor, or wielded an ax, or played the fool, the sun making a nimbus of his hair. Esko was in the landscape of his childhood, and she was the loving observer he thought he'd never have again.

The next day Kalliokoski came down from Vaasa in a big black Renault with a driver. He was older, grayer, sleeker, more pampered, and these days even more powerful. He recalled very well having met Katerina when she was a little girl. Hugging her, he offered condolences for the loss of her family.

He chided Esko only briefly about the churches. They were standing in the vicarage garden beside the burnished and still-gurgling Renault. "You're an undeserving soul in some respects," he said, his hand on Esko's shoulder.

"And I sometimes wonder why I have so much patience with you. Actually that's not true. I know very well."

He turned his ironic, self-amused eyes to Katerina, taking her arm and whispering to her. "When I was a young man I was very much in love with his mother. Oh, nothing happened, of course. But when she died I promised I'd always look out for him. A promise I hope I've kept. I've tried." He raised his voice. "We're all very proud of him now that he's done so well in America. And I hope that while he's back here he'll think about building me another church."

Kalliokoski stayed for dinner, during which he first entertained them and the youthful vicar with tales of Bolshevik bungling, and then shocked them with the story of how those same Bolsheviks had bungled several hundred Finnish socialists into a mass grave outside Leningrad, as Petrograd was now called. Esko felt his anger rise, reminded that Finland was a proud but small country jammed between powerful neighbors. America's power put its national identity beyond the anxieties of history and fate. America was so lucky, so young, so spoiled, so beautiful, so in love with the large gesture; no wonder its architectural idiom was the skyscraper.

He took another sip of wine, glancing at Kalliokoski over the guttering candle. "What do you hear about my father?"

"About Timo?" Kalliokoski said. "You should talk to Anna about that."

Esko turned his glass on the table. "To Anna? I'm not sure I understand."

"She's expecting to hear from you," Kalliokoski said, ignoring Esko's puzzled frown. "That's all I'm going to say."

After dinner the two men hugged, clasping each tightly, thumping each other on the back; Kalliokoski kissed Katerina on both cheeks, saying, "Good luck, my dear. Godspeed. Look after him!" And then they watched the Renault's taillights disappear into the midnight dusk, twinkling between rows of towering pine.

"I like him," Katerina said, after they themselves had set off for a late-night excursion, walking through the forest toward the lake, Esko carrying a basket that had in it a bottle of wine, a corkscrew, and two wine glasses wrapped in linen napkins. Esko was saddened, thinking about Anna, asking himself what Kalliokoski might have meant about his father, wondering what to do. More than six years since he'd left Finland. Six years! It was a long time, and a while since he and Anna had even exchanged letters.

Wisps of mist drifted from the lake, ensnaring the armies of spruce and birch, and in the mysterious silver-gray twilight Esko glimpsed hummocks in the forest, giant anthills waiting to trap the boot, or outcroppings of granite that had been deposited when the ice retreated all those millennia ago, glacial testaments to the movement of time, strange bumps in the summer landscape. When winter came, snow would cover these mounds and they would look like warriors' tombs. Or that was what he'd always thought when he was a kid, he now remembered as they came to the bright moonlit gleam of the lake, where a small boat was pulled up on the sand, the rowlocks still inside, and a pair of oars crossed over the bench in its belly.

Waves splashed gently at their feet; Esko looked at Katerina, remembering the boat rides he used to take with his mother, pushing off from this very same spot, and it felt as though an old wound was healing inside him, as if something that had burned for years could now be soothed.

"Shall we take out the boat?"

"Sure," she said.

A crash came from behind them, deep within the forest, a crunching and splintering of branches, and Esko turned, stiffening, thinking it might be a bear; but this approaching racket was soon accompanied by very human oaths and shouts.

"Elderberry boy!"

The nickname brought a long-forgotten face to mind: "Turkkila?"

A hatted figure pranced out from the undergrowth, raising his boots high in the air and nursing a bottle between his chest and his cradled elbow.

"Elderberry boy! Are you looking to steal me boat again? You did it just the other night."

Just the other night? Esko thought; it had been twenty-seven years ago, almost to the day.

"Turkkila? Is that really you?"

With one hand Turkkila flapped at his pockets, as if for matches, for tobacco, for something he'd forgotten; then he remembered the other arm, the one cradling the bottle. He took a last swig, belched, and then hurled the bottle over his shoulder; it flashed for a moment, bright in the gloom, and vanished without a sound, as if it hadn't fallen at all, but had been caught and stolen away by a Finnish forest god determined to extract the last drop.

Turkkila blew his nose in his hand. He inspected the hand, wiped it against the stiff, shiny lapel of his encrusted old jacket. He shook his right foot, shook his left foot, and began beating his clothes again. A match struck against its box, flashing light over cratered cheeks, a crushed nose, and a fang-like tooth that stuck out over a puffy lower lip.

"Elderberry boy!" he said, reeking of sulphur and cheap tobacco and fiendish home brew. "What is it that goes up in the sky?"

"An elevator."

"That's it. An elevator! I've been thinking about you, elderberry boy. You've been in my thoughts."

Turkkila noisily cleared his throat, spat, and shut his eyes. In a deep voice he began to chant, singing a song about five boys who left the village. One went for nuts, another for wheat, a third for fish, while the fourth set off to hunt for hare. The fifth? No one knew where he went, and he was still missing, long after the others had come back. So the villagers sent out a search party. They searched the great forests, they traversed the wide fields, they glided across the deep lake waters until at last they heard a voice calling to them from high above:

> Here I am everybody
> a cloud is holding my head
> the cloud's son has got my feet
> the cloud's uncles have grabbed my arms
> the clouds have taken me
> trapped me in the sky.

Turkkila opened his eyes and spat again now that the song was over. He brushed his fingers under his awful nose, touched his hat. "Who's that with you, elderberry boy? A woman? She looks like a dancer, a little dancer. Has she been dancing rings around you, elderberry boy?" he said, cackling, doubling up in a spasm of coughing. "Excuse me," he said at last, sniffed, spat. "You've found her now then, eh? The little girl in the motor car. The elderberry boy thought he could steal her away. The devil's daughter from the devil's own machine. Well, maybe old Turkkila got that bit wrong." A sly look dawned in his eyes. His nostrils quivered. "What you got in that basket then, a bottle? You folks take a little in your glasses—not too much now—and give the bottle to old Turkkila. He likes it best that way."

Katerina, having silently watched Turkkila all this while, now took his hand. "In the song," she said, "do the clouds ever let the little boy go?"

"Wouldn't know that, miss," he said, bashful now. "Take the boat; be my guests."

"Here—the wine," Esko said.

"Now there's a deal," Turkkila said. "Good-bye miss, good-bye elderberry boy. You remember what I said—watch out for them elevators. Beware elevators!"

Esko gave Katerina his hand as he helped her into the stern; he pushed the boat into the shallow water and jumped aboard, fixing the oars in the rowlocks, spitting on his hands, and then easing into his task, dipping the oars and pulling with smooth, clean strokes. The boat jerked ahead at first but was soon scooting smoothly along. Katerina lay back, trailing her hand in the cool water, not worried about soaking the sleeve of her dress.

"Who was the old man?" she said, her eyes closed.

"Turkkila? He used to be the gravedigger. It seems like he's been here forever. You talk to some people in the village, they'll tell you that he really *has* been here forever. They say he's in touch with the spirits, and not just the ones that come out of a bottle."

"It's unfortunate about the elevators." She'd opened her eyes now and was looking at him with a sly smile. "Since you're a skyscraper architect."

"Yes, that is a pity," Esko admitted, laughing.

She lifted her dripping sleeve from the water. "Is this the lake where your mother drowned herself?"

Esko nodded, lowering his head and pulling hard at the oars.

"Is it very strange for you to be back here?"

"It's like I'm being tracked by a ghost and the ghost is me. I keep looking around trees and seeing little Esko."

"I liked little Esko. He wore funny, stiff clothes. But he looked at me in a way I've never forgotten. It's taken a long time for me to learn to look at other people like that. Knowing that they can be hurt as badly as you've been hurt yourself."

Esko wondered whether he would ask her the question that had troubled him all these years. What had she really said on that long ago night? Had it really been *run him down*? He realized it didn't matter, because now she wasn't thinking that and never would again. "Will you ever go back to Petersburg, Leningrad—whatever we must call it?"

"Petersburg, for me always that. I go back every night, but only in my dreams," she said.

Esko pulled the oars from the water, and rested them in the belly of the boat; then he made his way gingerly to the stern, sitting down beside Katerina so they could lay back together in each other's arms and stare up, trying to make out a single star in this strange grayness of the midsummer sky. Little waves slapped the side of the boat. Two birds, cranes, called from far away; the smell of bonfire smoke drifted across the water. New York, the skyscraper, seemed more than an ocean away, and yet, Esko knew, if he were to glance a little to his left he might see the perfect skyscraper of his childhood rising from the lake.

"For years I've known how to be alone, how to be strict and silent with myself. I want that to change now. I want us to be together, Esko." Her fingers played across his chest. "Can we?"

"Of course."

"I don't know if this is possible for me, but I'd like for us to try to have a child."

Esko felt like he was standing on joyful tiptoe, his body tingling with every pleasure of the summer night. "I insist on a girl," he said in a very solemn voice. "I'll love her and she'll adore me. She must learn to play the piano."

"My mother played."

"It runs in the family. The Vaananen girl will be musical. Where will she be born?"

"In America, of course. Within sight of your skyscraper."

"I'll tell her that her mother is the most beautiful woman in the world and that everything I've done has been for her. Until now, I'll say. Now, I'll say, I'm doing it for my girl too."

And they talked for hours, drifting in that boat on the calm waters of the lake; they dreamed of the future with an optimism that seemed it could be a shaping influence and not only a state of their mingled hearts; they held each other until sunlight came again in a sky that had never grown dark.

6

Anna no longer wore the wedding ring he'd slipped on her finger more than six years before, a plain and modest gold band. Her shoulders were thrown back proudly and she looked well. She was on her feet, watching him from behind the desk in her office. He knew that he'd hurt her terribly, and he saw her struggling with that before her shoulders rose and fell with a sigh and her mouth relaxed into a smile. "Esko Vaananen," she said, coming round from behind the desk. "Esko *Vaananen.*"

Esko felt both his hands grasped in hers while she studied his face, intently comparing every detail of him with what she remembered, as though confirming that he wasn't, in fact, a ghost. "Here you are, yes, it's really you," she said, laughing, and stood on tiptoe to kiss him.

Esko hugged her tight, his anxiety about seeing her again ebbing away. "I'm sorry, Anna—for everything."

"*Shush,*" she said, holding up her hand to stop his mouth. "I know you, Esko. I know you're sorry. And so am I. We have lots to talk about. But first let me get another look at you."

Standing back, she regarded him with her intellect this time, not her love, and saw him changed. "A lot's happened, hasn't it? I want to hear all about it. Tell me. I've seen photographs of your East River project. It's fabulous, wonderful."

Esko shifted on his feet, shamed and gratified by her praise, and looked briskly about the office. With its drafting boards, its heavy oak desks, its stoves—unlit now—its windows thrown open to the summer heat, Esko was reminded of the well-ordered way things used to be at Arnefelt & Bromberg. The designs on the walls were different, of course; they were for churches, for a military barracks, a school, a couple of houses, all done in the clean-lined modernistic style; in one corner, framed, was the original drawing Esko had made for the Church of the Shadow Cross.

"You're doing very well," he said.

"We're pioneers," she said with a typically self-mocking shrug, though this was the truth; Anna had set up practice with three other architects, all women. "In the early days we kept all the money in an old cigar box so anyone who really needed it could take some. We were poor as mice."

They chatted for a while about her young partners, about the proposed Helsinki skyscraper project, about East River Plaza, about America, about the new work that was being done in Finland. Esko realized that even after everything that had happened, he could still talk to Anna about anything and everything in an intimate and easy way. She proposed they take a walk and so they set off down Mariankatu Street, strolling arm in arm in the sun, toward the harbor at the bottom of the hill. It was a perfect Helsinki day, warm but a fresh breeze coming off the sea. They were crossing the cobbles of the Senate Square when Anna stopped and raised her arms and put them around his neck. "Kalliokoski told me you're here with Katerina," she said. "I suppose that means you want a divorce."

"Same old Anna," he said, laughing, unmanned by her intuition; he and Katerina had discussed this very point. "Never avoid a bull if you can take it by the horns."

"Do you?"

"Only if you'll give me one."

"Same old Esko. You want what you want and you want to be a good man and you want me to help you, is that it?"

"Anna, I don't want to fight."

"Then we won't," she said firmly. "But you have to help me too. I gather Kalliokoski also mentioned that your father's back in Helsinki. The secret police arrested most of the Red underground six months ago. They didn't get Timo."

"No, I'm sure they didn't," Esko said; his father was one of the great escape artists.

"He's in hiding."

"Calling himself Offermans."

Now it was her turn to be surprised. "How on earth did you know that?"

Esko shrugged. "It's a family tradition."

"Will you see him?"

"When?"

"Now."

Esko glanced up at the steps of the cathedral, remembering the man he'd seen die there, shot by one of Timo's Red comrades. He honestly thought he could live the rest of his life without seeing his father again. Such a meeting was neither desired nor needed. But for Anna? "To help you—sure."

"Thanks, Esko."

"How will this help, exactly?" he said, with some effort pushing down the old fears and angers.

"You'll see. He's a difficult, trying man, but very brave," she said, leading him through the flower stalls at the harbor, past Vallgren's statue of the plump, alluring mermaid, among the crowds milling around the delicate wrought-iron tracery of the Kappeli Café at the bottom of the Esplanade Park.

During the war and afterward Esko had often seen pictures of his father in the newspapers, but last time he'd seen him in the flesh had been at the political meeting in 1917; before that, more than twenty-five years ago, in the village, in the bottom of the bell tower, fist raised. Now he was an old man, his face lined, his hair cropped where previously it had been long, still shock-white.

He was about twenty yards away, directly in front of Esko on the grass. He was down on his hands and knees, making piston motions with his arms, chuffing like a train: "Choo! Choo!"

"No, Grandpa," a little boy was saying. He was fair-haired, a little more than five years old, and he had an energized, very serious expression. He wore small leather boots, blue pants, and a thick blue shirt that filled with the wind as he rushed across the grass and shoved his grandfather in the chest. "You're the caboose. I'm the engine. *You* have to follow *me*."

Esko blinked, and looked again, feeling as though the whole architecture of his known world was crumbling inside him, yet one more tower toppling each time he saw his son move; for he knew that this was his son; he didn't need to ask; the information was planted inside him.

"What's his name?" Esko said, his throat hoarse and tightening.

"Sakari," Anna said.

"Why didn't you tell me? You wrote all those letters and never said a thing."

"You'd gone your own way, Esko, and with good reason. I didn't want to blackmail you. Besides, would it have made a difference?"

Esko was shocked, because he didn't know the answer. Would it have? Would he have left New York and come back? "Maybe not," he said.

"Let it make a difference now," she said. "Sakari! Sakari!" she called, waving her hand, and the little boy ran over, swinging his arms like a windmill, holding a little wooden train that he held out with an expression of fierce concentration, as though it were a trophy he'd gained and was now offering to her.

"Mama! Look what Grandpa gave me," he said, his voice confident and serious and alive with energy and enthusiasm.

"Oh-hoh, it's a good one," Anna said, ruffling his blond hair and kneeling down in front of him. "Sakari, sweetheart, do you remember what we were talking about at breakfast? Say hello to your father."

Anna stood up and Sakari quickly darted behind her skirts, peeping out at Esko with startling blue eyes whose expression was curious rather than fearful. "Mama, he's very ugly. He only has one eye. Is he a pirate?"

"Good question," Timo said, stepping forward. "Hello, Esko."

Esko glanced at his father's hand a moment before taking it.

"He looks just like you did at that age. Little scamp."

Esko nodded, his father's words washing over him, intent on his son.

"Sakari, I'm going to leave you here with your father for a while. I want you to be very good. Don't worry," she said, brushing his hair away from his forehead. "I won't be far away. Perhaps he'll take you for a pastry. Or an ice cream. Would you like that?"

Sakari's nod was a little uncertain. "Mama!" he called sharply, when Anna had taken Timo's arm and was turning away.

"What?" she said, concerned.

Sakari summoned all his fortitude, a Finn, and Esko felt a spurt of pride.

"See you later," Sakari said, waving his hand.

Esko, left facing this little person dressed all in blue, his son, realized he was suddenly being called upon to be capable in an area where he had no blueprint or hint of knowledge, let alone expertise. He coughed. "Well. Sakari. Shall we get that ice cream?" The words, he felt at once, came out stiff and awkward, trying too hard. He got down on his hands and knees in the grass and asked, man to man. "Why on earth are you wearing that thick shirt? Aren't you hot in it?"

"I like to be hot, I like to be sweaty," Sakari said, face puckering in a frown. "Why are you crying?"

"I don't know," Esko said, swallowing back tears. "Don't you ever cry?"

Sakari shook his head, appalled by the very idea, his blue eyes wide; the little boy was a bit of an actor—Timo's influence, Esko thought, which would have to be crushed.

"Never," he said. "I never cry."

"Good boy," Esko said, knowing that Sakari must cry sometimes, determined that he never should, not if he had anything to do with it. "Now let's go get that ice cream. You know where they have some?"

Sakari shook his head, blond locks flopping from side to side.

"The *train* station," Esko said.

Sakari whooped like an Indian.

7

You must stay here and get to know him," Katerina said, her eyes downcast, velvety mouth prim.

"You'll stay too?"

"No," she said quietly, deliberately. "I'll go to New York."

"Without me?" he said. An elderly lady in a feathered hat turned, startled by his raised voice, putting her finger to her lips. It was later the same afternoon and they were in a gallery in the Ateneum Museum, in front of a small bronze statue of a girl dancing, swirling in a diaphanous, flamelike garment. It occurred to him that this might have been why Katerina had wanted to come here—it was no place to make a scene. "Excuse me, madam," Esko said, raising his hat in apology to the old woman. Then, whispering: "We'll go together."

"You have a son. It's wonderful news," Katerina said, pacing slowly, raising her eyes only when they came to the next of Vallgren's statues: another girl in a flowing dress, this one begging at a door, a supplicant for admission. "You know what it's like to grow up without a father. He must be a part of our lives."

"Of course, he will be," Esko said, her coolness needling him, and yet reassured by the "our." There was something he didn't understand. She seemed to have become distant. He hadn't expected her to demand that he never see Anna or Sakari again and devote himself to her alone like a worshiper. Katerina was far too composed for that. Perhaps he'd half hoped it would happen, as a sign that she truly needed his love. He certainly hadn't thought she'd be so totally unsurprised and unconcerned. "You don't mind? Not at all?"

"Why should I? You married Anna when you thought I'd been killed."

Another thought struck him. "Anna doesn't want me back, if that's what you're thinking."

Her voice was patient. "I have to go back—my show's moving to Chicago."

"I'll come back with you. O'Geehan's probably fretting about my being away so long as it is."

She laid her hand on the sleeve of his jacket, leaning against him with a tolerant smile. "Just the other day you told me O'Geehan hated you fussing around so much," she said. "And the skyscraper's building itself, isn't it? You're not required to drive in every rivet."

"I thought you wanted us to be together. Isn't that what we talked about?"

"We *will* be together. But there's a child involved now—your child. Are you afraid you'll lose me?"

"Of course."

"When I was holding that gun, I chose you, Esko," she said, glancing about for a moment, whispering. "What makes you think I'm going to change my mind?"

They moved into the next gallery, standing beside a picture entitled *The Garden of Death*; it was a humorous picture, in fact, showing three skeletons working at gardeners' benches, lovingly tending potted plants with strange, frail flowers. Katerina smiled at it, saying: "Perhaps that's where souls wait before they get into heaven."

Esko touched his forehead. He had no desire to talk about art. "Can we get out of here?"

"I like these pictures," she said.

He sighed. "I *do* want to spend time with Sakari."

"So it's decided," she said.

"And I want you to stay with me here in Helsinki."

Katerina threw back her head, shut her eyes. "We went through this."

"I'm not letting you go. . . ."

"Please, do," she softly moaned.

". . . not for a minute," he said, his hand shooting out, grasping her before the impact of those last words sank in. *Please, do.* He dropped his arm, stood back. "You *want* to go."

"I have a confession to make," she said, and her face seemed to rush away from him, as if suddenly he were viewing her through the wrong end of a telescope.

"What?" She tried to take his hand but now he was the standoffish one, those other words coming back: *run him down.*

"I didn't want to have to tell you this," her coolness and imperturbability vanishing; she shook, and when she lifted her eyes to his, they were bright with tears. Taking a deep breath, she went on. "This morning, when you went to meet Anna, I followed you. I was on the other side of the street, with my camera. I thought I'd make a little movie—Esko in Helsinki. It sounds strange, even silly—I know. But it's what I do. It's a way I have of dealing with the world. And I was so proud, watching you stride along, dodging this way and that, looking up at buildings. That's my man, I thought. I could tell which ones you hated just by the scowl on your face. I waited while you were up in Anna's office and then I followed the two of you down into the square, past the big church, into the park. I filmed you with Sakari. And then I put the camera down. There was a man . . . an old man with white hair . . ." Her voice fell away.

"My father," Esko said, taking her hand, raising it and brushing his lips gently against her skin, to and fro. "Katerina—what is it?" he said, filled with dread at what she might be about to tell him.

"I'd never seen your father before, but I knew who he was. A Bolshevik. The man who once tried to kill my own father. This was so strange." She swallowed, pressing the inside of her palm against her mouth, eyes shut tight. "I'm sorry, Esko." She shook her head, sighed. "It was like an emotion with no memory attached. I was overwhelmed. I was back in Petersburg. The big brass handle on our front door was turning. The door was smashed down and those men came in. My mother—her throat cut. Papa . . . I looked at your father and felt a knife go between my legs. I looked at your father and thought I was going to die."

Esko gathered her in, pressing his arms around her, his hands stroking the back of her head and the warmth of her body that shivered through the thin summer fabric of her dress.

"He was one of them?"

"No," she said, settling her face snug against his chest. "But when I saw him—I went back there. My whole body went back there."

Esko understood now why Katerina couldn't stay another moment in

Helsinki. Ashamed of his own initially doubting response, he took her back to the hotel. He still wanted to leave with her. "No," she said. "Somehow the bad things have to stop. Maybe they won't, maybe they can't. But we have to try. We've found each other, and you've found that you have a son. Now you have to build lives for us all. You can do that, can't you Esko?"

Midnight found them in the domed shed of the Helsinki railway station, Esko loading her bags into a first-class sleeper compartment at the front of the train. The night had turned cool, even though there was still plenty of light in the sky, and Katerina had the collar of her coat turned up and her beret on her head. Esko was having to be brisk, for they'd made love at the hotel and arrived at the station deliberately late, trying to hold off those melancholy moments of departure. People and porters hurried all around them amid the smells of steam and oil and cinders. Katerina was traveling to Turku, by boat to Stockholm, and thence to Le Havre and New York. Doors slammed along the line of the coaches, a whistle blew, and Esko at last broke away from her arms and jumped down onto the platform.

"I'll see you in a couple of weeks, my darling," she said, blowing a kiss.

"I love you."

"I love you."

"Safe voyage."

"I love you."

Holding her hand through the open window, he lengthened his stride, running along the platform until the speed of the train took her fingers from his grasp, and then he watched, arm high above his head, waving, until her head was a speck, a blur, no longer visible against the clicking passage of the coaches.

8

The nights drew in, clouds settled over Helsinki, the temperature dropped, and the rain began to fall, at first a drizzle, then a downpour. Within a few days the end of the short Finnish summer became the beginning of an early Finnish autumn. When Esko walked out of the hotel and looked down the Esplanade toward the harbor it was impossible to discern where the sea ended and the sky began. The air was all moisture and the streets turned to mud. Horses were splashed in mud up to their blinkers, trolley cars hurled great clods of mud from beneath their swaying bellies, people slipped on the mud-encrusted cobbles and jostled each other with their mud-bespattered umbrellas. Trucks fretfully churned their wheels in the stuff, struggling to gain purchase outside the Aleksanterinkatu site where the Diktonius Building was already being demolished.

Sakari, Esko found, loved the mud. He was fond of jumping up and down in it, he liked sliding in it, and he particularly enjoyed throwing it at Esko. Anna complained that Esko always brought back their son covered in dirt. She didn't mind really. Esko would fill the tub in her apartment, plunge his hand into the water to check that it wasn't too hot, and then give Sakari his bath, soaping his hair, scrubbing his back, squeezing droplets from a sponge and onto his chest. He would wrap Sakari in a thick towel that Anna had warmed, dry his hair, and read him a story before bed. He was unprepared for, delighted by, the sudden flower of intimacy and trust that opened between them. Anna was pleased too.

"He's interested in God now," she told Esko one night when Sakari had fallen asleep and they were drinking wine. "The other day he wanted to know why he couldn't see God. I said it was because he couldn't see Him that we know God is everywhere."

Esko had been thinking about what Katerina had said the day she left—about him building lives for them all—and he told Anna that he was contemplating buying a house outside Helsinki, perhaps an old *jugend* place that he could so something with, for when he was working on the Aleksanterinkatu skyscraper and the church he hoped to build for Kalliokoski. He also wanted to get a new base in Manhattan. Why not, he thought? He was a successful enough architect these days to contemplate a career that spanned the two continents. He envisioned himself and Katerina bouncing to and fro quite a bit between New York and Helsinki in these next years, if she could ever be persuaded to come back here. "Katerina asked me to ask you," he said. "How would it be if Sakari came and stayed with us in America sometime?"

"How would that work?" Anna said, sipping at her wine, sitting with her knees tucked up under her on the sofa, the tender light from a coal fire glowing between them.

"I'd come here and get him. Take him with me on the boat. Bring him back. Or you could come to America too. Whatever you like."

"I'll think about it." She hesitated a moment. "All right—we'll try it."

Esko wanted to ask her to keep Timo away from Sakari, but he didn't know if this was fair, so he kept his silence for the moment. Anna too found Timo's relationship with Sakari trying, even though Timo loved the boy and always seemed softened and restored when in his company. Esko was vaguely horrified by the idea that at some point he was going to have to see his father again and deal with all that.

Those two weeks in Helsinki settled into a routine. In the morning he saw Sakari; at lunch he composed wires to Katerina, sending them courtesy of the French Line, while she was in passage, and then to the address of a friend in New York where she'd be staying until Esko got back and they had a chance to look for a place together; he dealt with whatever problems—and there seemed to be few—that O'Geehan saw fit to let him know about on East River Plaza; in the afternoon he sat down at the hotel, cleared off a table with his elbows, and spread out some drafting paper, going to work; the evenings were always with Sakari and Anna.

The day prior to his departure, having arranged to take Sakari to the movies, he arrived at Anna's apartment to find Timo there. He wore a fur hat and a brown, tweed overcoat too small for his bulky, bony frame. His white hands seemed to shoot out from the cloth. He'd arrived unannounced and, on hearing of Esko's plans for the evening, quickly invited himself along. "You'll pay for my ticket, of course," he said. "Then you can buy me an expensive dinner. Is the restaurant in the Kamp as good as they say? I've never been there."

"Bolsheviks aren't allowed," Esko said, with a sarcastic smile, feeling coerced.

Timo's shortsightedness, hitherto unannounced and unguessed at by Esko, required that they sit in the front row, puddles gathering at their feet from the water dripping off people's coats and boots and umbrellas and coursing down the theater's angled floor. Sakari took Esko's hand as the curtains drew back, the orange house lights dimmed, the pianist at the side struck up fortissimo, and a shuddering shaft of silver light shot above their heads and hit the screen like a bull's-eye. The first two films were shorts in which a hopeless fat man forever spoiled the plans of a mournful thin one; then it was Chaplin teeing up on a golf course, waggling and launching his club into a demonic swing only to discover that he had no golf ball. Sakari, Timo, and Esko burst out laughing at precisely the same moment, laughing with equal enthusiasm, howling really, as if some humor gene had passed untouched between the three generations. Esko was amused by the idea that Timo the revolutionary, Timo the firebrand, Timo the butcher laughed like a little boy at the man in the bowler hat and big floppy shoes.

Afterward, in the lobby, Timo looked at his grandson and said, "So you see, Sakari. Chaplin is a good man of the people."

Esko bit his lip, crouching down, buttoning Sakari's coat and straightening his cap. "Why do you like Chaplin, Sakari?"

"He's *funny*," Sakari said, twisting his fingers around Esko's.

"Good boy."

Timo took up battle once they'd dropped Sakari back at Anna's, had walked through the Esplanade Park to the hotel, and were seated at a table in the corner—the same table, Esko recalled, where he'd once confronted Oskari Bromberg about going to America. The same highly varnished oil painting of those same drunken Finns hung on the wall above the table. Timo glanced at it, grunting, saying nothing, and sitting down. He looks old, Esko thought; but then he knew Timo still had a rude and angry vigor.

Timo ate like a man who hadn't enjoyed a square meal in a month. Perhaps he hadn't, Esko thought, allowing himself to feel a little pity while his father demolished several herrings, a plate of salmon, two plates of roast beef with horseradish and beets and potatoes, all the while guzzling wine and snapping his fingers at the waiters and raising his eyes anxiously from his plate to the door as if he expected the secret police to burst through at any moment.

"He's a good boy," Timo said, waving at a waiter for more wine. "So were you."

"Thank you, Father," Esko said dryly, knowing that he was in for a lecture.

"I hear you're a capitalist now, little Esko. You build filing cabinets for businessmen."

Esko took some wine, not about to be drawn into an argument about architecture with a man whose ignorance concerning the subject was voluminous; then he put aside that snobbish thought, trying to be fair.

"It's caused me some trouble—if you must know. Even in Moscow some of the comrades ask me if I'm related to Vaananen, the architect."

Esko could imagine how much his father must enjoy that. "They asked me to enter a competition—to build a new skyscraper palace for the glory of Comrade Stalin and the party," he said.

"I know," Timo said, peeved. "I tried to tell them—the idea is absurd."

"Naturally—of course you tried to tell them that."

"You fought for the Whites in the war. It makes me ashamed."

"Father—can we please not talk about this."

"It is my *life*. A second revolution is just starting in Russia. Stalin is cleaning out the deadwood." He leaned back in his chair, his big hands on the table, nodding. "It can still happen here. It must."

Esko eyed his father warily, knowing that their minds could never meet, knowing that Timo's rigid utopianism was misplaced, not least because it was men like him who tended to be the scientists behind such experiments, believing they could put the world in a bottle and make it better with a few arrogant shakes. But Esko was scarcely in a position to talk, having achieved his own ambition through an unholy marriage of violence and high finance. So he kept his mouth shut. What was there to say? The world was a messy and mysterious place, and although the ends did not justify the means, the decency and common sense of one's goal was a better guarantee of the result than mystic fervor, be it of the religious or the political or indeed the architectural variety. That had been Kirby's position anyway; it was why he'd preferred Wright's visionary pragmatism to Le Corbusier's heroic white-box rigor. And Esko knew Kirby was right: the world itself was so pliable, so endlessly changing, so constantly turning from black to white, that the best style in the end was the style that was in constant flux and evolution. Dogma was dangerous; the shape-shifter would prevail. Timo was older, but he hadn't changed.

Esko watched his father's mouth and realized that for about five minutes he hadn't been listening to a single word coming out of it.

"You're very quiet, little Esko. Thinking of your money?"

"No, Father, I was thinking of a man I knew." He couldn't decide whether Timo was only trying to torment him a little, or whether there was real envy and anger and hatred involved.

"Do you remember when your mother died, little Esko?"

"Yes, of course I do."

Timo's eyes were filled with a wicked glimmer. "It was a black day," he said, fingering the stubble on his cheek, scratchy like sandpaper. "The blackest day of my life. And now I'm going to tell Mr. Esko Vaananen, American architect, something that he doesn't know."

Esko refused to be nettled. "Oh, and what's that?"

"She didn't drown in the lake."

"What are you talking about?"

"Remember when you ran inside? She was in the house."

Esko's heart stammered. A flutter of fear, almost panic, rose in his throat. "No, that's impossible."

"She burned, Esko. You could have saved her, but you failed. Because you didn't have the will."

Esko forced himself to sit back, swill the brandy in his glass and drink it, not letting his father see how disconcerted and stunned he was. Could it be so? Had he really failed? His memory of that day was clear until the moment when he had entered the burning house. After that—nothing; and however hard he strove, however hard he pushed, the shut door of what had happened after that would not open. Had Little Esko let his mother down so badly?

Esko swallowed, appalled by his father's mean-spiritedness. "Now listen here, you old . . ." he started to say, but at the sight of the smile that began to appear on his father's face, he pushed back his rage, knowing that, had his mother indeed been inside that fire he would have done everything he could to get to her. Little Esko would have run through flame.

"And what about your failure, Father?" he said in a calm voice. "You let her down, and me too."

Timo's face twitched, and Esko realized something else.

"You loved her very much, didn't you, Father? You loved her, you lost her, and you blamed me for it. Well, I'm not going to put up with it anymore."

Timo blinked, too proud to weep.

"I'm a father now myself, Father. And you're not going to infect Sakari with your hatred."

Timo's mouth dropped a little. "Are you telling me I can't see my grandson?"

"That would be easy for you, wouldn't it? That way you could blame me again. I'm saying that although you and I may never agree or like each other, you have to put that behind you, for his sake. This is personal politics—and you'd better start learning some."

"I love that little boy," he said, looking frail and afraid.

Esko sighed, with a sudden picture of his father's lifelong solitariness, his recalcitrance, his ceaseless striving. Timo had his tragedies too.

"I know," he said. "And from now on we're going to be civil—for Sakari's sake."

Timo stared down into his glass. Presently he raised his head with a jerk.

"I think Chaplin's funny too," he said, hurrying the phrase, almost choking on it.

Esko nodded, wanting this to end.

"I know you do," he said.

In the street, after he and Timo had shaken hands, Esko stood alone for a moment, watching his father, with his white hair and broad back, disappear in the direction from which he'd come. Then he turned quickly, and walked through the night to Anna's apartment.

Finding Sakari asleep, Esko kissed his son's forehead and breathed a blessing into his ear. He and Anna talked long into the night and parted with a connection he couldn't have imagined a month earlier. This had been a good time. He'd missed Katerina desperately, but he knew that he'd be seeing her soon and he felt happy, secure in the love they shared. It seemed to him that he would indeed find a way to fashion a life for them all, even if there was a long way to go and unforetold difficulties ahead.

9

Esko arrived on board at Le Havre with a couple of hours to spare, several as it happened, for the *Ile de France* was late getting underway. No explanation was offered, although up on deck, strolling past the splendid triple funnels, Esko saw a dockside crane swinging a gleaming yellow automobile on board like a stork delivering a baby. That's a Rolls-Royce, he said to himself, but thought no more of it.

Before unpacking he called the radio office and dictated a couple of wires, one to Katerina, and another to O'Geehan, telling him that he was on board and on his way. With his sketchbook in front of him on the desk, he noticed his hand tremble a little; the engines had started, filling the entire ship with the pulse of life. Soon, looking out of the brass-ringed porthole in his cabin, he glimpsed the seawall of Le Havre sliding by, and, beyond, the rolling waves of the Atlantic.

Having showered and dressed for dinner, he drank a martini in the first-class lounge and, finding that it was raining up top, strolled down through the decks. He stopped, listening with one ear, in the middle of a corridor. A door slammed. The faint strains of an orchestra played counterpoint to the throb of the engines. From nearby came the raucous celebratory sounds of someone's getting-underway party. Ahead of him stretched steel walls painted the color of clotted cream and lines of black varnished doors with numbers on them in gold.

And then Paul Mantilini burst around the corner, handsome face bronzed by the sun, wearing a black suit with a broad chalky pinstripe. His black hair was slicked back, and his teeth flashed in a cutting smile. He came closer and closer and Esko stepped to one side, heart pumping, something in him made quick and afraid.

"Paul—" he started to say, but Mantilini swept by, almost pushing him aside, walking fast and with a strange, swirling limp. Then Esko saw Gardella, hat set dead straight on his head, eyes impassive, and some others he recognized, familiar members of the entourage, and a number of new faces.

Esko realized he was holding his breath, thought he might be dreaming; but when he took his place for dinner that night, he raised his eye and there was Mantilini, not at the captain's table beneath the biblical mural, but surrounded by his own people at a circular table commanding the brilliantly chandeliered dining room from one corner. Esko touched his wineglass. He gulped water for the dryness in his throat while all around him people spoke Mantilini's name with excited pleasure, even awe.

"... Mantilini ..."

"... owns the governor ..."

"... Mantilini ..."

"... making a film with Chaplin ..."

"... Mantilini ..."

"... working on his tennis ..."

"... Mantilini ..."

"... cornering the coffee market ..."

"... Mantilini ... Mantilini ... Mantilini ..."

"... held up the ship for him ..."

"... Mantilini ... Mantilini ..."

Confronting the situation, pushing his glass back on the table, tossing down his napkin, Esko walked the length of the room, feeling everyone's eyes on him amid the hubbub of voices and the waiters weaving their way with shining tureens of soup.

"Paul—what's this all about?" he said.

Mantilini looked up sharply, mopping at his lips with a napkin. Still chewing, he sipped red wine. "Eleven o'clock," he said. "My cabin."

Esko had thought his own quarters sumptuous until he saw Mantilini's. Various bodyguards and associates stood about like double-breasted statues with toothpicks between their lips, posed among the marble tables, silk screens, crystal vases, chairs upholstered in shining satin. Mantilini himself was in the center of the room, seated beside a life-size effigy of a swan, sculpted in ice and topped with caviar; he was sitting for his portrait, while the artist, a wiry, hard Italian in his early thirties, worked away in oils. In one corner Ruthie was dancing to a melancholy jazz tune, weaving her sinuous body. On seeing Esko she paused to turn the hand-crank Victrola. Wondering how it was that Mantilini had sailed from New York with his wife and was returning there with his mistress, Esko held out hope that perhaps Mantilini's hostile mood was nothing to do with him at all.

Mantilini acknowledged his presence with the briefest of nods. "You ever do any painting, Esko?"

"Some."

"Tell me what you think."

The portrait was cleverly done, lifelike, but still with a Cubist influence, as if the facets of Paul Mantilini had been diced up and put back together to emphasize the flamboyant and gorgeous aspects of his persona, with a hint of sharp knives. This showed advanced artistic taste, but then he realized that by now nothing Paul Mantilini did should surprise him. "It's very good. You're going to like it."

Mantilini nodded slowly, with no suggestion of pleasure. "Everybody out," he said in that snappish voice of command. "Everybody out, come on now." Pointing an accusing finger at Esko, he said: "Not you."

Gardella quickly herded up the others, shooing them on their way.

"You too, Gardella—out," Mantilini said. "And you, Ruthie."

Gardella nodded his squashed, pulled-about face, showed his acres of back, while Ruthie merely flipped the record, set it back on the turntable, and cranked the Victrola. Dancing again, she smiled, fingering the pearls around her delicate black throat.

"Ruthie," Mantilini said, ice in his voice. "You might see something you don't want to see. You understand what I'm saying."

Ruthie looked down at the floor, kicked up an ankle, threw her head to one side, showed her very white, small, regular teeth. Her fingernails were painted pink; she looked like a willful schoolgirl who'd ingested opium rather than her daily milk ration.

Mantilini watched her in blank amazement for a moment or two. "Suit yourself," he said, shaking his head, turning coins in his pocket. "Stupid bitch."

He slammed the door, said to Esko: "MacCormick's body washed up out of the river. They arrested your Russian lady friend. She confessed. I want you to explain to me why I shouldn't kill you now and have her killed tomorrow."

The information was like a slap in the face. Esko stepped back, hand flying to the patch over his eye. "When? When did this happen?"

"No questions. I want an explanation. Why shouldn't I kill you—this moment?"

Esko didn't panic; he didn't try to bluff or wriggle his way out; nor did he turn his hand and show the scar claiming blood brotherhood. He had to save Katerina; therefore he had to stay alive. A calmness of purpose shivered through him and took root like a tree. His eye was alert, watchful.

"I'm waiting for an answer," Mantilini said.

"It wasn't me who shot MacCormick," Esko said. "We fought, like I told you. The gun went flying. Katerina picked it up. She shot him."

Mantilini didn't move. He was more still than Esko had ever seen him. A single bead of perspiration rolled down his cheek. He closed his eyes for a moment, jaw set, muscles tense, mouth tight, his whole face straining with disbelief, not at the story, but at the fact of Esko's having lied to him. He'd been deceived: deceived on the night of the killing, deceived thereafter.

"I sent her on her way," Esko said. "The rest you know."

Mantilini's face cracked, a frozen smile. "Not all of it," he said. "What does *she* know? Does she know about me?"

"Everything." Esko said.

Mantilini's head ducked in anger. A hand flew inside his pinstriped jacket, came out grasping the nickel-gleam of a pistol.

"She won't say a word."

Fire rippled from the muzzle, a crystal vase jumped and shattered, even as the noise of the shot shocked Esko's ears. Smoke and the smell of cordite wafted across the cabin while Esko, unflinching, never took his eye off Mantilini. "You'll be safe."

Mantilini's body was quite still once more, pistol leaking smoke in his hand. "Bet your life I will be. I kill her, I kill you. That way I'm safe."

"She's proud. She won't say a word about me, or about you."

Another bullet flew, this one shattering a wing on the ice sculpture. Lumps of ice flew and danced.

"I promise you, Paul—Katerina will say nothing of what I told her."

"Sure she won't. If she's dead." The gun, aimed at Esko's heart, was steady in Mantilini's hand.

Now Ruthie spoke. "Esko's right," she said. "She'll keep quiet."

Mantilini clutched at his head, the pistol still in his right hand. "Jesus, Ruthie—keep out of this, will you? What the hell do you know about it?"

"I know her," Ruthie said. "She won't say anything because she's crazy enough to protect him. Would you do the same for me, Mr. Paul Mantilini?" Her fingers played with the pearls about her neck. "I doubt it," she said. She cranked the Victrola again and raised her bangled wrists above her head, moving her lissome body to that same haunting refrain. "You're just a no-good gangster who doesn't give a shit."

"So what should I do?" Mantilini threw out his arms. "I'm surrounded by lunatics. Oh, hell," he said. Dropping the gun on the chair, he bunched his fist and struck Esko in the face.

On the floor, on his hands and knees, Esko watched thick blood running dripping from his nose.

"You're lucky, you know that," Mantilini was saying, shaking his fist as though he'd hurt it. "She killed him, she keeps quiet, she gets what's coming to her. That's just. That's the way it had better be," he said, his shoulders rolling, as if trying to burst out from beneath his suit.

Esko raised himself to his feet, clutching at the table, taking a napkin that he held to his nose. "That won't do," he said. "I have to get her out. And you're going to help me."

"Bullshit," Mantilini exclaimed.

Esko fingered caviar into his mouth, savoring the salty tang. "If you don't, I'll tell the cops what you did."

Mantilini, his rage having ebbed only moments ago, now thrust his hands in his pockets and laughed. "You're bluffing."

"Not at all," Esko said. "I'll walk out the door, go to the radio office, wire it to the world. 'Paul Mantilini Dumps Financier's Body in River.' You'll have to shoot me to stop me."

Ruthie moved away from the Victrola, sauntered past the wrecked ice sculpture, threw herself in a chair, lounging, lighting a cigarette and crossing her legs with a whisper of silk. She didn't want to miss a moment of the excitement; this was where she liked to be herself, dancing on the edge of some extremity. Her eyes moved from Mantilini to Esko and back.

"You've got lawyers," Esko said. "You can make it happen—I bet you've had one of your people go see the detectives and Katerina already, sniffing things out."

Mantilini shrugged. It was true.

"What evidence do they have against her?"

"Not much. No weapon. No witnesses. Just a couple of hundred million dollars worth of motive and the fact that when they asked her she said, 'I killed him.' A leaky case."

"Make it happen. Show me how powerful Paul Mantilini really is."

Mantilini had his hands in his pockets, smiling as though constrained to explain why he couldn't oblige. "The guy turned out to be a floater. He popped up out of the goddamn river. A well-known guy. A rich guy. The cops have a body and now they need a suspect because it's all over the newspapers. This won't just go away."

"Send a wire to New York. Tell your lawyers to tell them there's been a mistake, a miscarriage of justice. Tell them to say they know who Mac-Cormick's killer really is. Get Katerina out of there. Give them me."

"You? Are you crazy?"

"I'll leave her out of it, and you. You have my word on that. I'll tell them I killed him and got rid of the body myself. You can explain to me just how I did that—so my story will be far more convincing, won't it?"

Mantilini didn't like it. Walking, frowning, jingling his keys in his pockets, he snapped his fingers at Ruthie, signaling her to her feet; then he threw himself down in the chair, sat up, put his elbows on his knees, his head down in his hands. He sat up straight, drawing his hands along his face. A hand stretched out, sliding up Ruthie's silky leg.

"What about East River?" he said. "They'll arrest you at the dock."

"Doesn't matter," Esko said. "Doesn't matter whether I see the skyscraper again or whether the press kicks up all hell about a murderer having made it. It won't be the first time that a part of a city got made by a crook. And a few years from now everyone will forget that. The story will be gone—but East River will be there, and people will either like it or they won't. And Katerina will be free."

Mantilini sprang to his feet. "I can get her out. I can put you in. But you're gonna have to go through with this. They'll throw things at you. They'll trip you up. I don't own everybody and there'll be some little pissant puritan who'll thank his lucky stars thinking he can get to me through this. You'll have to stick with this, all the way to the chair."

Esko wiped his hands, threw aside the bloody napkin. "Not a problem," he said. "All the way to the chair. Just get Katerina out," he said, and clutched Mantilini by the shoulder.

The gangster nodded, the scar on his eyelid white as marble, his sleek, handsome face a blank, not smiling, not angry, not used to being bested, while Ruthie strutted across the cabin and the jazz began again.

✳   ✳   ✳

It was hot, New York hot, steaming hot, broiling hot, sapping hot, sagging hot the day they docked: from the rail, Esko watched the skyline rise above the soupy, slow-moving waters of the harbor; the skyscrapers danced, never in the same place for a minute at a time, constantly shuffling their orientations, moving and cutting different angles in the sky. It was East River Tower, his own building, that was now the tallest, the big figure in this millionaires' waltz, and beside him at the rail a plump husband turned to his plump wife. "That's Vaananen's building," he said, and Esko wondered what the man might have heard.

While the puttering tugboats towed the *Ile de France* to its pier, Esko didn't once take his eye off his skyscraper, not even when Mantilini came on deck, not even when the police sergeant appeared on the dock beneath the ship, surrounded by a score of uniformed officers, and raised a white megaphone to his mouth.

Esko felt a nudge in his ribs. "They've caught up with him at last," the man who'd been talking to his wife said, aiming his neat little beard at Paul Mantilini.

Esko shook his head in the heat. The police weren't waiting for Mantilini. They were waiting for him. They'd always been waiting.

10

The cell was five feet wide, six and a half feet long, and seven feet high. A steel-frame bed was bolted to the graffitied brick wall, thin mattress and gray blanket atop it; there was no window, no washbasin, just a tin bucket for Esko's slops. The black, barred grate in the black steel door looked onto a stone walkway and the prison's exterior wall, where light filtered down from steel-meshed windows set high above.

Lunch, or dinner as they called it in the Tombs, was at eleven-thirty in the morning—usually lentil soup and stew. The kid in the cell next to Esko's on murderers row would customarily shout, "Hey, flatfeet!" and regale the guard with long and detailed complaints about the menu. Exercise was between two and four. There was no courtyard or any outdoor facility; instead the entire two hours was devoted to walking around and around the runway that rimmed the cells. The nineteen-year-old kid from the cell next door had a fleshy, pockmarked face and a smile that showed two missing teeth. He'd shot a man after stealing a car. He was the pacesetter on the circular course, striding furiously, as if hoping by some miraculous chance to find himself on the open road. There were two other, older men, who stuck together—they looked like brothers—whispering about how they would beat the rap, or arguing loudly about horses and the fights. Another fellow—he had black hair and staring eyes—would pause in swaying resentment if anyone came near him, and Esko quickly learned to keep out of his way. A supper of corned beef hash and chocolate pudding was doled out at four o'clock and at five the cell doors were shut and locked.

Nights were the most difficult. Though the Tombs grew dark, the stinking air in the prison never seemed to cool, and echoed with fretful sounds that jangled the nerves. Men snored and moaned and blubbered. Footsteps came faintly on the runway, growing louder, growing closer, closer, and then fading away again. There were strange murmurs and metallic clangs, as if the building itself were alive and Esko merely a ghostly parasite.

Esko couldn't sleep. On this, the fourth night of his incarceration, he lay on his back on the bed with his arms behind his head and his eye shut, trying to concentrate on the day he and Katerina had spent in the forest in Finland, walking among silver birch trees that were like a thousand spears of light struck straight at the sky. Instead, more recent images crowded in—he saw himself handcuffed, bundled into the back of the police wagon; he remembered his interrogation first at the hands of a detective and then a skeptical deputy district attorney who'd been disinclined to believe his story. "I don't like the way these confessions keep falling into my lap," he'd said. Esko was nagged by memories of his arraignment in court, his arrival at the Tombs, the *Graphic* headline, which a guard had pushed against the bars of his cell— "Architect Confesses to Millionaire's Slaughter."

Tired, turning, restless, he rose and began walking back and forth across the cell, taking short steps to make the stretch a little longer, knowing that none of these memories would make him anxious, indeed they'd be welcome guests, could he be certain of one fact: that Katerina was free. But the lawyer who'd come to see him every day, sent by Mantilini, had thus far had nothing to say on that matter. What if she was still being held? he thought. What if Mantilini had betrayed him or been unable to pull it off? The idea tortured him, and there was nothing he could do about it now. He just had to wait.

Coins of silver light began to spangle the cell, rolling and dancing across the floor. Amazed, Esko drew himself up from the steel bed, feeling the lights drift across his face, watching the lights ripple across his body as he walked toward the door. Looking through the bars, looking up, looking toward the meshed window high in the outer wall he saw a sleek cigar of silver, a zeppelin, endlessly long, a hundred or more yards long, longer than a liner, slipping through the framed oblong of moonlit sky. It was as if a part of his subconscious, all of his longing, all of his guilt, had been released and was looming over the city, passing low over the prison, spilling the moon's bounty, spattering him with light. The soundless zeppelin seemed so close he could almost build a ladder to it, were it not for the bars of his cell, the steel mesh on the window. Esko shivered at this, one of the scariest, most wonderful things he'd ever seen, a miracle of man's ingenuity that had traveled all the way from Europe across the Atlantic. How amazing, he thought, that men had built such a thing. Then the zeppelin slid beyond his vision and the cell grew dark again.

Next morning a guard rapped the bars of the cell with a stick. "Vaana-nen—visitor!"

In the visiting room there were two rows of screened compartments slightly smaller than telephone booths set about eighteen inches apart; inmates sat on one side, visitors on the other; the space between was brilliantly lit by meshed bulbs in the low ceiling, but this only had the effect of emphasizing the darkness in the stalls themselves.

Esko sat down on the bolted wood-and-steel bench, leaning forward in the booth, eye dazzled by the glare. He couldn't see who was sitting opposite, if indeed his visitor had arrived yet. All around him there was a deafening babble of voices in different languages and dialects, prisoners and visitors yelling at each other across the harsh light that separated them. A woman's voice rose above the rest, pledging her sexual loyalty in tones more resembling a Comanche yell. Someone screamed about socks and underwear. There were snatches of Italian, Polish, Yiddish. At last he made out a shadow in front of him, and rising out of the cacophony he thought he heard a familiar voice:

"Esko!"

"What? Katerina—is that you?"

"I can hardly see you, my darling."

"Katerina!" His body went wire hard with recognition and then softened, relief flowing through him. "You're out!"

Someone was yelling in what sounded like Hungarian, and Katerina's voice struggled against the racket.

"You're getting out too!" she said.

"What? I can't hear you!"

"I said—I'll see you tomorrow! You're getting out too!"

"What?"

"Look!" She pushed something against the steel grille on her side: photographs. Esko couldn't make them out beneath the lights. "Your skyscraper! I'll see you on top of your skyscraper!"

"Katerina—are you crazy?"

"On the skyscraper—tomorrow!"

Esko spent the rest of the day, through dinner, exercise, and supper, and then the whole of a fitful night, trying to figure out what she might mean; after breakfast the next morning, his cell door opened and a guard thrust a parcel at him, the belongings that had been taken away when he came in. "Come on," the guard said, and led him down through the tiers of the prison into the reception area, where a clerk produced a ledger for him to sign. "You're free to go."

Moments later Esko found himself out on Center Street, looking back at the gloomy building from which he'd been disgorged with so little fuss. It was a bright October day, sun shining, a light breeze coming up from the tip of the island. A yellow Rolls-Royce purred to a halt beside him and a door was flung open.

"I'll give you a ride," Mantilini said.

Esko hesitated; at least part of the mystery had been explained—at least he knew now who had got him out; but how, and why?

"Come on, Esko. Don't you know me by now? I got you a suite at the Plaza," Mantilini said, wearing a white shirt and a suit of solid scarlet. "I thought you might need to freshen up."

Esko climbed in, closed the door, and settled himself in the plush leather and walnut of the interior while Gardella eased the Rolls uptown through the morning traffic.

"Ruthie says hi," Mantilini said.

"Where's Katerina? Is she safe?"

"Unless she hurt herself snapping up her stockings this morning," Mantilini said. He pushed Esko's knee with his hand. "Relax. She got out two days ago. You're out today. It's over. I've taken care of things. I happen to know some people who can do that."

Esko grappled with this.

"Did you really think I was going to let you go through with it? You're my brother, remember?" Mantilini said with a nod and a flash of his teeth. "You got the better of me back there on the boat, Esko. Not many people do."

He looked out the window, broody, as if still startled and unsettled by the memory. "Hey! Look—Esko, you gotta go see that movie," he said, pointing to one of the billboards in Times Square. He started telling Esko the plot, which involved a Chicago gunman and his molls, his eyes bright as he sketched in the details. "A great city in the dead of night . . . A lonely street . . . A skyscraper . . . A car screams around the corner."

He mimed the effects, glad that the motion picture business had woken up to the charms of his own profession. And, as far as he was concerned, there was another angle too. "It's a way of keeping tabs on things," he said. "On the American system."

He put on dark glasses, and let a little smile cut into his face, looking out over the marquees and unlit lights of Broadway, a king in his world. "Now I want my house. You owe me a house," he said.

11

In the suite at the Plaza, Esko found boxes of clothes that Mantilini had ordered from one of the big department stores. The shoes were Esko's size, and so were the collars on the shirts; the socks were silk, the suits looked like they would fit perfectly. Esko shaved, showered, and put on the clothes he'd been wearing before, waking up to the fact of his freedom and to all the choices he thought he'd never have to make but were starting to again stare him in the face. Picking up the phone, he had the operator place a call to the apartment of one of Katerina's friends, where he thought he might find her. There was no reply. But then there was a knock on the door and a bellboy bearing an envelope on a silver platter. Esko slipped the bellboy a bill and quickly ripped open the letter.

My love, it began.

> *I'll be waiting for you on top of the skyscraper, on top of your pilvenpiirtaja. I want to hold you, to feel your lips against mine, my love, and to kiss you in return—forever. Let's never be separated again. These last days have been an agony—but everything's wonderful now. I love you, Esko, with all my heart and soul.*
>
> *Katerina.*

Esko was running across the Plaza lobby when Marion Bennett sat up from one of the chairs in the lobby.

"Have a drink?" she said, taking his arm, looking up at him, her face pale and appearing hung over beneath the veil of her hat.

"It's a little early, isn't it?"

"It's never too early for a drink," she said. "Besides, I thought you might need one after everything you've been through."

"Not right now," he said.

She tugged at his arm. "Slow down. Can I have a word?" she said. "I wanted to apologize. I've always liked you, Esko. But for a while back there you really had me thinking that you'd killed MacCormick. I even wrote a story about it."

"That's all right," Esko said.

"I'm glad I was wrong. I'm glad it was another architect who killed him."

Esko had an odd ominous feeling. What was she talking about? "Another architect?"

Marion Bennett observed him from beneath her veil. "I guess you wouldn't have heard yet. The cops have issued a warrant for Joe Lazarus. Apparently they found a gun in his apartment. He's on the run."

"A diamond-studded revolver?"

"How did you know that?"

Esko sighed. This was Mantilini's work, obviously; Esko wondered what else, what other incriminating evidence might have been planted in Lazarus's apartment; he and Mantilini would have to talk about it. "Joe Lazarus didn't kill MacCormick," he said simply. "Tell them that, Marion. All right? Joe Lazarus is a bad man but he didn't kill Andrew MacCormick. Tell them."

Her expression was puzzled. "Who did then?"

A bell chimed behind them on the main desk. "Marion, excuse me, I have to rush," he said.

He was at the door when she called: "Hey, Esko!"

He turned; she'd lifted the veil now, and a cigarette hung from the rouged bow of her mouth. "Did you hear the news?" she said, hand on hip. "Someone announced another skyscraper yesterday. Gonna be two hundred feet higher than yours."

Esko smiled. "Good," he said.

*   *   *

His skyscraper, a white and unadorned slab, soared at the sky with elegant, rippling setbacks; around it, like seedlings, the other buildings were already starting to sprout, giving shape to the overall layout of the plaza. Structural steel on the two corner apartment buildings had almost been completed, likewise on the hotel. Excavations for the school and the hospital were underway. Lofty derrick cranes swung this way and that against the sky. Three trucks pulled up, one behind the other, growling. Cement mixers rattled and churned. The air was filled with the colliding smells of fresh concrete and dynamited bedrock. Men teemed down in the earth, swung high in the sky, and because of him, because of some drawings he'd made on a tablecloth one night in a restaurant with Kirby and Katerina. Just as it had taken the whole of France all of the Middle Ages to produce Notre Dame, so it had taken, not only the better part of Esko's life, but the entire jazz era, the whole of America—its good, its bad; its dark, its light; its greed, its generosity; its restless striving, its youthful appetite for violence—to make this.

Esko felt a strange, light-headed elation; he was at one with the world, proud, and yet . . . And yet: there was something missing, something lacking, an indefinable something he couldn't quite put his finger on that wasn't right. This striking and improbably tall skyscraper wasn't the *pilvenpiirtaja* he'd seen as a little boy on the ice. It wasn't pure; it wasn't crystalline; it wasn't enough. Its imperfect beauty drew not just pleasure from his heart but a yearning ache.

"It's a fine monster, a wonderful thing indeed," said O'Geehan, swinging toward him, snatching off his derby hat and wiping his forehead. "Is that what you're thinking, Esko?"

"Now then, O'Geehan," Esko said, the shadow passing as excited expectation filled him once more. I'm going to see Katerina, he thought, and threw his arm around the Irish contractor's shoulders. "Are you ready for the next one? Are you ready to build a *real* skyscraper? Because there's this idea I've had for quite some time."

O'Geehan laughed at his enthusiasm. "Really?" he said. "Deal me in."

"How high can we go?"

"Fifteen hundred feet?"

"Not high enough," Esko said.

"Eighteen hundred feet? Two thousand feet?"

"Higher," said Esko, lofting his arm to the sky. "Why not a mile high— why not the loveliest building in America, in all the world?"

They came into the marbled lobby of the main tower, walking toward the elevator core, toward the open doors of the express elevator. Glancing inside, Esko saw that the walls and ceiling of the car were already decorated with the murals that had been sent back from the Diktonius Building in Helsinki.

"This is some pretty nice work," O'Geehan said. "Where'd you find it?"

"I did these myself, a long time ago," Esko said.

"You don't say," O'Geehan said, tipping his derby hat back on his head. "I didn't know you painted."

"I wield a clumsy brush, O'Geehan," Esko said. "A clumsy brush, but I'll do better yet," he said, stepping into the elevator, looking up at his pictures — the woodpecker, the boat, the lake in winter, the wounded angel, and the blinded child — and drawing in breath, then letting it out again slowly with a huge feeling of gratitude and hope. He'd been lucky, he knew that, very lucky, and his conscience would make sure that he made the most of that luck. He didn't give a damn about what had happened in the past. It was only the stuff out of which he would design the future. He'd achieved some things but in truth the best was yet to come: love, a family, better buildings, a second skyscraper . . . a third . . . a fourth . . . He could still be someone, maybe even a good man. His heartbeat quickened. He felt the push of these hopeful, perhaps absurd dreams, and he smiled, reaching for the brass lever that would send the elevator hurtling upward.

A man came hurrying across the lobby. For a moment Esko paid no heed; he had only the impression of a bulky figure.

This man shoved O'Geehan aside, and then Esko saw a hand reaching into a pocket. He saw a beard, hair that was dyed black, too black. The man was Joe Lazarus.

There was no time even to be afraid.

A knife flashed, Lazarus lunged, and Esko felt a piercing pain in his gut. His hands clutched at the pain, at the handle of the knife, which he realized was his own *puukko*.

For a moment he was surprised. How on earth did Joe get hold of that? he thought. But then he remembered and looked up to see Lazarus's face, white with adrenaline, filled with concentration and fury.

Lazarus whipped out a pistol from beneath his overcoat; then the barrel flashed.

The first bullet struck Esko in the chest, throwing him against the back of the elevator car as if nailed there. The second missed. The third ripped through the patch over his blind left eye and traveled through his brain.

Esko's head was bowed, and he slid slowly down, smearing the back of the car with his blood, settling on the floor with his legs outstretched while the doors closed and the car began its smooth accelerating ascent. It seemed to him that he was weightless, traveling far within a second, his good eye star-

ing at the lake in the mural he'd painted, no longer seeing the flawed pig-
ment of the picture but speeding across the surface of the lake itself, where
ruffling wavelets brushed his face before he stretched his arms and soared up,
borne on the softest breeze. Is this dying? he thought.

A figure came toward him through the light, a woman, a beautiful
woman in a black dress. A voice was calling, begging him not to go; but the
voice was far away, and the light was tempting. His soul was a skyscraper soaring through the clouds, flying out and into space, zooming toward the heart
of the sun where Katerina was waiting. She'd always be waiting.

And then the light went out.

Katerina was kneeling down beside Esko, cradling his head. Briefly she
felt the pressure of his fingers around her own, staining her gloves with blood;
then they went limp. She wailed, whispering to her lover and breathing into
his mouth as if her kisses could bring a dead man back to life.

Epilogue: 1933

Anna Vaananen came to New York with her son, Sakari, at the end of 1933, three weeks before Christmas, during the bleak time of the depression. It was the year when Lindbergh's baby had been kidnapped and killed, an event that made her heart clutch. In Germany the Reichstag had burned and Hitler had passed laws requiring idiots and depressives and schizophrenics to be sterilized, and Jewish shopkeepers to be shunned and attacked. In Helsinki she'd tossed a glass of wine in the face of an older Finnish architect who'd said that Hitler was a good thing, because at least he was getting rid of the Communists. Europe was heading toward another mess and Finland, as usual, was hunkering down between its more powerful neighbors. Was Stalin really preferable to Hitler? A little, thought Anna—but what a choice to have to make. Things, in general, looked perilous and uncertain. Perhaps they would always be so.

She'd been invited to New York by a company that wanted to take out a license on several of Esko's wooden furniture designs and put them into mass production for schools and hospitals being built under the Federal Relief program. The rights in these designs belonged to her and Sakari now; it seemed they were going to be worth quite a lot of money, and Anna was pleased about that, for Sakari's sake.

The two of them stayed in Katerina's apartment, a five-room place in Greenwich Village. Anna had gathered that for a while Katerina had been rich in America, as she had once been rich in Russia, but that most everything had gone in the crash of twenty-nine and she'd been forced once again to start afresh. The apartment was painted white and sparsely furnished; it was almost antiseptically clean and tidy, anonymous, devoid of any personal touch, conveying the impression that Katerina had moved in only yesterday and might move out again at any moment.

There was only one photograph in the entire apartment, a brown-toned daguerrotype, far too ancient to have been taken by Katerina; it showed a young boy clad awkwardly in a stiff tweed suit, with a scarred face and a patch over one eye, gazing into the camera with a strange and surprised and almost dreamy confidence. It was Esko, of course, Esko as a little boy, photographed on the day that he and Katerina first met. Katerina had searched out that photograph, had traveled both to Oulu and Vaasa before at last finding the man who had taken it. This had been in those days late in 1928, soon after his death, when she'd brought his ashes to Finland. Anna and Katerina talked for a long time before deciding where his final resting place should be; in the end they'd taken him to Ostrobothnia, to the estate of his White Army colleague Selin, and a sheltered spot beneath the walls of the Church of the Shadow Cross.

She and Katerina were good friends now. They wrote to each other frequently, though rarely mentioning Esko or the circumstances that had brought them together; it was odd, perhaps, but understandable.

Katerina was out of town at the moment, taking pictures in the Carolinas. She was coming back to New York in a few days, and Anna and Sakari would see her then.

But it was on the first morning of their stay that Esko's former colleague, the Irish contractor O'Geehan, came to collect them. "Now then, young fella," he said, ruffling Sakari's blond hair, pushing back his hat, and handing over a big box. "Are you still interested in trains?"

Soon a red electric engine was tugging several freight and passenger cars around a metal track on the floor of the apartment while Anna and O'Geehan sipped coffee, and O'Geehan, having outlined the morning schedule, prowled about the place, shaking his head. "She's quite something, that Katerina," he said in his lilting brogue. "She goes places in this country I'd be afraid to go myself, let alone if I were a woman."

"I think she can take care of herself," said Anna, liking the Irishman on sight, but knowing that he underestimated her friend. "Some of the newspapers mentioned a racketeer, a bootlegger who'd known Esko."

"Paul Mantilini? I never knew the man. Prohibition's over now. I think I heard somewhere that he went to California. Or was it Nevada? Anyway his life proceeds. No doubt sensationally." O'Geehan smiled ruefully, rattling his cup in its saucer. "Is there more of this?"

"Will be. Soon," Anna said, busying herself in Katerina's kitchen while O'Geehan prattled on, the electric train clicking against its tracks in the living room of the apartment. Isn't this the strangest and most miraculous thing of all, she thought to herself—just to be here talking, moving, walking? People sipped coffee, or came across the sea to New York and disappeared to California, or back into Russia (as had that dutiful grandparent and still driven man, Timo Vaananen); or else—like Joseph Lazarus, Esko's killer—they were incarcerated in lunatic asylums, or they ventured to distant parts of the country and even the world just to take photographs. Their stories continued, making tracks in the snow.

Whatever happened, whoever died, the lake of things, of life, lived on regardless, rising and falling, freezing and melting, now rippled by the wind, now burnished by the sun, through season after season, year after year—that was mankind's tragedy, its saving grace in a way, just as the secret of Esko's spirit had been his perseverance, his struggling, combating, and in the end conquering heart, his caring too much and too passionately. His resolve had always been visible in the fire of his eye. He'd endured so much without ever giving up. He'd perished, but hadn't he won also?

*   *   *

East River Plaza was thick and busy with people sitting on benches, streaming in and out of the buildings, buying and selling food, standing and talking by the fountain, its plumes turned off, the water in the stone basin beneath frozen like a rink.

The skyscraper was one of the most gorgeous things Anna had ever seen, a great solitary finger aimed into the light blue winter sky. New York already had taller buildings, but none nobler or more inspiring, and as Anna's gaze

traveled down from that central tower, moving to the corner apartment building, to the school, to the hospital, to the motion picture palace, she found
herself thinking of the trip through Italy that she and Esko had once made,
and her husband's love for those piazzas that were both the architectural center of the city, and the main setting of its social life. There was something of
that here. This wasn't just a lonely office tower standing largely empty, as
were the Chrysler and the Empire State, because of the dire present eco-
nomic circumstance. There was dirt, there was bustle, there was noise and
ebb and flow; there were the bums and hobos in the soup line that snaked its
way outside the doors of the school, men and women who were revived for a
moment by being in the midst of what Esko had fashioned in stone, as if
they'd been caressed by his awkward boyish tenderness and longing.

Anna straightened Sakari's cap. "Your father made this," she said.

Sakari, almost eleven now, absorbed this without a nod or a blink, with that
look of single-minded concentration she remembered so well on Esko's face.

"He planned it in his head; he drew it; and now here it is," Anna said.

Sakari looked around, as if following the flight of a star. And then he ran,
skating and sliding across the frozen fountain.

Acknowledgments and Sources

I met my wife, Paivi Suvilehto, during the Finnish midsummer of 1990. Without her *The Cloud Sketcher* would not and could not exist. It's as simple as that. The novel is dedicated to her and to our children with all my love.

My editor Dan Conaway first held out a welcoming hand toward the book, goaded, advised, and supported me through various drafts, and sensitively and brilliantly edited the final ones. My debt is incalculable. Thank you, Dan— you're the best. And thanks too to Nikola Scott at HarperCollins, for the support and all her hard work.

Many thanks are also due to—

In Helsinki: Mika Kaurismaki, Aki Kaurismaki, Riitta Nikula, Jaakko Tapaninen, Sinikka Partanen, Niko Aula, and Soila Lehtonen and her invaluable magazine *Books from Finland*.

In Pyhajarvi: Erkki Suvilehto, Riitta Suvilehto, Eero Suvilehto, Juho-Pekka Suvilehto.

In New York: the architect and historian James Sanders, my friends Jon Levi and Ric Burns, and my wonderful agent Jeff Posternak.

In Los Angeles: Peter Loewenberg, Michael Sant, Robert Yager, Brad Auerbach, and especially to Mirja Covarrubias and all at the Finnish Consulate.

And to the staffs of the Museum of Architecture in Helsinki, the New York Public Library, and the UCLA Research Library, and all at the Monacelli Press, the Princeton Architectural Press, and the MIT Press, producers of desirable architectural books.

A particular joy, and not the least burden, of writing *The Cloud Sketcher* was the amount of reading involved. Research is an endless maze. I'm indebted to the following books as well as to innumerable newspaper and magazine articles from the period:

ON FINLAND

Jarl Kronlund: *Suomen Puolustuslaitos 1918–1939*

Yrjo Blomsedt et al: *Suomen Historia*. Volumes 6, 7

Veijo Meri: *Ei tule vaivatta vapaus, Suomi*

The Finnish Literature Society: *Finland, a Cultural Encyclopedia*

Eino Jutikkala and Kauko Pirinen: *A History of Finland*

A. F. Upton: *The Finnish Revolution 1917–1918; The Communist Parties of Scandinavia and Finland*

Tuomo Polvinen: *Imperial Borderland — Bobrikov and the Attempted Russification of Finland, 1898–1904*

George C. Schoolfield: *Helsinki of the Czars*

Stig Jagerskiold: *Mannerheim*

J. E. O. Screen: *Mannerheim — The Years of Preparation*

Seppo Zetterberg: *Finland after 1917*

Isaac Deutscher: *Stalin; Trotsky — The Prophet Armed*

Victor Serge: *Year One of the Russian Revolution*

Oksari Tokoi: *Sisu*

John Boulton Smith: *The Golden Age of Finnish Art*

Markku Valkonen: *The Golden Age; Finnish Art over the Centuries*

Timo Martin and Douglas Siven: *Akseli Gallen-Kallela*

Kai Laitinen: *Literature of Finland*

Kalevala, in both the W. P. Kirby and Keith Bosley translations

Matti Kuusi, Michael Branch and Keith Bosley (eds.): *Finnish Folk Poetry Epic*

Edmund Wilson: *To the Finland Station*

On New York

F. Scott Fitzgerald: *The Great Gatsby*; *The Crack-Up*

Ann Douglas: *Terrible Honesty*

Rem Koolhaas: *Delirious New York*

Luc Sante: *Low Life*

Lloyd Morris: *Incredible New York*

The WPA Guide to New York

Peter Conrad: *Art and the City*

Neal Gabler: *Walter Winchell*

Joseph Mitchell: *Up in the Old Hotel*

Lester Cohen: *The New York Graphic*

Paul Rosenfeld: *Port of New York*

Benjamin de Cessares: *Mirrors of New York*

Edmund Wilson: *The Twenties*; *The American Earthquake*

Frederick Lewis Allen: *Only Yesterday*

Berenice Abbott: *Changing New York*

Henry James: *The American Scene*

Weegee: *The Naked City*

Marion Meade: *Dorothy Parker*

John Kobler: *Al Capone*

Robert Lacey: *Little Man*

Jan Morris: *Manhattan '45*

Herbert Asbury: *Gangs of New York*; *The Great Illusion*

Gene Fowler: *Skyline*

Samuel Fuller: *New York in the 1930s*

ON ARCHITECTURE

Riitta Nikula: *Architecture and Landscape — The Building of Finland*
Marika Hausen et al: *Eliel Saarinen, Projects 1896–1923*
Albert Christ-Janer: *Eliel Saarinen*
Goran Schildt: *Alvar Aalto. The Early Years* and *The Decisive Years*
Malcolm Quantrill: *Alvar Aalto, A Critical Study*
Lars Pettersson et al: *Finnish Wooden Church*
Riitta Nikula, Janey Bennett et al.: *Erik Bryggman 1891–1955*
Robert Stern, Gregory Gilmartin, Thomas Mellins: *New York 1930*
Robert Stern: *Raymond Hood*
Deborah Nevins and Robert Stern: *The Architect's Eye*
Paul Goldberger: *The Skyscraper*
Walter H. Kilham: *Raymond Hood*
Frank Lloyd Wright: *Autobiography*
Henry Russell Hitchcock: *Architecture — Nineteenth and Twentieth Centuries*
Sheldon Cheney: *The New World Architecture*
Peter Blake: *The Master Builders*
Thomas A. P. van Leeuwen: *The Skyward Trend of Thought*
Carol Willis: *Form Follows Finance; Building the Empire State*
Hugh Ferriss: *The Metropolis of Tomorrow*
Robert Hughes: *The Shock of the New*
Erich Mendelsohn: *Letters of an Architect; Amerika*
Jean-Louis Cohen: *Scenes of the World to Come*
Lewis Mumford: *Sidewalk Critic*
John Tauranac: *The Empire State Building*
Merrill Schleier: *The Skyscraper in American Art 1890–1931*
Reyner Banham: *Theory and Design in the First Machine Age*

All faults are, of course, my own.
Richard Rayner

$((($ (LISTEN TO) $)))$

THE CLOUD
SKETCHER

PERFORMED BY
SIMON JONES

"Steeped with a deft sense of time and place,
The Cloud Sketcher is fiction at its most exuberant:
big, bursting, intricate, and alive."

—David Ebershoff, author of *The Danish Girl*

"Engrossing....Rayner is...
an assured and confident storyteller."

—*Los Angeles Times Book Review*

ISBN 0-694-52520-0 • $29.95 ($44.95 Can.)
9 Hours • 6 Cassettes
ABRIDGED

Available wherever books are sold, or call 1-800-331-3761 to order.

HarperAudio
An Imprint of HarperCollins*Publishers*
www.harperaudio.com